BEST STORIES OF

O. HENRY

BEST STORIES OF
O. HENRY

Heart of the West was first published in 1907
The Four Million was first published in 1906

This edition first published in the United States of America in 1987 by

Octopus Books Limited
59 Grosvenor Street
London W1

ISBN 0 7064 3025 5

Printed and bound in the United Kingdom by
William Clowes Ltd, Beccles

CONTENTS

HEART OF THE WEST

HEARTS AND CROSSES

BALDY WOODS REACHED FOR THE BOTTLE, and got it. Whenever Baldy went for anything he usually – but this not Baldy's story. He poured out a third drink that was larger by a finger than the first and second. Baldy was in consultation; and the consultee is worthy of his hire.

'I'd be king if I was you,' said Baldy, so positively that his holster creaked and his spurs rattled.

Webb Yeager pushed back his flat-brimmed Stetson, and made further disorder in his straw-colored hair. The tonsorial recourse being without avail, he followed the liquid example of the more resourceful Baldy.

'If a man marries a queen, it oughtn't to make him a two-spot,' declared Webb, epitomizing his grievances.

'Sure not,' said Baldy, sympathetic, still thirsty, and genuinely solicitous concerning the relative value of the cards. 'By rights you're a king. If I was you, I'd call for a new deal. The cards have been stacked on you – I'll tell you what you are, Webb Yeager.'

'What?' asked Webb, with a hopeful look in his pale-blue eyes.

'You're a prince-consort.'

'Go easy,' said Webb. 'I never black-guarded you none.'

'It's a title,' explained Baldy, 'up among the picture-cards; but it don't take no tricks. I'll tell you, Webb. It's a brand they've got for certain animals in Europe. Say that you or me or one of them Dutch dukes marries in a royal family. Well, by and by our wife gets to be queen. Are we king? Not in a million years. At the coronation ceremonies we march between little casino and the Ninth Grand Custodian of the Royal Hall Bedchamber. The only use we are is to appear in photographs, and accept the responsibility for the heir-apparent. That ain't any square deal. Yes, sir, Webb, you're a prince-consort; and if I was you, I'd start a interregnum or a habeas corpus or something'; and I'd be king if I had to turn from the bottom of the deck.'

Baldy emptied his glass to the ratification of his Warwick pose.

'Baldy,' said Webb, solemnly, 'me and you punched cows in the same outfit for years. We been runnin' on the same range, and ridin' the same trails since we was boys. I wouldn't talk about my family affairs to nobody but you. You was line-rider on the Nopalito Ranch when I married Santa McAllister. I was foreman then; but what am I now? I don't amount to a knot in a stake rope.'

'When old McAllister was the cattle king of West Texas,' continued Baldy with Satanic sweetness, 'you was some tallow. You had as much to say on the ranch as he did.'

'I did,' admitted Webb, 'up to the time he found out I was tryin' to get my rope over Santa's head. Then he kept me out on the range as far from the ranch-house as he could. When the old man died they commenced to call Santa the "cattle queen." I'm boss of the cattle – that's all. She 'tends to all the business; she handles all the money; I can't sell even a beef-steer to a party of campers, myself. Santa's the "queen"; and I'm Mr. Nobody.'

'I'd be a king if I was you,' repeated Baldy Woods, the royalist. 'When a man marries a queen he ought to grade up with her – on the hoof – dressed

– dried – corned – any old way from the chaparral to the packing-house. Lots of folks thinks it's funny, Webb, that you don't have the say-so on the Nopalito. I ain't reflectin' none on Miz Yeager – she's the finest little lady between the Rio Grande and next Christmas – but a man ought to be boss of his own camp.'

The smooth, brown face of Yeager lengthened to a mask of wounded melancholy. With that expression, and his rumpled yellow hair and guileless blue eyes, he might have been likened to a schoolboy whose leadership had been usurped by a youngster of superior strength. But his active and sinewy seventy-two inches and his girded revolvers forbade the comparison.

'What was that you called me, Baldy?' he asked. 'What kind of a concert was it?'

'A "consort," ' corrected Baldy – ' "a prince-consort." It's a kind of short-card pseudonym. You come in sort of between Jack-high and a four-card flush.'

Webb Yeager sighed, and gathered the strap of his Winchester scabbard from the floor.

'I'm ridin' back to the ranch to-day,' he said, half-heartedly. 'I've got to start a bunch of beeves for San Antone in the morning.'

'I'm your company as far as Dry Lake,' announced Baldy. 'I've got a round-up camp on the San Marcos cuttin' out two-year-olds.'

The two *compañeros* mounted their ponies and trotted away from the little railroad settlement, where they had foregathered in the thirsty morning.

At Dry Lake, where their routes diverged, they reined up for a party cigarette. For miles they had ridden in silence save for the soft drum of the ponies' hoofs on the matted mesquite grass, and the rattle of the chaparral against their wooden stirrups. But in Texas discourse is seldom continuous. You may fill in a mile, a meal, and a murder between your paragraphs without detriment to your thesis. So, without apology, Webb offered an addendum to the conversation that had begun ten miles away.

'You remember, yourself, Baldy, that there was a time when Santa wasn't quite so independent. You remember the days when old McAllister was keepin' us apart, and how she used to send me the sign that she wanted to see me? Old man Mac promised to make me look like a colander if I ever come in gun-shot of the ranch. You remember the sign she used to send, Baldy – the heart with a cross inside of it?'

'Me?' cried Baldy, with intoxicated archness. 'You old sugar-stealing coyote! Don't I remember! Why, you dadblamed old long-horned turtle-dove, the boys in camp was all cognoscious about them hieroglyphs. The "gizzard-and-crossbones" we used to call it. We used to see 'em on truck that was sent out from the ranch. They was marked in charcoal on the sacks of flour and in lead-pencil on the newspapers. I see one of 'em once chalked on the back of a new cook that old man McAllister sent out from the ranch – danged if I didn't.'

'Santa's father,' exclaimed Webb gently, 'got her to promise that she wouldn't write to me or send me any word. That heart-and-cross sign was her scheme. Whenever she wanted to see me in particular she managed to put that mark on somethin' at the ranch that she knew I'd see. And I never laid eyes on it but when I burnt the wind for the ranch the same night. I used to see her in that coma mott back of the little horse-corral.'

'We knowed it,' chanted Baldy; 'but we never let on. We was all for you.

We knowed why you always kept that fast paint in camp. And when we see that gizzard-and-crossbones figured out on the truck from the ranch we knowed old Pinto was goin' to eat up miles that night instead of grass. You remember Scurry – that educated horse-wrangler we had – the college fellow that tangle-foot drove to the range? Whenever Scurry saw that come-meet-your-honey brand on anything from the ranch, he'd wave his hand like that, and say, "Our friend Lee Andrews will again swim the Hell's point to-night."'

'The last time Santa sent me the sign,' said Webb, 'was once when she was sick. I noticed it as soon as I hit camp, and I galloped Pinto forty mile that night. She wasn't at the coma mott. I went to the house; and old McAllister met me at the door. "Did you come here to get killed?" says he; "I'll disoblige you for once. I just started a Mexican to bring you. Santa wants you. Go in that room and see her. And then come out here and see me."

'Santa was lyin' in bed pretty sick. But she gives out a kind of a smile, and her hand and mine lock horns, and I sets down by the bed – mud and spurs and chaps and all. "I've heard you ridin' across the grass for hours, Webb," she says. "I was sure you'd come. You saw the sign?" she whispers. "The minute I hit camp," says I. "'Twas marked on the bag of potatoes and onions." "They're always together," says she, soft like – "always together in life." "They go well together," I says, "in a stew." "I mean hearts and crosses," says Santa. "Our sign – to love and to suffer – that's what they mean."

'And there was old Doc Musgrove amusin' himself with whisky and a palm-leaf fan. And by and by Santa goes to sleep; and Doc feels her forehead; and he says to me: "You're not such a bad febrifuge. But you'd better slide out now, for the diagnosis don't call for you in regular doses. The little lady'll be all right when she wakes up."

'I seen old McAllister outside. "She's asleep," says I. "And now you can start in with your colander-work. Take your time; for I left my gun on my saddle-horn."

'Old Mac laughs, and he says to me: "Pumpin' lead into the best ranch-boss in West Texas don't seem to me good business policy. I don't know where I could get as good a one. It's the son-in-law idea, Webb, that makes me admire for to use you as a target. You ain't my idea for a member of the family. But I can use you on the Nopalito if you'll keep outside of a radius with the ranch-house in the middle of it. You go upstairs and lay down on a cot, and when you get some sleep we'll talk it over."'

Baldy Woods pulled down his hat, and uncurled his leg from his saddle-horn. Webb shortened his rein, and his pony danced, anxious to be off. The two men shook hands with Western ceremony.

'*Adios*, Baldy,' said Webb. 'I'm glad I seen you and had this talk.'

With a pounding rush that sounded like the rise of a covey of quail, the riders sped away toward different points of the compass. A hundred yards on his route Baldy reined in on the top of a bare knoll and emitted a yell. He swayed on his horse; had he been on foot, the earth would have risen and conquered him; but in the saddle he was a master of equilibrium, and laughed at whisky, and despised the centre of gravity.

Webb turned in his saddle at the signal.

'If I was you,' came Baldy's strident and perverting tones, 'I'd be king!'

At eight o'clock on the following morning Bud Turner rolled from his saddle in front of the Nopalito ranch-house, and stumbled with whizzing rowels toward the gallery. Bud was in charge of the bunch of beef-cattle that was to strike the trail that morning for San Antonio. Mrs. Yeager was on the gallery watering a cluster of hyacinths growing in a red earthenware jar.

'King' McAllister had bequeathed to his daughter many of his strong characteristics – his resolution, his gay courage, his contumacious self-reliance, his pride as a reigning monarch of hoofs and horns. *Allegro* and *fortissimo* had been McAllister's tempo and tone. In Santa they survived, transposed to the feminine key. Substantially, she preserved the image of the mother who had been summoned to wander in other and less finite green pastures long before the waxing herds of kine had conferred royalty upon the house. She had her mother's slim, strong figure and grave, soft prettiness that relieved in her the severity of the imperious McAllister eye and the McAllister air of royal independence.

Webb stood on one end of the gallery giving orders to two or three sub-bosses of various camps and outfits who had ridden in for instructions.

''Morning,' said Bud, briefly. 'Where do you want them beeves to go in town – to Barber's, as usual?'

Now, to answer that had been the prerogative of the queen. All the reins of business – buying, selling, and banking – had been held by her capable fingers. The handling of the cattle had been entrusted fully to her husband. In the days of 'King' McAllister, Santa had been his secretary and helper; and she had continued her work with wisdom and profit. But before she could reply, the prince-consort spake up with calm decision:

'You drive that bunch to Zimmerman and Nesbit's pens. I spoke to Zimmerman about it some time ago.'

Bud turned on his high boot-heels.

'Wait!' called Santa quickly. She looked at her husband with surprise in her steady gray eyes.

'Why, what do you mean, Webb?' she asked, with a small wrinkle gathering between her brows. 'I never deal with Zimmerman and Nesbit. Barber has handled every head of stock from this ranch in that market for five years. I'm not going to take the business out of his hands.' She faced Bud Turner. 'Deliver those cattle to Barber,' she concluded positively.

Bud gazed impartially at the water-jar hanging on the gallery, stood on his other leg, and chewed a mesquite-leaf.

'I want this bunch of beeves to go to Zimmerman and Nesbit,' said Webb, with a frosty light in his blue eyes.

'Nonsense,' said Santa impatiently. 'You'd better start on, Bud, so as to noon at the Little Elm waterhole. Tell Barber we'll have another lot of culls ready in about a month.'

Bud allowed a hesitating eye to steal upward and meet Webb's. Webb saw apology in his look, and fancied he saw commiseration.

'You deliver them cattle,' he said grimly, 'to—'

'Barber,' finished Santa sharply. 'Let that settle it. Is there anything else you are waiting for, Bud?'

'No, m'm,' said Bud. But before going he lingered while a cow's tail could have switched thrice; for a man is man's ally; and even the Philistines must have blushed when they took Samson in the way they did.

'You hear your boss!' cried Webb, sardonically. He took off his hat, and bowed until it touched the floor before his wife.

'Webb,' said Santa rebukingly, 'you're acting mighty foolish to-day.'

'Court fool, your Majesty,' said Webb, in his slow tones, which had changed their quality. 'What else can you expect? Let me tell you. I was a man before I married a cattle-queen. What am I now? The laughing-stock of the camps. I'll be a man again.'

Santa looked at him closely.

'Don't be unreasonable, Webb,' she said calmly. 'You haven't been slighted in any way. Do I ever interfere in your management of the cattle? I know the business side of the ranch much better than you do. I learned it from Dad. Be sensible.'

'Kingdoms and queendoms,' said Webb, 'don't suit me unless I am in the pictures, too. I punch the cattle and you wear the crown. All right. I'd rather be High Lord Chancellor of a cow-camp than the eight-spot in a queen-high flush. It's your ranch; and Barber gets the beeves.'

Webb's horse was tied to the rack. He walked into the house and brought out his roll of blankets that he never took with him except on long rides, and his 'slicker,' and his longest stake-rope of plaited rawhide. These he began to tie deliberately upon his saddle. Santa, a little pale, followed him.

Webb swung up into the saddle. His serious, smooth face was without expression except for a stubborn light that smouldered in his eyes.

'There's a herd of cows and calves,' said he, 'near the Hondo Waterhole on the Frio that ought to be moved away from timber. Lobos have killed three of the calves. I forgot to leave orders. You'd better tell Simms to attend to it.'

Santa laid a hand on the horse's bridle, and looked her husband in the eye.

'Are you going to leave me, Webb?' she asked quietly.

'I am going to be a man again,' he answered.

'I wish you success in a praiseworthy attempt,' she said, with a sudden coldness. She turned and walked directly into the house.

Webb Yeager rode to the southeast as straight as the topography of West Texas permitted. And when he reached the horizon he might have ridden on into blue space as far as knowledge of him on the Nopalito went. And the days, with Sundays at their head, formed into hebdomadal squads; and the weeks, captained by the full moon, close ranks into menstrual companies carrying 'Tempus fugit' on their banners; and the months marched on toward the vast camp-ground of the years; but Webb Yeager came no more to the dominions of his queen.

One day a being named Bartholomew, a sheep-man – and therefore of little account – from the lower Rio Grande country, rode in sight of the Nopalito ranch-house, and felt hunger assail him. *Ex consuetudine* he was soon seated at the mid-day dining-table of that hospitable kingdom. Talk like water gushed from him: he might have been smitten with Aaron's rod – that is your gentle shepherd when an audience is vouchsafed him whose ears are not overgrown with wool.

'Missis Yeager,' he babbled, 'I see a man the other day on the Rancho Seco down in Hidalgo County by your name – Webb Yeager was his. He'd just been engaged as manager. He was a tall, light-haired man, not saying much. Maybe he was some kin of yours, do you think?'

'A husband,' said Santa cordially. 'The Seco has done well. Mr. Yeager is one of the best stockmen in the West.'

The dropping out of a prince-consort rarely disorganizes a monarchy. Queen Santa had appointed as *mayordomo* of the ranch, a trusty subject, named Ramsay, who had been one of her father's faithful vassals. And there was scarcely a ripple on the Nopalito ranch save when the gulf-breeze created undulations in the grass of its wide acres.

For several years the Nopalito had been making experiments with an English breed of cattle that looked down with aristocratic contempt upon the Texas long-horns. The experiments were found satisfactory; and a pasture had been set apart for the blue-bloods. The fame of them had gone forth into the chaparral and pear as far as men ride in saddles. Other ranches woke up, rubbed their eyes, and looked with new dissatisfaction upon the long-horns.

As a consequence, one day a sunburned, capable, silk-kerchiefed nonchalant youth, garnished with revolvers, and attended by three Mexican *vaqueros*, alighted at the Nopalito ranch and presented the following business-like epistle to the queen thereof.

Mrs. Yeager – The Nopalito Ranch:

Dear Madam:
I am instructed by the owners of the Rancho Seco to purchase 100 head of two and three-year-old cows of the Sussex breed owned by you. If you can fill the order please deliver the cattle to the bearer; and a check will be forwarded to you at once.

Respectfully,
Webster Yeager,
Manager of the Rancho Seco.

Business is business, even – very scantily did it escape being written 'especially' – in a kingdom.

That night the 100 head of cattle were driven up from the pasture and penned in a corral near the ranch-house for delivery in the morning.

When night closed down and the house was still, did Santa Yeager throw herself down, clasping that formal note to her bosom, weeping, and calling out a name that pride (either in one or the other) had kept from her lips many a day? Or did she file the letter, in her business way, retaining her royal balance and strength?

Wonder, if you will; but royalty is sacred; and there is a veil. But this much you shall learn.

At midnight Santa slipped softly out of the ranch-house, clothed in something dark and plain. She paused for a moment under the live-oak trees. The prairies were somewhat dim, and the moonlight was pale orange, diluted with particles of an impalpable, flying mist. But the mockbird whistled on every bough of vantage; leagues of flowers scented the air; and a kindergarten of little shadowy rabbits leaped and played in an open space near by. Santa turned her face to the southeast and threw kisses thitherward; for there was none to see.

Then she sped silently to the blacksmith-shop, fifty yards away; and what she did there can only be surmised. But the forge glowed red; and there was a faint hammering such as Cupid might make when he sharpens his arrow-points.

Later she came forth with a queer-shaped, handled thing in one hand, and a portable furnace, such as are seen in branding-camps, in the other. To the corral where the Sussex cattle were penned she sped with these things swiftly in the moonlight.

She opened the gate and slipped inside the corral. The Sussex cattle were mostly a dark red. But among this bunch was one that was milky white – notable among the others.

And now Santa shook from her shoulder something that we had not seen before – a rope lasso. She freed the loop of it, coiling the length in her left hand, and plunged into the thick of the cattle.

The white cow was her object. She swung the lasso, which caught one horn and slipped off. The next throw encircled the forefeet and the animal fell heavily. Santa made for it like a panther; but it scrambled up and dashed against her, knocking her over like a blade of grass.

Again she made the cast, while the aroused cattle milled round the four sides of the corral in a plunging mass. This throw was fair; the white cow came to earth again; and before it could rise Santa had made the lasso fast around a post of the corral with a swift and simple knot, and had leaped upon the cow again with the rawhide hobbles.

In one minute the feet of the animal were tied (no record-breaking deed) and Santa leaned against the corral for the same space of time, panting and lax.

And then she ran swiftly to her furnace at the gate and brought the branding-iron, queerly shaped and white-hot.

The bellow of the outraged white cow, as the iron was applied, should have stirred the slumbering auricular nerves and consciences of the nearby subjects of the Nopalito, but it did not. And it was amid the deepest nocturnal silence that Santa ran like a lapwing back to the ranch-house and there fell upon a cot and sobbed – sobbed as though queens had hearts as simple ranchmen's wives have, and as though she would gladly make kings of prince-consorts, should they ride back again from over the hills and far away.

In the morning the capable, revolvered youth and his *vaqueros* set forth, driving the bunch of Sussex cattle across the prairies to the Rancho Seco. Ninety miles it was; a six days' journey, grazing and watering the animals on the way.

The beasts arrived at Rancho Seco one evening at dusk; and were received and counted by the foreman of the ranch.

The next morning at eight o'clock a horseman loped out of the brush to the Nopalito ranch-house. He dismounted stiffly, and strode, with whizzing spurs, to the house. His horse gave a great sigh and swayed foam-streaked, with down-drooping head and closed eyes.

But waste not your pity upon Belshazzar, the flea-bitten sorrel. Today, in Nopalito horse-pasture he survives, pampered, beloved, unridden, cherished record-holder of long-distance rides.

The horseman stumbled into the house. Two arms fell around his neck and someone cried out in the voice of woman and queen alike: 'Webb – oh, Webb!'

'I was a skunk,' said Webb Yeager.

'Hush,' said Santa, 'did you see it?'

'I saw it,' said Webb.

What they meant God knows; and you shall know, if you rightly read the primer of events.

'Be the cattle-queen,' said Webb; 'and overlook it if you can. I was a mangy, sheep-stealing coyote.'

'Hush!' said Santa again, laying her fingers upon his mouth. 'There's no queen here. Do you know who I am? I am Santa Yeager, First Lady of the Bedchamber. Come here.'

She dragged him from the gallery into the room to the right. There stood a cradle with an infant in it – a red, ribald, unintelligible, babbling, beautiful infant, sputtering at life in an unseemly manner.

'There's no queen on this ranch,' said Santa again. 'Look at the king. He's got your eyes, Webb. Down on your knees and look at his Highness.'

But jingling rowels sounded on the gallery, and Bud Turner stumbled there again with the same query that he had brought, lacking a few days, a year ago.

"Morning. Them beeves is just turned out on the trail. Shall I drive 'em to Barber's, or – '

He saw Webb and stopped, open-mouthed.

'Ba-ba-ba-ba-ba-ba!' shrieked the king in his cradle, beating the air with his fists.

'You hear your boss, Bud,' said Webb Yeager, with a broad grin – just as he had said a year ago.

And that is all, except that when old man Quinn, owner of the Rancho Seco, went out to look over the herd of Sussex cattle that he had bought from the Nopalito ranch, he asked his new manager:

'What's the Nopalito ranch brand, Wilson?'

'X Bar Y,' said Wilson.

'I thought so,' said Quinn. 'But look at that white heifer there; she's got another brand – a heart with a cross inside of it. What brand is that?'

THE RANSOM OF MACK

ME AND OLD MACK LONSBURY, we got out of that Little Hide-and-Seek gold mine affair with about $40,000 apiece. I say 'old' Mack; but he wasn't old. Forty-one, I should say; but he always seemed old.

'Andy,' he says to me, 'I'm tired of hustling. You and me have been working hard together for three years. Say we knock off for a while, and spend some of this idle money we've coaxed our way.'

'The proposition hits me just right,' says I. 'Let's be nabobs a while and see how it feels. What'll we do – take in the Niagara Falls, or buck at faro?'

'For a good many years,' says Mack, 'I've thought that if I ever had extravagant money I'd rent a two-room cabin somewhere, hire a Chinaman to cook, and sit in my stocking feet and read Buckle's History of Civilization.'

'That sounds self-indulgent and gratifying without vulgar ostentation,' says I; 'and I don't see how money could be better invested. Give me a cuckoo clock and a Sep Winner's Self-Instructor for the Banjo, and I'll join you.'

A week afterward me and Mack hits this small town of Piña, about thirty miles out from Denver, and finds an elegant two-room house that just suits us. We deposited half-a-peck of money in the Piña bank and shook hands with every one of the 340 citizens in the town. We brought along the Chinaman and the cuckoo clock and Buckle and the Instructor with us from Denver; and they made the cabin seem like home at once.

Never believe it when they tell you riches don't bring happiness. If you could have seen old Mack sitting in his rocking-chair with his blue-yarn sock feet up in the window and absorbing in that Buckle stuff through his specs you'd have seen a picture of content that would have made Rockefeller jealous. And I was learning to pick out 'Old Zip Coon' on the banjo, and the cuckoo was on time with his remarks, and Ah Sing was messing up the atmosphere with the handsomest smell of ham and eggs that ever laid the honeysuckle in the shade. When it got too dark to make out Buckle's nonsense and the notes in the Instructor, me and Mack would light our pipes and talk about science and pearl diving and sciatica and Egypt and spelling and fish and trade-winds and leather and gratitude and eagles, and a lot of subjects that we'd never had time to explain our sentiments about before.

One evening Mack spoke up and asked me if I was much apprised in the habits and policies of women folks.

'Why, yes,' says I, in a tone of voice; 'I know 'em from Alfred to Omaha. The feminine nature and similitude,' says I, 'is as plain to my sight as the Rocky Mountains is to a blue-eyed burro. I'm onto all their little sidesteps and punctual discrepancies.'

'I tell you, Andy,' says Mack, with a kind of sigh. 'I never had the least amount of intersection with their predispositions. Maybe I might have had a proneness in respect to their vicinity, but I never took the time. I made my own living since I was fourteen; and I never seemed to get my ratiocinations equipped with the sentiments usually depicted toward the sect. I sometimes wish I had,' says old Mack.

'They're an adverse study,' says I, 'and adapted to points of view. Although they vary in rationale, I have found 'em quite often obviously differing from each other in divergences of contrast.'

'It seems to me,' goes on Mack, 'that a man had better take 'em in and secure his inspirations of the sect when he's young and so preordained. I let my chance go by; and I guess I'm too old now to go hopping into the curriculum.'

'Oh, I don't know,' I tells him. 'Maybe you better credit yourself with a barrel of money and a lot of emancipation from a quantity of uncontent. Still, I don't regret my knowledge of 'em,' I says. 'It takes a man who understands the symptoms and by-plays of women-folks to take care of himself in this world.'

We stayed on in Piña because we liked the place. Some folks might enjoy their money with noise and rapture and locomotion; but me and Mack we had had plenty of turmoils and hotel towels. The people were friendly; Ah Sing got the swing of the grub we liked; Mack and Buckle were as thick as two body-snatchers, and I was hitting out a cordial resemblance to 'Buffalo Gals, Can't You Come Out To-night,' on the banjo.

One day I got a telegram from Speight, the man that was working a mine I had an interest in out in New Mexico. I had to go out there; and I was gone two months. I was anxious to get back to Piña and enjoy life once more.

When I struck the cabin I nearly fainted. Mack was standing in the door; and if angels ever wept, I saw no reason why they should be smiling then.

That man was a spectacle. Yes; he was worse; he was a spyglass; he was the great telescope in the Lick Observatory. He had on a coat and shiny shoes and a white vest and a high silk hat; and a geranium as big as an order of spinach was spiked onto his front. And he was smirking and warping his face like an infernal storekeeper or a kid wit colic.

'Hello, Andy,' says Mack, out of his face. 'Glad to see you back. Things have happened since you went away.'

'I know it,' says I, 'and a sacrilegious sight it is. God never made you that way, Mack Lonsbury. Why do you scarify His works with this presumptious kind of ribaldry?'

'Why, Andy,' said he, 'they've elected me justice of the peace since you left.'

I looked at Mack close. He was restless and inspired. A justice of the peace ought to be disconsolate and assuaged.

Just then a young woman passed on the sidewalk; and I saw Mack kind of half snicker and blush, and then he raised up his hat and smiled and bowed, and she smiled and bowed, and went on by.

'No hope for you,' says I, 'if you've got the Mary-Jane infirmity at your age. I thought it wasn't going to take on you. And patent leather shoes! All this in two little short months!'

'I'm going to marry the young lady who just passed to-night,' says Mack, in a kind of a flutter.

'I forgot something at the post-office,' says I, and walked away quick.

I overtook that young woman a hundred yards away. I raised my hat and told her my name. She was about nineteen; and young for her age. She blushed, and then looked at me cool, like I was the snow scene from the 'Two Orphans.'

'I understand you are to be married to-night,' I said.

'Correct,' says she. 'You got any objections?'

'Listen, sissy,' I begins.

'My name is Miss Rebosa Reed,' says she in a pained way.

'I know it,' says I. 'Now, Rebosa, I'm old enough to have owed money to your father. And that old specious, dressed-up, garbled, seasick ptomaine prancing around avidiously like an irremediable turkey gobbler with patent leather shoes on is my best friend. Why did you go and get him invested in this marriage business?'

'Why, he was the only chance there was,' answered Miss Rebosa.

'Nay,' says I, giving a sickening look of admiration at her complexion and style of features; 'with your beauty you might pick any kind of a man. Listen, Rebosa. Old Mack ain't the man you want. He was twenty-two when you was *née* Reed, as the papers say. This bursting into bloom won't last with him. He's all ventilated with oldness and rectitude and decay. Old Mack's down with a case of Indian summer. He overlooked his bet when he was young; and now he's suing Nature for the interest on the promissory note he took from Cupid instead of the cash. Rebosa, are you bent on having this marriage occur?'

'Why, sure I am,' says she, oscillating the pansies on her hat, 'and so is somebody else, I reckon.'

'What time is it to take place?' I asks.

'At six o'clock,' says she.

I made up my mind right away what to do. I'd save old Mack if I could. To have a good, seasoned, ineligible man like that turn chicken for a girl that hadn't quit eating slate pencils and buttoning in the back was more than I could look on with easiness.

'Rebosa,' says I, earnest, drawing upon my display of knowledge concerning the feminine intuitions of reason – 'ain't there a young man in Piña – a nice young man that you think a heap of?'

'Yep,' says Rebosa, nodding her pansies – 'Sure there is! What do you think! Gracious!'

'Does he like you?' I asks. 'How does he stand in the matter?'

'Crazy,' says Rebosa. 'Ma has to wet down the front steps to keep him from sitting there all the time. But I guess that'll be all over after to-night,' she winds up with a sigh.

'Rebosa,' says I, 'you don't really experience any of this adoration called love for old Mack, do you?'

'Lord! no,' says the girl, shaking her head. 'I think he's as dry as a lava bed. The idea!'

'Who is this young man that you like, Rebosa?' I inquires.

'It's Eddie Bayles,' says she. 'He clerks in Crosby's grocery. But he don't make but thirty-five a month. Ella Noakes was wild about him once.'

'Old Mack tells me,' I says, 'that he's going to marry you at six o'clock this evening.'

'That's the time,' says she. 'It's to be at our house.'

'Rebosa,' says I, 'listen to me. If Eddy Bayles had a thousand dollars cash – a thousand dollars, mind you, would buy him a store of his own – if you and Eddie had that much to excuse matrimony on, would you consent to marry him this evening at five o'clock?'

The girl looks at me a minute; and I can see these inaudible cogitations going on inside of her, as women will.

'A thousand dollars?' says she. 'Of course I would.'

'Come on,' says I. 'We'll go and see Eddie.'

We went up to Crosby's store and called Eddie outside. He looked to be estimable and freckled; and he had chills and fever when I made my proposition.

'At five o'clock?' says he, 'for a thousand dollars? Please don't wake me up! Well, you *are* the rich uncle retired from the spice business in India. I'll buy out old Crosby and run the store myself.'

We went inside and got old man Crosby apart and explained it. I wrote my check for a thousand dollars and handed it to him. If Eddie and Rebosa married each other at five he was to turn the money over to them.

And then I gave 'em my blessing, and went to wander in the wild-wood for a season. I sat on a log and made cogitations on life and old age and the zodiac and the ways of women and all the disorder that goes with a lifetime. I passed myself congratulations that I had probably saved my old friend Mack from his attack of Indian summer. I knew when he got well of it and shed his infatuation and his patent leather shoes, he would feel grateful. 'To keep old Mack disinvolved,' thinks I, 'from relapses like this, is worth more than a thousand dollars.' And most of all I was glad that I'd made a study of women, and wasn't to be deceived any by their means of conceit and evolution.

It must have been half-past five when I got back home. I stepped in; and there sat old Mack on the back of his neck in his old clothes with his blue socks on the window and the History of Civilization propped up on his knees.

'This don't look like getting ready for a wedding at six,' I says, to seem innocent.

'Oh,' says Mack, reaching for his tobacco, 'that was postponed back to five o'clock. They sent me a note saying the hour had been changed. It's all over now. What made you stay away so long, Andy?'

'You heard about the wedding?' I asks.

'I operated it,' says he. 'I told you I was justice of the peace. The preacher is off East to visit his folks, and I'm the only one in town that can perform the dispensations of marriage. I promised Eddie and Rebosa a month ago I'd marry 'em. He's a busy lad; and he'll have a grocery of his own some day.'

'He will,' says I.

'There was lots of women at the wedding,' says Mack, smoking up. 'But I didn't seem to get any ideas from 'em. I wish I was informed in the structure of their attainments like you said you was.'

'That was two months ago,' says I, reaching up for the banjo.

TELEMACHUS, FRIEND

RETURNING FROM A HUNTING TRIP, I waited at the little town of Los Piños, in New Mexico, for the south-bound train, which was one hour late. I sat on the porch of the Summit House and discussed the functions of life with Telemachus Hicks, the hotel proprietor.

Perceiving that personalities were not out of order, I asked him what species of beast had long ago twisted and mutilated his left ear. Being a hunter, I was concerned in the evils that may befall one in the pursuit of game.

'That ear,' said Hicks, 'is the relic of true friendship.'

'An accident?' I persisted.

'No friendship is an accident,' said Telemachus; and I was silent.

'The only perfect case of true friendship I ever knew,' went on my host, 'was a cordial intent between a Connecticut man and a monkey. The monkey climbed palms in Barranquilla and threw down cocoanuts to the man. The man sawed them in two and made dippers, which he sold for two *reales* each and bought rum. The monkey drank the milk of the nuts. Through each being satisfied with his own share of the graft, they lived like brothers.

'But in the case of human beings, friendship is a transitory act, subject to discontinuance without further notice.

'I had a friend once, of the entitlement of Paisley Fish, that I imagined was sealed to me for an endless space of time. Side by side for seven years we had mined, ranched, sold patent churns, herded sheep, took photographs and other things, built wire fences, and picked prunes. Thinks I, neither homicide nor flattery nor riches nor sophistry nor drink can make trouble between me and Paisley Fish. We was friends an amount you could hardly guess at. We was friends in business, and we let our amicable qualities lap over and season our hours of recreation and folly. We certainly had days of Damon and nights of Pythias.

'One summer me and Paisley gallops down into these San Andrés mountains for the purpose of a month's surcease and levity, dressed in the natural store habiliments of man. We hit this town Los Piños, which certainly was a roof-garden spot of the world, and flowing with condensed milk and honey. It had a street or two, and air, and hens, and a eating-house; and that was enough for us.

'We strikes the town after supper-time, and we concludes to sample whatever efficacy there is in this eating-house down by the railroad tracks. By the time we had set down and pried up our plates with a knife from the red oil-cloth, along intrudes Widow Jessup with the hot biscuit and fried liver.

'Now, there was a woman that would have tempted an anchovy to forget his vows. She was not so small as she was large; and a kind of welcome air seemed to mitigate her vicinity. The pink of her face was the *in hoc signo* of a culinary temper and a warm disposition, and her smile would have brought out the dogwood blossoms in December.

'Widow Jessup talks to us a lot of garrulousness about the climate and history and Tennyson and prunes and the scarcity of mutton, and finally wants to know where we came from.

' "Spring Valley," says I.

' "Big Spring Valley," chips in Paisley, out of a lot of potatoes and knuckle-bone of ham in his mouth.

'That was the first sign I notices that the old *fidus Diogenes* business between me and Paisley Fish was ended forever. He knew how I hated a talkative person, and yet he stampedes into the conversation with his amendments and addendums of syntax. On the map it was Big Spring Valley; but I had heard Paisley himself call it Spring Valley a thousand times.

'Without saying any more, we went out after supper and set on the railroad track. We had been pardners too long not to know what was going on in each other's mind.

' "I reckon you understand," says Paisley, "that I've made up my mind to accrue that widow woman as part and parcel in and to my hereditaments forever, both domestic, sociable, legal, and otherwise, until death us do part."

' "Why, yes," says I, "I read it between the lines, though you only spoke one. And I suppose you are aware," says I, "that I have a movement on foot that leads up to the widow's changing her name to Hicks, and leaves you writing to the society column to inquire whether the best man wears a japonica or seamless socks at the wedding!"

' "There'll be some hiatuses in your program," says Paisley, chewing up a piece of a railroad tie. "I'd give in to you," says he, "in 'most any respect if it was secular affairs, but this is not so. The smiles of woman," goes on Paisley, "is the whirlpool of Squills and Chalybeates, into which vortex the good ship Friendship is often drawn and dismembered. I'd assault a bear that was annoying you," says Paisley, "or I'd indorse your note, or rub the place between your shoulder-blades with opodeldoc the same as ever; but there my sense of etiquette ceases. In this fracas with Mrs. Jessup we play it alone. I've notified you fair."

'And then I collaborates with myself, and offers the following resolutions and by-laws:

' "Friendship between man and man," says I, "is an ancient historical virtue enacted in the days when men had to protect each other against lizards with eighty-foot tails and flying turtles. And they've kept up the habit to this day, and stand by each other till the bellboy comes up and tells them the animals are not really there. I've often heard," I says, "about ladies stepping in and breaking up a friendship between men. Why should that be? I'll tell you, Paisley, the first sight and hot biscuit of Mrs. Jessup appears to have inserted a oscillation into each of our bosoms. Let the best man of us have her. I'll play you a square game, and won't do any underhanded work. I'll do all of my courting of her in your presence, so you will have an equal opportunity. With that arrangement I don't see why our steamboat of friendship should fall overboard in the medicinal whirlpools you speak of, whichever of us wins out."

' "Good old hoss!" says Paisley, shaking my hand. "And I'll do the same," says he. "We'll court the lady synonymously, and without any of the prudery and bloodshed usual to such occasions. And we'll be friends still, win or lose."

'At one side of Mrs. Jessup's eating-house was a bench under some trees where she used to sit in the breeze after the south-bound had been fed and gone. And there me and Paisley used to congregate after supper and make partial payments on our respects to the lady of our choice. And we was so honorable and circuitous in our calls that if one of us got there first we waited for the other before beginning any gallivantery.

'The first evening that Mrs. Jessup knew about our arrangement I got to the bench before Paisley did. Supper was just over, and Mrs. Jessup was out there with a fresh pink dress on, and almost cool enough to handle.

'I sat down by her and made a few specifications about the moral surface of nature as set forth by the landscape and the contiguous perspective. That evening was surely a case in point. The moon was attending to business in the section of sky where it belonged, and the trees was making shadows on the ground according to science and nature, and there was a kind of conspicuous hullabaloo going on in the bushes between the bull-bats and the orioles and the jack-rabbits and other feathered insects of the forest. And the wind out of the mountains was singing like a jew's-harp in the pile of old tomato-cans by the railroad track.

I felt a kind of sensation in my left side — something like dough rising in a crock by the fire. Mrs. Jessup had moved up closer.

' "Oh, Mr. Hicks," says she, 'when one is alone in the world, don't they feel it more aggravated on a beautiful night like this?"

'I rose up off the bench at once.

' "Excuse me, ma'am," says I, "but I'll have to wait till Paisley comes before I can give a audible hearing to leading questions like that."

'And then I explained to her how we was friends cinctured by years of embarrassment and travel and complicity, and how we had agreed to take no advantage of each other in any of the more mushy walks of life, such as might be fomented by sentiment and proximity. Mrs. Jessup appears to think serious about the matter for a minute, and then she breaks into a species of laughter that makes the wildwood resound.

'In a few minutes Paisley drops around, with oil of bergamot on his hair, and sits on the other side of Mrs. Jessup, and inaugurates a sad tale of adventure in which him and Pieface Lumley has a skinning-match of dead cows in '95 for a silver-mounted saddle in the Santa Rita valley during the nine months' drought.

'Now, from the start of that courtship I had Paisley Fish hobbled and tied to a post. Each one of us had a different system of reaching out for the easy places in the female heart. Paisley's scheme was to petrify 'em with wonderful relations of events that he had either come across personally or in large print. I think he must have got his idea of subjugation from one of Shakespeare's shows I see once called "Othello." There is a colored man in it who acquires a duke's daughter by disbursing to her a mixture of the talk turned out by Rider Haggard, Lew Dockstader, and Dr. Parkhurst. But that style of courting don't work well off the stage.

'Now, I give you my own recipe for inveigling a woman into that state of affairs when she can be referred to as "*née* Jones." Learn how to pick up her hand and hold it, and she's yours. It ain't so easy. Some men grab at it so much like they was going to set a dislocation of the shoulder that you can smell the arnica and hear 'em tearing off bandages. Some take it up like a hot horseshoe, and hold it off at arm's length like a druggist pouring tincture of asafoetida in a bottle. And most of 'em catch hold of it and drag it right out before the lady's eyes like a boy finding a baseball in the grass, without giving her a chance to forget that the hand is growing on the end of her arm. Them ways are all wrong.

'I'll tell you the right way. Did you ever see a man sneak out in the backyard and pick up a rock to throw at a tomcat that was sitting on a fence looking at him? He pretends he hasn't got a thing in his hand, and that the cat don't see him, and that he don't see the cat. That's the idea. Never drag her hand out where she'll have to take notice of it. Don't let her know that you think she knows you have the least idea she is aware you are holding her hand. That was my rule of tactics; and as far as Paisley's serenade about hostilities and misadventure went, he might as well have been reading to her a time-table of the Sunday trains that stop at Ocean Grove, New Jersey.

'One night when I beat Paisley to the bench by one pipeful, my friendship gets subsidized for a minute, and I asks Mrs. Jessup if she didn't think a "H" was easier to write than a "J." In a second her head was mashing the oleander flower in my button-hole, and I learned over and – but I didn't.

' "If you don't mind," says I, standing up "we'll wait for Paisley to come before finishing this. I've never done anything dishonorable yet to our friendship, and this won't be quite fair."

' "Mr. Hicks," says Mrs. Jessup, looking at me peculiar in the dark, "if it wasn't for but one thing, I'd ask you to hike yourself down the gulch and never disresume your visits to my house."

' "And what is that, ma'am?" I asks.

' "You are too good a friend not to make a good husband," says she.

'In five minutes Paisley was on his side of Mrs. Jessup.

' "In Silver City, in the summer of '98," he begins, "I see Jim Batholomew chew off a Chinaman's ear in the Blue Light Saloon on account of a crossbarred muslin shirt that – what was that noise?"

'I had resumed matters again with Mrs. Jessup right where we had left off.

' "Mrs. Jessup," says I, "has promised to make it Hicks. And this is another of the same sort."

'Paisley winds his feet around a leg of the bench and kind of groans.

' "Lem," says he, "we been friends for seven years. Would you mind not kissing Mrs. Jessup quite so loud? I'd do the same for you."

' "All right," says I. "The other kind will do as well."

' "This Chinaman," goes on Paisley, "was the one that shot a man named Mullins in the spring of '97, and that was — "

'Paisley interrupted himself again.

' "Lem," says he, "if you was a true friend you wouldn't hug Mrs. Jessup quite so hard. I felt the bench shake all over just then. You know you told me you would give me an even chance as long as there was any."

' "Mr. Man," says Mrs. Jessup, turning around to Paisley, "if you was to drop in to the celebration of mine and Mr. Hicks's silver wedding, twenty-five years from now, do you think you could get it into that Hubbard squash you call your head that you are *nix cum rous* in this business? I've put up with you a long time because you was Mr. Hicks's friend; but it seems to me it's time for you to wear the willow and trot off down the hill."

' "Mrs. Jessup," says I, without losing my grasp on the situation as fiancé, "Mr. Paisley is my friend, and I offered him a square deal and a equal opportunity as long as there was a chance."

' "A chance!" says she. "Well, he may think he has a chance; but I hope he won't think he's got a cinch, after what he's been next to all the evening."

'Well, a month afterwards me and Mrs. Jessup was married in the Los Piños Methodist Church; and the whole town closed up to see the performance.

'When we lined up in front and the preacher was beginning to sing out his rituals and observances, I looks around and misses Paisley. I calls time on the preacher. "Paisley ain't here," says I. "We've got to wait for Paisley. A friend once, a friend always – that's Telemachus Hicks," says I. Mrs. Jessup's eyes snapped some; but the preacher holds up the incantations according to instructions.

'In a few minutes Paisley gallops up the aisle, putting on a cuff as he comes. He explains that the only dry-goods store in town was closed for the wedding, and he couldn't get the kind of a boiled shirt that his taste called for until he had broke open the back window of the store and helped himself. Then he ranges up on the other side of the bride, and the wedding goes on. I always imagined that Paisley calculated as a last chance that the preacher might marry him to the widow by mistake.

'After the proceedings was over we had tea and jerked antelope and canned apricots, and then the populace hiked itself away. Last of all Paisley shook me by the hand and told me I'd acted square and on the level with him and he was proud to call me a friend.

'The preacher had a small house on the side of the street that he'd fixed up to rent; and he allowed me and Mrs. Hicks to occupy it till the ten-forty train the next morning, when we was going on a bridal tour to El Paso. His wife had decorated it all up with hollyhocks and poison ivy, and it looked real festal and bowery.

'About ten o'clock that night I sets down in the front door and pulls of my boots a while in the cool breeze, while Mrs. Hicks was fixing around in the room. Right soon the light went out inside; and I sat there a while, reverberating over old times and scenes. And then I heard Mrs. Hicks call out, "Ain't you coming in soon, Lem?"

' "Well, well!" says I, kind of rousing up. "Durn me if I wasn't waiting for old Paisley to—"

'But when I got that far,' concluded Telemachus Hicks, 'I thought somebody had shot this left ear of mine off with a forty-five. But it turned out to be only a lick from a broomhandle in the hands of Mrs. Hicks.'

THE HANDBOOK OF HYMEN

'TIS THE OPINION OF MYSELF, Sanderson Pratt, who sets this down, that the educational system of the United States should be in the hands of the weather bureau. I can give you good reasons for it; and you can't tell me why our college professors shouldn't be transferred to the meteorological department. They have been learned to read; and they could very easily glance at the morning papers and then wire in to the main office what kind of weather to expect. But there's the other side of the proposition. I am going on to tell you how the weather furnished me and Idaho Green with an elegant education.

We was up in the Bitter Root Mountains over the Montana line prospecting for gold. A chin-whiskered man in Walla-Walla, carrying a line of hope as excess baggage, grubstaked us; and there we was in the foothills pecking away, with enough grub on hand to last an army through a peace conference.

Along one day comes a mail-rider over the mountains from Carlos, and stops to eat three cans of green-gages, and leave us a newspaper of modern date. This paper prints a system of premonitions of the weather, and the card it dealt Bitter Root Mountains from the bottom of the deck was 'warmer and fair, with light westerly breezes.'

That evening it began to snow, with the wind strong in the east. Me and Idaho moved camp into an old empty cabin higher up the mountain, thinking it was only a November flurry. But after falling three foot on a level it went to work in earnest; and we knew we was snowed in. We got in plenty of firewood before it got deep, and we had grub enough for two months, so we let the elements rage and cut up all they thought proper.

If you want to instigate the art of manslaughter just shut two men up in a eighteen-by-twenty-foot cabin for a month. Human nature won't stand it.

When the first snowflakes fell me and Idaho Green laughed at each other's jokes and praised the stuff we turned out of a skillet and called bread. At the end of three weeks Idaho makes this kind of a edict to me. Says he:

'I never exactly heard sour milk dropping out of a balloon on the bottom of a tin pan, but I have an idea it would be music of the spears compared to this attenuated stream of asphyxiated thought that emanates out of your organs of conversation. The kind of half-masticated noises that you emit every day puts me in mind of a cow's cud, only she's lady enough to keep hers to herself, and you ain't.'

'Mr. Green,' says I, 'you having been friend of mind once, I have some hesitations in confessing to you that if I had my choice for society between you and a common yellow three-legged cur pup, one of the inmates of this here cabin would be wagging a tail just at present.'

This way we goes on for two or three days, and then we quits speaking to one another. We divides up the cooking implements, and Idaho cooks his grub on one side of the fireplace, and me on the other. The snow is up to the windows, and we have to keep a fire all day.

You see me and Idaho never had any education beyond reading and doing 'if John had three apples and James five' on a slate. We never felt any special need for a university degree, though we had acquired a species of intrinsic intelligence in knocking around the world that we could use in emergencies.

But snowbound in that cabin in the Bitter Roots, we felt for the first time that if we had studied Homer or Greek and fractions and the higher branches of information, we'd have had some resources in the line of meditation and private thought. I've seen them Eastern college fellows working in camps all through the West, and I never noticed but what education was less of a drawback to 'em than you would think. Why, once over on Snake River, when Andrew McWilliams' saddle horse got the botts, he sent a buckboard ten miles for one of these strangers that claimed to be a botanist. But that horse died.

One morning Idaho was poking around with a stick on top of a little shelf that was too high to reach. Two books fell down to the floor. I started toward 'em but caught Idaho's eye. He speaks for the first time in a week.

'Don't burn your fingers,' says he. 'In spite of the fact that you're only fit to be the companion of a sleeping mud-turtle, I'll give you a square deal. And that's more than your parents did when they turned you loose in the world with the sociability of a rattlesnake and the bedside manner of a frozen turnip. I'll play you a game of seven-up, the winner to pick up his choice of the book, the loser to take the other.'

We played; and Idaho won. He picked up his book; and I took mine. Then each of us got on his side of the house and went to reading.

I never was as glad to see a ten-ounce nugget as I was that book. And Idaho looked at his like a kid looks at a stick of candy.

Mine was a little book about five by six inches called 'Herkimer's Handbook of Indispensable Information.' I may be wrong, but I think that was the greatest book that ever was written. I've got it to-day; and I can stump you or any man fifty times in five minutes with the information in it. Talk about Solomon or the New York *Tribune!* Herkimer had cases on both of 'em. That man must have put in fifty years and travelled a million miles to find out all that stuff. There was the population of all cities in it, and the way to tell a girl's age, and the number of teeth a camel has. It told you the longest tunnel in the world, the number of the stars, how long it takes for chicken pox to break out, what a lady's neck ought to measure, the veto powers of Governors, the dates of the Roman aqueducts, how many pounds of rice going without three beers a day would buy, the average annual temperature of Augusta, Maine, the quantity of seed required to plant an acre of carrots in drills, antidotes for poisons, the number of hairs on a blond lady's head, how to preserve eggs, the height of all the mountains in the world, and the dates of all wars and battles, and how to restore drowned persons, and sunstroke, and the number of tacks in a pound, and how to make dynamite and flowers and beds, and what to do before the doctor comes – and a hundred times as many things besides. If there was anything Herkimer didn't know I didn't miss it out of the book.

I sat and read that book for four hours. All the wonders of education was compressed in it. I forgot the snow, and I forgot that me and old Idaho was on the outs. He was sitting still on a stool reading away with a kind of partly soft and partly mysterious look shining through his tan-bark whiskers.

'Idaho,' says I, 'what kind of a book is yours?'

Idaho must have forgot, too, for he answered moderate, without any slander or malignity.

'Why,' says he, 'this here seems to be a volume by Homer K. M.'

'Homer K. M. what?' I asked.

'Why, just Homer K. M.,' says he.

'You're a liar,' says I, a little riled that Idaho should try to put me up a tree. 'No man is going 'round signing books with his initials. If it's Homer K. M. Spoopendyke, or Homer K. M. McSweeney, or Homer K. M. Jones, why don't you say so like a man instead of biting off the end of it like a calf chewing off the tail of a shirt on a clothesline?'

'I put it to you straight, Sandy,' says Idaho, quiet. 'It's a poem book,' says he, 'by Homer K. M. I couldn't get color out of it at first, but there's a vein if you follow it up. I wouldn't have missed this book for a pair of red blankets.'

'You're welcome to it,' says I. 'What I want is a disinterested statement of facts for the mind to work on, and that's what I seem to find in the book I've drawn.'

'What you've got,' said Idaho, 'is statistics, the lowest grade of information that exists. They'll poison your mind. Give me old K. M.'s system of surmises. He seems to be a kind of a wine agent. His regular toast is "nothing doing," and he seems to have a grouch, but he keeps it so well lubricated with booze that his worst kicks sound like an invitation to split a quart. But it's poetry,' says Idaho, 'and I have sensations of scorn for that truck of yours that tries to convey sense in feet and inches. When it comes to explaining the instict of philosophy through the art of nature, old K. M. has got your man beat by drills, rows, paragraphs, chest measurement, and average annual rainfall.'

So that's the way me and Idaho had it. Day and night all the excitement we got was studying our books. That snowstorm sure fixed us with a fine lot of attainments apiece. By the time the snow melted, if you had stepped up to me suddenly and said: 'Sanderson Pratt, what would it cost per square foot to lay a roof with twenty by twenty-eight tin at nine dollars and fifty cents per box?' I'd have told you as quick as light could travel the length of a spade handle at the rate of one hundred and ninety-two thousand miles per second. How many can do it? You wake up 'most any man you know in the middle of the night, and ask him quick to tell you the number of bones in the human skeleton exclusive of the teeth, or what percentage of the vote of the Nebraska Legislature overrules a veto. Will he tell you? Try him and see.

About what benefit Idaho got out of his poetry book I didn't exactly know, Idaho boosted the wine-agent every time he opened his mouth; but I wasn't so sure.

This Homer K. M., from what leaked out of his libretto through Idaho, seemed to me to be a kind of a dog who looked at life like it was a tin can tied to his tail. After running himself half to death, he sits down, hangs his tongue out, and looks at the can and says:

'Oh, well, since we can't shake the growler, let's get filled at the corner, and all have a drink on me.'

Besides that, it seems he was a Persian; and I never hear of Persia producing anything worth mentioning unless it was Turkish rugs and Maltese cats.

That spring me and Idaho struck pay ore. It was a habit of ours to sell out quick and keep moving. We unloaded on our grubstaker for eight thousand dollars apiece; and then we drifted down to this little town of Rosa, on the Salmon River, to rest up, and get some human grub, and have our whiskers harvested.

Rosa was no mining-camp. It laid in the valley, and was as free of uproar and pestilence as one of them rural towns in the country. There was a

three-mile trolley line champing its bit in the environs; and me and Idaho
spent a week riding on one of the cars, dropping off of nights at the Sunset
View Hotel. Being now well read as well as travelled, we was soon *pro re
nata* with the best society in Rosa, and was invited out to the most
dressed-up and high-toned entertainments. It was at a piano recital and
quail-eating contest in the city hall, for the benefit of the fire company, that
me and Idaho first met Mrs. D. Ormond Sampson, the queen of Rosa society.

Mrs. Sampson was a widow, and owned the only two-story house in town.
It was painted yellow, and whichever way you looked from you could see
it as plain as egg on the chin of an O'Grady on a Friday. Twenty-two men
in Rosa besides me and Idaho was trying to stake a claim on that yellow
house.

There was a dance after the song books and quail bones had been raked
out of the Hall. Twenty-three of the bunch galloped over to Mrs. Sampson
and asked for a dance. I side-stepped the two-step, and asked permission to
escort her home. That's where I made a hit.

On the way home says she:

'Ain't the stars lovely and bright to-night, Mr. Pratt?'

'For the chance they've got,' says I, 'they're humping themselves in a
mighty creditable way. That big one you see is sixty-six billions of miles
distant. It took thirty-six years for light to reach us. With an eighteen-foot
telescope you can see forty-three millions of 'em, including them of the
thirteenth magnitude, which, if one was to go out now, you would keep on
seeing it for twenty-seven hundred years.'

'My!' says Mrs. Sampson. 'I never knew that before. How warm it is! I'm
as damp as I can be from dancing so much.'

'That's easy to account for,' says I, 'when you happen to know that you've
got two million sweat-glands working all at once. If every one of your
perspiratory ducts, which are a quarter of an inch long, was placed end to
end, they would reach a distance of seven miles.'

'Lawsy!' says Mrs. Sampson. 'It sounds like an irrigation ditch you was
describing, Mr. Pratt. How do you get all this knowledge of information?'

'From observation, Mrs. Sampson,' I tells her. 'I keep my eyes open when
I go about the world.'

'Mr. Pratt,' says she, 'I always did admire a man of education. There are
so few scholars among the sap-headed plug-uglies of this town that it is a real
pleasure to converse with a gentleman of culture. I'd be gratified to have you
call at my house whenever you feel so inclined.'

And that was the way I got the goodwill of the lady in the yellow house.
Every Tuesday and Friday evenings I used to go there and tell her about the
wonders of the universe as discovered, tabulated, and compiled from nature
by Herkimer. Idaho and the other gay Lutherans of the town got every
minute of the rest of the week that they could.

I never imagined that Idaho was trying to work on Mrs. Sampson with old
K. M.'s rules of courtship till one afternoon when I was on my way over to
take her a basket of wild hog-plums. I met the lady coming down the lane
that led to her house. Her eyes were snapping, and her hat made a dangerous
dip over one eye.

'Mr. Pratt,' she opens up, 'this Mr. Green is a friend of yours, I believe.'

'For nine years,' says I.

'Cut him out,' says she. 'He's no gentleman!'

'Why, ma'am,' says I, 'he's a plain incumbent of the mountain, with asperities and the usual failings of a spendthrift and a liar, but I never on the most momentous occasion had the heart to deny that he was a gentleman. It may be that in haberdashery and the sense of arrogance and display Idaho offends the eye, but inside, ma'am, I've found him impervious to the lower grades of crime and obesity. After nine years of Idaho's society, Mrs. Sampson,' I winds up, 'I should hate to impute him, and I should hate to see him imputed.'

'It's right plausible of you, Mr. Pratt,' says Mrs. Sampson, 'to take up the curmudgeons in your friend's behalf; but it don't alter the fact that he has made proposals to me sufficiently obnoxious to ruffle the ignominy of any lady.'

'Why, now, now, now!' says I, 'Old Idaho do that! I could believe it of myself sooner. I never knew but one thing to deride in him; and a blizzard was responsible for that. Once while we was snowbound in the mountains he became a prey to a kind of spurious and uneven poetry, which may have corrupted his demeanor.'

'It has,' says Mrs. Sampson. 'Ever since I knew him he has been reciting to me a lot of irreligious rhymes by some person he calls Ruby Ott, and who is no better than she should be, if you judge by her poetry.'

'Then Idaho has struck a new book,' says I, 'for one he had was by a man who writes under the *nom de plume* of K. M.'

'He'd better have stuck to it,' says Mrs. Sampson, 'whatever it was. And to-day he caps the vortex. I get a bunch of flowers from him, and on 'em is pinned a note. Now, Mr. Pratt, you know a lady when you see her; and you know how I stand in Rosa society. Do you think for a moment that I'd skip out to the woods with a man along with a jug of wine and a loaf of bread, and go singing and cavorting up and down under the trees with him? I take a little claret with my meals, but I'm not in the habit of packing a jug of it into the brush and raising Cain in any such style as that. And of course he'd bring his book of verses along, too. He said so. Let him go on his scandalous picnics alone! Or let him take his Ruby Ott with him. I reckon she wouldn't kick unless it was on account of there being too much bread along. And what do you think of your gentleman friend now, Mr. Pratt?'

'Well, 'm,' says I, 'it may be that Idaho's invitation was a kind of poetry, and meant no harm. Maybe it belonged to the class of rhymes they call figurative. They offend law and order, but they get sent through the mails on the grounds that they mean something that they don't say. I'd be glad on Idaho's account if you'd overlook it,' says I, 'and let us extricate our minds from the low regions of poetry to the higher planes of fact and fancy. On a beautiful afternoon like this, Mrs. Sampson,' I goes on, 'we should let our thoughts dwell accordingly. Though it is warm here, we should remember that at the equator the line of perpetual frost is at an altitude of fifteen thousand feet. Between the latitudes of forty degrees and forty-nine degrees it is from four thousand to nine thousand feet.'

'Oh, Mr. Pratt,' says Mrs. Sampson, 'It's such a comfort to hear you say them beautiful facts after getting such a jar from that minx of a Ruby's poetry!'

'Let us sit on this log at the roadside,' says I, 'and forget the inhumanity and ribaldry of the poets. It is in the glorious columns of ascertained facts and legalized measures that beauty is to be found. In this very log we sit upon, Mrs. Sampson,' says I, 'is statistics more wonderful than any poem. The rings show it was sixty years old. At the depth of two thousand feet it would become coal in three thousand years. The deepest coal mine in the world is at Killingworth, near Newcastle. A box four feet long, three feet wide, and two feet eight inches deep will hold one ton of coal. If an artery is cut, compress it above the wound. A man's leg contains thirty bones. The Tower of London was burned in 1841.'

'Go on, Mr. Pratt,' says Mrs. Sampson. 'Them ideas is so original and soothing. I think statistics are just as lovely as they can be.'

But it wasn't till two weeks later that I got all that was coming to me out of Herkimer.

One night I was waked up by folks hollering 'Fire!' all around. I jumped up and dressed and went out of the hotel to enjoy the scene. When I seen it was Mrs. Sampson's house, I gave forth a kind of yell, and I was there in two minutes.

The whole lower story of the yellow house was in flames, and every masculine, feminine, and canine in Rosa was there, screeching and barking and getting in the way of the firemen. I saw Idaho trying to get away from six firemen who were holding him. They was telling him the whole place was on fire downstairs, and no man could go in it and come out alive.

'Where's Mrs. Sampson?' I asks.

'She hasn't been seen,' says one of the firemen. 'She sleeps upstairs. We've tried to get in, but we can't, and our company hasn't got any ladders yet.'

I runs around to the light of the big blaze, and pulls the Handbook out of my inside pocket. I kind of laughed when I felt it in my hands – I reckon I was some daffy with the sensation of excitement.

'Herky, old boy,' I says to it, as I flipped over the pages, 'you ain't ever lied to me yet, and you ain't ever throwed me down at a scratch yet. Tell me what, old boy, tell me what!' says I.

I turned to 'What to do in Case of Accidents,' on page 117. I run my finger down the page, and struck it. Good old Herkimer, he never overlooked anything! It said:

SUFFOCATION FROM INHALING SMOKE OR GAS. – There is nothing better than flaxseed. Place a few seeds in the corner of the eye.

I shoved the Handbook back in my pocket, and grabbed a boy that was running by.

'Here,' says I, giving him some money, 'run to the drug store and bring a dollar's worth of flaxseed. Hurry, and you'll get another one for yourself. Now,' I sings out to the crowd, 'we'll have Mrs. Sampson!' And I throws away my coat and hat.

Four of the firemen and citizens grabs hold of me. It's sure death, they say, to go in the house, for the floors was beginning to fall through.

'How in blazes,' I sings out, kind of laughing yet, but not feeling like it, 'do you expect me to put flaxseed in a eye without the eye?'

I jabbed each elbow in a fireman's face, kicked the bark off of one citizen's shin, and tripped the other one with a side hold. And then I busted into the house. If I die first I'll write you a letter and tell you if it's any worse down there than the inside of that yellow house was; but don't believe it yet. I was a heap more cooked than the hurry-up orders of broiled chicken that you get in restaurants. The fire and smoke had me down on the floor twice, and was about to shame Herkimer, but the firemen helped me with their little stream of water, and I got to Mrs. Sampson's room. She'd lost conscientiousness from the smoke, so I wrapped her in the bed clothes and got her on my shoulder. Well, the floors wasn't as bad as they said, or I never could have done it – not by no means.

I carried her out fifty yards from the house and laid her on the grass. Then, of course, every one of them other twenty-two plantiffs to the lady's hand crowded around with tin dippers of water ready to save her. And up runs the boy with the flaxseed.

I unwrapped the covers from Mrs. Sampson's head. She opened her eyes and says:

'Is that you, Mr. Pratt?'

'S-s-sh,' says I. 'Don't talk till you've had the remedy.'

I runs my arm around her neck and raises her head, gentle, and breaks the bag of flaxseed with the other hand; and as easy as I could I bends over and slips three or four of the seeds in the outer corner of her eye.

Up gallops the village doc by this time, and snorts around, and grabs at Mrs. Sampson's pulse, and wants to know what I mean by any such sandblasted nonsense.

'Well, old Jalap and Jersulem oak seed,' says I, 'I'm no regular practitioner, but I'll show you my authority, anyway.'

They fetched my coat, and I gets out the Handbook.

'Look on page 117,' says I, 'at the remedy for suffocation by smoke or gas. Flaxseed in the outer corner of the eye, it says. I don't know whether it works as a smoke consumer or whether it hikes the compound gastro-hippopotamus nerve into action, but Herkimer says it, and he was called to the case first. If you want to make it a consultation, there's no objection.'

Old doc takes the book and looks at it by means of his specs and a fireman's lantern.

'Well, Mr. Pratt,' says he, 'you evidently got on the wrong line in reading your diagnosis. The recipe for suffocation says: "Get the patient into fresh air as quickly as possible, and place in a reclining position." The flaxseed remedy is for "Dust and Cinders in the Eye," on the line above. But, after all – '

'See here,' interrupts Mrs. Sampson, 'I reckon I've got something to say in this consultation. That flaxseed done me more good than anything I ever tried.' And then she raises up her head and lays it back on my arm again, and says: 'Put some in the other eye, Sandy dear.'

And so if you was to stop off at Rosa to-morrow, or any other day, you'd see a fine new yellow house with Mrs. Pratt, that was Mrs. Sampson, embellishing and adorning it. And if you was to step inside you'd see on the marble-top centre table in the parlor, 'Herkimer's Handbook of Indispensable Information,' all rebound in red morocco, and ready to be consulted on any subject pertaining to human happiness and wisdom.

THE PIMIENTA PANCAKES

WHILE WE WERE ROUNDING UP a bunch of the Triangle-O cattle in the Frio bottoms a projecting branch of a dead mesquite caught my wooden stirrup and gave my ankle a wrench that laid me up in camp for a week.

On the third day of my compulsory idleness I crawled out near the grub wagon, and reclined helpless under the conversational fire of Judson Odom, the camp cook. Jud was a monologist by nature, whom Destiny, with customary blundering, had set in a profession wherein he was bereaved, for the greater portion of his time, of an audience.

Therefore, I was manna in the desert of Jud's obmutescence.

Betimes I was stirred by invalid longings for something to eat that did not come under the caption of 'grub.' I had visions of the maternal pantry 'deep as first love, and wild with all regret,' and then I asked:

'Jud, can you make pancakes?'

Jud laid down his sixshooter, with which he was preparing to pound an antelope steak, and stood over me in what I felt to be a menacing attitude. He further indorsed my impression that his pose was resentful by fixing upon me with his light blue eyes a look of cold suspicion.

'Say, you,' he said, with candid, though not excessive, choler, 'did you mean that straight, or was you trying to throw the gaff into me? Some of the boys been telling you about me and that pancake racket?'

'No, Jud,' I said, sincerely, 'I meant it. It seems to me I'd swap my pony and saddle for a stack of buttered brown pancakes with some first crop, open kettle, New Orleans sweetening. Was there a story about pancakes?'

Jud was mollified at once when he saw that I had not been dealing in allusions. He brought some mysterious bags and tin boxes from the grub wagon and set them in the shade of the hackberry where I lay reclined. I watched him as he began to arrange them leisurely and untie their many strings.

'No, not a story,' said Jud, as he worked, 'but just the logical disclosures in the case of me and that pink-eyed snoozer from Mired Mule Cañada and Miss Willella Learight. I don't mind telling you.

'I was punching then for old Bill Toomey, on the San Miguel. One day I gets all ensnared up in aspirations for to eat some canned grub that hasn't even mooed or baaed or grunted or been in peck measures. So, I gets on my bronc and pushed the wind for Uncle Emsley Telfair's store at the Pimienta Crossing on the Neuces.

'About three in the afternoon I throwed my bridle over a mesquite limb and walked the last twenty yards into Uncle Emsley's store. I got up on the counter and told Uncle Emsley that the signs pointed to the devastation of the fruit crop of the world. In a minute I had a bag of crackers and a long-handled spoon, with an open can each of apricots and pineapples and cherries and green-gages beside of me with Uncle Emsley busy chopping away with the hatchet at the yellow clings. I was feeling like Adam before the apple stampede, and was digging my spurs into the side of the counter and working with my twenty-four-inch spoon when I happened to look out of the window into the yard of Uncle Emsley's house, which was next to the store.

'There was a girl standing there – an imported girl with fixings on – philandering with a croquet maul and amusing herself by watching my style of encouraging the fruit canning industry.

'I slid off the counter and delivered up my shovel to Uncle Emsley.

' "That's my niece," says he; "Miss Willella Learight, down from Palestine on a visit. Do you want that I should make you acquainted?"

' "The Holy Land," I says to myself, my thought milling some as I tried to run 'em into the corral. "Why not? There was sure angels in Pales — Why yes, Uncle Emsley," I says out loud, "I'd be awful edified to meet Miss Learight."

'So Uncle Emsley took me out in the yard and gave us each other's entitlements.

'I never was shy about women. I never could understand why some men who can break a mustang before breakfast and shave in the dark, get all left-handed and full of perspiration and excuses when they see a bolt of calico draped around what belongs in it. Inside of eight minutes me and Miss Willella was aggravating the croquet balls around as amiable as second cousins. She gave me a dig about the quantity of canned fruit I had eaten, and I got back at her, flat-footed, about how a certain lady named Eve started the fruit trouble in the first free-grass pasture – "Over in Palestine, wasn't it?" says I, as easy and pat as roping a one-year-old.

'That was how I acquired cordiality for the proximities of Miss Willella Learight; and the disposition grew larger as time passed. She was stopping at Pimienta Crossing for her health, which was very good, and for the climate, which was forty per cent. hotter than Palestine. I rode over to see her once every week for a while; and then I figured it out that if I doubled the number of trips I would see her twice as often.

'One week I slipped in a third trip; and that's where the pancakes and the pink-eyed snoozer busted into the game.

'That evening, while I set on the counter with a peach and two damsons in my mouth, I asked Uncle Emsley how Miss Willella was.

' "Why," says Uncle Emsley, "she's gone riding with Jackson Bird, the sheep man from over at Mired Mule Cañada."

'I swallowed the peach seed and the two damsons seeds. I guess somebody held the counter by the bridle while I got off; and then I walked out straight ahead till I butted against the mesquite where my roan was tied.

' "She's gone riding," I whispered in my bronc's ear, "with Birdstone Jack, the hired mule from Sheep Man's Cañada. Did you get that, old Leather-and-Gallops?"

'That bronc of mine wept, in his way. He'd been raised a cow pony and he didn't care for snoozers.

'I went back and said to Uncle Emsley: "Did you say a sheep man?"

' "I said a sheep man," says Uncle again. "You must have heard tell of Jackson Bird. He's got eight sections of grazing and four thousand head of the finest Merinos south of the Arctic Circle."

'I went out and sat on the ground in the shade of the store and leaned against a prickly pear. I sifted sand into my boots with unthinking hands while I soliloquized a quantity about this bird with the Jackson plumage to his name.

'I never had believed in harming sheep men. I see one, one day, reading a Latin grammar on hossback, and I never touched him! They never irritated me like they do most cowmen. You wouldn't go to work now, and impair and disfigure snoozers, would you, that eat on tables and wear little shoes and speak to you on subjects? I had always let 'em pass, just as you would a jack-rabbit; with a polite word and a guess about the weather, but no stopping to swap canteens. I never thought it was worth while to be hostile with a snoozer. And because I'd been lenient, and let 'em live, here was one going around riding with Miss Willella Learight!

'An hour by sun they come loping back, and stopped at Uncle Emsley's gate. The sheep person helped her off; and they stood throwing each other sentences all sprightful and sagacious for a while. And then this feathered Jackson flies up in his saddle and raises his little stewpot of a hat, and trots off in the direction of his mutton ranch. By this time I had turned the sand out of my boots and unpinned myself from the prickly pear; and by the time he gets half a mile out of Pimienta, I singlefoots up beside him on my bronc.

'I said that snoozer was pink-eyed, but he wasn't. His seeing arrangement was gray enough, but his eye-lashes was pink and his hair was sandy, and that gave you the idea. Sheep man – he wasn't more than a lamb man, anyhow – a little thing with his neck involved in a yellow silk handkerchief, and shoes tied up in bowknots.

' "Afternoon!" says I to him. "You now ride with a equestrian who is commonly called Dead-Moral-Certainty Judson, on account of the way I shoot. When I want a stranger to know me I always introduce myself before the draw, for I never did like to shake hands with ghosts."

' "Ah," says he, just like that – "Ah, I'm glad to know you, Mr. Judson. I'm Jackson Bird, from over at Mired Mule Ranch."

'Just then one of my eyes saw a roadrunner skipping down the hill with a young tarantula in his bill, and the other eye noticed a rabbit-hawk sitting on a dead limb in a water-elm. I popped over one after the other with my forty-five just to show him. "Two out of three," said I. "Birds just naturally seem to draw my fire wherever I go."

' "Nice shooting," says the sheep man, without a flutter. "But don't you sometimes ever miss the third shot? Elegant fine rain that was last week for the young grass, Mr. Judson," says he.

' "Willie," says I, riding over close to his palfrey, "your infatuated parents may have denounced you by the name of Jackson, but you sure moulted into a twittering Willie – let us slough of this here analysis of rain and the elements, and get down to talk that is outside the vocabulary of parrots. That is a bad habit you have got of riding with young ladies over at Pimienta. I've known birds," says I, "to be served on toast for less than that. Miss Willella," says I, "don't ever want any nest made out of sheep's wool by a tomtit of the Jacksonian branch of ornithology. Now, are you going to quit, or do you wish for to gallop up against this Dead-Moral-Certainty attachment to my name, which is good for two hyphens and at least one set of funeral obsequies?"

'Jackson Bird flushed up some, and then he laughed.

' "Why, Mr. Judson," says he, "you've got the wrong idea. I've called on Miss Learight a few times; but not for the purpose you imagine. My object is purely a gastronomical one."

'I reached for my gun.

' "Any coyote," says I, "that would boast of dishonorable — "

' "Wait a minute," says this Bird, "till I explain. What would I do with a wife? If you ever saw that ranch of mine! I do my own cooking and mending. Eating – that's all the pleasure I get out of sheep raising. Mr. Judson, did you ever taste the pancakes that Miss Learight makes?"

' "Me? No," I told him. "I never was advised that she was up to any culinary maneuvers."

' "They're golden sunshine," says he, "honey-browned by the ambrosial fires of Epicurus. I'd give two years of my life to get the recipe for making them pancakes. That's what I went to see Miss Learight for," says Jackson Bird, "but I haven't been able to get it from her. It's an old recipe that's been in the family for seventy-five years. They hand it down from one generation to another, but they don't give it away to outsiders. If I could get that recipe, so I could make them pancakes for myself on my ranch, I'd be a happy man," says Bird.

' "Are you sure," I says to him, "that it ain't the hand that mixes the pancakes that you're after?"

' "Sure," says Jackson. "Miss Learight is a mighty nice girl, but I can assure you my intentions go no further than the gastro—" but he seen my hand going down to my holster and he changed his similitude – "than the desire to procure a copy of the pancake recipe," he finishes.

' "You ain't such a bad little man," says I, trying to be fair. "I was thinking some of making orphans of your sheep, but I'll let you fly away this time. But you stick to pancakes," says I, "as close as the middle one of a stack; and don't go and mistake sentiments for syrup, or there'll be singing at your ranch, and you won't hear it."

' "To convince you that I am sincere," says the sheep man, "I'll ask you to help me. Miss Learight and you being closer friends, maybe she would do for you what she wouldn't for me. If you will get me a copy of that pancake recipe, I give you my word that I'll never call upon her again."

' "That's fair," I says, and I shook hands with Jackson Bird. "I'll get it for you if I can, and glad to oblige." And he turned off down the big pear flat on the Piedra, in the direction of Mired Mule; and I steered north-west for old Bill Toomey's ranch.

'It was five days afterward when I got another chance to ride over to Pimienta. Miss Willella and me passed a gratifying evening at Uncle Emsley's. She sang some, and exasperated the piano quite a lot with quotations from the operas. I gave imitations of a rattlesnake, and told her about Snaky McFee's new way of skinning cows, and described the trip I made to Saint Louis once. We was getting along in one another's estimations fine. Thinks I, if Jackson can now be persuaded to migrate, I win. I recollect his promise about the pancake receipt, and I thinks I will persuade it from Miss Willella and give it to him; and then if I catches Birdie off of Mired Mule again, I'll make him hop the twig.

'So, along about ten o'clock, I put on a wheedling smile and says to Miss Willella: "Now, if there's anything I do like better than the sight of a red steer on green grass it's the taste of a nice hot pancake smothered in sugarhouse molasses."

'Miss Willella gives a little jump on the piano stool, and looked at me curious.

' "Yes," says she, "they're real nice. What did you say was the name of that street in Saint Louis, Mr. Odom, where you lost your hat?"

' "Pancake Avenue," says I, with a wink, to show her that I was on about the family receipt, and couldn't be side-corralled off of the subject. "Come now, Miss Willella," I says; "let's hear how you make 'em. Pancakes is just whirling in my head like wagon wheels. Start her off, now – pound of flour, eight dozen eggs, and so on. How does the catalogue of constituents run?"

' "Excuse me for a moment, please," says Willella, and she gives me a quick kind of sideways look, and slides off the stool. She ambled out into the other room and directly Uncle Emsley comes in in his shirt sleeves, with a pitcher of water. He turns around to get a glass on the table, and I see a forty-five in his hip pocket. "Great post-holes!" thinks I, "but here's a family thinks a heap of cooking receipts, protecting it with firearms. I've known outfits that wouldn't do that much by a family feud."

' "Drink this here down," says Uncle Emsley, handing me the glass of water. "You've rid too far to-day, Jud, and got yourself over-excited. Try to think about something else now."

' "Do you know how to make them pancakes, Uncle Emsley?" I asked.

' "Well, I'm not as apprised in the anatomy of them as some," says Uncle Emsley, "but I reckon you take a sifter of plaster of paris and a little dough and saleratus and corn meal, and mix 'em with eggs and buttermilk as usual. Is old Bill going to ship beeves to Kansas City again this spring, Jud?"

'That was all the pancake specifications I could get that night. I didn't wonder that Jackson Bird found it uphill work. So I dropped the subject and talked with Uncle Emsley a while about hollow-horn and cyclones. And then Miss Willella came and said "Good-night." and I hit the breeze for the ranch.

'About a week afterward I met Jackson Bird riding out of Pimienta as I rode in, and we stopped in the road for a few frivolous remarks.

' "Got the bill of particulars for them flap-jacks yet?" I asked him.

' "Well, no," says Jackson. "I don't seem to have any success in getting hold of it. Did you try?"

' "I did," says I, "and 'twas like trying to dig a prairie dog out of his hole with a peanut hull. That pancake receipt must be a jooka-lorum, the way they hold on to it."

' "I'm 'most ready to give it up," says Jackson, so discouraged in his pronunciations that I felt sorry for him; "but I did want to know how to make them pancakes to eat on my lonely ranch," says he. "I lie awake at nights thinking how good they are."

' "You keep on trying for it," I tells him, "and I'll do the same. One of us is bound to get a rope over its horns before long. Well, so-long, Jacksy."

'You see, by this time we was on the peacefullest of terms. When I saw that he wasn't after Miss Willella I had more endurable contemplations of that sandy-haired snoozer. In order to help out the ambitions of his appetite I kept on trying to get that receipt from Miss Willella. But every time I would say "pancakes" she would get sort of remote and fidgety about the eye, and try to change the subject. If I held her to it she would slide out and round up Uncle Emsley with his pitcher of water and hip-pocket howitzer.

'One day I galloped over to the store with a fine bunch of blue verbenas that I cut out of a herd of wild flowers over on Poisoned Dog Prairie. Uncle Emsley looked at 'em with one eye shut and says:

' "Haven't ye heard the news?"

' "Cattle up?" I asks.

' "Willella and Jackson Bird was married in Palestine yesterday," says he. "Just got a letter this morning."

'I dropped them flowers in a cracker-barrel, and let the news trickle in my ears and down toward my upper left-hand shirt pocket until it got to my feet.

' "Would you mind saying that over again once more, Uncle Emsley?" says I. "Maybe my hearing has got wrong, and you only said that prime heifers was 4.80 on the hoof, or something like that."

' "Married yesterday," says Uncle Emsley, "and gone to Waco and Niagara Falls on a wedding tour. Why, didn't you see none of the signs all along? Jackson Bird has been courting Willella ever since that day he took her out riding."

' "Then," says I, in a kind of a yell, "what was all this zizzaparoola he gives me about pancakes? Tell me *that*."

'When I said "pancakes" Uncle Emsley sort of dodged and stepped back.

' "Somebody's been dealing me pancakes from the bottom of the deck," I says, "and I'll find out. I believe you know. Talk up," says I, "or we'll mix a panful of batter right here."

'I slid over the counter after Uncle Emsley. He grabbed at his gun, but it was in a drawer, and he missed it two inches. I got him by the front of his shirt and shoved him in a corner.

' "Talk pancakes," says I, "or be made into one. Does Miss Willella make 'em?"

' "She never made one in her life and I never saw one," says Uncle Emsley, soothing. "Calm down now, Jud – calm down. You've got excited, and that wound in your head is contaminating your sense of intelligence. Try not to think about pancakes."

' "Uncle Emsley," says I, "I'm not wounded in the head except so far as my natural cogitative instincts run to runts. Jackson Bird told me he was calling on Miss Willella for the purpose of finding out her system of producing pancakes, and he asked me to help him get the bill of lading of the ingredients. I done so, with the results as you see. Have I been sodded down with Johnson grass by a pink-eyed snoozer, or what?"

' "Slack up your grip on my dress shirt," says Uncle Emsley, "and I'll tell you. Yes, it looks like Jackson Bird has gone and humbugged you some. The day after he went riding with Willella he came back and told me and her to watch out for you whenever you go to talking about pancakes. He said you was in camp once where they was cooking flapjacks, and one of the fellows cut you over the head with a frying pan. Jackson said that whenever you got over-hot or excited that wound hurt you and made you kind of crazy, and you went raving about pancakes. He told us to just get you worked off of the subject and soothed down, and you wouldn't be dangerous. So, me and Willella done the best by you we knew how. Well, well," says Uncle Emsley, "that Jackson Bird is sure a seldom kind of a snoozer." '

During the progress of Jud's story he had been slowly but deftly combining certain portions of the contents of his sacks and cans. Toward the close of it he set before me the finished product – a pair of red-hot, rich-hued pancakes on a tin plate. From some secret hoarding place he also brought a lump of excellent butter and a bottle of golden syrup.

'How long ago did these things happen?' I asked him.

'Three years,' said Jud. 'They're living on the Mired Mule Ranch now.

But I haven't seen either of 'em since. They say Jackson Bird was fixing his ranch up fine with rocking chairs and window curtains all the time he was putting me up the pancake tree. Oh, I got over it after a while. But the boys kept the racket up.'

'Did you make these cakes by the famous recipe?' I asked.

'Didn't I tell you there wasn't no receipt?' said Jud. 'The boys hollered pancakes till they got pancake hungry, and I cut this receipt out of a newspaper. How does the truck taste?'

'They're delicious,' I answered. 'Why don't you have some, too, Jud?' I was sure I heard a sigh.

'Me?' said Jud. 'I don't never eat 'em.'

SEATS OF THE HAUGHTY

GOLDEN BY DAY AND SILVER BY NIGHT, a new trail now leads to us across the Indian Ocean. Dusky kings and princes have found out our Bombay of the West; and few be their trails that do not lead down Broadway on their journey for to admire and for to see.

If chance should ever lead you near a hotel that transiently shelters some one of these splendid touring grandees, I counsel you to seek Lucullus Polk among the republican tuft-hunters that besiege its entrances. He will be there. You will know him by his red, alert, Wellington-nosed face, by his manner of nervous caution mingled with determination, by his assumed promoter's or broker's air of busy impatience, and by his bright-red necktie, gallantly redressing the wrongs of his maltreated blue serge suit, like a battle standard, still waving above a lost cause. I found him profitable; and so may you. When you do look for him, look among the light-horse troop of Bedouins that besiege the picket-line of the travelling potentate's guards and secretaries – among the wild-eyed genii of Arabian Afternoons that gather to make astounding and egregious demands upon the prince's coffers.

I first saw Mr. Polk coming down the steps of the hotel at which sojourned His Highness the Gaekwar of Baroda, most enlightened of the Mahratta princes, who, of late, ate bread and salt in our Metropolis of the Occident.

Lucullus moved rapidly, as though propelled by some potent moral force that imminently threatened to become physical. Behind him closely followed the impetus – a hotel detective, if ever white Alpine hat, hawk's nose, implacable watch chain, and loud refinement of manner spoke the truth. A brace of uniformed porters at his heels preserved the smooth decorum of the hotel, repudiating by their air of disengagement any suspicion that they formed a reserve squad of ejectment.

Safe on the sidewalk, Lucullus Polk turned and shook a freckled fist at the caravansary. And, to my joy, he began to breathe deep invective in strange words.

'Rides in howdahs, does he?' he cried loudly and sneeringly. 'Rides on elephants in howdahs and calls himself a prince! Kings – yah! Comes over here and talks horse till you would think he was a president; and then goes home and rides in a private dining-room strapped onto an elephant. Well, well, well!'

The ejecting committee quietly retired. The scorner of princes turned to me and snapped his fingers.

'What do you think of that?' he shouted derisively. 'The Gaekwar of Baroda rides on an elephant in a howdah! And there's old Bikram Shamsher Jang scorching up and down the pig-paths of Khatmandu on a motor-cycle. Wouldn't that maharajah you? And the Shah of Persia, that ought to have been Muley-on-the-spot for at least three, he's got the palanquin habit. And that funny-hat prince from Korea – wouldn't you think he could afford to amble around on a milk-white palfrey once in a dynasty or two? Nothing doing! His idea of a Balaklava charge is to tuck his skirts under him and do his mile in six days over the hog-wallows of Seoul on a bull-cart. That's the kind of visiting potentates that come to this country now. It's a hard deal, friend.'

I murmured a few words of sympathy. But it was uncomprehending, for I did not know his grievance against the rulers who flash, meteor-like, now and then upon our shores.

'The last one I sold,' continued the displeased one, 'was to that three-horse-tailed Turkish pasha that came over a year ago. Five hundred dollars he paid for it, easy. I says to his executioner or secretary – he was a kind of a Jew or a Chinaman – " 'Tis Turkey Giblets is fond of horses, then?"

' "Him?" says the secretary. "Well, no. He's got a big, fat wife in the harem named Bad Dora that he don't like. I believe he intends to saddle her up and ride her up and down the board-walk in the Bulbul Gardens a few times every day. You haven't got a pair of extra long spurs you could throw in on the deal, have you?" Yes, sir, there's mighty few real rough-riders among the royal sports these days.'

As soon as Lucullus Polk got cool enough I picked him up, and with no greater effort than you would employ in persuading a drowning man to clutch a straw, I inveigled him into accompanying me to a cool corner in a dim café.

And it came to pass that men-servants set before us brewage; and Lucullus Polk spake unto me, relating the wherefores of his beleaguering the ante-chambers of the princes of the earth.

'Did you ever hear of the S. A. & A. P. Railroad in Texas? Well, that don't stand for Samaritan Actor's Aid Philanthropy. I was down that way managing a summer bunch of the gum and syntax-chewers that play the Idlewild Parks in the Western hamlets. Of course, we went to pieces when the soubrette ran away with a prominent barber of Beeville. I don't know what became of the rest of the company. I believe there were some salaries due; and the last I saw of the troupe was when I told them that forty-three cents was all the treasury contained. I say I never saw any of them after that; but I heard them for about twenty minutes. I didn't have time to look back. But after dark I came out of the woods and struck the S. A. & A. P. agent for means of transportation. He at once extended to me the courtesies of the entire railroad, kindly warning me, however, not to get aboard any of the rolling stock.

'About ten the next morning I steps off the ties into a village that calls itself Atascosa City. I bought a thirty-cent breakfast and a ten-cent cigar, and stood on Main Street jingling the three pennies in my pocket – dead broke. A man in Texas with only three cents in his pocket is no better off than a man that has no money and owes two cents.

'One of luck's favorite tricks is to soak a man for his last dollar so quick that he don't have time to look it. There I was in a swell St. Louis tailor-made, blue-and-green plaid suit, and an eighteen-carat sulphate-of-copper scarf pin, with no hope in sight except the two great Texas industries, the cotton fields, and grading new railroads. I never picked cotton, and I never cottoned to a pick, so the outlook had ultramarine edges.

'All of a sudden, while I was standing on the edge of the wooden sidewalk, down out of the sky falls two fine gold watches into the middle of the street. One hits a chunk of mud and sticks. The other falls hard and flies open, making a fine drizzle of little springs and screws and wheels. I looks up for a balloon or an airship; but not seeing any, I steps off the sidewalk to investigate.

'But I hear a couple of yells and see two men running up the street in leather overalls and high-heeled boots and carwheel hats. One man is six or eight feet high, with open-plumbed joints and a heartbroken cast of countenance. He picks up the watch that has stuck in the mud. The other man, who is little, with pink hair and white eyes, goes for the empty case, and says, "I win." Then the elevated pessimist goes down under his leather leg-holsters and hands a handful of twenty-dollar gold pieces to his albino friend. I don't know how much money it was; it looked as big as an earthquake-relief fund to me.

' "I'll have this here case filled up with the works," says Shorty, "and throw you again for five hundred."

' "I'm your company," says the high man. "I'll meet you at the Smoked Dog Saloon an hour from now."

'The little man hustles away with a kind of Swiss movement toward a jewelry store. The heartbroken person stoops over and takes a telescopic view of my haberdashery.

' "Them's a mighty slick outfit of habiliments you have got on, Mr. Man," says he. "I'll bet a hoss you never acquired the right, title, and interest in and to them clothes in Atascosa City."

' "Why no," says I, being ready enough to exchange personalities with this moneyed monument of melancholy. "I had this suit tailored from a special line of coatericks, vestures, and paintings in St. Louis. Would you mind putting me sane," says I, "on this watch-throwing contest? I've been used to seeing timepieces treated with more politeness and esteem – except women's watches, of course, which by nature they abuse by cracking walnuts with 'em and having 'em taken showing in tintype pictures."

' "Me and George," he explains, "are up from the ranch, having a spell of fun. Up to last month we owned four sections of watered grazing down on the San Miguel. But along comes one of these oil prospectors and begins to bore. He strikes a gusher that flows out twenty thousand – or maybe it was twenty million – barrels of oil a day. And me and George gets one hundred and fifty thousand dollars – seventy-five thousand dollars apiece – for the land. So now and then we saddles up and hits the breeze for Atascosa City for a few days of excitement and damage. Here's a little bunch of the *dinero* that I drawed out of the bank this morning," says he, and shows a roll of twenties and fifties as big around as a sleeping-car pillow. The yellowbacks glowed like a sun set on the gable end of Joh D's barn. My knees got weak, and I sat down on the edge of the board sidewalk.

' "You must have knocked around a right smart," goes on this oil Greaseus.

"I shouldn't be surprised if you have saw towns more livelier than what Atascosa City is. Sometimes it seems to me that there ought to be some more ways of having a good time than there is here, 'specially when you've got plenty of money and don't mind spending it."

'Then this Mother Cary's chick of the desert sits down by me and we hold a conversationfest. It seems that he was money-poor. He'd lived in ranch camps all his life; and he confessed to me that his supreme idea of luxury was to ride into camp, tired out from a roundup, eat a peck of Mexican beans, hobble his brains with a pint of raw whisky, and go to sleep with his boots for a pillow. When this bargeload of unexpected money came to him and his pink but perky partner, George, and they hied themselves to this clump of outhouses called Atascosa City, you know what happened to them. They had money to buy anything they wanted; but they didn't know what to want. Their ideas of spendthriftiness were limited to three – whisky, saddles, and gold watches. If there was anything else in the world to throw away fortunes on, they had never heard about it. So, when they wanted to have a hot time, they'd ride into town and get a city directory and stand in front of the principal saloon and call up the population alphabetically for free drinks. Then they would order three or four new California saddles from the storekeeper, and play crackloo on the sidewalk with twenty-dollar gold pieces. Betting who could throw his gold watch the farthest was an inspiration of George's; but even that was getting to be monotonous.

'Was I on to the opportunity? Listen.

'In thirty minutes I had dashed off a word picture of metropolitan joys that made life in Atascosa City look as dull as a trip to Coney Island with your own wife. In ten minutes more we shook hands on an agreement that I was to act as his guide, interpreter and friend in and to the aforesaid wassail and amenity. And Solomon Mills, which was his name, was to pay all expenses for a month. At the end of that time, if I had made good as director-general of the rowdy life, he was to pay me one thousand dollars. And then, to clinch the bargain, we called the roll of Atascosa City and put all of its citizens except the ladies and minors under the table, except one man named Horace Westervelt St. Claire. Just for that we bought a couple hatfuls of cheap silver watches and egged him out of town with 'em. We wound up by dragging the harness-maker out of bed and setting him to work on three new saddles; and then we went to sleep across the railroad track at the depot, just to annoy the S. A. & A. P. Think of having seventy-five thousand dollars and trying to avoid the disgrace of dying rich in a town like that!

'The next day George, who was married or something, started back to the ranch. Me and Solly, as I now called him, prepared to shake off our moth balls and wing our way against the arc-lights of the joyous and tuneful East.

' "No way-stops," says I to Solly, "except long enough to get you barbered and haberdashed. This is no Texas feet shampetter," says I, "where you eat chili-con-carne-con-huevos and then holler 'Whoopee!' across the plaza. We're now going against the real high life. We're going to mingle with the set that carries a Spitz, wears spats, and hits the ground in high spots."

'Solly puts six thousand dollars in century bills in one pocket of his brown ducks, and bills of lading for ten thousand dollars on Eastern banks in another. Then I resume diplomatic relations with the S. A. & A. P., and we hike in a northwesterly direction on our circuitous route to the spice gardens of the Yankee Orient.

'We stopped in San Antonio long enough for Solly to buy some clothes, and eight rounds of drinks for the guests and employees of the Menger Hotel, and order four Mexican saddles with silver trimmings and white Angora *suaderos* to be shipped down to the ranch. From there we made a big jump to St. Louis. We got there in time for dinner; and I put our thumb-prints on the register of the most expensive hotel in the city.

' "Now," says I to Solly, with a wink at myself, "here's the first dinner-station we've struck where we can get a real good plate of beans." And while he was up in his room trying to draw water out of the gas-pipe, I got one finger in the buttonhole of the head waiter's Tuxedo, drew him apart, inserted a two-dollar bill, and closed him up again.

' "Frankoyse," says I, "I have a pal here for dinner that's been subsisting for years on cereals and short stogies. You see the chef and order a dinner for us such as you serve to Dave Francis and the general passenger agent of the Iron Mountain when they eat here. We've got more than Bernhardt's tent full of money; and we want the nosebags crammed with all the Chief Deveries *de cuisine*. Object is no expense. Now, show us."

'At six o'clock me and Solly sat down to dinner. Spread! There's nothing been seen like it since the Cambon snack. It was all served at once. The chef called it *dinnay à la poker*. It's a famous thing among the gormands of the West. The dinner comes in threes of a kind. There was guinea-fowls, guinea-pigs, and Guinness's stout; roast veal, mock turtle soup, and chicken pâté; shad-roe, caviar, and tapioca; canvas-back duck, canvas-back ham, and cottontail rabbit; Philadelphia capon, fried snails, and sloe-gin – and so on, in threes. The idea was that you eat nearly all you can of them, and then the waiter takes away the discard and gives you pears to fill on.

'I was sure Solly would be tickled to death with these hands, after the bob-tail flushes he'd been eating on the ranch; and I was a little anxious that he should, for I didn't remember his having honored my efforts with a smile since we left Atascosa City.

'We were in the main dining room, and there was a fine-dressed crowd there, all talking loud and enjoyable about the two St. Louis topics, the water supply and the color line. They mix the two subjects so fast that strangers often think they are discussing water-colors; and that has given the old town something of a rep as an art centre. And over in the corner was a fine brass band playing; and now, thinks I, Solly will become conscious of the spiritual oats of life nourishing and exhilarating his system. But *nong, mong frang*.

'He gazed across the table at me. There was four square yards of it, looking like the path of a cyclone that has wandered through a stock-yard, a poultry-farm, a vegetable-garden, and an Irish linen mill. Solly gets up and comes around to me.

' "Luke," says he, "I'm pretty hungry after our ride. I thought you said they had some beans here. I'm going out and get something I can eat. You can stay and monkey with this artificial layout of grub if you want to."

' "Wait a minute," says I.

'I called the waiter, and slapped "S. Mills" on the back of the check for thirteen dollars and fifty cents.

' "What do you mean," says I, "by serving gentlemen with a lot of truck only suitable for deck hands on a Mississippi steamboat? We're going out to get something decent to eat."

'I walked up the street with the unhappy plainsman. He saw a saddle-shop open, and some of the sadness faded from his eyes. We went in, and he ordered and paid for two more saddles – one with a solid silver horn and nails and ornaments and a six-inch border of rhinestones and imitation rubies around the flaps. The other one had to have a gold-mounted horn, quadruple-plated stirrups, and the leather inlaid with silver bead-work wherever it would stand it. Eleven hundred dollars the two cost him.

'Then he goes out and heads toward the river, following his nose. In a little side street, where there was no street and no sidewalks and no houses, he finds what he is looking for. We go into a shanty and sit on high stools among stevedores and boatmen, and eat beans with tin spoons. Yes, sir, beans – beans boiled with salt pork.

' "I kind of thought we'd strike some over this way," says Solly.

' "Delightful," says I. "That stylish hotel grub may appeal to some; but for me, give me the husky *table d'goat*."

'When we had succumbed to the beans I leads him out of the tarpaulin-steam under a lamp post and pulls out a daily paper with the amusement column folded out.

' "But now, what ho for a merry round of pleasure," says I. "Here's one of Hall Caine's shows, and a stock-yard company in 'Hamlet,' and skating at the Hollowhorn Rink, and Sara Bernhardt, and the Shapely Syrens Burlesque Company. I should think, now, that the Shapely —'

'But what does this healthy, wealthy, and wise man do but reach his arms up to the second-story windows and gape noisily.

' "Reckon I'll be going to bed," says he, "it's about my time. St. Louis is a kind of quiet place, ain't it?"

' "Oh, yes," says I; "ever since the railroads ran in here the town's been practically ruined. And the building-and-loan associations and the fair have about killed it. Guess we might as well go to bed. Wait till you see Chicago though. Shall we get tickets for the Big Breeze to-morrow?"

' "Mought as well," says Solly. "I reckon all these towns are about alike."

'Well, maybe the wise cicerone and personal conductor didn't fall hard in Chicago; Loolooville-on-the-Lake is supposed to have one or two things in it calculated to keep the rural visitor awake after the curfew rings. But not for the grass-fed man of the pampas! I tried him with theatres, rides in automobiles, sails on the lake, champagne suppers, and all those little inventions that hold the simple life in check; but in vain. Solly grew sadder day by day. And I got fearful about my salary, and knew I must play my trump card. So I mentioned New York to him, and informed him that these Western towns were no more than gateways to the great walled city of the whirling dervishes.

'After I bought the tickets I missed Solly. I knew his habits by then; so in a couple of hours I found him in a saddle-shop. They had some new ideas there in the way of trees and girths that had strayed down from the Canadian mounted police; and Solly was so interested that he almost looked reconciled to live. He invested about nine hundred dollars in there.

'At the depot I telegraphed a cigar-store man I knew in New York to meet me at the Twenty-third Street ferry with a list of all the saddle-stores in the city. I wanted to know where to look for Solly when he got lost.

'Now I'll tell you what happened in New York. I says to myself: "Friend

Heherezade, you want to get busy and make Bagdad look pretty to the sad sultan of the sour countenance, or it'll be the bow string for yours." But I never had any doubt I could do it.

'I began with him like you'd feed a starving man. I showed him the horse-cars on Broadway and the Staten Island ferry-boats. And then I piled up the sensations on him, but always keeping a lot of warmer ones up my sleeve.

'At the end of the third day he looked like a composite picture of five thousand orphans too late to catch a picnic steamboat, and I was wilting down a collar every two hours wondering how I could please him and whether I was going to get my thou. He went to sleep looking at the Brooklyn Bridge; he disregarded the sky-scrapers above the third story; it took three ushers to wake him up at the liveliest vaudeville in town.

'Once I thought I had him. I nailed a pair of cuffs on him one morning before he was awake; and I dragged him that evening to the palm-cage of one of the biggest hotels in the city – to see the Johnnies and the Alice-sit-by-the-hours. They were out in numerous quantities, with the fat of the land showing in their clothes. While we were looking them over, Solly divested himself of a fearful, rusty kind of laugh – like moving a folding bed with one roller broken. It was his first in two weeks, and it gave me hope.

' "Right you are," says I. "They're a funny lot of post-cards, aren't they?"

' "Oh, I wasn't thinking of them dudes and culls on the hoof," says he. "I was thinking of the time me and George put sheep-dip in Horsehead Johnson's whisky. I wish I was back in Atascosa City," says he.

'I felt a cold chill run down my back. "Me to play and mate in one move," says I to myself.

'I made Solly promise to stay in the café for half an hour and I hiked out in a cab to Lolabelle Delatour's flat on Forty-third Street. I knew her well. She was a chorus-girl in a Broadway musical comedy.

' "Jane," says I when I found her, "I've got a friend from Texas here. He's all right, but – well, he carries weight. I'd like to give him a little whirl after the show this evening – bubbles, you know, and a buzz out to a casino for the whitebait and pickled walnuts. Is it a go?"

' "Can he sing?" asks Lolabelle.

' "You know," says I, "that I wouldn't take him away from home unless his notes were good. He's got pots of money – bean-pots full of it."

' "Bring him around after the second act," says Lolabelle, "and I'll examine his credentials and securities."

'So about ten o'clock that evening I led Solly to Miss Delatour's dressing-room, and her maid let us in. In ten minutes in comes Lolabelle, fresh from the stage, looking stunning in the costume she wears when she steps from the ranks of the lady grenadiers and says to the king, "Welcome to our May-day revels." And you can bet it wasn't the way she spoke the lines that got her the part.

'As soon as Solly saw her he got up and walked straight out through the stage entrance into the street. I followed him. Lolabelle wasn't paying my salary. I wondered whether anybody was.

' "Luke," says Solly, outside, "that was an awful mistake. We must have got into the lady's private room. I hope I'm gentleman enough to do anything possible in the way of apologies. Do you reckon she'd ever forgive us?"

' "She may forget it," says I. "Of course it was a mistake. Let's go find some beans."

'That's the way it went. But pretty soon afterward Solly failed to show up at dinner time for several days. I cornered him. He confessed that he had found a restaurant on Third Avenue where they cooked beans in Texas style. I made him take me there. The minute I set foot inside the door I threw up my hands.

'There was a young woman at the desk, and Solly introduced me to her. And then we sat down and had beans.

'Yes, sir, sitting at the desk was the kind of a young woman that can catch any man in the world as easy as lifting a finger. There's a way of doing it. She knew. I saw her working it. She was healthy-looking and plain dressed. She had her hair drawn back from her forehead and face – no curls or frizzes; that's the way she looked. Now I'll tell you the way they work the games; it's simple. When she wants a man, she manages it so that every time he looks at her he finds her looking at him. That's all.

'The next evening Solly was to go to Coney Island with me at seven. At eight o'clock he hadn't showed up. I went out and found a cab. I felt sure there was something wrong.

' "Drive to the Back Home Restaurant on Third Avenue," says I. "And if I don't find what I want there, take in these saddle-shops." I handed him the list.

' "Boss," says the cabby, "I et a steak in that restaurant once. If you're real hungry, I advise you to try the saddle-shops first."

' "I'm a detective," says I, "and I don't eat. Hurry up!"

'As soon as I got to the restaurant I felt in the lines of my palms that I should beware of a tall, red, damfool man, and I was going to lose a sum of money.

'Solly wasn't there. Neither was the smooth-haired lady.

'I waited; and in an hour they came in a cab and got out, hand in hand. I asked Solly to step around the corner for a few words. He was grinning clear across his face; but I had not administered the grin.

' "She's the greatest that ever sniffed the breeze," says he.

' "Congrats," says I. "I'd like to have my thousand now if you please."

' "Well, Luke," says he, "I don't know that I've had such a skyhoodlin' fine time under your tutelage and dispensation. But I'll do the best I can for you – I'll do the best I can," he repeats. "Me and Miss Skinner was married an hour ago. We're leaving for Texas in the morning."

' "Great!" says I. "Consider yourself covered with rice and Congress gaiters. But don't let's tie so many satin bows on our business relations that we lose sight of 'em. How about my honorarium?"

' "Missis Mills," says he, "has taken possession of my money and papers except six bits. I told her what I'd agreed to give you; but she says it's an irreligious and illegal contract, and she won't pay a cent of it. But I ain't going to see you treated unfair," says he. "I've got eighty-seven saddles on the ranch what I've bought on this trip; and when I get back I'm going to pick out the best six in the lot and send 'em to you." '

'And did he?' I asked, when Lucullus ceased talking.

'He did. And they are fit for kings to ride on. The six he sent me must have cost him three thousand dollars. But where is the market for 'em? Who would buy one except one of these rajahs and princes of Asia and Africa? I've

got 'em all on the list. I know ever tan royal dub and princerino from
Mindanao to the Caspian Sea.'

'It's a long time between customers,' I ventured.

'They're coming faster,' said Polk. 'Nowadays, when one of the murdering
mutts gets civilized enough to abolish suttee and quite using his whiskers for
a napkin, he calls himself the Roosevelt of the East, and comes over to
investigate our Chautauquas and cocktails. I'll place 'em all yet. Now look
here.'

From an inside pocket he drew a tightly folded newspaper with much-
worn edges, and indicated a paragraph.

'Read that,' said the saddler to royalty. The paragraph ran thus:

His Highness Seyyid Feysal bin Turkee, Imam of Muskat, is one of
the most progressive and enlightened rulers of the Old World. His
stables contain more than a thousand horses of the purest Persian breeds.
It is said that this powerful prince contemplates a visit to the United
States at an early date.

'There!' said Mr. Polk triumphantly. 'My best saddle is as good as sold –
the one with turquoises set in the rim of the cantle. Have you three dollars
that you could loan me for a short time?'

It happened that I had; and I did.

If this should meet the eye of the Imam of Muskat, may it quicken his
whim to visit the land of the free! Otherwise I fear that I shall be longer
than a short time separated from my dollars three.

HYGEIA AT THE SOLITO

IF YOU ARE KNOWING IN THE CHRONICLES of the ring you will recall to mind an
event in the early 'nineties when, for a minute and sundry odd seconds, a
champion and a 'would-be' faced each other on the alien side of an international river. So brief a conflict had rarely imposed upon the fair promise
of true sport. The reporters made what they could of it, but, divested of
padding, the action was sadly fugacious. The champion merely smote his
victim, turned his back upon him, remarking, 'I know what I done to dat
stiff,' and extended an arm like a ship's mast for his glove to be removed.

Which accounts for a trainload of extremely disgusted gentlemen in uproar
of fancy vests and neckwear being spilled from their Pullman in San Antonio
in the early morning following the fight. Which also partly accounts for the
unhappy predicament in which 'Cricket' McGuire found himself as he
tumbled from his car and sat upon the depot platform, torn by a spasm of
that hollow, racking cough so familiar to San Antonian ears. At that time,
in the uncertain light of dawn, that way passed Curtis Raidler, the Nueces
County cattleman – may his shadow never measure under six feet two.

The cattleman, out this early to catch the south-bound for his ranch
station, stopped at the side of the distressed patron of sport and spoke in the
kindly drawl of his ilk and region, 'Got it pretty bad, bud?'

'Cricket' McGuire, exfeather-weight prize-fighter, tout, jockey, follower of the 'ponies,' all-around sport, and manipulator of the gum balls and walnut shells, looked up pugnaciously at the imputation cast by 'bud.'

'G'wan,' he rasped, 'telegraph pole. I didn't ring for yer.'

Another paroxysm wrung him, and he leaned limply against a convenient baggage truck. Raidler waited patiently, glancing around at the white hats, short overcoats, and big cigars thronging the platform. 'You're from the No'th ain't you, bud?' he asked when the other was partially recovered. 'Come down to see the fight?'

'Fight!' snapped McGuire. 'Puss-in-the-corner. 'Twas a hypodermic injection. Handed him just one like a squirt of dope, and he's asleep, and no tanbark needed in front of his residence. Fight!' He rattled a bit, coughed, and went on, hardly addressing the cattleman, but rather for the relief of voicing his troubles. 'No more dead sure t'ings for me. But Rus Sage himself would have snatched at it. Five to one dat de boy from Cork wouldn't stay t'ree rounds is what I invested in. Put my last cent on, and could already smell the sawdust in dat all-night joint of Jimmy Delaney's on T'irty-seventh Street I was goin' to buy. And den – say, telegraph pole, what a gazaboo a guy is to put his whole roll on one turn of the gaboozlum!'

'You're plenty right,' said the big cattleman; 'more 'specially when you lose. Son, you get up and light out for a hotel. You got a mighty bad cough. Had it long?'

'Lungs,' said McGuire comprehensively. 'I got it. The croaker says I'll come to time for six months longer – maybe a year if I hold my gait. I wanted to settle down and take care of myself. Dat's why I speculated on dat five to one perhaps. I had a t'ousand iron dollars saved up. If I winned I was goin' to buy Delaney's café. Who'd a t'ought dat stiff would take a nap in de foist round – say?'

'It's a hard deal,' commented Raidler, looking down at the diminutive form of McGuire crumpled against the truck. 'But you go to a hotel and rest. There's the Menger and the Maverick, and —'

'And the Fi'th Av'noo, and the Waldorf-Astoria,' mimicked McGuire. 'Told you I went broke. I'm on de bum proper. I've got one dime left. Maybe a trip to Europe or a sail in me private yacht would fix me up – pa'per!'

He flung his dime at a newsboy, got his *Express*, propped his back against the truck, and was at once rapt in the account of his Waterloo, as expanded by the ingenious press.

Custis Raidler interrogated an enormous gold watch, and laid his hand on McGuire's shoulder.

'Come on, bud,' he said. 'We got three minutes to catch the train.'

Sarcasm seemed to be McGuire's vein.

'You ain't seen me cash in any chips or call a turn since I told you I was broke, a minute ago, have you? Friend, chase yourself away.'

'You're going down to my ranch,' said the cattleman, 'and stay till you get well. Six months'll fix you good as new.' He lifted McGuire with one hand, and half-dragged him in the direction of the train.

'What about the money?' said McGuire, struggling weakly to escape.

'Money for what?' asked Raidler, puzzled. They eyed each other, not understanding, for they touched only as at the gear of bevelled cog-wheels – at right angles, and moving upon different axes.

Passengers on the south-bound saw them seated together, and wondered at the conflux of two such antipodes. McGuire was five feet one, with a

countenance belonging to either Yokohama or Dublin. Bright-beady of eye,
bony of cheek and jaw, scarred, toughened, broken and reknit, indestructible,
grisly, gladiatorial as a hornet, he was a type neither new nor unfamiliar.
Raidler was the product of a different soil. Six feet two in height, miles broad,
and no deeper than a crystal brook, he represented the union of the West
and South. Few accurate pictures of his kind have been made, for art galleries
are so small and the mutoscope is as yet unknown in Texas. After all, the
only possible medium of portrayal of Raidler's kind would be the fresco –
something high and simple and cool and unframed.

They were rolling southward on the International. The timber was
huddling into little, dense green motts at rare distances before the inundation
of the downright, vert prairies. This was the land of the ranches; the domain
of the kings of the kine.

McGuire sat, collapsed into his corner of the seat, receiving with acid
suspicion the conversation of the cattleman. What was the 'game' of this big
'geezer' who was carrying him off? Altruism would have been McGuire's
last guess. 'He ain't no farmer,' thought the captive, 'and he ain't no con
man, for sure. W'at's his lay? You trail in, Cricket, and see how many cards
he draws. You're up against it, anyhow. You get a nickel and gallopin'
consumption, and you better lay low. Lay low and see w'at's his game.'

At Rincon, a hundred miles from San Antonio, they left the train for a
buckboard which was waiting there for Raidler. In this they travelled the
thirty miles between the station and their destination. If anything could,
this drive should have stirred the acrimonious McGuire to a sense of his
ransom. They sped upon velvet wheels across an exhilarant savanna. The
pair of Spanish ponies struck a nimble, tireless trot, which gait they occa-
sionally relieved by a wild, untrammelled gallop. The air was wine and
seltzer, perfumed, as they absorbed it, with the delicate redolence of prairie
flowers. The road perished, and the buckboard swam the uncharted billows
of the grass itself, steered by the practised hand of Raidler, to whom each
tiny distant mott of trees was a signboard, each convolution of the low hills
a voucher of course and distance. But McGuire reclined upon his spine,
seeing nothing but a desert, and receiving the cattleman's advances with
sullen distrust. 'W'at's he up to?' was the burden of his thoughts; 'w'at kind
of a gold brick has the big guy got to sell?' McGuire was only applying the
measure of the streets he had walked to a range bounded by the horizon and
the fourth dimension.

A week before, while riding the prairies, Raidler had come upon a sick
and weakling calf deserted and bawling. Without dismounting he had reached
and slung the distressed bossy across his saddle, and dropped it at the ranch
for the boys to attend to. It was impossible for McGuire to know or
comprehend that, in the eyes of the cattleman, his case and that of the calf
were identical in interest and demand upon his assistance. A creature was ill
and helpless; he had the power to render aid – these were the only postulates
required for the cattleman to act. They formed his system of logic and the
most of his creed. McGuire was the seventh invalid whom Raidler had
picked up thus casually in San Antonio, where so many thousand go for the
ozone that is said to linger about its contracted streets. Five of them had been
guests of Solito Ranch until they had been able to leave, cured or better, and
exhausting the vocabulary of tearful gratitude. One came too late, but rested
very comfortably, at last, under a ratama tree in the garden.

So, then, it was no surprise to the ranchhold when the buckboard spun to the door, and Raidler took up his debile *protégé* like a handful of rags and set him down upon the gallery.

McGuire looked upon things strange to him. The ranch-house was the best in the country. It was built of brick hauled one hundred miles by wagon, but it was of but one story, and its four rooms were completely encircled by a mud floor 'gallery.' The miscellaneous setting of horses, dogs, saddles, wagons, guns, and cow-punchers' paraphernalia oppressed the metropolitan eye of the wrecked sportsman.

'Well, here we are at home,' said Raidler, cheeringly.

'It's a h – l of a looking place,' said McGuire promptly, as he rolled upon the gallery floor, in a fit of coughing.

'We'll try to make it comfortable for you, buddy,' said the cattleman, gently. 'It ain't fine inside; but it's the outdoors, anyway, that'll do you the most good. This'll be your room, in here. Anything we got, you ask for it.'

He led McGuire into the east room. The floor was bare and clean. White curtains waved in the gulf breeze through the open windows. A big willow rocker, two straight chairs, a long table covered with newspapers, pipes, tobacco, spurs, and cartridges stood in the centre. Some well-mounted heads of deer and one of an enormous black javeli projected from the walls. A wide, cool cot-bed stood in a corner. Nueces County people regarded this guest chamber as fit for a prince. McGuire showed his eye teeth at it. He took out his nickel and spun it up to the ceiling.

'T'ought I was lyin' about the money, did ye? Well, you can frisk me if you wanter. Dat's the last simoleon in the treasury. Who's goin' to pay?'

The cattleman's clear gray eyes looked steadily from under his grizzly brows into the huckleberry optics of his guest. After a little he said simply, and not ungraciously, 'I'll be much obliged to you, son, if you won't mention money any more. Once was quite a plenty. Folks I ask to my ranch don't have to pay anything, and they very scarcely ever offers it. Supper'll be ready in half an hour. There's water in the pitcher, and some, cooler, to drink in that red jar hanging on the gallery.'

'Where's the bell?' asked McGuire, looking about.

'Bell for what?'

'Bell to ring for things. I can't – see here,' he exploded in a sudden weak fury, 'I never asked you to bring me here. I never held you up for a cent. I never gave you a hard-luck story till you asked me. Here I am fifty mile from a bellboy or a cocktail. I'm sick. I can't hustle. Gee! but I'm up against it!' McGuire fell upon the cot and sobbed shiveringly.

Raidler went to the door and called. A slender, bright-complexioned Mexican youth about twenty came quickly. Raidler spoke to him in Spanish.

'Ylario, it is in my mind that I promised you the position of *vaquero* on the San Carlos range at the fall *rodeo*.'

'*Sí señor*, such was your goodness.'

'Listen. This *señorito* is my friend. He is very sick. Place yourself at his side. Attend to his wants at all times. Have much patience and care with him. And when he is well, or – and when he is well, instead of *vaquero* I will make you *mayordomo* of the Rancho de las Piedras. *Está bueno?*'

'*Sí, sí – mil gracias, señor*.' Ylario tried to kneel upon the floor in his gratitude, but the cattleman kicked at him benevolently, growling, 'None of your opery-house antics, now.'

Ten minutes later Ylario came from McGuire's room and stood before Raidler.

'The little *señor*,' he announced, 'presents his compliments' (Raidler credited Ylario with the preliminary) 'and desires some pounded ice, one hot bath, one gin feez-z, that the windows be all closed, toast, one shave, one Newyorkheral', cigarettes, and to send one telegram.'

Raidler took a quart bottle of whisky from his medicine cabinet. 'Here, take him this,' he said.

Thus was instituted the reign of terror at the Solito Ranch. For a few weeks McGuire blustered and boasted and swaggered before the cow-punchers who rode in for miles around to see this latest importation of Raidler's. He was an absolutely new experience to them. He explained to them all the intricate points of sparring and the tricks of training and defence. He opened to their minds' view all the indecorous life of a tagger after professional sports. His jargon of slang was a continuous joy and surprise to them. His gestures, his strange poses, his frank ribaldry of tongue and principle fascinated them. He was like a being from a new world.

Strange to say, this new world he had entered did not exist to him. He was an utter egoist of bricks and mortar. He had dropped out, he felt, in open space for a time, and all it contained was an audience for his reminiscences. Neither the limitless freedom of the prairie days nor the grand hush of the close-drawn, spangled nights touched him. All the hues of Aurora could not win him from the pink pages of a sporting journal. 'Get something for nothing,' was his mission in life; 'T'irty-seventh' Street was his goal.

Nearly two months after his arrival he began to complain that he felt worse. It was then that he became the ranch's incubus, its harpy, its Old Man of the Sea. He shut himself in his room like some venomous kobold or flibbertigibbet, whining, complaining, cursing, accusing. The keynote of his plaint was that he had been inveigled into a gehenna against his will; that he was dying of neglect and lack of comforts. With all his dire protestations of increasing illness, to the eye of others he remained unchanged. His currant-like eyes were as bright and diabolic as ever; his voice was as rasping; his callous face, with the skin drawn tense as a drum-head, had no flesh to lose. A flush on his prominent cheek bones each afternoon hinted that a clinical thermometer might have revealed a symptom, and percussion might have established the fact that McGuire was breathing with only one lung, but his appearance remained the same.

In constant attendance upon him was Ylario, whom the coming reward of the *mayordomoship* must have greatly stimulated, for McGuire chained him to a bitter existence. The air – the man's only chance for life – he commanded to be kept out by closed windows and drawn curtains. The room was always blue and foul with cigarette smoke; whosoever entered it must sit, suffocating, and listen to the imp's interminable gasconade concerning his scandalous career.

The oddest thing of all was the relation existing between McGuire and his benefactor. The attitude of the invalid toward the cattleman was something like that of a peevish, perverse child toward an indulgent parent. When Raidler would leave the ranch McGuire would fall into a fit of malevolent, silent sullenness. When he returned, he would be met by a string of violent and stinging reproaches. Raidler's attitude toward his charge was quite inexplicable in its way. The cattleman seemed actually to assume and feel the character assigned him by McGuire's intemperate accusations – the character of tyrant and guilty oppressor. He seemed to have adopted the responsibility of the fellow's condition, and he always met his tirades with a pacific, patient, and even remorseful kindness that never altered.

One day Raidler said to him, 'Try more air, son. You can have the buckboard and a driver every day if you'll go. Try a week or two in one of the cow camps. I'll fix you up plum comfortable. The ground, and the air next to it – them's the things to cure you. I knowed a man from Philadelphy, sicker than you are, got lost on the Guadalupe, and slept on the bare grass in sheep camps for two weeks. Well, sir, it started him getting well, which he done. Close to the ground – that's where the medicine in the air stays. Try a little hossback riding now. There's a gentle pony – '

'What've I done to yer?' screamed McGuire. 'Did I ever double-cross yer? Did I ask you to bring me here? Drive me out to your camps if you wanter; or stick a knife in me and save trouble. Ride! I can't lift my feet. I couldn't sidestep a jar from a five-year-old kid. That's what your d – d ranch has done for me. There's nothing to eat, nothing to see, and nobody to talk to but a lot of Reubens who don't know a punching bag from lobster salad.'

'It's a lonesome place, for certain,' apologized Raidler abashedly. 'We got plenty, but it's rough enough. Anything you think of you want, the boys'll ride up and fetch it down for you.'

It was Chad Murchison, a cow-puncher from the Circle Bar outfit, who first suggested that McGuire's illness was fraudulent. Chad had brought a basket of grapes for him thirty miles, and four out of his way, tied to his saddle-horn. After remaining in the smoke-tainted room for a while, he emerged and bluntly confided his suspicions to Raidler.

'His arm,' said Chad, 'is harder'n a diamond. He interduced me to what he called a shore-perplexus punch, and 'twas like being kicked twice by a mustang. He's playin' it low down on you, Curt. He ain't no sicker'n I am. I hate to say it, but the runt's workin' you for range and shelter.'

The cattleman's ingenuous mind refused to entertain Chad's view of the case, and when, later, he came to apply the test, doubt entered not into his motives.

One day, about noon, two men drove up to the ranch, alighted, hitched, and came in to dinner; standing and general invitations being the custom of the country. One of them was a great San Antonio doctor, whose costly services had been engaged by a wealthy cowman who had been laid low by an accidental bullet. He was now being driven to the station to take the train back to town. After dinner Raidler took him aside, pushed a twenty-dollar bill against his hand, and said:

'Doc, there's a young chap in that room I guess has got a bad case of consumption. I'd like for you to look him over and see just how bad he is, and if we can do anything for him.'

'How much was that dinner I just ate, Mr. Raidler?' said the doctor bluffly, looking over his spectacles. Raidler returned the money to his pocket. The doctor immediately entered McGuire's room, and the cattleman seated himself upon a heap of saddles on the gallery, ready to reproach himself in the event the verdict should be unfavorable.

In ten minutes the doctor came briskly out. 'Your man,' he said promptly, 'is as sound as a new dollar. His lungs are better than mine. Respiration, temperature, and pulse normal. Chest expansion four inches. Not a sign of weakness anywhere. Of course I didn't examine for the bacillus, but it isn't there. You can put my name to the diagnosis. Even cigarettes and a vilely close room haven't hurt him. Coughs, does he? Well, you tell him it isn't necessary. You asked if there is anything we could do for him. Well, I advise you to set him digging post-holes or breaking mustangs. There's our team ready. Good-day, sir.' And like a puff of wholesome, blustery wind the doctor was off.

Raidler reached out and plucked a leaf from a mesquite bush by the railing, and began chewing it thoughtfully.

The branding season was at hand, and the next morning Ross Hargis, foreman of the outfit, was mustering his force of some twenty-five men at the ranch, ready to start for the San Carlos range, where the work was to begin. By six o'clock the horses were all saddled, the grub wagon ready, and the cow-punchers were swinging themselves upon their mounts, when Raidler bade them wait. A boy was bringing up an extra pony, bridled and saddled, to the gate. Raidler walked to McGuire's room and threw open the door. McGuire was lying on his cot, not yet dressed, smoking.

'Get up,' said the cattleman, and his voice was clear and brassy, like a bugle.

'How's that?' asked McGuire, a little startled.

'Get up and dress. I can stand a rattlesnake, but I hate a liar. Do I have to tell you again?' He caught McGuire by the neck and stood him on the floor.

'Say, friend,' cried McGuire wildly, 'are you bug-house? I'm sick – see? I'll croak if I got to hustle. What've I done to yer?' he began his chronic whine – 'I never asked yer to—'

'Put on your clothes,' called Raidler, in a rising tone.

Swearing, stumbling, shivering, keeping his amazed, shiny eyes upon the now menacing form of the aroused cattleman, McGuire managed to tumble into his clothes. Then Raidler took him by the collar and shoved him out and across the yard to the extra pony hitched at the gate. The cow-punchers lolled in their saddles, open-mouthed.

'Take this man,' said Raidler to Ross Hargis, 'and put him to work. Make him work hard, sleep hard, and eat hard. You boys know I done what I could for him, and he was welcome. Yesterday the best doctor in San Antone examined him, and says he's got the lungs of a burro and the constitution of a steer. You know what to do with him, Ross.'

Ross Hargis only smiled grimly.

'Aw,' said McGuire, looking intently at Raidler, with a peculiar expression upon his face, 'the croaker said I was all right, did he? Said I was fakin', did he? You put him onto me. You t'ought I wasn't sick. You said I was a liar. Say, friend, I talked rough, I know, but I didn't mean most of it. If you felt like I did – aw! I forgot – I ain't sick, the croaker says. Well, friend, now I'll go work for yer. Here's where you play even.'

He sprang into the saddle easily as a bird, got the quirt from the horn, and gave his pony a slash with it. 'Cricket,' who once brought in Good Boy by a neck at Hawthorne – and a 10 to 1 shot – had his foot in the stirrups again.

McGuire led the cavalcade as they dashed away from San Carlos, and the cow-punchers gave a yell of applause as they closed in behind his dust.

But in less than a mile he had lagged to the rear, and was last man when they struck the patch of high chaparral below the horse pens. Behind a clump of this he drew rein, and held a handkerchief to his mouth. He took it away drenched with bright, arterial blood, and threw it carefully into a clump of prickly pear. Then he slashed with his quirt again, gasped 'G'wan' to his astonished pony, and galloped after the gang.

That night Raidler received a message from his old home in Alabama. There had been a death in the family; an estate was to divide, and they called for him to come. Daylight found him in the buckboard, skimming the prairies for the station. It was two months before he returned. When he arrived at the ranch-house he found it well-nigh deserted save for Ylario, who acted as a kind of steward during his absence. Little by little the youth made him acquainted with the work done while he was away. The branding camp, he was informed, was still doing business. On account of many severe storms the cattle had been badly scattered, and the branding had been accomplished but slowly. The camp was now in the valley of the Guadalupe, twenty miles away.

'By the way,' said Raidler, suddenly remembering, 'that fellow I sent along with them – McGuire – is he working yet?'

'I do not know,' said Ylario. 'Man's from the camp come verree few times to the ranch. So plentee work with the leetle calves. They no say. Oh, I think that fellow McGuire he dead much time ago.'

'Dead!' said Raidler. 'What you talking about?'

'Verree sick fellow, McGuire,' replied Ylario, with a shrug of his shoulder. 'I theenk he no live one, two month when he go away.'

'Shucks!' said Raidler. 'He humbugged you too, did he? The doctor examined him and said he was sound as a mesquite knot.'

'That doctor,' said Ylario, smiling, 'he tell you so? That doctor no see McGuire.'

'Talk up,' ordered Raidler. 'What the devil do you mean?'

'McGuire,' continued the boy tranquilly, 'he getting drink water outside when that doctor come in room. That doctor take me and pound me all over here with his fingers' – putting his hand to his chest – 'I not know for what. He put his ear here and here and here, and listen – I not know for what. He put his little glass stick in my mouth. He feel my arm here. He make me count like whisper – so – twenty, *treinta, cuarenta*. Who knows,' concluded Ylario, with a deprecating spread of his hands, 'for what that doctor do those verree droll and such-like things?'

'What horses are up?' asked Raidler, shortly.

'Paisano is grazing out behind the little corral, *señor*.'

'Saddle him for me at once.'

Within a very few minutes the cattleman was mounted and away. Paisano, well named after that ungainly but swift-running bird, struck into his long lope that ate up the road like a strip of macaroni. In two hours and a quarter Raidler, from a gentle swell, saw the branding camp by a water hole in the Guadalupe. Sick with expectancy of the news he feared, he rode up, dismounted, and dropped Paisano's reins. So gentle was his heart that at that moment he would have pleaded guilty to the murder of McGuire.

The only being in the camp was the cook, who was just arranging the hunks of barbecued beef, and distributing the tin coffee cups for supper. Raidler evaded a direct question concerning the one subject in his mind.

'Everything all right in camp, Pete?' he managed to inquire.

'So, so,' said Pete, conservatively. 'Grub give out twice. Wind scattered the cattle, and we've had to rake the brush for forty mile. I need a new coffee-pot. And the mosquitoes is some more hellish than common.'

'The boys – all well?'

Pete was no optimist. Besides, inquiries concerning the health of cow-punchers were not only superfluous, but bordered on flaccidity. It was not like the boss to make them.

'What's left of 'em don't miss no calls to grub,' the cook conceded.

'What's left of 'em?' repeated Raidler in a husky voice. Mechanically he began to look around for McGuire's grave. He had in his mind a white slab such as he had seen in the Alabama church-yard. But immediately he knew that was foolish.

'Sure,' said Pete; 'what's left. Cow camps change in two months. Some's gone.'

Raidler nerved himself.

'That – chap – I sent along – McGuire – did – he—'

'Say,' interrupted Pete, rising with a chunk of corn bread in each hand, that was a dirty shame, sending that poor, sick kid to a cow camp. A doctor that couldn't tell he was graveyard meat ought to be skinned with a cinch buckle. Game as he was, too – it's a scandal among snakes – lemme tell you what he done. First night in camp the boys started to initiate him in the leather breeches degree. Ross Hargis busted him one swipe with his chaparreras, and what do you reckon the poor child did? Got up, the little skeeter, and licked Ross. Licked Ross Hargis. Licked him good. Hit him plenty and everywhere and hard. Ross'd just get up and pick out a fresh place to lay down on agin.

'Then that McGuire goes off there and lays down with his head in the grass and bleeds. A hem'ridge they calls it. He lays there eighteen hours by the watch, and they can't budge him. Then Ross Hargis, who loves any man who can lick him, goes to work and damns the doctors from Greenland to Poland Chiny; and him and Green Branch Johnson they gets McGuire in a tent, and spells each other feedin' him chopped raw meat and whisky.

'But it looks like the kid ain't got no appetite to git well, for they misses him from the tent in the night and finds him rootin' in the grass, and likewise a drizzle fallin'. "Gwan," he says, "lemme go and die like I wanter. He said I was a liar and a fake and I was playin' sick. Lemme alone."

'Two weeks,' went on the cook, 'he laid around, not noticin' nobody, and then—'

A sudden thunder filled the air, and a score of galloping centaurs crashed through the brush into camp.

'Illustrious rattlesnakes!' exclaimed Pete, springing all ways at once: 'here's the boys come, and I'm an assassinated man if supper ain't ready in three minutes.'

But Raidler saw only one thing. A little brown-faced, grinning chap, springing from his saddle in the full light of the fire. McGuire was not like that, and yet—

In another instant the cattleman was holding him by the hand and shoulder.

'Son, son, how goes it?' was all he found to say.

'Close to the ground, says you,' shouted McGuire, crunching Raidler's fingers in a grip of steel; 'and dat's where I found it – healt' and strengt', and tumbled to what a cheap skate I been actin'. T'anks fer kickin' me out, old man. And – say! de joke's on dat croaker, ain't it? I looked t'rough the window and see him playin' tag on dat Dago kid's solar plexus.'

'You son of a tinker,' growled the cattleman, 'whyn't you talk up and say the doctor never examined you?'

'Aw – g'wan!' said McGuire, with a flash of his old asperity, 'no-body can't bluff me. You never ast me. You made your spiel, and you t'rowed me out, and I let it go at dat. And, say, friend, dis chasin' cows is outer sight. Dis is de whitest bunch of sports I ever travelled with. You'll let me stay, won't yer, old man?'

Raidler looked wonderingly toward Ross Hargis.

'That cussed little runt,' remarked Ross tenderly, 'is the Jo-dartin'est hustler – and the hardest hitter in anybody's cow camp.'

AN AFTERNOON MIRACLE

AT THE UNITED STATES END of an international river bridge, four armed rangers sweltered in a little 'dobe hut, keeping a fairly faithful espionage upon the lagging trail of passengers from the Mexican side.

Bud Dawson, proprietor of the Top Notch Saloon, had, on the evening previous, violently ejected from his premises one Leandro Garcia, for alleged violation of the Top Notch code of behavior. Garcia had mentioned twenty-four hours as a limit, by which time he would call and collect plentiful indemnity for personal satisfaction.

This Mexican, although a tremendous braggart, was thoroughly courageous, and each side of the river respected him for one of these attributes. He and a following of similar bravos were addicted to the pastime of retrieving towns from stagnation.

The day designated by Garcia for retribution was to be further signalized on the American side by a cattlemen's convention, a bull fight, and an old settlers' barbecue and picnic. Knowing the avenger to be a man of his word, and believing it prudent to court peace while three such gently social relaxations were in progress, Captain McNulty, of the ranger company stationed there, detailed his lieutenant and three men for duty at the end of the bridge. Their instructions were to prevent the invasion of Garcia, either alone or attended by his gang.

Travel was slight that sultry afternoon, and rangers swore gently, and mopped their brows in their convenient but close quarters. For an hour no one had crossed save an old woman enveloped in a brown wrapper and a black mantilla, driving before her a burro loaded with kindling wood tied in small bundles for peddling. Then three shots were fired down the street, the sound coming clear and snappy through the still air.

The four rangers quickened from sprawling, symbolic figures of indolence to alert life, but only one rose to his feet. Three turned their eyes beseechingly but hopelessly upon the fourth, who had gotten nimbly up and was buckling his cartridge-belt around him. The three knew that Lieutenant Bob Buckley, in command, would allow no man of them the privilege of investigating a row when he himself might go.

The agile, broad-chested lieutenant, without a change of expression in his smooth, yellow-brown, melancholy face, shot the belt strap through the

guard of the buckle, hefted his sixes in their holsters as a belle gives the
finishing touches to her toilette, caught up his Winchester, and dived for the
door. There he paused long enough to caution his comrades to maintain their
watch upon the bridge, and then plunged into the broiling highway.

The three relapsed into resigned inertia and plaintive comment.

'I've heard of fellows,' grumbled Broncho Leathers, 'what was wedded to
danger, but if Bob Buckley ain't committed bigamy with trouble, I'm a son
of a gun.'

'Peculiarness of Bob is,' inserted the Nueces Kid, 'he ain't had proper
trainin'. He never learned how to git skeered. Now, a man ought to be
skeered enough when he tackles a fuss to hanker after readin' his name on
the list of survivors, anyway.'

'Buckley,' commented Ranger No. 3, who was a misguided Eastern man,
burdened with an education, 'scraps in such a solemn manner that I have
been led to doubt its spontaneity. I'm not quite onto his system, but he fights,
like Tybalt, by the book of arithmetic.'

'I never heard,' mentioned Broncho, 'about any of Dibble's ways of mixin'
scrappin' and cipherin'.'

'Triggernometry?' suggested the Nueces infant.

'That's rather better than I hoped from you,' nodded the Easterner,
approvingly. 'The other meaning is that Buckley never goes into a fight
without giving away weight. He seems to dread taking the slightest advantage.
That's quite close to foolhardiness when you are dealing with horse-thieves
and fence-cutters who would ambush you any night, and shoot you in the
back if they could. Buckley's too full of sand. He'll play Horatius, and hold
the bridge once too often some day.'

'I'm on there,' drawled the Kid; 'I mind that bridge gang in the reader.
Me, I go instructed for the other chap – Spurious Somebody – the one that
fought and pulled his freight, to fight 'em on some other date.'

'Anyway,' summed up Broncho, 'Bob's about the gamest man I ever see
along the Rio Bravo. Great Sam Houston! If she gets any hotter she'll sizzle!'
Broncho whacked at a scorpion with his four-pound Stetson felt, and the
three watchers relapsed into comfortless silence.

How well Bob Buckley had kept his secret, since these men, for two years
his side comrades in countless border raids and dangers, thus spake of him,
not knowing that he was the most arrant physical coward in all that Rio
Bravo country! Neither his friends nor his enemies had suspected him of
aught else than the finest courage. It was purely a physical cowardice, and
only by an extreme, grim effort of will had he forced his craven body to do
the bravest deeds. Scourging himself always, as a monk whips his besetting
sin, Buckley threw himself with apparent recklessness into every danger,
with the hope of some day ridding himself of the despised affliction. But
each successive test brought no relief, and the ranger's face by nature adapted
to cheerfulness and good humor, became set to the guise of gloomy melancholy. Thus, while the frontier admired his deeds, and his prowess was
celebrated in print and by word of mouth in many campfires in the valley
of the Bravo, his heart was sick within him. Only himself knew of the
horrible tightening of the chest, the dry mouth, the weakening of the spine,
the agony of the strung nerves – the never-failing symptoms of his shameful
malady.

One mere boy in his company was wont to enter a fray with a leg perched flippantly about the horn of his saddle, a cigarette hanging from his lips, which emitted smoke and original slogans of clever invention. Buckley would have given a year's pay to attain that devil-may-care method. Once the debonair youth said to him: 'Buck, you go into a scrap like it was a funeral. Not,' he added, with a complimentary wave of his tin cup, 'but what it generally is.'

Buckley's conscience was of the New England order with Western adjustments, and he continued to get his rebellious body into as many difficulties as possible; wherefore, on that sultry afternoon he chose to drive his own protesting limbs to investigation of that sudden alarm that had startled the peace and dignity of the State.

Two squares down the street stood the Top Notch Saloon. Here Buckley came upon signs of recent upheaval. A few curious spectators pressed about its front entrance, grinding beneath their heels the fragments of a plate-glass window. Inside, Buckley found Bud Dawson utterly ignoring a bullet wound in his shoulder, while he feelingly wept at having to explain why he failed to drop the 'blamed masquerooter,' who shot him. At the entrance of the ranger Bud turned appealingly to him for confirmation of the devastation he might have dealt.

'You know, Buck, I'd 'a' plum got him, first rattle, if I'd thought a minute. Come in amasquerootin', playin' female till he got the drop, and turned loose. I never reached for a gun, thinkin' it was sure Chihuahua Betty, or Mrs. Atwater, or anyhow one of the Mayfield girls comin' a-gunnin', which they might, liable as not. I never thought of that blamed Garcia until—'

'Garcia!' snapped Buckley. 'How did he get over here?'

Bud's bartender took the ranger by the arm and led him to the side door. There stood a patient gray burro cropping the grass along the gutter, with a load of kindling wood tied across its back. On the ground lay a black shawl and a voluminous brown dress.

'Masquerootin' in them things,' called Bud, still resisting attempted ministrations to his wounds. 'Thought he was a lady till he give a yell and winged me.'

'He went down this side street, ' said the bartender. 'He was alone, and he'll hide out till night when his gang comes over. You ought to find him in that Mexican lay-out below the depot. He's got a girl down there – Pancha Sales.'

'How was he armed?' asked Buckley.

'Two pearl-handled sixes, and a knife.'

'Keep this for me, Billy,' said the ranger, handing over his Winchester. Quixotic, perhaps, but it was Bob Buckley's way. Another man – and a braver one – might have raised a posse to accompany him. It was Buckley's rule to discard all preliminary advantage.

The Mexican had left behind him a wake of closed doors and an empty street, but now people were beginning to emerge from their places of refuge with assumed unconsciousness of anything having happened. Many citizens who knew the ranger pointed out to him with alacrity the course of Garcia's retreat.

As Buckley swung along upon the trail he felt the beginning of the suffocating constriction about his throat, the cold sweat under the brim of his hat, the old, shameful, dreaded sinking of his heart as it went down, down, down in his bosom.

The morning train of the Mexican Central had that day been three hours late, thus failing to connect with the I. & G. N. on the other side of the river. Passengers for *Los Estados Unidos* grumblingly sought entertainment in the little swaggering mongrel town of two nations, for until the morrow, no other train would come to rescue them. Grumblingly, because two days later would begin the great fair and races in San Antone. Consider that at that time San Antone was the hub of the wheel of Fortune, and the names of its spokes were Cattle, Wool, Faro, Running Horses, and Ozone. In those times cattlemen played at crack-loo on the side-walks with double-eagles, and gentlemen backed their conception of the fortuitous card with stacks limited in height only by the interference of gravity. Wherefore, thither journeyed the sowers and the reapers – they who stampeded the dollars, and they who rounded them up. Especially did the caterers to the amusement of the people haste to San Antone. Two greatest shows on earth were already there, and dozens of smallest ones were on the way.

On a side track near the mean little 'dobe depot stood a private car, left there by the Mexican train that morning and doomed by an ineffectual schedule to ignobly await, amid squalid surroundings, connection with the next day's regular.

The car had been once a common day-coach, but those who had sat in it and cringed to the conductor's hatbands slips would never have recognized it in its transformation. Paint and gilding and certain domestic touches had liberated it from any suspicion of public servitude. The whitest of lace curtains judiciously screened its windows. From its fore end dropped in the torrid air the flag of Mexico. From its rear projected the Stars and Stripes and a busy stovepipe, the latter reinforcing in its suggestion of culinary comforts the general suggestion of privacy and ease. The beholder's eye, regarding its gorgeous sides, found interest to culminate in a single name in gold and blue letters extending almost its entire length – a single name, the audacious privilege of royalty and genius. Doubly, then, was this arrogant nomenclature here justified; for the name was that of 'Alvarita, Queen of the Serpent Tribe.' This, her car, was back from a triumphant tour of the principal Mexican cities, and now headed for San Antonio, where, according to promissory advertisement, she would exhibit her 'Marvellous Dominion and Fearless Control over Deadly and Venomous Serpents, Handling them with Ease as they Coil and Hiss to the Terror of Thousands of Tongue-tied Tremblers!'

One hundred in the shade kept the vicinity somewhat depeopled. This quarter of the town was a ragged edge; its denizens the bubbling froth of five nations; its architecture tent, *jacal*, and 'dobe; its distractions the hurdy-gurdy and the informal contribution to the sudden stranger's store of experience. Beyond this dishonorable fringe upon the old town's jowl rose a dense mass of trees, surmounting and filling a little hollow. Through this bickered a small stream that perished down the sheer and disconcerting side of the great cañon of the Rio Bravo del Norte.

In this sordid spot was condemned to remain for certain hours the impotent transport of the Queen of the Serpent Tribe.

The front door of the car was open. Its forward end was curtained off into a small reception room. Here the admiring and propitiatory reporters were wont to sit and transpose the music of Señorita Alvarita's talk into the more florid key of the press. A picture of Abraham Lincoln hung against a wall;

one of a cluster of school-girls grouped upon stone steps was in another place; a third was Easter lilies in a blood-red frame. A neat carpet was under foot. A pitcher, sweating cold drops, and a glass stood upon a fragile stand. In a willow rocker, reading a newspaper, sat Alvarita.

Spanish, you would say, Andalusian, or, better still, Basque; that compound, like a diamond, of darkness and fire. Hair, the shade of purple grapes viewed at midnight. Eyes, long, dusky, and disquieting with their untroubled directness of gaze. Face, haughty and bold, touched with a pretty insolence that gave it life. To hasten conviction of her charm, but glance at the stacks of handbills in the corner, green, and yellow, and white. Upon them you see an incompetent presentment of the señorita in her professional garb and pose. Irresistible, in black lace and yellow ribbons, she faces you; a blue racer is spiralled upon each bare arm; coiled twice about her waist and once about her neck, his horrid head close to hers; you perceive Kuku, the great eleven-foot Asian python.

A hand drew aside the curtain that partitioned the car, and a middle-aged faded woman holding a knife and a half-peeled potato looked in and said:

'Alviry, are you right busy?'

'I'm reading the home paper, ma. What do you think! that pale, tow-headed Matilda Price got the most votes in the *News* for the prettiest girl in Gallipo – *lees*.'

'Shuh! She wouldn't of done it if *you'd* been home, Alviry. Lord knows, I hope we'll be there before fall's over. I'm tired gallopin' round the world playin' we are dagoes, and givin' snake shows. But that ain't what I wanted to say. That there biggest snake's gone again. I've looked all over the car and can't find him. He must have been gone an hour. I remember hearin' somethin' rustlin' along the floor, but I thought it was you.'

'Oh, blame that old rascal!' exclaimed the Queen, throwing down her paper. 'This is the third time he's got away. George never *will* fasten down the lid to his box properly. I do believe he's *afraid* of Kuku. Now I've got to go hunt him.'

'Better hurry; somebody might hurt him.'

The Queen's teeth showed in a gleaming, contemptuous smile. 'No danger. When they see Kuku outside they simply scoot away and buy bromides. There's a crick over between here and the river. That old scamp'd swap his skin any time for a drink of running water. I guess I'll find him there, all right.'

A few minutes later Alvarita stepped upon the forward platform, ready for her quest. Her handsome black skirt was shaped to the most recent proclamation of fashion. Her spotless shirt-waist gladdened the eye in that desert of sunshine, a swelling oasis, cool and fresh. A man's split-straw hat sat firmly upon her coiled abundant hair. Beneath her serene, round, impudent chin a man's four-in-hand tie was jauntily knotted about a man's high, stiff collar. A parasol she carried, of white silk, and its fringe was lace, yellowly genuine.

I will grant Gallipolis as to her costume, but firmly to Seville or Valladolid I am held by her eyes; castanets, balconies, mantillas, serenades, ambuscades, escapades – all these their dark depths guaranteed.

'Ain't you afraid to go out alone, Alviry?' queried the Queen-mother anxiously. 'There's so many rough people about. Mebbe you'd better—'

'I never saw anything I was afraid of yet, ma. 'Specially people. And men

in particular. Don't you fret. I'll trot along back as soon as I find that runaway
scamp.'

The dust lay thick upon the bare ground near the tracks. Alvarita's eye
soon discovered the serrated trail of the escaped python. It led across the
depot grounds and away down a smaller street in the direction of the little
cañon, as predicted by her. A stillness and lack of excitement in the
neighborhood encouraged the hope that, as yet, the inhabitants were unaware
that so formidable a guest traversed their highways. The heat had driven
them indoors, whence outdrifted occasional shrill laughs, or the depressing
·whine of a maltreated concertina. In the shade a few Mexican children, like
vivified stolid idols in clay, stared from their play, vision-struck and silent,
as Alvarita came and went. Here and there a woman peeped from a door and
stood dumb, reduced to silence by the aspect of the white silk parasol.

A hundred yards and the limits of the town were passed, scattered chaparral
succeeding, and then a noble grove, overflowing the bijou cañon. Through
this a small bright stream meandered. Park-like it was, with a kind of cockney
ruralness further indorsed by the waste papers and rifled tins of picnickers.
Up this stream, and down it, among its pseudo-sylvan glades and depressions,
wandered the bright and unruffled Alvarita. Once she saw evidence of the
recreant reptile's progress in his distinctive trail across a spread of fine sand
in the arroyo. The living water was bound to lure him; he could not be far
away.

So sure was she of his immediate proximity that she perched herself to
idle for a time in the curve of a great creeper that looped down from a giant
water-elm. To reach this she climbed from the pathway a little distance up
the side of a steep and rugged incline. Around her chaparral grew thick and
high. A late-blooming ratama tree dispensed from its yellow petals a sweet
and persistent odor. Adown the ravine rustled a sedative wind, melancholy
with the taste of sodden, fallen leaves.

Alvarita removed her hat, and undoing the oppressive convolutions of her
hair, began to slowly arrange it in two long, dusky plaits.

From the obscure depths of a thick clump of evergreen shrubs five feet
away, two small jewel-bright eyes were steadfastly regarding her. Coiled
there lay Kuku, the great python; Kuku, the magnificent, he of the plated
muzzle, the grooved lips, the eleven-foot stretch of elegantly and brilliantly
mottled skin. The great python was viewing his mistress without a sound or
motion to disclose his presence. Perhaps the splendid truant forfeit his
capture, but, screened by the foliage, thought to prolong the delight of his
escapade. What pleasure it was, after the hot and dusty car, to lie thus,
smelling the running water, and feeling the agreeable roughness of the earth
and stones against his body! Soon, very soon the Queen would find him, and
he, powerless as a worm in her audacious hands, would be returned to the
dark chest in the narrow house that ran on wheels.

Alvarita heard a sudden crunching of the gravel below her. Turning her
head she saw a big, swarthy Mexican, with a daring and evil expression,
contemplating her with an ominous, dull eye.

'What do you want?' she asked as sharply as five hairpins between her lips
would permit, continuing to plait her hair, and looking him over with placid
contempt. The Mexican continued to gaze at her, and showed his teeth in
a white, jagged smile.

'I no hurt-y you, Señorita,' he said.

'You bet you won't,' answered the Queen, shaking back one finished, massive plait. 'But don't you think you'd better move on?'

'Not hurt-y you – no. But maybeso take one *beso* – one li'l kees, you call him.'

The man smiled again, and set his foot to ascend the slope. Alvarita leaned swiftly and picked up a stone the size of a cocoanut.

'Vamoose, quick,' she ordered peremptorily, 'you *coon!*'

The red of insult burned through the Mexican's dark skin.

'*Hidalgo, Yo!*' he shot between his fangs. 'I am not neg-r-ro! *Diabla bonita*, for that you shall pay me.'

He made two quick upward steps this time, but the stone, hurled by no weak arm, struck him square in the chest. He staggered back to the footway, swerved half around, and met another sight that drove all thoughts of the girl from his head. She turned her eyes to see what had diverted his interest. A man with red-brown, curling hair and a melancholy, sunburned, smooth-shaven face was coming up the path, twenty yards away. Around the Mexican's waist was buckled a pistol belt with two empty holsters. He had laid aside his sixes – possibly in the *jacal* of the fair Pancha – and had forgotten them when the passing of -the fairer Alvarita had enticed him to her trail. His hands now flew instinctively to the holsters, but finding the weapons gone, he spread his fingers outward with the eloquent, abjuring, deprecating Latin gesture, and stood like a rock. Seeing his plight, the newcomer unbuckled his own belt containing two revolvers, threw it upon the ground, and continued to advance.

'Splendid!' murmured Alvarita, with flashing eyes .

As Bob Buckley, according to the mad code of bravery that his sensitive conscience imposed upon his cowardly nerves, abandoned his guns and closed in upon his enemy, the old, inevitable nausea of abject fear wrung him. His breath whistled through his constricted air passages. His feet seemed like lumps of lead. His mouth was dry as dust. His heart, congested with blood, hurt his ribs as it thumped against them. The hot June day turned to moist November. And still he advanced, spurred by a mandatory pride that strained its uttermost against his weakling flesh.

The distance between the two men slowly lessened. The Mexican stood, immovable, waiting. When scarce five yards separated them a little shower of loosened gravel rattled down from above to the ranger's feet. He glanced upward with instinctive caution. A pair of dark eyes, brilliantly soft, and fierily tender, encountered and held his own. The most fearful heart and the boldest one in all the Rio Bravo country exchanged a silent and inscrutable communication. Alvarita, still seated within her vine, leaned forward above the breast-high chaparral. One hand was laid across her bosom. One great dark braid curved forward over her shoulder. Her lips were parted; her face was lit with what seemed but wonder – great and absolute wonder. Her eyes lingered upon Buckley's. Let no one ask or presume to tell through what subtle medium the miracle was performed. As by a lightning flash two clouds will accomplish counterpoise and compensation of electric surcharge, so on that eye glance the man received his complement of manhood, and the maid concealed what enriched her womanly grace by its loss.

The Mexican, suddenly stirring, ventilated his attitude of apathetic waiting by conjuring swiftly from his bootleg a long knife. Buckley cast aside his hat, and laughed once aloud, like a happy schoolboy at a frolic. Then, empty-handed, he sprang nimbly, and Garcia met him without default.

So soon was the engagement ended that disappointment imposed upon the ranger's war-like ecstasy. Instead of dealing the traditional downward stroke, the Mexican lunged straight with his knife. Buckley took the precarious chance, and caught his wrist, fair and firm. Then he delivered the good Saxon knock-out blow – always so pathetically disastrous to the fistless Latin races – and Garcia was down and out, with his head under a clump of prickly pears. The ranger looked up again to the Queen of the Serpents.

Alvarita scrambled down to the path.

'I'm mighty glad I happened along when I did,' said the ranger.

'He – he frightened me so,' cooed Alvarita.

They did not hear the long, low hiss of the python under the shrubs. Wiliest of the beasts, no doubt he was expressing the humiliation he felt at having so long dwelt in subjection to this trembling and coloring mistress of his whom he had deemed so strong and potent and fearsome.

Then came galloping to the spot the civic authorities; and to them the ranger awarded the prostrate disturber of the peace, whom they bore away limply across the saddle of one of their mounts. But Buckley and Alvarita lingered.

Slowly, slowly they walked. The ranger regained his belt of weapons. With a fine timidity she begged the indulgence of fingering the great .45's with little 'Ohs' and 'Ahs' of new-born delicious shyness.

The *cañoncito* was growing dusky. Beyond its terminus in the river bluff they could see the outer world yet suffused with the waning glory of sunset.

A scream – a piercing scream of fright from Alvarita. Back she cowered, and the ready, protecting arm of Buckley formed her refuge. What terror so dire as to thus beset the close of the reign of the never-before-daunted Queen?

Across the path there crawled a *caterpillar* – a horrid, fuzzy, two-inch caterpillar! Truly, Kuku, thou wert avenged. Thus abdicated the Queen of the Serpent Tribe – *viva la reina!*

THE HIGHER ABDICATION

CURLY THE TRAMP SIDLED TOWARD the free-lunch counter. He caught a fleeting glance from the bartender's eye, and stood still, trying to look like a business man who had just dined at the Menger and was waiting for a friend who had promised to pick him up in his motor car. Curly's histrionic powers were equal to the impersonation; but his make-up was wanting.

The bartender rounded the bar in a casual way, looking up at the ceiling as though he was pondering some intricate problem of kalsomining, and then fell upon Curly so suddenly that the roadster had no excuses ready. Irresistibly, but so composedly that it seemed almost absentmindedness on his part, the dispenser of drinks pushed Curly to the swinging doors and kicked him out, with a nonchalance that almost amounted to sadness. That was the way of the Southwest.

Curly arose from the gutter leisurely. He felt no anger or resentment toward his ejector. Fifteen years of tramphood spent out of the twenty-two years of his life had hardened the fibres of his spirit. The slings and arrows of outrageous fortune fell blunted from the buckler of his armored pride. With especial resignation did he suffer contumely and injury at the hands of bartenders. Naturally, they were his enemies; and unnaturally, they were often his friends. He had to take his chances with them. But he had not yet learned to estimate these cool, languid, Southwestern knights of the bung-starter, who had the manners of an Earl of Pawtucket, and who, when they disapproved of your presence, moved you with the silence and despatch of a chess automaton advancing a pawn.

Curly stood a few moments in the narrow, mesquite-paved street. San Antonio puzzled and disturbed him. Three days he had been a non-paying guest of the town, having dropped off there from a box car of an I. & G. N. freight, because Greaser Johnny had told him in Des Moines that the Alamo City was manna fallen, gathered, cooked, and served free with cream and sugar. Curly had found the tip partly a good one. There was hospitality in plenty of a careless, liberal, irregular sort. But the town itself was a weight upon his spirits after his experience with the rushing, business-like, system-atized cities of the North and East. Here he was often flung a dollar, but too frequently a good-natured kick would follow it. Once a band of hilarious cowboys had roped him on Military Plaza and dragged him across the black soil until no respectable rag-bag would have stood sponsor for his clothes. The winding, doubling streets, leading nowhere, bewildered him. And then there was a little river, crooked as a pot-hook, that crawled through the middle of the town, crossed by a hundred little bridges so nearly alike that they got on Curly's nerves. And the last bartender wore a number nine shoe.

The saloon stood on a corner. The hour was eight o'clock. Homefarers and outgoers jostled Curly on the narrow stone sidewalk. Between the buildings to his left he looked down a cleft that proclaimed itself another thoroughfare. The alley was dark except for one patch of light. Where there was a light there were sure to be human beings. Where there were human beings after nightfall in San Antonio there might be food, and there was sure to be drink. So Curly headed for the light.

The illumination came from Schwegel's Café. On the sidewalk in front of it Curly picked up an old envelope. It might have contained a check for a million. It was empty; but the wanderer read the address, 'Mr. Otto Schwegel,' and the name of the town and State. The postmark was Detroit.

Curly entered the saloon. And now in the light it could be perceived that he bore the stamp of many years of vagabondage. He had none of the tidiness of the calculating and shrewd professional tramp. His wardrobe represented the cast-off specimens of half a dozen fashions and eras. Two factories had combined their efforts in providing shoes for his feet. As you gazed at him there passed through your mind vague impressions of mummies, wax figures, Russian exiles, and men lost on desert islands. His face was covered almost to his eyes with a curly brown beard that he kept trimmed short with a pocket-knife, and that had furnished him with his *nom de route*. Light-blue eyes, full of sullenness, fear, cunning, impudence, and fawning, witnessed the stress that had been laid upon his soul.

The saloon was small, and in its atmosphere the odors of meat and drink struggled for the ascendency. The pig and the cabbage wrestled with hydrogen and oxygen. Behind the bar Schwegel labored with an assistant whose epidermal pores showed no signs of being obstructed. Hot wiernerwurst and sauerkraut were being served to purchasers of beer. Curly shuffled to the end of the bar, coughed hollowly, and told Schwegel that he was a Detroit cabinet-maker out of a job.

It followed as the night the day that he got his schooner and lunch.

'Was you acquainted maybe mit Heinrich Strauss in Detroit?' asked Schwegel.

'Did I know Heinrich Strauss?' repeated Curly, affectionately. 'Why, say, 'Bo, I wish I had a dollar for every game of pinochle me and Heine has played on Sunday afternoons.'

More beer and a second plate of steaming food was set before the diplomat. And then Curly, knowing to a fluid-drachm how far a 'con' game would go, shuffled out into the unpromising street.

And now he began to perceive the inconveniences of this stony Southern town. There was none of the outdoor gaiety and brilliancy and music that provided distraction even to the poorest in the cities of the North. Here, even so early, the gloomy, rock-walled houses were closed and barred against the murky dampness of the night. The streets were mere fissures through which flowed gray wreaths of river mist. As he walked he heard laughter and the chink of coin and chips behind darkened windows, and music coming from every chink of wood and stone. But the diversions were selfish; the day of popular pastimes had not yet come to San Antonio.

But at length Curly, as he strayed, turned the sharp angle of another lost street and came upon a rollicking band of stockmen from the outlying ranches celebrating in the open in front of an ancient wooden hotel. One great roisterer from the sheep country who had just instigated a movement toward the bar, swept Curly in like a stray goat with the rest of his flock. The princes of kine and wool hailed him as a new zoölogical discovery, and uproariously strove to preserve him in the diluted alcohol of their compliments and regards.

An hour afterward Curly staggered from the hotel barroom, dismissed by his fickle friends, whose interest in him had subsided as quickly as it had risen. Full – stoked with alcoholic fuel and cargoed with food, the only question remaining to disturb him was that of shelter and bed.

A drizzling, cold Texas rain had begun to fall – an endless, lazy, unintermittent downfall that lowered the spirits of men and raised a reluctant steam from the warm stones of the streets and houses. Thus comes the 'norther' dousing gentle spring and amiable autumn with the chilling salutes and adieux of coming and departing winter.

Curly followed his nose down the first tortuous street into which his irresponsible feet conducted him. At the lower end of it, on the bank of the serpentine stream, he perceived an open gate in a cemented rock wall. Inside he saw camp fires and a row of low wooden sheds built against three sides of the enclosing wall. He entered the enclosure. Under the sheds many horses were champing at their oats and corn. Many wagons and buckboards stood about with their teams' harness thrown carelessly upon the shafts and doubletrees. Curly recognized the place as a wagon yard, such as is provided by merchants for their out-of-town friends and customers. No one was in sight. No doubt the drivers of those wagons were scattered about the town 'seeing the elephant and hearing the owl.' In their haste to become patrons of the town's dispensaries of mirth and good cheer the last ones to depart must have left the great wooden gate swinging open.

Curly had satisfied the hunger of an anaconda and the thirst of a camel, so he was neither in the mood nor the condition of an explorer. He zigzagged his way to the first wagon that his eyesight distinguished in the semi-darkness under the shed. It was a two-horse wagon with a top of white canvas. The wagon was half filled with loose piles of wool sacks, two or three great bundles of gray blankets, and a number of bales, bundles, and boxes. A reasoning eye would have estimated the load at once as ranch supplies, bound on the morrow for some outlying hacienda. But to the drowsy intelligence of Curly they represented only warmth and softness and protection against the cold humidity of the night. After several unlucky efforts, at last he conquered gravity so far as to climb over a wheel and pitch forward upon the best and warmest bed he had fallen upon in many a day. Then he became instinctively a burrowing animal, and dug his way like a prairie-dog down among the sacks and blankets, hiding himself from the cold air as snug and safe as a bear in his den. For three nights sleep had visited Curly only in broken and shivering doses. So now, when Morpheus condescended to pay him a call, Curly got such a strangle hold on the mythological old gentleman that it was a wonder that any one else in the whole world got a wink of sleep that night.

Six cow-punchers of the Cibolo Ranch were waiting around the door of the ranch store. Their ponies cropped grass near by, tied in the Texas fashion – which is not tied at all. Their bridle reins had been dropped to the earth, which is a more effectual way of securing them (such is the power of habit and imagination) than you could devise out of a half-inch rope and a live-oak tree.

These guardians of the cow lounged about, each with a brown cigarette paper in his hand, and gently but unceasingly cursed Sam Revell, the storekeeper. Sam stood in the door, snapping the red elastic bands on his pink madras shirtsleeves and looking down affectionately at the only pair of tan shoes within a forty-mile radius. His offence had been serious, and he was divided between humble apology and admiration for the beauty of his raiment. He had allowed the ranch stock of 'smoking' to become exhausted.

'I thought sure there was another case of it under the counter, boys,' he explained. 'But it happened to be catterdges.'

'You've sure got a case of happendicitis,' said Poky Rodgers, fence rider of the Largo Verde *potrero*. 'Somebody ought to happen to give you a knock on the head with the butt end of a quirt. I've rode in nine miles for some tobacco; and it don't appear natural and seemly that you ought to be allowed to live.'

'The boys was smokin' cut plug and dried mesquite leaves mixed when I left,' sighed Mustang Taylor, horse wrangler of the Three Elm camp. 'They'll be lookin' for me back by nine. They'll be settin' up, with their papers ready to roll a whiff of the real thing before bedtime. And I've got to tell 'em that this pink-eyed, sheep-headed, sulphur-footed, shirt-waisted son of a calico broncho, Sam Revell, hasn't got no tobacco on hand.'

Gregorio Falcon, Mexican vaquero and best thrower of the rope on the Cibolo, pushed his heavy, silver-embroidered straw sombrero back upon his thicket of jet-black curls and scraped the bottoms of his pockets for a few crumbs of the precious weed.

'Ah, Don Samuel,' he said, reproachfully, but with his touch of Castilian manners, 'escuse me. Dthey say dthe jackrabbeet and dthe sheep have the most leetle *sesos* – how you call dthem – brain-es? Ah, don't believe dthat, Don Samuel – escuse me. Ah dthink people w'at don't keep esmokin' tobacco, dthey – bot you weel escuse me, Don Samuel.'

'Now, what's the use of chewin' the rag, boys,' said the untroubled Sam, stooping over to rub the toes of his shoes with a red-and-yellow handkerchief. 'Ranse took the order for some more smokin' to San Antone with him Tuesday. Pancho rode Ranse's hoss back yesterday; and Ranse is goin' to drive the wagon back himself. There wa'n't much of a load – just some woolsacks and blankets and nails and canned peaches an a few things we was out of. I look for Ranse to roll in to-day sure. He's a early starter and a hell-to-split driver, and he ought to be here not far from sundown.'

'What plugs is he drivin'?' asked Mustang Taylor, with a smack of hope in his tones.

'The buckboard grays,' said Sam.

'I'll wait a spell, then,' said the wrangler. 'Them plugs eat up a trail like a road-runner swallowin' a whip snake. And you may bust me open a can of green-gage plums, Sam, while I'm waitin' for somethin' better.'

'Open me some yellow clings,' ordered Poky Rodgers. 'I'll wait, too.'

The tobaccoless punchers arranged themselves comfortably on the steps of the store. Inside Sam chopped open with a hatchet the tops of the cans of fruit.

The store, a big, white wooden building like a barn, stood fifty yards from the ranch-house. Beyond it were the horse corrals; and still farther the wool sheds and the brush-topped shearing pens – for the Rancho Cibolo raised both cattle and sheep. Behind the store, at a little distance, were the grass-thatched *jacals* of the Mexicans who bestowed their allegiance upon the Cibolo.

The ranch-house was composed of four large rooms, with plastered adobe walls, and a two-room wooden cell. A twenty-feet-wide 'gallery' circumvented the structure. It was set in a grove of immense live-oaks and water-elms near a lake – a long, not very wide, and tremendously deep lake in which, at nightfall, great gars leaped to the surface and plunged with the noise of hippopotamuses frolicking at their bath. From the trees hung garlands and massive pendants of the melancholy gray moss of the South. Indeed, the Cibolo ranch-house seemed more of the South than of the West. It looked as if old 'Kiowa' Truesdell might have brought it with him from the lowlands of Mississippi when he came to Texas with his rifle in the hollow of his arm in '55.

But, though he did not bring the family mansion, Truesdell did bring something in the way of a family inheritance that was more lasting than brick or stone. He brought one end of the Truesdell-Curtis family feud. And when a Curtis bought the Rancho de los Olmos, sixteen miles from the Cibolo, there were lively times on the pear flats and in the chaparral thickets of the Southwest. In those days Truesdell cleaned the brush of many a wolf and tiger cat and Mexican lion; and one or two Curtises fell heirs to notches on his rifle stock. Also he buried a brother with a Curtis bullet in him on the bank of the lake at Cibolo. And then the Kiowa Indians made their last raid upon the ranches between the Frio and the Rio Grande, and Truesdell at the head of his rangers rid the earth of them to the last brave, earning his sobriquet. Then came prosperity in the form of waxing herds and broadening lands. And then old age and bitterness, when he sat, with his great mane of hair as white as the Spanish-dagger blossoms and his fierce, pale-blue eyes, on the shaded gallery at Cibolo, growling like the pumas that he had slain. He snapped his fingers at old age; the bitter taste of life did not come from that. The cup that stuck at his lips was that his only son Ransom wanted to marry a Curtis, the last youthful survivor of the other end of the feud.

For a while the only sounds to be heard at the store were the rattling of the tin spoons and the gurgling intake of the juicy fruits by the cow-punchers, the stamping of the grazing ponies, and the singing of a doleful song by Sam as he contentedly brushed his stiff auburn hair for the twentieth time that day before a crinkly mirror.

From the door of the store could be seen the irregular, sloping stretch of prairie to the south, with its reaches of light-green, billowing mesquite flats in the lower places, and its rises crowned with nearly black masses of short chaparral. Through the mesquite flat wound the ranch road that, five miles away, flowed into the old government trail to San Antonio. The sun was so low that the gentlest elevation cast its gray shadow miles into the green-gold of sunshine.

That evening ears were quicker than eyes.

The Mexican held up a tawny finger to still the scraping of tin against tin.

'One waggeen,' said he, 'cross dthe Arroyo Hodo. Ah hear dthe wheel. Verree rockee place, dthe Hondo.'

'You've got good ears, Gregorio,' said Mustang Taylor. 'I never heard nothin' but the song-bird in the bush and the zephyr skally-hootin' across the peaceful dell.'

In ten minutes Taylor remarked: 'I see the dust of a wagon risin' right above the fur end of the flat.'

'You have verree good eyes, señor,' said Gregorio smiling.

Two miles away they saw a faint cloud dimming the green ripples of the mesquites. In twenty minutes they heard the clatter of horses' hoofs: in five minutes more the gray plugs dashed out of thicket, whickering for oats and drawing the light wagon behind them like a toy.

From the *jacals* came a cry of: 'El Amo! El Amo!' Four Mexican youths raced to unharness the grays. The cow-punchers gave a yell of greeting and delight.

Ranse Truesdell, driving, threw the reins to the ground and laughed.

'It's under the wagon sheet, boys,' he said. 'I know what you're waiting for. If Sam lets it run out again we'll use them yellow shoes of his for a target. There's two cases. Pull 'em out and light up. I know you'll want a smoke.'

After striking dry country Ranse had removed the wagon sheet from the bows and thrown it over the goods in the wagon. Six pairs of hasty hands dragged it off and grabbled beneath the sacks and blankets for the cases of tobacco.

Long Collins, tobacco messenger from the San Gabriel outfit, who rode with the longest stirrups west of the Mississippi, delved with an arm like the tongue of a wagon. He caught something harder than a blanket and pulled out a fearful thing – a shapeless, muddy bunch of leather tied together with wire and twine. From its ragged end, like the head and claws of a disturbed turtle, protruded human toes.

'Who-ee!' yelled Long Collins. 'Ranse, are you a-packin' around of corpuses?
Here's a – howlin' grasshoppers!'

Up from his long slumber popped Curly, like some vile worm from its
burrow. He clawed his way out and sat blinking like a disreputable, drunken
owl. His face was as bluish red and puffed and seamed and crosslined as the
cheapest round steak of the butcher. His eyes were swollen slits; his nose a
pickled beet; his hair would have made the wildest thatch of a Jack-in-the-
box look like the satin poll of a Cléo de Mérode. The rest of him was
scarecrow done to the life.

Ranse jumped down from his seat and looked at his strange cargo with
wide-open eyes.

'Here, you maverick, what are you doing in my wagon? How did you get
in there?'

The punchers gathered around in delight. For the time they had forgotten
tobacco.

Curly looked around him slowly in every direction. He snarled like a
Scotch terrier through his ragged beard.

'Where is this,' he rasped through his parched throat. 'It's a damn farm in
an old field. What'd you bring me here for – say? Did I say I wanted to come
here? What are you Reubs rubberin' at – hey? G'wan or I'll punch some of
your faces.'

'Drag him out, Collins,' said Ranse.

Curly took a slide and felt the ground rise up and collide with his shoulder
blades. He got up and sat on the steps of the store shivering from outraged
nerves, hugging his knees and sneering. Taylor lifted out a case of tobacco
and wrenched off its top. Six cigarettes began to glow, bringing peace and
forgiveness to Sam.

'How'd you come in my wagon?' repeated Ranse, this time in a voice that
drew a reply.

Curly recognized the tone. He had heard it used by freight brakemen and
large persons in blue carrying clubs.

'Me?' he growled. 'Oh, was you talkin' to me? Why, I was on my way to
the Menger, but my valet had forgot to pack my pajamas. So I crawled into
that wagon in the wagon-yard – see? I never told you to bring me out to this
bloomin' farm – see?'

'What is it, Mustang?' asked Poky Rodgers, almost forgetting to smoke in
his ecstasy. 'What do it live on?'

'It's a galliwampus, Poky,' said Mustang. 'It's the thing that hollers
"williwallo" up in ellum trees in the low grounds of nights. I don't know if
it bites.'

'No, it ain't, Mustang,' volunteered Long Collins. 'Them galliwampuses
has fins on their backs, and eighteen toes. This here is a hicklesnifter. It lives
under the ground and eats cherries. Don't stand so close to it. It wipes out
villages with one stroke of its prehensile tail.'

Sam, the cosmopolite, who called bartenders in San Antone by their first
name, stood in the door. He was a better zoölogist.

'Well, ain't that a Willie for your whiskers?' he commented. 'Where'd
you dig up the hobo, Ranse? Goin' to make an auditorium for inbreviates out
of the ranch?'

'Say,' said Curly, from whose panoplied breast all shafts of wit fell blunted.

'Any of you kiddin' guys got a drink on you? Have your fun. Say, I've been hittin' the stuff till I don't know straight up.'

He turned to Ranse. 'Say, you shanghaied me on your d—d old prairie schooner – did I tell you to drive me to a farm? I want a drink. I'm goin' all to little pieces. What's doin'?'

Ranse saw that the tramp's nerves were racking him. He despatched one of the Mexican boys to the ranch-house for a glass of whisky. Curly gulped it down; and into his eyes came a brief, grateful glow – as human as the expression in the eye of a faithful setter dog.

'Thanky, boss,' he said, quietly.

'You're thirty miles from a railroad, and forty miles from a saloon,' said Ranse.

Curly fell back weakly against the steps.

'Since you are here,' continued the ranchman, 'come along with me. We can't turn you out on the prairie. A rabbit might tear you to pieces.'

He conducted Curly to a large shed where the ranch vehicles were kept. There he spread out a canvas cot and brought blankets.

'I don't suppose you can sleep,' said Ranse, 'since you've been pounding your ear for twenty-four hours. But you can camp here till morning. I'll have Pedro fetch you up some grub.'

'Sleep!' said Curly. 'I can sleep a week. Say, sport, have you got a coffin nail on you?'

Fifty miles had Ransom Truesdell driven that day. And yet this is what he did.

Old 'Kiowa' Truesdell sat in his great wicker chair reading by the light of an immense oil lamp. Ranse laid a bundle of newspapers fresh from town at his elbow.

'Back, Ranse?' said the old man, looking up.

'Son,' old 'Kiowa' continued, 'I've been thinking all day about a certain matter that we have talked about. I want you to tell me again. I've lived for you. I've fought wolves and Indians and worse white men to protect you. You never had any mother that you can remember. I've taught you to shoot straight, ride hard, and live clean. Later on I've worked to pile up dollars that'll be yours. You'll be a rich man, Ranse, when my chunk goes out. I've made you. I've licked you into shape like a leopard cat licks its cubs. You don't belong to yourself – you've got to be a Truesdell first. Now, is there to be any more nonsense about this Curtis girl?'

'I'll tell you once more,' said Ranse, slowly. 'As I am a Truesdell and as you are my father, I'll never marry a Curtis.'

'Good boy,' said old 'Kiowa.' 'You'd better go get some supper.'

Ranse went to the kitchen at the rear of the house. Pedro, the Mexican cook, sprang up to bring the food he was keeping warm in the stove.

'Just a cup of coffee, Pedro,' he said, and drank it standing. And then:

'There's a tramp on a cot in the wagon-shed. Take him something to eat. Better make it enough for two.'

Ranse walked out toward the *jacals.* A boy came running.

'Manuel, can you catch Vaminos, in the little pasture, for me?'

'Why not, señor? I saw him near the *puerta* but two hours past. He bears a drag-rope.'

'Get him and saddle him as quick as you can.'

'*Prontito, señor.*'

Soon mounted, on Vaminos, Ranse leaned in the saddle, pressed with his knees, and galloped eastward past the store, where sat Sam trying his guitar in the moonlight.

Vaminos shall have a word – Vaminos the good dun horse. The Mexicans, who have a hundred names for the colors of a horse, called him *gruyo*. He was a mouse-colored, slate-colored, flea-bitten road-dun, if you can conceive it. Down his back from his mane to his tail went a line of black. He would live forever; and surveyors have not laid off as many miles in the world as he could travel in a day.

Eight miles east of the Cibolo ranch-house Ranse loosened the pressure of his knees, and Vaminos stopped under a big ratama tree. The yellow ratama blossoms showered fragrance that would have undone the roses of France. The moon made the earth a great concave bowl with a crystal sky for a lid. In a glade five jack-rabbits leaped and played together like kittens. Eight miles farther east shone a faint star that appeared to have dropped below the horizon. Night riders, who often steered their course by it, knew it to be the light in the Rancho de los Olmos.

In ten minutes Yenna Curtis galloped to the tree on her sorrel pony Dancer. The two leaned and clasped hands heartily.

'I ought to have ridden nearer your home,' said Ranse. 'But you never will let me.'

Yenna laughed. And in the soft light you could see her strong white teeth and fearless eyes. No sentimentality there, in spite of the moonlight, the odor of the ratamas, and the admirable figure of Ranse Truesdell, the lover. But she was there, eight miles from her home, to meet him.

'How often have I told you, Ranse,' she said, 'that I am your half-way girl? Always half-way.'

'Well?' said Ranse, with a question in his tones.

'I did,' said Yenna, with almost a sigh. 'I told him after dinner when I thought he would be in a good humor. Did you ever wake up a lion, Ranse, with the mistaken idea that he would be a kitten? He almost tore the ranch to pieces. It's all up. I love my daddy, Ranse, and I'm afraid – I'm afraid of him, too. He ordered me to promise that I'd never marry a Truesdell. I promised. That's all. What luck did you have?'

'The same,' said Ranse, slowly. 'I promised him that his son would never marry a Curtis. Somehow I couldn't go against him. He's mighty old. I'm sorry, Yenna.'

The girl leaned in her saddle and laid one hand on Ranse's, on the horn of his saddle.

'I never thought I'd like you better for giving me up,' she said ardently, 'but I do. I must ride back now, Ranse. I slipped out of the house and saddled Dancer myself. Good-night, neighbor.'

'Good-night,' said Ranse. 'Ride carefully over them badger holes.'

They wheeled and rode away in opposite directions. Yenna turned in her saddle and called clearly:

'Don't forget I'm your half-way girl, Ranse.'

'Damn all family feuds and inherited scraps,' muttered Ranse vindictively to the breeze as he rode back to the Cibolo.

Ranse turned his horse into the small pasture and went to his own room. He opened the lowest drawer of an old bureau to get out the packet of letters that Yenna had written him one summer when she had gone to Mississippi for a visit. The drawer stuck, and he yanked at it savagely – as a man will. It came out of the bureau, and bruised both his shins – as a drawer will. An old, folded yellow letter without an envelope fell from somewhere – probably from where it had lodged in one of the upper drawers. Ranse took it to the lamp and read it curiously.

Then he took his hat and walked to one of the Mexican *jacals*.

'Tía Juana,' he said, 'I would like to talk with you awhile.'

An old, old Mexican woman, white-haired and wonderfully wrinkled, rose from a stool.

'Sit down,' said Ranse, removing his hat and taking the one chair in the *jacal*. 'Who am I, Tía Juana?' he asked, speaking Spanish.

'Don Ransom, our good friend and employer. Why do you ask?' answered the old woman wonderingly.

'Tía Juana, who am I?' he repeated, with his stern eyes looking into hers.

A frightened look came in the old woman's face. She fumbled with her black shawl.

'Who am I, Tía Juana?' said Ranse once more.

'Thirty-two years I have lived on the Rancho Cibolo,' said Tía Juana. 'I thought to be buried under the coma mott beyond the garden before these things should be known. Close the door, Don Ransom, and I will speak. I see in your face that you know.'

An hour Ranse spent behind Tía Juana's closed door. As he was on his way back to the house Curly called to him from the wagon-shed.

The tramp sat on his cot, swinging his feet and smoking.

'Say, sport,' he grumbled. 'This is no way to treat a man after kidnappin' him. I went up to the store and borrowed a razor from that fresh guy and had a shave. But that ain't all a man needs. Say – can't you loosen up for about three fingers more of that booze? I never asked you to bring me to your d—d farm.'

'Stand up out here in the light,' said Ranse, looking at him closely.

Curly got up sullenly and took a step or two.

His face, now shaven smooth, seemed transformed. His hair had been combed, and it fell back from the right side of his forehead with a peculiar wave. The moonlight charitably softened the ravages of drink; and his aquiline, well-shaped nose and small, square-cleft chin almost gave distinction to his looks.

Ranse sat on the foot of the cot and looked at him curiously.

'Where did you come from – have you got any home or folks anywhere?'

'Me? Why, I'm a dook,' said Curly. 'I'm Sir Reginald – oh, cheese it. No; I don't know anything about my ancestors. I've been a tramp ever since I can remember. Say, old pal, are you going to set 'em up again tonight or not?'

'You answer my questions and maybe I will. How did you come to be a tramp?'

'Me,' answered Curly. 'Why, I adopted that profession when I was an infant. Case of had to. First thing I can remember, I belonged to a big, lazy hobo called Beefsteak Charley. He sent me around to houses to beg. I wasn't hardly big enough to reach the latch of a gate.'

'Did he ever tell you how he got you?' asked Ranse.

'Once when he was sober he said he bought me for an old six-shooter and six bits from a band of drunken Mexican sheep-shearers. But what's the diff? That's all I know.'

'All right,' said Ranse. 'I reckon you're a maverick for certain. I'm going to put the Rancho Cibolo brand on you. I'll start you to work in one of the camps to-morrow.'

'Work!' sniffed Curly, disdainfully. 'What do you take me for? Do you think I'd chase cows, and hop-skip-and-jump around after crazy sheep like that pink-and-yellow guy at the store says these Reubs do? Forget it.'

'Oh, you'll like it when you get used to it,' said Ranse. 'Yes. I'll send you up one more drink by Pedro. I think you'll make a first-class cowpuncher before I get through with you.'

'Me?' said Curly. 'I pity the cows you set me to chaperon. They can go chase themselves. Don't forget my nightcap, please, boss.'

Ranse paid a visit to the store before going to the house. Sam Revell was taking off his tan shoes regretfully and preparing for bed.

'Any of the boys from the San Gabriel camp riding in early in the morning?' asked Ranse.

'Long Collins,' said Sam, briefly. 'For the mail.'

'Tell him,' said Ranse, 'to take that tramp out to camp with him and keep him till I get there.'

Curly was sitting on his blankets in the San Gabriel camp cursing talentedly when Ranse Truesdell rode up and dismounted on the next afternoon. The cow-punchers were ignoring the stray. He was grimy with dust and black dirt. His clothes were making their last stand in favor of the conventions.

Ranse went up to Buck Rabb, the camp boss, and spoke briefly.

'He's a plum buzzard,' said Buck. 'He won't work, and he's the lowdownest passel of inhumanity I ever see. I didn't know what you wanted done with him, Ranse, so I just let him set. That seems to suit him. He's been condemned to death by the boys a dozen times, but I told 'em maybe you was savin' him for torture.'

Ranse took off his coat.

'I've got a hard job before me, Buck, I reckon, but it has to be done. I've got to make a man out of that thing. That's what I've come to camp for.'

He went up to Curly.

'Brother,' he said, 'don't you think if you had a bath it would allow you to take a seat in the company of your fellow-man with less injustice to the atmosphere?'

'Run away, farmer,' said Curly, sardonically. 'Willie will send for nursey when he feels like having his tub.'

The *charco*, or water hole, was twelve yards away. Ranse took one of Curly's ankles and dragged him like a sack of potatoes to the brink. Then with the strength and sleight of a hammer-thrower he hurled the offending member of society far into the lake.

Curly crawled out and up the bank spluttering like a porpoise.

Ranse met him with a piece of soap and a coarse towel in his hands.

'Go to the other end of the lake and use this,' he said. 'Buck will give you some dry clothes at the wagon.'

The tramp obeyed without protest. By the time supper was ready he had returned to camp. He was hardly to be recognized in his new blue shirt and brown duck clothes. Ranse observed him out of the corner of his eye.

'Lordy, I hope he ain't a coward,' he was saying to himself. 'I hope he won't turn out to be a coward.'

His doubts were soon allayed. Curly walked straight to where he stood. His light-blue eyes were blazing.

'Now I'm clean,' he said, meaningly, 'maybe you'll talk to me. Think you've got a picnic here, do you? You clodhoppers think you can run over a man because you know he can't get away. All right. Now, what do you think of that?'

Curly planted a stinging slap against Ranse's left cheek. The print of his hand stood out a dull red against the tan.

Ranse smiled happily.

The cow-punchers talk to this day of the battle that followed.

Somewhere in his restless tour of the cities Curly had acquired the art of self-defence. The ranchman was equipped only with the splendid strength and equilibrium of perfect health and the endurance conferred by decent living. The two attributes nearly matched. There were no formal rounds. At last the fibre of the clean liver prevailed. The last time Curly went down from one of the ranchman's awkward but powerful blows he remained on the grass, but looking up with an unquenched eye.

Ranse went to the water barrel and washed the red from a cut on his chin in the stream from the faucet.

On his face was a grin of satisfaction.

Much benefit might accrue to educators and moralists if they could know the details of the curriculum of reclamation through which Ranse put his waif during the month that he spent in the San Gabriel camp. The ranchman had no fine theories to work out – perhaps his whole stock of pedagogy embraced only a knowledge of horse-breaking and a belief in heredity.

The cow-punchers saw that their boss was trying to make a man out of the strange animal that he had sent among them; and they tacitly organized themselves into a faculty of assistants. But their system was their own.

Curly's first lesson stuck. He became on friendly and then on intimate terms with soap and water. And the thing that pleased Ranse most was that his 'subject' held his ground at each successive higher step. But the steps were sometimes far apart.

Once he got at the quart bottle of whisky kept sacredly in the grub tent for rattlesnake bites, and spent sixteen hours on the grass, magnificently drunk. But when he staggered to his feet his first move was to find his soap and towel and start for the *charco*. And once, when a treat came from the ranch in the form of a basket of fresh tomatoes and young onions, Curly devoured the entire consignment before the punchers reached the camp at supper time.

And then the punchers punished him in their own way. For three days they did not speak to him, except to reply to his own questions or remarks. And they spoke with absolute and unfailing politeness. They played tricks on one another; they pounded one another hurtfully and affectionately; they heaped upon one another's heads friendly curses and obloquy; but they were polite to Curly. He saw it, and it stung him as much as Ranse hoped it would.

Then came a night that brought a cold, wet norther. Wilson, the youngest of the outfit, had lain in camp two days, ill with a fever. When Joe got up at daylight to begin breakfast he found Curly sitting asleep against a wheel of the grub wagon with only a saddle blanket around him, while Curly's blankets were stretched over Wilson to protect him from the rain and wind.

Three nights after that Curly rolled himself in his blanket and went to sleep. Then the other punchers rose up softly and began to make preparations. Ranse saw Long Collins tie a rope to the horn of a saddle. Others were getting out their six-shooters.

'Boys,' said Ranse, 'I'm much obliged. I was hoping you would. But I didn't like to ask.'

Half a dozen six-shooters began to pop – awful yells rent the air – Long Collins galloped wildly across Curly's bed, dragging the saddle after him. That was merely their way of gently awaking their victim. Then they hazed him for an hour, carefully and ridiculously, after the code of cow camps. Whenever he uttered protest they held him stretched over a roll of blankets and thrashed him woefully with a pair of leather leggins.

And all this meant that Curly had won his spurs, that he was receiving the punchers' accolade. Nevermore would they be polite to him. But he would be their 'pardner' and stirrup-brother, foot to foot.

When the fooling was ended all hands made a raid on Joe's big coffeepot by the fire for a Java nightcap. Ranse watched the new knight carefully to see if he understood and was worthy. Curly limped with his cup of coffee to a log and sat upon it. Long Collins followed and sat by his side. Buck Rabb went and sat at the other. Curly – grinned.

And then Ranse furnished Curly with mounts and saddle and equipment, and turned him over to Buck Rabb, instructing him to finish the job.

Three weeks later Ranse rode from the ranch into Rabb's camp, which was then in Snake Valley. The boys were saddling for the day's ride. He sought out Long Collins among them.

'How about that bronco?' he asked.

Long Collins grinned.

'Reach out your hand, Ranse Truesdell,' he said, 'and you'll touch him. And you can shake his'n, too, if you like, for he's plumb white and there's none better in no camp.'

Ranse looked again at the clear-faced, bronzed, smiling cow-puncher who stood at Collins's side. Could that be Curly? He held out his hand, and Curly grasped it with the muscles of a bronco-buster.

'I want you at the ranch,' said Ranse.

'All right, sport,' said Curly, heartily. 'But I want to come back again. Say, pal, this is a dandy farm. And I don't want any better fun than hustlin' cows with this bunch of guys. They're all to the merry merry.'

At the Cibolo ranch-house they dismounted. Ranse bade Curly wait at the door of the living room. He walked inside. Old 'Kiowa' Truesdell was reading at a table.

'Good-morning, Mr. Truesdell,' said Ranse.

The old man turned his white head quickly.

'How is this?' he began. 'Why do you call me "Mr. –"?'

When he looked at Ranse's face he stopped, and the hand that held his newspaper shook slightly.

'Boy,' he said slowly, 'how did you find it out?'

'It's all right,' said Ranse, with a smile. 'I made Tía Juana tell me. It was kind of by accident, but it's all right.'

'You've been like a son to me,' said old 'Kiowa,' trembling.

'Tía Juana told me all about it,' said Ranse. 'She told me how you adopted me when I was knee-high to a puddle duck out of a wagon train of prospectors that was bound West. And she told me how the kid – your own kid, you know – got lost or was run away with. And she said it was the same day that the sheep-shearers got on a bender and left the ranch.'

'Our boy strayed from the house when he was two years old,' said the old man. 'And then along came these emigrant wagons with a youngster they didn't want; and we took you. I never intended you to know, Ranse. We never heard of our boy again.'

'He's right outside, unless I'm mighty mistaken,' said Ranse, opening the door and beckoning.

Curly walked in.

No one could have doubted. The old man and the young had the same sweep of hair, the same nose, chin, line of face, and prominent light-blue eyes.

Old 'Kiowa' rose eagerly.

Curly looked about the room curiously. A puzzled expression came over his face. He pointed to the wall opposite.

'Where's the tick-tock?' he asked, absentmindedly.

'The clock,' cried old 'Kiowa' loudly. 'The eight-day clock used to stand there. Why—'

He turned to Ranse, but Ranse was not there.

Already a hundred yards away, Vaminos, the good flea-bitten dun, was bearing him eastward like a racer through dust and chaparral towards the Rancho de los Olmos.

CUPID À LA CARTE

'THE DISPOSITIONS OF WOMAN,' said Jeff Peters, after various opinions on the subject had been advanced, 'run, regular, to diversions. What a woman wants is what you're out of. She wants more of a thing when it's scarce. She likes to have souvenirs of things she never heard of. A one-sided view of objects is disjointing to the female composition.

''Tis a misfortune of mine, begotten by nature and travel,' continued Jeff, looking thoughtfully between his elevated feet at the grocery stove, 'to look deeper into some subjects than most people do. I've breathed gasoline smoke talking to street crowds in nearly every town in the United States. I've held 'em spellbound with music, oratory, sleight of hand, and prevarications, while I've sold 'em jewelry, medicine, soap, hair tonic, and junk of other nominations. And during my travels, as a matter of recreation and expiation, I've taken cognizance some of women. It takes a man a lifetime to find out about one particular woman; but if he puts in, say, ten years, industrious and curious, he can acquire the general rudiments of the sex. One lesson I picked up was when I was working the West with a line of Brazilian diamonds and a patent fire kindler just after my trip from Savannah down through the cotton belt with Dalby's Anti-explosive Lamp Oil Powder. 'Twas when the Oklahoma country was in first bloom. Guthrie was rising in the middle of it like a lump of self-raising dough. It was a boom town of the regular kind – you stood in line to get a chance to wash your face; if you ate over ten minutes you had a lodging bill added on; if you slept on a plank at night they charged it to you as board the next morning.

'By nature and doctrines I am addicted to the habit of discovering choice places wherein to feed. So I looked around and found a proposition that exactly cut the mustard. I found a restaurant tent just opened up by an outfit that had drifted in on the tail of the boom. They had knocked together a box house, where they lived and did the cooking, and served the meals in a tent pitched against the side. That tent was joyful with placards on it calculated to redeem the world-worn pilgrim from the sinfulness of boarding houses and pick-me-up hotels. "Try Mother's Home-Made Biscuits," "What's the Matter with Our Apple Dumplings and Hard Sauce?" "Hot Cakes and Maple Syrup Like You Ate When a Boy," "Our Fried Chicken Never Was Heard to Crow" – there was literature doomed to please the digestions of man! I said to myself that mother's wandering boy should munch there that night. And so it came to pass. And there is where I contracted my case of Mame Dugan.

'Old Man Dugan was six feet by one of Indiana loafer, and he spent his time sitting on his shoulder blades in a rocking-chair in the shanty memorializing the great corn-crop failure of '86. Ma Dugan did the cooking, and Mame waited on table.

'As soon as I saw Mame I knew there was a mistake in the census reports. There wasn't but one girl in the United States. When you come to specifications it isn't easy. She was about the size of an angel, and she had eyes, and ways about her. When you come to the kind of a girl she was, you'll find a belt of 'em reaching from the Brooklyn Bridge west as far as the courthouse in Council Bluffs, Ia. They earn their own living in stores, restaurants, factories, and offices. They're descended straight from Eve, and they're the crowd that's got woman's rights, and if a man wants to dispute it he's in line to get one of them against his jaw. They're chummy and honest and free and tender and sassy, and they look life straight in the eye. They've met man face to face, and discovered that he's a poor creature. They've dropped to it that the reports in the Seaside Library about his being a fairy prince lack confirmation.

'Mame was that sort. She was full of life and fun, and breezy; she passed the repartee with the boarders quick as a wink; you'd have smothered laughing. I am disinclined to make excavations into the insides of a personal affection. I am glued to the theory that the diversions and discrepancies of the indisposition known as love should be as private a sentiment as a toothbrush. 'Tis my opinion that the biographies of the heart should be confined with the historical romances of the liver to the advertising pages of the magazines. So, you'll excuse the lack of an itemized bill of my feelings toward Mame.

'Pretty soon I got a regular habit of dropping into the tent to eat at irregular times when there wasn't so many around. Mame would sail in with a smile, in a black dress and white apron, and say: "Hello, Jeff – why don't you come at mealtime. Want to see how much trouble you can be, of course. Fried-chickenbeefsteakporkchopshamandeggspotpie" – and so on. She called me Jeff, but there was no significations attached. Designations was all she meant. The front names of any of us she used as they came to hand. I'd eat about two meals before I left, and string 'em out like a society spread where they changed plates and wives, and josh one another festively between bites.

Mame stood for it, pleasant, for it wasn't up to her to take any canvas off the tent by declining dollars just because they were chipped in after meal times.

'It wasn't long until there was another fellow named Ed Collier got the between-meals affliction, and him and me put in bridges between breakfast and dinner, and dinner and supper, that made a three-ringed circus of that tent, and Mame's turn as waiter a continuous performance. That Collier man was saturated with designs and contrivings. He was in well-boring or insurance or claim-jumping or something – I've forgotten which. He was a man well lubricated with gentility and his words were such as recommended you to his point of view. So Collier and me infested the grub tent with care and activity. Mame was level full of impartiality. 'Twas like a casino hand the way she dealt out her favors – one to Collier and one to me and one to the board and not a card up her sleeve.

'Me and Collier naturally got acquainted, and gravitated together some on the outside. Divested of his stratagems, he seemed to be a pleasant chap, full of an amiable sort of hostility.

' "I notice you have an affinity for grubbing in the banquet hall after the guests have fled," says I to him one day, to draw his conclusions.

' "Well, yes," says Collier, reflecting; "the tumult of a crowded board seems to harass my sensitive nerves."

' "It exasperates mine some, too," says I. "Nice little girl, don't you think?"

' "I see," says Collier, laughing. "Well, now that you mention it, I have noticed that she doesn't seem to displease the optic nerve."

' "She's a joy to mine," says I, "and I'm going after her. Notice is hereby served."

' "I'll be as candid as you," admits Collier, "and if the drug stores don't run out of pepsin I'll give you a run for your money that'll leave you a dyspeptic at the wind-up."

'So Collier and me begins the race; the grub department lays in new supplies; Mame waits on us, jolly and kind and agreeable and it looks like an even break, with Cupid and the cook working overtime in Dugan's restaurant.

"Twas one night in September when I got Mame to take a walk after supper when the things were all cleared away. We strolled out a distance and sat on a pile of lumber at the edge of town. Such opportunities was seldom, so I spoke my piece, explaining how the Brazilian diamonds and the fire kindler were laying up sufficient treasure to guarantee the happiness of two, and that both of 'm together couldn't equal the light from somebody's eyes, and that the name of Dugan should be changed to Peters, or reasons why not would be in order.

'Mame didn't say anything right away. Directly she gave a kind of shudder, and I began to learn something.

' "Jeff," she says. "I'm sorry you spoke. I like you as well as any of them, but there isn't the man in the world I'd ever marry, and there never will be. Do you know what a man is in my eye? He's a tomb. He's a sarcophagus for the interment of Beefsteakporkchopsliver'nbaconhamandeggs. He's that and nothing more. For two years I've watched men eat, eat, eat, until they represent nothing on earth to me but ruminant bipeds. They're absolutely nothing but something that goes in front of a knife and fork and plate at the table. They're fixed that way in my mind and memory. I've tried to overcome it, but I can't. I've heard girls rave about their sweethearts, but I never could understand it. A man and a sausage grinder and a pantry awake in me exactly the same sentiments. I went to a matinée once to see an actor the girls were crazy about. I got interested enough to wonder whether he liked his steak rare, medium, or well done, and his eggs over or straight up. That was all. No, Jeff; I'll marry no man and see him set at the breakfast table and eat and come back to dinner and eat, and happen in again at supper to eat, eat, eat."

' "But, Mame," says I, "it'll wear off. You've had too much of it. You'll marry some time, of course. Men don't eat always."

' "As far as my observation goes, they do. No, I'll tell you what I'm going to do." Mame turns, suddenly to animation and bright eyes. "There's a girl named Susie Foster in Terre Haute, a chum of mine. She waits in the railroad eating house there. I worked two years in a restaurant in that town. Susie has it worse than I do, because the men who eat at railroad stations gobble. They try to flirt and gobble at the same time. Whew! Susie and I have it all planned out. We're saving our money, and when we get enough we're going to buy a little cottage and five acres we know of, and live together, and grow violets for the Eastern market. A man better not bring his appetite within a mile of that ranch."

' "Don't girls ever—" I commenced, but Mame heads me off sharp.

' "No, they don't. They nibble a little bit sometimes; that's all."

' "I thought the confect—"

' "For goodness' sake, change the subject." says Mame.

'As I said before, that experience put me wise that the feminine arrangement ever struggles after deceptions and illusions. Take England – beef made her; wieners elevated Germany; Uncle Sam owes his greatness to fried chicken and pie, but the young ladies of the Shetalkyou schools, they'll never believe it. Shakespeare, they allow, and Rubinstein, and the Rough Riders is what did the trick.

"Twas a situation calculated to disturb. I couldn't bear to give up Mame; and yet it pained me to think of abandoning the practice of eating. I had acquired the habit too early. For twenty-seven years I had been blindly rushing upon my fate, yielding to the insidious lures of that deadly monster, food. It was too late. I was a ruminant biped for keeps. It was lobster salad to a doughnut that my life was going to be blighted by it.

'I continued to board at the Dugan tent, hoping that Mame would relent. I had sufficient faith in true love to believe that since it has often outlived the absence of a square meal it might, in time, overcome the presence of one. I went on ministering to my fatal vice, although I felt that each time I shoved a potato into my mouth in Mame's presence I might be burying my fondest hopes.

'I think Collier must have spoken to Mame and got the same answer, for one day he orders a cup of coffee and a cracker, and sits nibbling the corner of it like a girl in the parlor, that's filled up in the kitchen, previous, on cold roast and fried cabbage. I caught on and did the same, and maybe we thought we'd made a hit! The next day we tried it again, and out comes Old Man Dugan fetching in his hands the fairy viands.

' "Kinder off yer feed, ain't ye, gents?" he asks, fatherly and some sardonic. "Thought I'd spell Mame a bit, seein' the work was light, and my rheumatiz can stand the strain."

'So back me and Collier had to drop to the heavy grub again. I noticed about that time that I was seized by a most uncommon and devastating appetite. I ate until Mame must have hated to see me darken the door. Afterward I found out that I had been made the victim of the first dark and irreligious trick played on me by Ed Collier. Him and me had been taking drinks together uptown regular trying to drown our thirst for food. That man had bribed about ten bartenders to always put a big slug of Appletree's Anaconda Appetite Bitters in every one of my drinks. But the last trick he played me was hardest to forget.

'One day Collier failed to show up at the tent. A man told me he left town that morning. My only rival now was the bill of fare. A few days before he left Collier had presented me with a two-gallon jug of fine whisky which he said a cousin had sent him from Kentucky. I now have reason to believe that it contained Appletree's Anaconda Appetite Bitters almost exclusively. I continued to devour tons of provisions. In Mame's eyes I remained a mere biped, more ruminant than ever.

'About a week after Collier pulled his freight there came a kind of side-show to town, and hoisted a tent near the railroad. I judged it was a sort of fake museum and curiosity business. I called to see Mame one night, and Ma Dugan said she and Thomas, her younger brother, had gone to the show. That same thing happened for three nights that week. Saturday night I caught her on the way coming back, and got to sit on the steps a while and talk to her. I noticed she looked different. Her eyes were softer, and shiny like. Instead of a Mame Dugan to fly from the voracity of man and raise violets, she seemed to be a Mame more in line as God intended her, approachable, and suited to bask in the light of the Brazilians and the Kindler.

' "You seem to be right smart inveigled," says I, "with the Unparalleled Exhibition of the World's Living Curiosities and Wonders."

' "It's a change," says Mame.

' "You'll need another," says I, "if you keep on going every night."

' "Don't be cross Jeff," says she; "it takes my mind off business."

' "Don't the curiosities eat?" I ask.

' "Not all of them. Some of them are wax."

' "Look out, then, that you don't get stuck," says I, kind of flip and foolish.

'Mame blushed. I didn't know what to think about her. My hopes raised some that perhaps my attentions had palliated man's awful crime of visibly introducing nourishment into his system. She talked some about the stars, referring to them with respect and politeness, and I drivelled a quantity about united hearts, homes made bright by true affection, and the Kindler. Mame listened without scorn and I says to myself, "Jeff, old man, you're removing the hoodoo that has clung to the consumer of victuals; you're setting your heel upon the serpent that lurks in the gravy bowl."

'Monday night I drop around. Mame is at the Unparalleled Exhibition with Thomas.

' "Now, may the curse of the forty-one seven-sided sea cooks," says I, "and the bad luck of the nine impenitent grasshoppers rest upon this selfsame sideshow at once and forever. Amen. I'll go to see it myself tomorrow night and investigate its baleful charm. Shall man that was made to inherit the earth be bereft of his sweetheart first by a knife and fork and then by a ten-cent circus?"

'The next night before starting out for the exhibition tent I inquire and find out that Mame is not at home. She is not at the circus with Thomas this

time, for Thomas waylays me in the grass outside of the grub tent with a
scheme of his own before I had time to eat supper.

' "What'll you give me, Jeff," says he, "if I tell you something?"

' "The value of it, son," I says.

' "Sis is stuck on a freak," says Thomas, "one of the side-show freaks. I
don't like him. She does. I overheard 'em talking. Thought maybe you'd like
to know. Say, Jeff, does it put you wise two dollars' worth? There's a target
rifle up town that—"

'I frisked my pockets and commenced to dribble a stream of halves and
quarters into Thomas's hat. The information was of the pile-driver system
of news, and it telescoped my intellects for a while. While I was leaking
small change and smiling foolish on the outside, and suffering disturbances
internally, I was saying, idiotically and pleasantly:

' "Thank you, Thomas – thank you – er – a freak, you said, Thomas.
Now, could you make out the monstrosity's entitlements a little clearer if
you please, Thomas?"

' "This is the fellow," says Thomas, pulling out a yellow handbill from
his pocket and shoving it under my nose. "He's the Champion Faster of the
Universe. I guess that's why Sis got soft on him. He don't eat nothing. He's
going to fast forty-nine days. This is the sixth. That's him."

'I looked at the name Thomas pointed out – "Professor Eduardo Collieri"
"Ah!" says I, in admiration, "that's not so bad, Ed Collier. I give you credit
for the trick. But I don't give you the girl until she's Mrs. Freak."

'I hit the sod in the direction of the show. I came up to the rear of the tent,
and, as I did so, a man wiggled out like a snake from under the bottom of the
canvas, scrambled to his feet, and ran into me like a locoed bronco. I gathered
him by the neck and investigated him by the light of the stars. It is Professor
Eduardo Collieri, in human habiliments, with a desperate look in one eye
and impatience in the other.

' "Hello, Curiosity," says I. "Get still a minute and let's have a look at
your freakship. How do you like being the willopus-wallopus or the bim-
bam from Borneo, or whatever name you are denounced by in the sideshow
business?"

' "Jeff Peters," says Collier, in a weak voice. "Turn me loose, or I'll slug
you one. I'm in the extremest kind of a large hurry. Hands off!"

' "Tut, tut, Eddie," I answers, holding him hard; "let an old friend gaze on
the exhibition of your curiousness. It's an eminent graft you fell onto, my
son. But don't speak of assaults and battery, because you're not fit. The best
you've got is a lot of nerve and a mighty empty stomach." And so it was.
The man was as weak as a vegetarian cat.

' "I'd argue this case with you, Jeff," says he, regretful in his style, "for an
unlimited number of rounds if I had half an hour to train in and a slab of
beefsteak two feet square to train with. Curse the man, I say, that invented
the art of going foodless. May his soul in eternity be chained up within two
feet of a bottomless pit of red-hot hash. I'm abandoning the conflict, Jeff; I'm
deserting to the enemy. You'll find Miss Dugan inside contemplating the
only living mummy and the informed hog. She's a fine girl, Jeff. I'd have
beat you out if I could have kept up the grubless habit a little while longer.
You'll have to admit that the fasting dodge was aces-up for a while. I figured
it out that way. But, say, Jeff, it's said that love makes the world go around.
Let me tell you, the announcement lacks verification. It's the wind from the

dinner horn that does it. I love that Mame Dugan. I've gone six days without food in order to coincide with her sentiments. Only one bite did I have. That was when I knocked the tattooed man down with a war club and got a sandwich he was gobbling. The manager fined me all my salary; but salary wasn't what I was after. 'Twas that girl. I'd give my life for her, but I'd endanger my immortal soul for a beef stew. Hunger is a horrible thing, Jeff. Love and business and family and religion and art and patriotism are nothing but shadows of words when a man's starving!''

'In such language Ed Collier discoursed to me, pathetic. I gathered the diagnosis that his affections and his digestions had been implicated in a scramble and the commissary had won out. I never disliked Ed Collier. I searched my internal admonitions of suitable etiquette to see if I could find a remark of a consoling nature, but there was none convenient.

' "I'd be glad, now," says Ed, "if you'll let me go. I've been hard hit, but I'll hit the ration supply harder. I'm going to clean out every restaurant in town. I'm going to wade waist deep in sirloins and swim in ham and eggs. It's an awful thing, Jeff Peters, for a man to come to this pass – to give up his girl for something to eat – it's worse than that man Esau, that swapped his copyright for a partridge – but then, hunger's a fierce thing. You'll excuse me, now, Jeff, for I smell a pervasion of ham frying in the distance, and my legs are crying out to stampede in that direction."

' "A hearty meal to you, Ed Collier," I says to him, "and no hard feelings. For myself, I am projected to be an unseldom eater, and I have condolence for your predicaments."

'There was a sudden big whiff of frying ham smell on the breeze; and the Champion Faster gives a snort and gallops off in the dark toward fodder.

'I wish some of the cultured outfit that are always advertising the extenuating circumstances of love and romance had been there to see. There was Ed Collier, a fine man full of contrivances and flirtations, abandoning the girl of his heart and ripping out into the contiguous territory in the pursuit of sordid grub. 'Twas a rebuke to the poets and a slap at the best-paying element of fiction. An empty stomach is a sure antidote to an overfull heart.

'I was naturally anxious to know how far Mame was infatuated with Collier and his stratagems. I went inside the Unparalleled Exhibition, and there she was. She looked surprised to see me, but unguilty.

' "It's an elegant evening outside," says I. "The coolness is quite nice and gratifying, and the stars are lined out, first class, up where they belong. Wouldn't you shake these by-products of the animal kingdom long enough to take a walk with a common human who never was on a programme in his life?"

'Mame gave a sort of sly glance around, and I knew what that meant.

' "Oh," says I, "I hate to tell you; but the curiosity that lives on wind has flew the coop. He just crawled out under the tent. By this time he has amalgamated himself with half the delicatessen truck in town."

' "You mean Ed Collier?" says Mame.

' "I do," I answers; "and a pity it is that he has gone back to crime again. I met him outside the tent, and he exposed his intentions of devastating the food crop of the world. 'Tis enormously sad when one's ideal descends from his pedestal to make a seventeen-year locust of himself."

'Mame looked me straight in the eye until she had corkscrewed my reflections.

' "Jeff," says she, "it isn't quite like you to talk that way. I don't care to hear Ed Collier ridiculed. A man may do ridiculous things, but they don't look ridiculous to the girl he does 'em for. That was the man in a hundred. He stopped eating just to please me. I'd be hardhearted and ungrateful if I didn't feel kindly toward him. Could you do what he did?"

' "I know," says I, seeing the point. "I'm condemned. I can't help it. The brand of the consumer is upon my brow. Mrs. Eve settled that business for me when she made the dicker with the snake. I fell from the fire into the frying-pan. I guess I'm the Champion Feaster of the Universe." I spoke humble, and Mame mollified herself a little.

' "Ed Collier and I are good friends," she said, "the same as me and you. I gave him the same answer I did you – no marrying for me. I liked to be with Ed and talk to him. There was something mighty pleasant to me in the thought that here was a man who never used a knife and fork, and all for my sake."

' "Wasn't you in love with him?" I asks, all injudicious. "Wasn't there a deal on for you to become Mrs. Curiosity?"

'All of us do it sometimes. All of us get jostled out of the line of profitable talk now and then. Mame put on that little lemon *glacé* smile that runs between ice and sugar, and says, much too pleasant: "You're short on credentials for asking that question, Mr. Peters. Suppose you do a forty-nine day fast, just to give you ground to stand on, and then maybe I'll answer it."

'So, even after Collier was kidnapped out of the way by the revolt of his appetite, my own prospects with Mame didn't seem to be improved. And then business played out in Guthrie.

'I had stayed too long there. The Brazilians I had sold commenced to show signs of wear, and the Kindler refused to light up right frequent on wet mornings. There is always a time, in my business, when the star of success says, "Move on to the next town." I was traveling by wagon at that time so as not to miss any of the small towns; so I hitched up a few days later and went down to tell Mame good-bye. I wasn't abandoning the game; I intended running over to Oklahoma City and work it for a week or two. Then I was coming back to institute fresh proceedings against Mame.

'What do I find at the Dugan's but Mame all conspicuous in a blue traveling dress, with her little trunk at the door. It seems that sister Lottie Bell, who is a typewriter in Terre Haute, is going to be married next Thursday, and Mame is off for a week's visit to be an accomplice at the ceremony. Mame is waiting for a freight wagon that is going to take her to Oklahoma, but I condemns the freight wagon with promptness and scorn, and offers to deliver the goods myself. Ma Dugan sees no reason why not, as Mr. Freighter wants pay for the job; so, thirty minutes later Mame and I pull out in my light spring wagon with white canvas cover, and head due south.

'That morning was of a praiseworthy sort. The breeze was lively, and smelled excellent of flowers and grass, and the little cottontail rabbits entertained themselves with skylarking across the road. My two Kentucky bays went for the horizon until it come sailing in so fast you wanted to dodge it like a clothesline. Mame was full of talk and rattled on like a kid about her old home and her school pranks and the things she liked and the hateful ways of those Johnson girls just across the street, 'way up in Indiana. Not a word was said about Ed Collier or victuals or such solemn subjects.

About noon Mame looks and finds that the lunch she had put up in a basket had been left behind. I could have managed quite a collation, but Mame didn't seem to be grieving over nothing to eat, so I made no lamentations. It was a sore subject with me, and I ruled provender in all its branches out of my conversation.

'I am minded to touch light on explanations how I came to lose the way. The road was dim and well grown with grass; and there was Mame by my side confiscating my intellects and attention. The excuses are good or they are not, as they may appear to you. But I lost it, and at dusk that afternoon, when we should have been in Oklahoma City, we were seesawing along the edge of nowhere in some undiscovered river bottom, and the rain was falling in large, wet bunches. Down there in the swamps we saw a little log house on a small knoll of high ground. The bottom grass and the chaparral and the lonesome timber crowded all around it. It seemed to be a melancholy little house, and you felt sorry for it. 'Twas that house for the night, the way I reasoned it. I explained to Mame, and she leaves it to me to decide. She doesn't become galvanic and prosecuting, as most women would, but she says it's all right; she knows I didn't mean to do it.

'We found the house was deserted. It had two empty rooms. There was a little shed in the yard where beasts had once been kept. In a loft of it was a lot of old hay. I put my horses in there and gave them some of it, for which they looked at me sorrowful, expecting apologies. The rest of the hay I carried into the house by armfuls, with a view to accommodations. I also brought in the patent Kindler and the Brazilians, neither of which are guaranteed against the action of water.

'Mame and I sat on the wagon seats on the floor, and I lit a lot of the Kindler on the hearth, for the night was chilly. If I was any judge, that girl enjoyed it. It was a change for her. It gave her a different point of view. She laughed and talked, and the Kindler made a dim light compared to her eyes. I had a pocketful of cigars, and as far as I was concerned there had never been any fall of man. We were at the same old stand in the Garden of Eden. Out there somewhere in the rain and the dark was the river of Zion, and the angel with the flaming sword had not yet put up the keep-off-the-grass sign. I opened up a gross or two of the Brazilians and made Mame put them on – rings, brooches, necklaces, eardrops, bracelets, girdles, and lockets. She flashed and sparkled like a million-dollar princess until she had pink spots in her cheeks and almost cried for a looking-glass.

'When it got late I made a fine bunk on the floor for Mame with the hay and my lap robes and blankets out of the wagon and persuaded her to lie down. I sat in the other room burning tobacco and listening to the pouring rain and meditating on the many vicissitudes that come to a man during the seventy years or so immediately preceding his funeral.

'I must have dozed a little before morning, for my eyes were shut, and when I opened them it was daylight, and there stood Mame with her hair all done up neat and correct, and her eyes bright with admiration of existence.

' "Gee whiz, Jeff!" she exclaims, "but I'm hungry. I could eat a—"

'I looked up and caught her eye. Her smile went back in and she gave me a cold look of suspicion. Then I laughed, and laid down on the floor to laugh easier. It seemed funny to me. By nature and geniality I am a hearty laugher, and I went the limit. When I came to, Mame was sitting with her back to me, all contaminated with dignity.

' "Don't be angry, Mame," I says, "for I couldn't help it. It's the funny way you've done up your hair. If you could only see it!"

' "You needn't tell stories, sir," said Mame, cool and advised. "My hair is all right. I know what you were laughing about. Why, Jeff, look outside," she winds up, peeping through a chink between the logs. I opened the little wooden window and looked out. The entire river bottom was flooded, and the knob of land on which the house stood was an island in the middle of a rushing stream of yellow water a hundred yards wide. And it was still raining hard. All we could do was to stay there till the dove brought in the olive branch.

'I am bound to admit that conversations and amusements languished during the day. I was aware that Mame was getting a too prolonged onesided view of things again, but I had no way to change it. Personally, I was wrapped up in the desire to eat. I had hallucinations of hash and visions of ham, and I kept saying to myself all the time, "What'll you have to eat Jeff? – what'll you order, now, old man, when the waiter comes?" I picks out to myself all sorts of favorites from the bill of fare, and imagines them coming. I guess it's that way with all very hungry men. They can't get their cogitations trained on anything but something to eat. It shows that the little table with the broken-legged caster and the imitation Worcester sauce and the napkin covering up the coffee stains is the paramount issue, after all, instead of the question of immortality or peace between nations.

'I sat there, musing along, arguing with myself quite heated as to how I'd have my steak – with mushrooms or à la créole. Mame was on the other seat, pensive, her head leaning on her hand. "Let the potatoes come home-fried," I states in my mind, "and brown the hash in the pan, with nine poached eggs on the side." I felt, careful, in my own pockets to see if I could find a peanut or a grain or two of popcorn.

'Night came on again with the river still rising and the rain still falling. I looked at Mame and I noticed that desperate look on her face that a girl always wears when she passes an ice-cream lair. I knew that poor girl was hungry – maybe for the first time in her life. There was that anxious look in her eye that a woman has only when she has missed a meal or feels her skirt unfastened in the back.

'It was about eleven o'clock or so on the second night when we sat, gloomy, in our ship-wrecked cabin. I kept jerking my mind away from the subject of food, but it kept flopping back again before I could fasten it. I thought of everything good to eat I had ever heard of. I went away back to my kidhood and remembered the hot biscuit sopped in sorghum and bacon gravy with partiality and respect. Then I trailed along up the years, pausing at green apples and salt, flapjacks and maple, lye hominy, fried chicken Old Virginia style, corn on the cob, spareribs and sweet potato pie, and wound up with Georgia Brunswick stew, which is the top notch of good things to eat, because it comprises 'em all.

'They say a drowning man sees a panorama of his whole life pass before him. Well, when a man's starving he sees the ghost of every meal he ever ate set out before him, and he invents new dishes that would make the fortune of a chef. If somebody would collect the last words of men who starved to death they'd have to sift 'em mighty fine to discover the sentiment, but they'd compile into a cook book that would sell into the millions.

'I guess I must have had my conscience pretty well inflicted with culinary mediations, for, without intending to do so, I says, out loud, to the imaginary waiter, "Cut it thick and have it rare, with the French fried, and six, soft-scrambled, on toast."

'Mame turned her head quick as a wink. Her eyes were sparkling and she smiled sudden.

' "Medium for me," she rattles on, "with the Juliennes, and three, straight up. Draw one, and brown the wheats, double order to come. Oh, Jeff, wouldn't it be glorious! And then I'd like to have a half fry, and a little chicken curried with rice, and a cup custard with ice cream, and—"

' "Go easy," I interrupts; "where's the chicken liver pie, and the kidney *sauté* on toast, and the roast lamb, and—"

' "Oh," cuts in Mame, all excited, "with mint sauce, and the turkey salad, and stuffed olives, and raspberry tarts, and—"

' "Keep it going," says I. "Hurry up with the fried squash, and the hot corn pone with sweet milk, and don't forget the apple dumpling with hard sauce, and the cross-barred dewberry pie—"

'Yes, for ten minutes we kept up that kind of restaurant repartee. We ranges up and down and backward and forward over the main trunk lines and the branches of the victual subject, and Mame leads the game, for she is apprised in the ramifications of grub, and the dishes she nominates aggravates my yearnings. It seems that there is set up a feeling that Mame will line up friendly again with food. It seems that she looks upon the obnoxious science of eating with less contempt than before.

'The next morning we find that the flood has subsided. I geared up the bays, and splashed out through the mud, some precarious, until we found the road again. We were only a few miles wrong, and in two hours we were in Oklahoma City. The first thing we saw was a big restaurant sign, and we piled into there in a hurry. Here I finds myself sitting with Mame at table, with knives and forks and plates between us, and she not scornful, but smiling with starvation and sweetness.

"Twas a new restaurant and well stocked. I designated a list of quotations from the bill of fare that made the waiter look out toward the wagon to see how many more might be coming.

'There we were, and there was the order being served. 'Twas a banquet for a dozen, but we felt like a dozen. I looked across the table at Mame and smiled, for I had recollections. Mame was looking at the table like a boy looks at his first stem-winder. Then she looked at me, straight in the face, and two big tears came in her eyes. The waiter was gone after more grub.

' "Jeff," she says, soft like, "I've been a foolish girl. I've looked at things from the wrong side. I never felt this way before. Men get hungry every day like this, don't they? They're big and strong, and they do the hard work of the world, and they don't eat just to spite silly waiter girls in restaurants, do they, Jeff? You said once – that is, you asked me – you wanted me to – well, Jeff, if you still care – I'd be glad and willing to have you always sitting across the table from me. Now give me something to eat, quick, please."

'So, as I've said, a woman needs to change her point of view now and then. They get tired of the same old sights – the same old dinner table, washtub, and sewing machine. Give 'em a touch of the various – a little travel and a little rest, a little tomfoolery along with the tragedies of keeping house, a little petting after the blowing-up, a little upsetting and jostling around – and everybody in the game will have chips added to their stack by the play.'

THE CABALLERO'S WAY

THE CISCO KID HAD KILLED six men in more or less fair scrimmages, had murdered twice as many (mostly Mexicans), and had winged a larger number whom he modestly forebore to count. Therefore a woman loved him.

The Kid was twenty-five, looked twenty; and a careful insurance company would have estimated the probable time of his demise at, say, twenty-six. His habitat was anywhere between the Frio and the Rio Grande. He killed for the love of it – because he was quick-tempered – to avoid arrest – for his own amusement – any reason that came to his mind would suffice. He had escaped capture because he could shoot five-sixths of a second sooner than any sheriff or ranger in the service, and because he rode a speckled roan horse that knew every cowpath in the mesquite and pear thickets from San Antonio to Matamoras.

Tonia Perez, the girl who loved the Cisco Kid, was half Carmen, half Madonna, and the rest – oh, yes, a woman who is half Carmen and half Madonna can always be something more – the rest, let us say, was humming-bird. She lived in a grass-roofed *jacal* near a little Mexican settlement at the Lone Wolf Crossing of the Frio. With her lived a father or grandfather, a lineal Aztec, somewhat less than a thousand years old, who herded a hundred goats and lived in a continuous drunken dream from drinking *mescal*. Back of the *jacal* a tremendous forest of bristling pear, twenty feet high at its worst, crowded almost to its door. It was along the bewildering maze of this spinous thicket that the speckled roan would bring the Kid to see his girl. And once, clinging like a lizard to the ridge-pole, high up under the peaked grass roof, he had heard Tonia, with her Madonna face and Carmen beauty and humming-bird soul, parley with the sheriff's posse, denying knowledge of her man in her soft *mélange* of Spanish and English.

One day the adjutant-general of the State, who is, *ex officio*, commander of the ranger forces, wrote some sarcastic lines to Captain Duval of Company X, stationed at Laredo, relative to the serene and undisturbed existence led by murderers and desperadoes in the said captain's territory.

The captain turned the color of brick dust under his tan, and forwarded the letter, after adding a few comments, per ranger Private Bill Adamson, to ranger Lieutenant Sandridge, camped at a water hole on the Nueces with a squad of five men in preservation of law and order.

Lieutenant Sandridge turned a beautiful *couleur de rose* through his ordinary strawberry complexion, tucked the letter in his hip pocket, and chewed off the end of his gamboge moustache.

The next morning he saddled his horse and rode alone to the Mexican settlement at the Lone Wolf Crossing of the Frio, twenty miles away.

Six feet two, blond as a Viking, quiet as a deacon, dangerous as a machine gun, Sandridge moved among the *Jacales*, patiently seeking news of the Cisco Kid.

Far more than the law, the Mexicans dreaded the cold and certain vengeance of the lone rider that the ranger sought. It had been one of the Kid's pastimes to shoot Mexicans 'to see them kick': if he demanded from them moribund Terpsichorean feats, simply that he might be entertained, what terrible and extreme penalties would be certain to follow should they anger him! One and all they lounged with upturned palms and shrugging shoulders, filling the air with 'quién sabes' and denials of the Kid's acquaintance.

But there was a man named Fink who kept a store at the Crossing – a man of many nationalities, tongues, interests, and ways of thinking.

'No use to ask them Mexicans,' he said to Sandridge. 'They're afraid to tell. This hombre they call the Kid – Goodall is his name, ain't it? – he's been in my store once or twice. I have an idea you might run across him at – but I guess I don't keer to say, myself. I'm two seconds later in pulling a gun than I used to be and the difference is worth thinking about. But this Kid's got a half-Mexican girl at the Crossing that he comes to see. She lives in that jacal a hundred yards down the arroyo at the edge of the pear. Maybe she – no, I don't suppose she would, but that jacal would be a good place to watch, anyway.'

Sandridge rode down to the jacal of Perez. The sun was low, and the broad shade of the great pear thicket already covered the grass-thatched hut. The goats were enclosed for the night in a brush corral near by. A few kids walked the top of it, nibbling the chaparral leaves. The old Mexican lay upon a blanket on the grass, already in a stupor from his mescal, and dreaming, perhaps, of the nights when he and Pizarro touched glasses to their New World fortunes – so old his wrinkled face seemed to proclaim him to be. And in the door of the jacal stood Tonia. And Lieutenant Sandridge sat in his saddle staring at her like a gannet agape at a sailorman.

The Cisco Kid was a vain person, as all eminent and successful assassins are, and his bosom would have been ruffled had he known that at a simple exchange of glances two persons, in whose minds he had been looming large, suddenly abandoned (at least for the time) all thought of him.

Never before had Tonia seen such a man as this. He seemed to be made of sunshine and blood-red tissue and clear weather. He seemed to illuminate the shadow of the pear when he smiled, as though the sun were rising again. The men she had known had been small and dark. Even the Kid, in spite of his achievements, was a stripling no larger than herself, with black straight hair and a cold marble face that chilled the noonday.

As for Tonia, though she sends description to the poorhouse, let her make a millionaire of your fancy. Her blue-black hair, smoothly divided in the middle and bound close to her head, and her large eyes full of the Latin melancholy, gave her the Madonna touch. Her motions and air spoke of the concealed fire and the desire to charm that she inherited from the gitanas of the Basque province. As for the humming-bird part of her, that dwelt in her heart; you could not perceive it unless her bright red skirt and dark blue blouse gave you a symbolic hint of the vagarious bird.

The newly lighted sun-god asked for a drink of water. Tonia brought it from the red jar hanging under the brush shelter. Sandridge considered it necessary to dismount so as to lessen the trouble of her ministrations.

I play no spy; nor do I assume to master the thoughts of any human heart; but I assert, by the chronicler's right, that before a quarter of an hour had sped, Sandridge was teaching her how to plait a six-strand rawhide stake-rope, and Tonia had explained to him that were it not for her little English book that the peripatetic padre had given her and the little crippled chivo, that she fed from a bottle, she would be very, very lonely indeed.

Which leads to a suspicion that the Kid's fences needed repairing, and that the adjutant-general's sarcasm had fallen upon unproductive soil.

In his camp by the water hole Lieutenant Sandridge announced and reiterated his intention of either causing the Cisco Kid to nibble the black loam of the Frio country prairies or of hailing him before a judge and jury. That sounded business-like. Twice a week he rode over to the Lone Wolf Crossing of the Frio, and directed Tonia's slim, slightly lemon-tinted fingers among the intricacies of the slowly growing lariat. A six-strand plait is hard to learn and easy to teach.

The ranger knew that he might find the Kid there at any visit. He kept his armament ready, and had a frequent eye for the pear thicket at the rear of the *jacal*. Thus he might bring down the kite and the humming-bird with one stone.

While the sunny-haired ornithologist was pursuing his studies the Cisco Kid was also attending to his professional duties. He moodily shot up a saloon in a small cow village on Quintana Creek, killed the town marshal (plugging him neatly in the centre of his tin badge), and then rode away, morose and unsatisfied. No true artist is uplifted by shooting an aged man carrying an old-style .38 bulldog.

On his way the Kid suddenly experienced the yearning that all men feel when wrong-doing loses its keen edge of delight. He yearned for the woman he loved to reassure him that she was his in spite of it. He wanted her to call his bloodthirstiness bravery and his cruelty devotion. He wanted Tonia to bring him water from the red jug under the brush shelter, and tell him how the *chivo* was thriving on the bottle.

The Kid turned the speckled roan's head up the ten-mile pear flat that stretches along the Arroyo Hondo until it ends at the Lone Wolf Crossing of the Frio. The roam whickered; for he had a sense of locality and direction equal to that of a belt-line street-car horse; and he knew he would soon be nibbling the rich mesquite grass at the end of a forty-foot stake rope while Ulysses rested his head in Circe's straw-roofed hut.

More weired and lonesome than the journey of an Amazonian explorer is the ride of one through a Texas pear flat. With dismal monotony and startling variety the uncanny and multiform shapes of the cacti lift their twisted trunks and fat, bristly hands to encumber the way. The demon plant, appearing to live without soil or rain, seems to taunt the parched traveler with its lush gray greenness. It warps itself a thousand times about what look to be open and inviting paths, only to lure the rider into blind and impassable spine-defended 'bottoms of the bag,' leaving him to retreat if he can, with the points of the compass whirling in his head.

To be lost in the pear is to die almost the death of the thief on the cross, pierced by nails and with grotesque shapes of all the fiends hovering about.

But it was not so with the Kid and his mount. Winding, twisting, circling, tracing the most fantastic and bewildering trail ever picked out, the good roan lessened the distance to the Lone Wolf Crossing with every coil and turn that he made.

While they fared the Kid sang. He knew but one tune and he sang it, as he knew but one code and lived it, and but one girl and loved her. He was a single-minded man of conventional ideas. He had a voice like a coyote with bronchitis, but whenever he chose to sing his song he sang it. It was a conventional song of the camps and trail, running at its beginning as near as may be to these words:

> Don't you monkey with my Lulu girl
> Or I'll tell you what I'll do —

and so on. The roan was inured to it, and did not mind.

But even the poorest singer will, after a certain time, gain his own consent to refrain from contributing to the world's noises. So the Kid, by the time he was within a mile or two of Tonia's *jacal*, had reluctantly allowed his song to die away – not because his vocal performance had become less charming to his own ears, but because his laryngeal muscles were aweary.

As though he were in a circus ring the speckled roan wheeled and danced through the labyrinth of pear until at length his rider knew by certain landmarks that the Lone Wolf Crossing was close at hand. Then, where the pear was thinner, he caught sight of the grass roof of the *jacal* and the hackberry tree on the edge of the arroyo. A few yards farther the Kid stopped the roan and gazed intently through the prickly openings. Then he dismounted, dropped the roan's reins, and proceeded on foot, stooping and silent, like an Indian. The roan, knowing his part, stood still, making no sound.

The Kid crept noiselessly to the very edge of the pear thicket and reconnoitered between the leaves of a clump of cactus.

Ten yards from his hiding-place, in the shade of the *jacal*, sat his Tonia calmly plaiting a raw-hide lariat. So far she might surely escape condemnation; women have been known, from time to time, to engage in more mischievous occupations. But if all must be told, there is to be added that her head reposed against the broad and comfortable chest of a tall red-and-yellow man, and that his arm was about her, guiding her nimble small fingers that required so many lessons at the intricate six-strand plait.

Sandridge glanced quickly at the dark mass of pear when he heard a slight squeaking sound that was not altogether unfamiliar. A gun-scabbard will make that sound when one grasps the handle of a six-shooter suddenly. But the sound was not repeated; and Tonia's fingers needed close attention.

And then, in the shadow of death, they began to talk of their love; and in the still July afternoon every word they uttered reached the ears of the Kid.

'Remember, then,' said Tonia, 'you must not come again until I send for you. Soon he will be here. A *vaquero* at the *tienda* said to-day he saw him on the Guadalupe three days ago. When he is that near he always comes. If he comes and finds you here he will kill you. So, for my sake, you must come no more until I send you the word.'

'All right,' said the ranger. 'And then what?'

'And then,' said the girl, 'you must bring your men here and kill him. If not, he will kill you.'

'He ain't a man to surrender, that's sure,' said Sandridge. 'It's kill or be killed for the officer that goes up against Mr. Cisco Kid.'

'He must die,' said the girl. 'Otherwise there will not be any peace in the world for thee and me. He has killed many. Let him so die. Bring your men, and give him no chance to escape.'

'You used to think right much of him,' said Sandridge.

Tonia dropped the lariat, twisted herself around, and curved a lemon-tinted arm over the ranger's shoulder.

'But then,' she murmured in liquid Spanish, 'I had not beheld thee, thou great, red mountain of a man! And thou art kind and good, as well as strong. Could one choose him, knowing thee? Let him die; for then I will not be filled with fear by day and night lest he hurt thee or me.'

'How can I know when he comes?' asked Sandridge.

'When he comes,' said Tonia, 'he remains two days, sometimes three. Gregorio, the small son of Old Luisa, the *lavandera*, has a swift pony. I will write a letter to thee and send it by him, saying how it will be best to come upon him. By Gregorio will the letter come. And bring many men with thee, and have such care, oh, dear red one, for the rattlesnake is not quicker to strike than is "*El Chivato*," as they call him, to send a ball from his *pistola*.'

'The Kid's handy with his gun, sure enough,' admitted Sandridge, 'but when I come for him I shall come alone. I'll get him by myself or not at all. The Cap wrote one or two things to me that make me want to do the trick without any help. You let me know when Mr. Kid arrives, and I'll do the rest.'

'I will send you the message by the boy Gregorio,' said the girl. 'I knew you were braver than that small slayer of men who never smiles. How could I ever have thought I cared for him?'

It was time for the ranger to ride back to his camp on the water hole. Before he mounted his horse he raised the slight form of Tonia with one arm high from the earth for a parting salute. The drowsy stillness of the torpid summer air still lay thick upon the dreaming afternoon. The smoke from the fire in the *jacal*, where the *frijoles* blubbered in the iron pot, rose straight as a plumb-line above the clay-daubed chimney. No sound or movement disturbed the serenity of the dense pear thicket ten yards away.

When the form of Sandridge had disappeared, loping his big dun down the steep banks of the Frio crossing, the Kid crept back to his own horse, mounted him, and rode back along the tortuous trail he had come.

But not far. He stopped and waited in the silent depths of the pear until half an hour had passed. And then Tonia heard the high, untrue notes of his unmusical singing coming nearer and nearer; and she ran to the edge of the pear to meet him.

The Kid seldom smiled; but he smiled and waved his hat when he saw her. He dismounted, and his girl sprang into his arms. The Kid looked at her fondly. His thick black hair clung to his head like a wrinkled mat. The meeting brought a slight ripple of some undercurrent of feeling to his smooth, dark face that was usually as motionless as a clay mask.

'How's my girl?' he asked, holding her close.

'Sick of waiting so long for you, dear one,' she answered. 'My eyes are dim with always gazing into that devil's pincushion through which you come. And I can see into it such a little way, too. But you are here, beloved one, and I will not scold. *Qué mal muchacho*! not to come to see your *alma* more often. Go in and rest, and let me water your horse and stake him with the long rope. There is cool water in the jar for you.'

The Kid kissed her affectionately.

'Not if the court knows itself do I let a lady stake my horse for me,' said he. 'But if you'll run in, *chica*, and throw a pot of coffee together while I attend to the *caballo*, I'll be a good deal obliged.'

Besides his marksmanship the Kid had another attribute for which he admired himself greatly. He was *muy caballero*, as the Mexicans express it, where the ladies were concerned. For them he had always gentle words and consideration. He could not have spoken a harsh word to a woman. He might ruthlessly slay their husbands and brothers, but he could not have laid the weight of a finger in anger upon a woman. Wherefore many of that interesting division of humanity who had come under the spell of his politeness declared their disbelief in the stories circulated about Mr. Kid. One shouldn't believe everything one heard, they said. When confronted by their indignant men folk with proof of the *caballero's* deeds of infamy, they said maybe he had been driven to it, and that he knew how to treat a lady, anyhow.

Considering this extremely courteous idiosyncrasy of the Kid and the pride that he took in it, one can perceive that the solution of the problem that was presented to him by what he saw and heard from his hiding-place in the pear that afternoon (at least as to one of the actors) must have been obscured by difficulties. And yet one could not think of the Kid overlooking little matters of that kind.

At the end of the short twilight they gathered around a supper of *frijoles*, goat steaks, canned peaches, and coffee, by the light of a lantern in the *jacal*. Afterward, the ancestor, his flock corralled, smoked a cigarette and became a mummy in a gray blanket. Tonia washed the few dishes while the Kid dried them with the flour-sacking towel. Her eyes shone; she chatted volubly of the inconsequent happenings of her small world since the Kid's last visit; it was as all his other home-comings had been.

Then outside Tonia swung in a grass hammock with her guitar and sang sad *canciones de amor*.

'Do you love me just the same, old girl?' asked the Kid, hunting for his cigarette papers.

'Always the same, little one,' said Tonia, her dark eyes lingering upon him.

'I must go over to Fink's,' said the Kid, rising, 'for some tobacco. I thought I had another sack in my coat. I'll be back in a quarter of an hour.'

'Hasten,' said Tonia, 'and tell me – how long shall I call you my own this time? Will you be gone again to-morrow, leaving me to grieve, or will you be longer with your Tonia?'

'Oh, I might stay two or three days this trip,' said the Kid, yawning. 'I've been on the dodge for a month, and I'd like to rest up.'

He was gone half an hour for his tobacco. When he returned Tonia was still lying in the hammock.

'It's funny,' said the Kid, 'how I feel. I feel like there was somebody lying behind every bush and tree waiting to shoot me. I never had mully-grubs like them before. Maybe it's one of them presumptions. I've got half a notion to light out in the morning before day. The Guadalupe country is burning up about that old Dutchman I plugged down there.'

'You are not afraid – no one could make my brave little one fear.'

'Well, I haven't been usually regarded as a jack-rabbit when it comes to scrapping; but I don't want a posse smoking me out when I'm in your *jacal*. Somebody might get hurt that oughtn't to.'

'Remain with your Tonia; no one will find you here.'

The Kid looked keenly into the shadows up and down the arroyo and toward the dim lights of the Mexican village.

'I'll see how it looks later on,' was his decision.

At midnight a horseman rode into the ranger's camp, blazing his way by noisy 'halloes' to indicate a pacific mission. Sandridge and one or two others turned out to investigate the row. The rider announced himself to be Domingo Sales, from the Lone Wolf Crossing. He bore a letter for Señor Sandridge. Old Luisa, the *lavandera*, had persuaded him to bring it, he said, her son Gregorio being too ill of a fever to ride.

Sandridge lighted the camp lantern and read the letter. These were its words:

Dear One: He has come. Hardly had you ridden away when he came out of the pear. When he first talked he said he would stay three days or more. Then as it grew later he was like a wolf or a fox, and walked about without rest, looking and listening. Soon he said he must leave before daylight when it is dark and stillest. And then he seemed to suspect that I be not true to him. He looked at me so strange that I am frightened. I swear to him that I love him, his own Tonia. Last of all he said I must prove to him I am true. He thinks that even now men are waiting to kill him as he rides from my house. To escape he says he will dress in my clothes, my red skirt and the blue waist I wear and the brown mantilla over the head, and thus ride away. But before that he says that I must put on his clothes, his *pantalones* and *camisa* and hat, and ride away on his horse from the *jacal* as far as the big road beyond the crossing and back again. This before he goes, so he can tell if I am true and if men are hidden to shoot him. It is a terrible thing. An hour before daybreak this is to be. Come, my dear one, and kill this man and take me for your Tonia. Do not try to take hold of him alive, but kill him quickly. Knowing all, you should do that. You must come long before the time and hide yourself in the little shed near the *jacal* where the wagon and saddles are kept. It is dark in there. He will wear my red skirt and blue waist and brown mantilla. I send you a hundred kisses. Come surely and shoot quickly and straight.

Thine Own Tonia

Sandridge quickly explained to his men the official part of the missive. The rangers protested against his going alone.

'I'll get him easy enough,' said the lieutenant. 'The girl's got him trapped. And don't even think he'll get the drop on me.'

Sandridge saddled his horse and rode to the Lone Wolf Crossing. He tied his big dun in a clump of brush on the arroyo, took his Winchester from his scabbard, and carefully approached the Perez *jacal*. There was only the half of a high moon drifted over by ragged, milk-white gulf clouds.

The wagon-shed was an excellent place for ambush; and the ranger got inside it safely. In the black shadow of the brush shelter in front of the *jacal* he could see a horse tied and hear him impatiently pawing the hard-trodden earth.

He waited almost an hour before two figures came out of the *jacal*. One, in man's clothes, quickly mounted the horse and galloped past the wagon-shed toward the crossing and village. And then the other figure, in skirt, waist, and mantilla over its head, stepped out into the faint moonlight, gazing after the rider. Sandridge thought he would take his chance then before Tonia rode back. He fancied she might not care to see it.

'Throw up your hands,' he ordered, loudly, stepping out of the wagon-shed with his Winchester at his shoulder.

There was a quick turn of the figure, but no movement to obey, so the ranger pumped in the bullets – one – two – three – and then twice more; for you never could be too sure of bringing down the Cisco Kid. There was no danger of missing at ten paces, even in that half moonlight.

The old ancestor, asleep on his blanket, was awakened by the shots. Listening further, he heard a great cry from some man in mortal distress or anguish, and rose up grumbling at the disturbing ways of moderns.

The tall, red ghost of a man burst into the *jacal*, reaching one hand, shaking like a *tule* reed, for the lantern hanging on its nail. The other spread a letter on the table.

'Look at this letter, Perez,' cried the man. 'Who wrote it?'

'*Ah, Dios*! it is Señor Sandridge,' mumbled the old man, approaching. '*Pues, señor*, that letter was written by "*El Chivata*," as he is called – by the man of Tonia. They say he is a bad man; I do not know. While Tonia slept he wrote the letter and sent it by this old hand of mine to Domingo Sales to be brought to you. Is there anything wrong in the letter? I am very old; and I did not know. *Valgame Dios*! it is a very foolish world; and there is nothing in the house to drink – nothing to drink.'

Just then all that Sandridge could think of to do was to go outside and throw himself face downward in the dust by the side of his humming-bird, of whom not a feather fluttered. He was not a *caballero* by instinct, and he could not understand the niceties of revenge.

A mile away the rider who had ridden past the wagon-shed struck up a harsh, untuneful song, the words of which began:

Don't you monkey with my Lulu girl
Or I'll tell you what I'll do—

THE SPHINX APPLE

TWENTY MILES OUT FROM PARADISE, and fifteen miles short of Sunrise City, Bildad Rose, the stage-driver, stopped his team. A furious snow had been falling all day. Eight inches it measured now, on a level. The remainder of the road was not without peril in daylight, creeping along the ribs of a bijou range of ragged mountains. Now, when both snow and night masked its dangers, further travel was not to be thought of, said Bildad Rose. So he pulled up his four stout horses, and delivered to his five passengers oral deductions of his wisdom.

Judge Menefee, to whom men granted leadership and the initiatory as upon a silver salver, sprang from the coach at once. Four of his fellow-passengers followed, inspired by his example, ready to explore, to objurgate, to resist, to submit, to proceed, according as their prime factor might be inclined to sway them. The fifth passenger, a young woman, remained in the coach.

Bildad had halted upon the shoulder of the first mountain spur. Two rail-fences, ragged-black, hemmed the road. Fifty yards above the upper fence, showing a dark blot in the white drifts, stood a small house. Upon this house descended – or rather ascended – Judge Menefee and his cohorts with boyish whoops born of the snow and stress. They called; they pounded at window and door. At the inhospitable silence they waxed restive; they assaulted and forced the pregnable barriers, and invaded the premises.

The watchers from the coach heard stumblings and shoutings from the interior of the ravaged house. Before long a light within flickered, glowed, flamed high and bright and cheerful. Then came running back through the driving flakes the exuberant explorers. More deeply pitched than the clarion – even orchestral in volume – the voice of Judge Menefee proclaimed the succor that lay in apposition with their state of travail. The one room of the house was uninhabited, he said, and bare of furniture; but it contained a great fireplace; and they had discovered an ample store of chopped wood in a lean-to at the rear. Housing and warmth against the shivering night were thus assured. For the placation of Bildad Rose there was news of a stable, not ruined beyond service, with hay in a loft, near the house.

'Gentlemen,' cried Bildad Rose from his seat, swathed in coats and robes, 'tear me down two panels of that fence, so I can drive in. That is old man Redruth's shanty. I thought we must be nigh it. They took him to the foolish house in August.'

Cheerfully the four passengers sprang at the snow-capped rails. The exhorted team tugged the coach up the slant to the door of the edifice from which a mid-summer madness had ravished its proprietor. The driver and two of the passengers began to unhitch. Judge Menefee opened the door of the coach, and removed his hat.

'I have to announce, Miss Garland,' said he, 'the enforced suspension of our journey. The driver asserts that the risk in traveling the mountain road by night is too great even to consider. It will be necessary to remain in the shelter of this house until morning. I beg that you will feel that there is nothing to fear beyond a temporary inconvenience. I have personally inspected the house, and find that there are means to provide against the rigor of the weather, at least. You shall be made as comfortable as possible. Permit me to assist you to alight.'

To the Judge's side came the passenger whose pursuit in life was the placing of the Little Goliath windmill. His name was Dunwoody; but that matters not much. In traveling merely from Paradise to Sunrise City one needs little or no name. Still, one who would seek to divide honors with Judge Madison L. Menefee deserves a cognominal peg upon which Fame may hang a wreath. Thus spake, loudly and buoyantly, the aërial miller:

'Guess you'll have to climb out of the ark, Mrs. McFarland. This wigwam ain't exactly the Palmer House, but it turns snow, and they won't search your grip for souvenir spoons when you leave. *We've* got a fire going, and *we'll* fix you up with dry Trilbys and keep the mice away, anyhow, all right, all right.'

One of the two passengers who were struggling in a *mêlée* of horses, harness, snow, and the sarcastic injunctions of Bildad Rose, called loudly from the whirl of his volunteer duties: 'Say, some of you fellows get Miss Solomon into the house, will you? Whoa, there! you confounded brute!'

Again must it be gently urged that in traveling from Paradise to Sunrise City an accurate name is prodigality. When Judge Menefee – sanctioned to the act by his grey hair and widespread repute – had introduced himself to the lady passenger, she had, herself, sweetly breathed a name, in response, that the hearing of the male passengers had variously interpreted. In the not unjealous spirit of rivalry that eventuated, each clung stubbornly to his own theory. For the lady passenger to have reasseverated or corrected would have seemed didactic if not unduly solicitous of a specific acquaintance. Therefore the lady passenger permitted herself to be Garlanded and McFarlanded and Solomoned with equal and discreet complacency. It is thirty-five miles from Paradise to Sunrise City. *Compagnon de voyage* is name enough, by the gripsack of the Wandering Jew! for so brief a journey.

Soon the little party of wayfarers were happily seated in a cheerful arc before the roaring fire. The robes, cushions and removable portions of the coach had been brought in and put to service. The lady passenger chose a place near the hearth at one end of the arc. There she graced almost a throne that her subjects had prepared. She sat upon cushions and leaned against an empty box and barrel, robe bespread, which formed a defence from the invading draughts. She extended her feet, delectably shod, to the cordial heat. She ungloved her hands, but retained about her neck her long fur boa. The unstable flames half revealed, while the warding boa half submerged, her face – a youthful face, altogether feminine, clearly moulded and calm with beauty's unchallenged confidence. Chivalry and manhood were here vying to please and comfort her. She seemed to accept their devoirs – not piquantly, as one courted and attended; not preeningly, as many of her sex unworthily reap their honors; nor yet stolidly, as the ox receives his hay; but concordantly with nature's own plan – as the lily ingests the drop of dew foreordained to its refreshment.

Outside the wind roared mightily, the fine snow whizzed through the cracks, the cold besieged the backs of the immolated six; but the elements did not lack a champion that night. Judge Menefee was attorney for the storm. The weather was his client, and he strove by special pleading to convince his companions in that frigid jury-box that they sojourned in a bower of roses, beset only by benignant zephyrs. He drew upon a fund of gaiety, wit, and anecdote, sophistical, but crowned with success. His cheerfulness communicated itself irresistibly. Each one hastened to contribute his quota toward the general optimism. Even the lady passenger was moved to expression.

'I think it is quite charming,' she said, in her slow, crystal tones.

At intervals some one of the passengers would rise and humorously explore the room. There was little evidence to be collected of its habitation by old man Redruth.

Bildad Rose was called upon vivaciously for the ex-hermit's history. Now, since the stage-driver's horses were fairly comfortable and his passengers appeared to be so, peace and comity returned to him.

'The old didapper,' began Bildad, somewhat irreverently, 'infested this here house about twenty year. He never allowed nobody to come nigh him. He'd duck his head inside and slam the door whenever a team drove along. There was spinning-wheels up in his loft, all right. He used to buy his groceries and tobacco at Sam Tilly's store, on the Little Muddy. Last August he went up there dressed in a red bedquilt, and told Sam he was King Solomon, and that the Queen of Sheba was coming to visit him. He fetched along all the money he had – a little bag full of silver – and dropped it in

Sam's well. "She won't come," says old man Redruth to Sam, "if she knows I've got any money."

'As soon as folks heard he had that sort of a theory about women and money they know he was crazy; so they sent down and packed him to the foolish asylum.'

'Was there a romance in his life that drove him to a solitary existence?' asked one of the passengers, a young man who had an Agency.

'No,' said Bildad, 'not that I ever heard spoke of. Just ordinary trouble. They say he had had unfortunateness in the way of love derangements with a young lady when he was young; before he contracted red bedquilts and had his financial conclusions disqualified. I never heard of no romance.'

'Ah!' exclaimed Judge Menefee, impressively; 'a case of unrequited affection, no doubt.'

'No, sir,' returned Bildad, 'not at all. She never married him. Marmaduke Muligan, down at Paradise, seen a man once that come from old Redruth's town. He said Redruth was a fine young man, but when you kicked him on the pocket all you could hear jingle was a cuff-fastener and a bunch of keys. He was engaged to this young lady – Miss Alice – something was her name; I've forgot. This man said she was the kind of a girl you like to have reach across you in a car to pay the fare. Well, there come to the town a young chap all affuent and easy, and fixed up with buggies and mining stock and leisure time. Although she was a staked claim, Miss Alice and the new entry seemed to strike a mutual kind of a clip. They had calls and coincidences of going to the post office and such things as sometimes make a girl send back the engagement ring and other presents – "a rift within the loot," the poetry man calls it.'

'One day folks seen Redruth and Miss Alice standing talking at the gate. Then he lifts his hat and walks away, and that was the last anybody in that town seen of him, as far as this man knew.'

'What about the young lady?' asked the young man who had an Agency.

'Never heard,' answered Bildad. 'Right there is where my lode of information turns to an old spavined crowbait, and folds its wings, for I've pumped it dry.'

'A very sad—' began Judge Menefee, but his remark was curtailed by a higher authority.

'What a charming story!' said the lady passenger, in flute-like tones.

A little silence followed, except for the wind and the crackling of the fire.

The men were seated upon the floor, having slightly mitigated its inhospitable surface with wraps and stray pieces of boards. The man who was placing Little Goliath windmills arose and walked about to ease his cramped muscles.

Suddenly a trimphant shout came from him. He hurried back from a dusky corner of the room, bearing aloft something in his hand. It was an apple – a large, red-mottled, firm pippin, pleasing to behold. In a paper bag on a high shelf in that corner he had found it. It could have been no relic of the love-wrecked Redruth, for its glorious soundness repudiated the theory that it had laid on that musty shelf since August. No doubt some recent bivouackers, lunching in the deserted house, had left it there.

Dunwoody – again his exploits demand for him the honors of nomenclature – flaunted his apple in the faces of his fellow-marooners. 'See what I found, Mrs. McFarland!' he cried, vaingloriously. He held the apple high up in the light of the fire, where it glowed a still richer red. The lady passenger smiled calmly – always calmly.

'What a charming apple!' she murmured, clearly.

For a brief space Judge Menefee felt crushed, humiliated, relegated. Second place galled him. Why had this blatant, obtrusive, unpolished man of windmills been selected by Fate instead of himself to discover the sensational apple? He could have made of the act a scene, a function, a setting for some impromptu fanciful discourse or piece of comedy – and have retained the rôle of cynosure. Actually, the lady passenger was regarding this ridiculous Dunboddy or Woodbundy with an admiring smile, as if the fellow had performed a feat! And the windmill man swelled and gyrated like a sample of his own goods, puffed up with the wind that ever blows from the chorus land toward the domain of the star.

While the transported Dunwoody, with his Aladdin's apple, was receiving the fickle attentions of all, the resourceful jurist formed a plan to recover his own laurels.

With his courtliest smile upon his heavy but classic features, Judge Menefee advanced, and took the apple, as if to examine it, from the hand of Dunwoody. In his hand it became Exhibit A.

'A fine apple,' he said, approvingly. 'Really, my dear Mr. Dunwindy, you have eclipsed all of us as a forager. But I have an idea. This apple shall become an emblem, a token, a symbol, a prize bestowed by the mind and heart of beauty upon the most deserving.'

The audience, except one, applauded. 'Good on the stump, ain't he?' commented the passenger who was nobody in particular to the young man who had an Agency.

The unresponsive one was the windmill man. He saw himself reduced to the ranks. Never would the thought have occurred to him to declare his apple an emblem. He had intended after it had been divided and eaten, to create diversion by sticking the seeds against his forehead and naming them for young ladies of his acquaintance. One he was going to name Mrs. McFarland. The seed that fell off first would be – but 'twas too late now.

'The apple,' continued Judge Menefee, charging his jury, 'in modern days occupies, though undeservedly, a lowly place in our esteem. Indeed, it is so constantly associated with the culinary and the commercial that it is hardly to be classed among the polite fruits. But in ancient times this was not so. Biblical, historical, and mythological lore abounds with evidences that the apple was the aristocrat of fruits. We still say "the apple of the eye" when we wish to describe something superlatively precious. We find in Proverbs the comparison to "apples of silver." No other product of tree or vine has been so utilized in figurative speech. Who has not heard of and longed for the "apples of the Hesperides"? I need not call your attention to the most tremendous and significant instance of the apple's ancient prestige when its consumption by our first parents occasioned the fall of man from his state of goodness and perfection.'

'Apples like them,' said the windmill man, lingering with the objective article, 'are worth $3.50 a barrel in the Chicago market.'

'Now, what I have to propose,' said Judge Menefee, conceding an indulgent smile to his interrupter, 'is this: We must remain here, perforce, until morning. We have wood in plenty to keep us warm. Our next need is to entertain ourselves as best we can, in order that the time shall not pass too slowly. I propose that we place this apple in the hands of Miss Garland. It is no longer a fruit, but, as I said, a prize, in award, representing a great human idea. Miss Garland, herself, shall cease to be an individual – but only temporarily, I am happy to add' – (a low bow, full of the old-time grace). 'She shall represent her sex; she shall be the embodiment, the epitome of womankind – the heart and brain, I may say, of God's masterpiece of creation. In this guise she shall judge and decide the question which follows:

'But a few minutes ago our friend, Mr. Rose, favored us with an entertaining but fragmentary sketch of the romance in the life of the former possessor of this habitation. The few facts that we have learned seem to me to open up a fascinating field for conjecture, for the study of human hearts, for the exercise of the imagination – in short, for story-telling. Let us make use of the opportunity. Let each one of us relate his own version of the story of Redruth, the hermit, and his lady-love, beginning where Mr. Rose's narrative ends – at the parting of the lovers at the gate. This much should be assumed and conceded – that the young lady was not necessarily to blame for Redruth's becoming a crazed and world-hating hermit. When we have done, Miss Garland shall render the JUDGMENT OF WOMAN. As the Spirit of her Sex she shall decide which version of the story best and most truly depicts human and love interest, and most faithfully estimates the character and acts of Redruth's betrothed according to the feminine view. The apple shall be bestowed upon him who is awarded the decision. If you are all agreed, we shall be pleased to hear the first story from Mr. Dinwiddie.'

The last sentence captured the windmill man. He was not one to linger in the dumps.

'That's a first-rate scheme, Judge,' he said heartily. 'Be a regular short-story vaudeville, won't it? I used to be correspondent for a paper in Springfield, and when there wasn't any news I faked it. Guess I can do my turn all right.'

'I think the idea is charming,' said the lady passenger, brightly. 'It will be almost like a game.'

Judge Menefee stepped forward and placed the apple in her hand impressively.

'In olden days,' he said, profoundly, 'Paris awarded the golden apple to the most beautiful.'

'I was at the Exposition,' remarked the windmill man, now cheerful again, 'but I never heard of it. And I was on the Midway, too, all the time I wasn't at the machinery exhibit.'

'But now,' continued the Judge, 'the fruit shall translate to us the mystery and wisdom of the feminine heart. Take the apple, Miss Garland. Hear our modest tales of romance, and then award the prize as you may deem it just.'

The lady passenger smiled sweetly. The apple lay in her lap beneath her robes and wraps. She reclined against her protecting bulwark, brightly and cosily at ease. But for the voices and the wind one might have listened hopefully to hear her purr. Someone cast fresh logs upon the fire. Judge Menefee nodded suavely. 'Will you oblige us with the initial story?' he asked.

The windmill man sat as sits a Turk, with his hat well back on his head on account of the draughts.

'Well,' he began, without any embarrassment, 'this is about the way I size up the difficulty: Of course Redruth was jostled a good deal by this duck who had money to play ball with who tried to cut him out of his girl. So he goes around, naturally, and asks her if the game is still square. Well, nobody wants a guy cutting in with buggies and gold bonds when he's got an option on a girl. Well, he goes around to see her. Well, maybe he's hot, and talks like the proprietor, and forgets that an engagement ain't always a lead-pipe cinch. Well, I guess that makes Alice warm under the lace yoke. Well, she answers back sharp. Well, he—'

'Say!' interrupted the passenger who was nobody in particular, 'if you could put up a windmill on every one of them "wells" you're using, you'd be able to retire from business, wouldn't you?'

The windmill man grinned good-naturedly.

'Oh, I ain't no *Guy de Mopassong*,' he said, cheerfully. 'I'm giving it to you in straight American. Well, she says something like this: "Mr. Gold Bonds is only a friend," says she; "but he takes me riding and buys me theatre tickets, and that's what you never do. Ain't I to never have any pleasure in life while I can?" "Pass this chatfield-chatfield thing along," says Redruth; "hand out the mitt to the Willie with creases in it or you don't put your slippers under my wardrobe."

'Now that kind of train orders don't go with a girl that's got any spirit. I bet that girl loved her honey all the time. Maybe she only wanted, as girls do, to work the good thing for a little fun and caramels before she settled down to patch George's other pair, and be a good wife. But he is glued to the high horse, and won't come down. Well, she hands him back the ring, proper enough; and George goes away and hits the booze. Yep. That's what done it. I bet that girl fired the cornucopia with the fancy vest two days after her steady left. George boards a freight and checks his bag of crackers for parts unknown. He sticks to Old Booze for a number of years; and then the aniline and aquafortis gets the decision. "Me for the hermit's hut," says George, "and the long whiskers, and the buried can of money that isn't there."

'But that Alice, in my mind, was on the level. She never married, but took up typewriting as soon as the wrinkles began to show, and kept a cat that came when you said "weeny – weeny – weeny!" I got too much faith in good women to believe they throw down the fellow they're stuck on every time for the dough.' The windmill man ceased.

'I think,' said the lady passenger, slightly moving upon her lowly throne, 'that that is a char—'

'Oh, Miss Garland!' interposed Judge Menefee, with uplifted hand, 'I beg of you, no comments! It would not be fair to the other contestants. Mr. – er – will you take the next turn?' The Judge addressed the young man who had the Agency.

'My version of the romance,' began the young man, diffidently clasping his hands, 'would be this: They did not quarrel when they parted. Mr. Redruth bade her good-bye and went out into the world to seek his fortune. He knew his love would remain true to him. He scorned the thought that his rival could make an impression upon a heart so fond and faithful. I would say that Mr. Redruth went out to the Rocky Mountains in Wyoming to seek for gold. One day a crew of pirates landed and captured him while at work, and—'

'Hey! what's that?' sharply called the passenger who was nobody in particular – 'a crew of pirates landed in the Rocky Mountains! Will you tell us how they sailed—'

'Landed from a train,' said the narrator, quietly and not without some readiness. 'They kept him prisoner in a cave for months, and then they took him hundreds of miles away to the forests of Alaska. There a beautiful Indian girl fell in love with him, but he remained true to Alice. After another year of wandering in the woods, he set out with the diamonds—'

'What diamonds?' asked the unimportant passenger, almost with acerbity.

'The ones the saddlemaker showed him in the Peruvian temple,' said the other, somewhat obscurely. 'When he reached home, Alice's mother led him, weeping, to a green mound under a willow tree. "Her heart was broken when you left," said her mother. "And what of my rival – of Chester McIntosh?" asked Mr. Redruth, as he knelt sadly by Alice's grave. "When he found out," she answered, "that her heart was yours, he pined away day by day until, at length, he started a furniture store in Grand Rapids. We heard lately that he was bitten to death by an infuriated moose near South Bend, Ind., where he had gone to try to forget scenes of civilization." With which, Mr. Redruth forsook the face of mankind and became a hermit, as we have seen.

'My story,' concluded the young man with an Agency, 'may lack the literary quality; but what I want it to show is that the young lady remained true. She cared nothing for wealth in comparison with true affection. I admire and believe in the fair sex too much to think otherwise.'

The narrator ceased, with a sidelong glance at the corner where reclined the lady passenger.

Bildad Rose was next invited by Judge Menefee to contribute his story in the contest for the apple of judgment. The stage-driver's essay was brief.

'I'm not one of them lobo wolves,' he said, 'who are always blaming on women the calamities of life. My testimony in regards to the fiction story you ask for, Judge, will be about as follows: What ailed Redruth was pure laziness. If he had up and slugged this Percival De Lacey that tried to give him the outside of the road, and had kept Alice in the grape-vine swing with the blind-bridle on, all would have been well. The woman you want is sure worth taking pains for.

' "Send for me if you want me again," says Redruth, and hoists his Stetson, and walks off. He'd have called it pride, but the nixycomlògical name for it is laziness. No woman don't like to run after a man. "Let him come back, hisself," says the girl; and I'll be bound she tells the boy with the pay ore to trot; and then spends her time watching out the window for the man with the empty pocket-book and the tickly moustache.

'I reckon Redruth waits about nine year expecting her to send him a note by a nigger asking him to forgive her. But she don't. "This game won't work," says Redruth; "then so won't I." And he goes in the hermit business and raises whiskers. Yes; laziness and whiskers was what done the trick. They travel together. You ever hear of a man with long whiskers and hair striking a bonanza? No. Look at the Duke of Marlborough and this Standard Oil snooper. Have they got 'em?

'Now, this Alice didn't never marry, I'll bet a hoss. If Redruth had married somebody else she might have done so, too. But he never turns up. She has these here things they call fond memories, and maybe a lock of hair and a corset steel that he broke, treasured up. Them sort of articles is as good as a husband to some women. I'd say she played out a lone hand. I don't blame no woman for old man Redruth's abandonment of barber shops and clean shirts.'

Next in order came the passenger who was nobody in particular. Nameless to us, he travels the road from Paradise to Sunrise City.

But him you shall see, if the firelight be not too dim, as he responds to the Judge's call.

A lean form, in rusty-brown clothing, sitting like a frog, his arms wrapping about his legs, his chin resting upon his knees. Smooth, oakum-colored hair; long nose; mouth like a satyr's, with upturned, tobacco-stained corners. An eye like a fish's; a red necktie with a horseshoe pin. He began with a rasping chuckle that gradually formed itself into words.

'Everybody wrong so far. What! a romance without any orange blossoms! Ho, ho! My money on the lad with the butterfly tie and the certified checks in his trouserings.

'Take 'em as they parted at the gate? All right. "You never loved me," says Redruth, wildly, "or you wouldn't speak to a man who can buy you the ice cream." "I hate him," says she. "I loathe his side-bar buggy; I despise the elegant cream bonbons he sends me in gilt boxes covered with real lace; I feel that I could stab him to the heart when he presents me with a solid medallion locket with turquoises and pearls running in a vine around the border. Away with them! 'Tis only you I love." "Back to the cosy corner!" says Redruth. "Was I bound and lettered in East Aurora? Get platonic, if you please. No jack-pots for mine. Go and hate your friend some more. For me the Nickerson girl on Avenue B, and gum, and a trolley ride."

'Around that night comes John W. Croesus. "What! tears?" says he, arranging his pearl pin. "You have driven my lover away," says little Alice sobbing. "I hate the sight of you." "Marry me, then," says John W., lighting a Henry Clay. "What!" she cries, indignantly, "marry you! Never," she says, "until this blows over, and I can do some shopping, and you see about the license. There's a telephone next door if you want to call up the county clerk." '

The narrator paused to give vent to his cynical chuckle.

'Did they marry?' he continued. 'Did the duck swallow the June-bug? And then I take up the case of Old Boy Redruth. There's where you are all wrong again, according to my theory. What turned him into a hermit? One says laziness; one says remorse; one says booze. I say women did it. How old is the old man now?' asked the speaker, turning to Bildad Rose.

'I should say about sixty-five.'

'All right. He conducted his hermit shop here for twenty years. Say he was twenty-five when he took off his hat at the gate. That leaves twenty years for him to account for, or else be docked. Where did he spend that ten and two fives? I'll give you my idea. Up for bigamy. Say there was the fat blonde in Saint Jo, and the panatela brunette at Skillet Ridge, and the gold tooth down in the Kaw valley. Redruth gets his cases mixed, and they send him up the road. He gets out after they are through with him, and says: "Any line for me except the crinoline. The hermit trade is not overdone, and the stenographers never apply to 'em for work. The jolly hermit's life for me. No more long hairs in the comb or dill pickles lying around in the cigar tray." You tell me they pinched old Redruth for the noodle villa just because he said he was King Solomon? Figs! He *was* Solomon. That's all of mine. I guess it don't call for any apples. Enclosed find stamps. It don't sound much like a prize winner.'

Respecting the stricture laid by Judge Menefee against comments upon the stories, all were silent when the passenger who was nobody in particular had concluded. And then the ingenious originator of the contest cleared his throat to begin the ultimate entry for the prize. Though seated with small comfort upon the floor, you might search in vain for any abatement of dignity in Judge Menefee. The now diminishing firelight played softly upon his face, as clearly chiselled as a Roman emperor's on some old coin, and upon the thick waves of his honorable gray hair.

'A woman's heart!' he began, in even but thrilling tones – 'who can hope to fathom it? The ways and desires of men are various. I think that the hearts of all women beat with the same rhythm, and to the same old tune of love. Love, to a woman, means sacrifice. If she be worthy of the name, no gold or rank will outweigh with her a genuine devotion.

'Gentlemen of the – er – I should say, my friends, the case of Redruth versus love and affection has been called. Yet, who is on trial? Not Redruth, for he has been punished. Not those immortal passions that clothe our lives with the joy of the angels. Then who? Each man of us here tonight stands at the bar to answer if chivalry or darkness inhabits his bosom. To judge us sits womankind in the form of one of its fairest flowers. In her hand she holds the prize, intrinsically insignificant, but worthy of our noblest efforts to win as a guerdon of approval from so worthy a representative of feminine judgment and taste.

'In taking up the imaginary history of Redruth and the fair being to whom he gave his heart, I must, in the beginning, raise my voice against the unworthy insinuation that the selfishness or perfidy or love of luxury of any woman drove him to renounce the world. I have not found woman to be so unspiritual or venal. We must seek elsewhere, among man's baser nature and lower motives for the cause.

'There was, in all probability, a lovers' quarrel as they stood at the gate on that memorable day. Tormented by jealousy, young Redruth vanished from his native haunts. But had he just cause to do so? There is no evidence for or against. But there is something higher than evidence: there is the grand, eternal belief in woman's goodness, in her steadfastness against temptation, in her loyalty even in the face of proffered riches.

'I picture to myself the rash lover, wandering, self-tortured, about the world. I picture his gradual descent, and, finally, his complete despair when he realizes that he has lost the most precious gift life had to offer him. Then his withdrawal from the world of sorrow and the subsequent derangement of his faculties becomes intelligible.

'But what do I see on the other hand? A lonely woman fading away as the years roll by; still faithful, still waiting, still watching for a form and listening for a step that will come no more. She is old now. Her hair is white and smoothly banded. Each day she sits at the door and gazes longingly down the dusty road. In spirit she is waiting there at the gate, just as he left her – his forever, but not here below. Yes; my belief in woman paints that picture in my mind. Parted forever on earth, but waiting! She in anticipation of a meeting in Elysium; he in the Slough of Despond.'

'I thought he was in the bughouse,' said the passenger who was nobody in particular.

Judge Menefee stirred, a little impatiently. The men sat, drooping, in grotesque attitudes. The wind had abated its violence; coming now in fitful, virulent puffs. The fire had burned to a mass of red coals which shed but a dim light within the room. The lady passenger in her cosy nook looked to be but a formless dark bulk, crowned by a mass of coiled, sleek hair and showing but a small space of snowy forehead above her clinging boa.

Judge Menefee got stiffly to his feet.

'And now, Miss Garland,' he announced, 'we have concluded. It is for you to award the prize to the one of us whose argument – especially, I may say, in regard to his estimate of true womanhood – approaches nearest to your own conception.'

No answer came from the lady passenger. Judge Menefee bent over solicitously. The passenger who was nobody in particular laughed low and harshly. The lady was sleeping sweetly. The Judge essayed to take her hand to awaken her. In doing so he touched a small, cold, round, irregular something in her lap.

'She has eaten the apple,' announced Judge Menefee, in awed tones, as he held up the core for them to see.

THE MISSING CHORD

I STOPPED OVERNIGHT at the sheep-ranch of Rush Kinney, on the Sandy Fork of the Nueces. Mr. Kinney and I had been strangers up to the time when I called 'Hallo!' at his hitching-rack; but from that moment until my departure on the next morning we were, according to the Texas code, undeniable friends.

After supper the ranchman and I lugged our chairs outside the two-room house, to its floorless gallery roofed with chaparral and sacuista grass. With the rear legs of our chairs sinking deep into the hard-packed loam, each of us reposed against an elm pillar of the structure and smoked El Toro tobacco, while we wrangled amicably concerning the affairs of the rest of the world.

As for conveying adequate conception of the engaging harm of that prairie evening, despair waits upon it. It is a bold chronicler who will undertake the descrption of a Texas night in the early spring. An inventory must suffice.

The ranch rested upon the summit of a lenient slope. The ambient prairie, diversified by arroyos and murky patches of brush and pear, lay around us like a darkened bowl at the bottom of which we reposed as dregs. Like a turquoise cover the sky pinned us there. The miraculous air, heady with ozone and made memorably sweet by leagues of wild flowerets, gave tang and savor to the breath. In the sky was a great, round, mellow searchlight which we knew to be no moon, but the dark lantern of summer, who came to hunt northward the cowering spring. In the nearest corral a flock of sheep lay silent until a groundless panic would send a squad of them huddling together with a drumming rush. For other sounds a shrill family of coyotes yapped beyond the shearing-pen, and whippoorwills twittered in the long grass. But even these dissonances hardly rippled the clear torrent of the mocking-birds' notes that fell from a dozen neighboring shrubs and trees. It would not have been preposterous for one to tiptoe and essay to touch the stars, they hung so bright and imminent.

Mr. Kinney's wife, a young and capable woman, we had left in the house. She remained to busy herself with the domestic round of duties in which I had observed that she seemed to take a buoyant and contented pride. In one room we had supped. Presently, from the other, as Kinney and I sat without, there burst a volume of sudden and brilliant music. If I could justly estimate the art of piano-playing, the construer of that rollicking fantasia had creditably mastered the secrets of the keyboard. A piano, and one so well played, seemed to me to be an unusual thing to find in that small and unpromising ranchhouse. I must have looked my surprise at Rush Kinney, for he laughed in his soft Southern way, and nodded at me through he moonlit haze of our cigarettes.

'You don't often hear as agreeable a noise as that on a sheep-ranch,' he remarked; 'but I never see any reason for not playing up to the arts and graces just because we happen to live out in the brush. It's a lonesome life for a woman; and if a little music can make it any better, why not have it? That's the way I look at it.'

'A wise and generous theory,' I assented. 'And Mrs. Kinney plays well. I am not learned in the science of music, but I should call her an uncommonly good performer. She has technic and more than ordinary power.'

The moon was very bright, you will understand, and I saw upon Kinney's face a sort of amused and pregnant expression, as though there were things behind it that might be expounded.

'You came up the trail from the Double-Elm Fork,' he said, promisingly. 'As you crossed it you must have seen an old deserted *jacal* to your left under a coma mott.'

'I did,' said I. 'There was a drove of *invalis* rooting around it. I could see by the broken corrals that no one lived there.'

'That's where this music proposition started,' said Kinney. 'I don't mind telling you about it while we smoke. That's where old Cal Adams lived. He had about eight hundred graded merinos and a daughter that was solid silk and as handsome as a new stake-rope on a thirty-dollar pony. And I don't mind telling you that I was guilty in the second degree of hanging around old Cal's ranch all the time I could spare away from lambing and shearing. Miss Marilla was her name; and I had figured it out by the rule of two that she was destined to become the chatelaine and lady superior of Rancho Lomito, belonging to R. Kinney, Esq., where you are now a welcome and honored guest.

'I will say that old Cal wasn't distinguished as a sheepman. He was a little, old stoop-shouldered *hombre* about as big as a gun scabbard, with scraggy white whiskers, and condemned to the continuous use of language. Old Cal was so obscure in his chosen profession that he wasn't even hated by the cowmen. And when a sheepman don't get eminent enough to acquire the hostility of the cattlemen, he is mighty apt to die unwept and considerably unsung.

'But that Marilla girl was a benefit to the eye. And she was the most elegant kind of a housekeeper. I was the nearest neighbour, and I used to ride over to the Double-Elm anywhere from nine to sixteen times a week with fresh butter or a quarter of venison or a sample of new sheep-dip just as a frivolous excuse to see Marilla. Marilla and me got to be extensively inveigled with each other, and I was pretty sure I was going to get my rope around her neck and lead her over to the Lomito. Only she was so everlastingly permeated with filial sentiments toward old Cal that I never could get her to talk about serious matters.

'You never saw anybody in your life that was as full of knowledge and had less sense than old Cal. He was advised about all the branches of information contained in learning, and he was up to all the rudiments of doctrines and enlightenment. You couldn't advance him any ideas on any of the parts of speech or lines of thought. You would have thought he was a professor of the weather and politics and chemistry and natural history and the origin of derivations. Any subject you brought up old Cal could give you an abundant synopsis of it from the Greek root up to the time it was sacked and on the market.

'One day just after the fall shearing I rides over to the Double-Elm with a lady's magazine about fashions for Marilla and a scientific paper for old Cal.

'While I was tying my pony to a mesquite, out run Marilla, 'tickled to death' with some news that couldn't wait.

' "Oh, Rush," she says, all flushed up with esteem and gratification, "what do you think! Dad's going to buy me a piano. Ain't it grand? I never dreamed I'd ever have one."

' "It's sure joyful," says I. "I always admired the agreeable uproar of a piano. It'll be lots of company for you. That's mighty good of Uncle Cal to do that."

' "I'm all undecided," says Marilla, "between a piano and a organ. A parlor organ is nice."

' "Either of 'em," says I, "is first-class for mitigating the lack of noise around a sheep-ranch. For my part," I says, "I shouldn't like anything better than to ride home of an evening and listen to a few waltzes and jigs, with somebody about your size sitting on the piano-stool and rounding up the notes."

' "Oh, hush about that," says Marilla, "and go on in the house. Dad hasn't rode out to-day. He's not feeling well."

'Old Cal was inside, lying on a cot. He had a pretty bad cold and cough. I stayed to supper.

' "Going to get Marilla a piano, I hear," says I to him.

' "Why, yes, something of the kind, Rush," says he. "She's been hankering for music for a long spell; and I allow to fix her up with something in that line right away. The sheep sheared six pounds all round this fall; and I'm going to get Marilla an instrument if it takes the price of the whole clip to do it."

' "*Star wayno*," says I. "The little girl deserves it."

' "I'm going to San Antone on the last load of wool," says Uncle Cal, "and select an instrument for her myself."

' "Wouldn't it be better," I suggest, "to take Marilla along and let her pick out one that she likes?"

'I might have known that would set Uncle Cal going. Of course, a man like him, that knew everything about everything, would look at that as a reflection on his attainments.

' "No, sir, it wouldn't," says he, pulling at his white whiskers. "There ain't a better judge of musical instruments in the whole world than what I am. I had an uncle," says he, "that was a partner in a piano-factory, and I've seen thousands of 'em put together. I know all about musical instruments from a pipe-organ to a corn-stalk fiddle. There ain't a man lives, sir, that can tell me any news about any instrument that has to be pounded, blowed, scraped, grinded, picked, or wound with a key."

' "You get me what you like, dad," says Marilla, who couldn't keep her
feet on the floor from joy. "Of course you know what to select. I'd just as lief
it was a piano or a organ or what."

' "I see in St. Louis once what they call a orchestrion," says Uncle Cal,
"that I judged was about the finest thing in the way of music ever invented.
But there ain't room in this house for one. Anyway, I imagine they'd cost
a thousand dollars. I reckon something in the piano line would suit Marilla
the best. She took lessons in that respect for two years over at Birdstail. I
wouldn't trust the buying of an instrument to anybody else but myself. I
reckon if I hadn't took up sheep-raising I'd have been one of the finest
composers or piano-and-organ manufacturers in the world."

'That was Uncle Cal's style. But I never lost any patience with him, on
account of his thinking so much of Marilla. And she thought just as much
of him. He sent her to the academy over at Birdstail for two years when it
took nearly every pound of wool to pay the expenses.

'Along about Tuesday Uncle Cal put out for San Antone on the last
wagon-load of wool. Marilla's Uncle Ben, who lived in Birdstail, come over
and stayed at the ranch while Uncle Cal was gone.

'It was ninety miles to San Antone, and forty to the nearest railroad-station,
so Uncle Cal was gone about four days. I was over at the Double-Elm when
he came rolling back one evening about sundown. And up there in the
wagon, sure enough, was a piano or a organ – we couldn't tell which – all
wrapped up in wool-sacks, with a wagon-sheet tied over it in case of rain.
And out skips Marilla, hollering, "Oh, oh!" with her eyes shining and her
hair a-flying. "Dad – dad," she sings out, "have you brought it – have you
brought it?" – and it right there before her eyes, as women will do.

' "Finest piano in San Antone," says Uncle Cal, waving his hand, proud.
"Genuine rosewood, and the finest, loudest tone you ever listened to. I
heard the storekeeper play it, and I took it on the spot and paid cash down."

'Me and Ben and Uncle Cal and a Mexican lifted it out of the wagon and
carried it in the house and set it in a corner. It was one of them upright
instruments, and not very heavy or very big.

'And then all of a sudden Uncle Cal flops over and says he's mighty sick.
He's got a high fever, and he complains of his lungs. He gets into bed, while
me and Ben goes out to unhitch and put the horses in the pasture, and
Marilla flies around to get Uncle Cal something hot to drink. But first she
puts both arms on that piano and hugs it with a soft kind of a smile, like you
see kids doing with their Christmas toys.

'When I came in from the pasture, Marilla was in the room where the
piano was. I could see by the strings and wool-sacks on the floor that she had
had it unwrapped. But now she was tying the wagon-sheet over it again, and
there was a kind of solemn, whitish look on her face.

' "Ain't wrapping up the music again, are you, Marilla?" I asks. "What's
the matter with just a couple of tunes for to see how she goes under the
saddle?"

' "Not to-night, Rush," says she. "I don't want to play any to-night. Dad's
too sick. Just think, Rush, he paid three hundred dollars for it – nearly a
third of what the wool-clip brought!"

' "Well, it ain't anyways in the neighborhood of a third of what you are
worth," I told her. "And I don't think Uncle Cal is too sick to hear a little
agitation of the piano-keys just to christen the machine."

' "Not to-night, Rush," says Marilla, in a way that she had when she wanted to settle things.

'But it seems that Uncle Cal was plenty sick, after all. He got so bad that Ben saddled up and rode over to Birdstail for Doc Simpson. I stayed around to see if I'd be needed for anything.

'When Uncle Cal's pain let up on him a little he called Marilla and says to her: "Did you look at your instrument, honey? And do you like it?"

' "It's lovely, dad,' says she, leaning down by his pillow; "I never saw one so pretty. How dear and good it was of you to buy it for me!"

' "I haven't heard you play on it any yet," says Uncle Cal; "and I've been listening. My side don't hurt quite so bad now – won't you play a piece, Marilla?"

'But no; she puts Uncle Cal off and soothes him down like you've seen women do with a kid. It seems she's made up her mind not to touch that piano at present.

'When Doc Simpson comes over he tells us that Uncle Cal has pneumonia the worst kind; and as the old man was past sixty and nearly on the lift anyhow, the odds was against his walking on grass any more.

'On the fourth day of his sickness he calls for Marilla again and wants to talk piano. Doc Simpson was there, and so was Ben and Mrs. Ben, trying to do all they could.

' "I'd have made a wonderful success in anything connected with music," says Uncle Cal. "I got the finest instrument for the money in San Antone. Ain't that piano all right in every respect, Marilla?"

' "It's just perfect, dad," says she. "It's got the finest tone I ever heard. But don't you think you could sleep a little now, dad?"

' "No, I don't," says Uncle Cal. "I want to hear that piano. I don't believe you've even tried it yet. I went all the way to San Antone and picked it out for you myself. It took a third of the fall clip to buy it; but I don't mind that if it makes any good girl happier. Won't you play a little bit for dad, Marilla?"

'Doc Simpson beckoned Marilla to one side and recommended her to do what Uncle Cal wanted, so it would get him quieted. And her Uncle ben and his wife asked her, too.

' "Why not hit out a tune or two with the soft pedal on?" I asks Marilla. "Uncle Cal has begged you so often. It would please him a good deal to hear you touch up the piano he's bought for you. Don't you think you might?"

'But Marilla stands there with big tears rolling down from her eyes and says nothing. And then she runs over and slips her arm under Uncle Cal's neck and hugs him tight.

' "Why, last night, dad," we heard her say, "I played ever so much. Honest – I have been playing it. And it's such a splendid instrument, you don't know how I love it. Last night I played "Bonnie Dundee" and the "Anvil Polka" and the "Blue Danube" – and lots of pieces. You must surely have heard me playing a little, didn't you, dad? I didn't like to play loud when you was so sick."

' "Well, well," says Uncle Cal, "maybe I did. Maybe I did and forgot about it. My head is a little cranky at times. I heard the man in the store play it fine. I'm mighty glad you like it, Marilla. Yes, I believe I could go to sleep a while if you'll stay right beside me till I do."

'There was where Marilla had me guessing. Much as she thought of that old man, she wouldn't strike a note on that piano that he'd bought her. I couldn't imagine why she told him she'd been playing it, for the wagon-sheet hadn't even been off of it since she put it back on the same day it come. I knew she could play a little anyhow, for I'd once heard her snatch some pretty fair dance-music out of an old piano at the Charco Largo Ranch.

'Well, in about a week the pneumonia got the best of Uncle Cal. They had the funeral over at Birdstail, and all of us went over. I brought Marilla back home in my buckboard. Her Uncle Ben and his wife were going to stay there a few days with her.

'That night Marilla takes me in the room where the piano was, while the others were out on the gallery.

' "Come here, Rush," says she; "I want you to see this now."

'She unties the rope, and drags off the wagon-sheet.

'If you ever rode a saddle without a horse, or fired off a gun that wasn't loaded, or took a drink out of an empty bottle, why, then you might have been able to scare an opera or two out of the instrument Uncle Cal had bought.

'Instead of a piano, it was one of them machines they've invented to play the piano with. By itself it was about as musical as the holes of a flute without the flute.

'And that was the piano that Uncle Cal had selected; and standing by it was the good, fine, all-wool girl that never let him know it.

'And what you heard playing a while ago,' concluded Mr. Kinney, 'was that same deputy-piano machine; only just at present it's shoved up against a six-hundred-dollar piano that I bought for Marilla as soon as we was married.'

A CALL LOAN

IN THOSE DAYS THE CATTLEMEN were the anointed. They were the grandees of the grass, kings of the kine, lords of the lea, barons of beef and bone. They might have ridden in golden chariots had their tastes so inclined. The cattleman was caught in a stampede of dollars. It seemed to him that he had more money than was decent. But when he had bought a watch with precious stones set in the case so large that they hurt his ribs, and a California saddle with silver nails and Angora skin *suaderos*, and ordered everybody up to the bar for whisky – what else was there for him to spend money for?

Not so circumscribed in expedient for the reduction of surplus wealth were those lairds of the lariat who had womenfolk to their name. In the breast of the rib-sprung sex the genius of purse lightening may slumber through years of inopportunity, but never, my brothers, does it become extinct.

So, out of the chaparral came Long Bill Longley ıfrom the Bar Circle Ranch on the Frio – a wife-driven man – to taste the urban joys of success. Something like half a million dollars he had, with an income steadily increasing.

Long Bill was a graduate of the camp and trail. Luck and thrift, a cool head, and a telescopic eye for mavericks had raised him from cowboy to be a cowman. Then came the boom in cattle, and Fortune, stepping gingerly among the cactus thorns, came and emptied her cornucopia at the doorstep of the ranch.

In the little frontier city of Chaparosa, Longley built a costly residence. Here he became a captive, bound to the chariot of social existence. He was doomed to become a leading citizen. He struggled for a time like a mustang in his first corral, and then he hung up his quirt and spurs. Time hung heavily on his hands. He organized the First National Bank of Chaparosa, and was elected its president.

One day a dyspeptic man, wearing double-magnifying glasses, inserted an official-looking card between the bars of the cashier's window of the First National Bank. Five minutes later the bank force was dancing at the beck and call of a national bank examiner.

This examiner, Mr. J. Edgar Todd, proved to be a thorough one.

At the end of it all the examiner put on his hat, and called the president, Mr. William R. Longley, into the private office.

'Well, how do you find things?' asked Longley, in his slow, deep tones. 'Any brands in the round-up you didn't like the looks of?'

'The bank checks up all right, Mr. Longley,' said Todd; 'and I find your loans in very good shape – with one exception. You are carrying one very bad bit of paper – one that is so bad that I have been thinking that you surely do not realize the serious position it places you in. I refer to a call loan of $10,000 made to Thomas Merwin. Not only is the amount in excess of the maximum sum the bank can loan any individual legally, but it is absolutely without endorsement or security. Thus you have doubly violated the national banking laws, and have laid yourself open to criminal prosecution by the Government. A report of the matter to the Comptroller of the Currency – which I am bound to make – would, I am sure, result in the matter being turned over to the Department of Justice for action. You see what a serious thing it is.'

Bill Longley was leaning his lengthy, slowly moving frame back in his swivel chair. His hands were clasped behind his head, and he turned a little to look the examiner in the face. The examiner was surprised to see a smile creep about the rugged mouth of the banker, and a kindly twinkle in his light-blue eyes. If he saw the seriousness of the affair, it did not show in his countenance.

'Of course, you don't know Tom Merwin,' said Longley, almost genially. 'Yes, I know about that loan. It hasn't any security except Tom Merwin's word. Somehow, I've always found that when a man's word is good, it's the best security there is. Oh, yes, I know the Government doesn't think so. I guess I'll see Tom about that note.'

Mr. Todd's dyspepsia seemed to grow suddenly worse. He looked at the chaparral banker through his double-magnifying glasses in amazement.

'You see,' said Longley, easily explaining the thing away, 'Tom heard of 2,000 head of two-year-olds down near Rocky Ford on the Rio Grande that could be had for $8 a head. I reckon 'twas one of old Laendro Garcia's outfits that he had smuggled over, and he wanted to make a quick turn on 'em. Those cattle are worth $15 on the hoof in Kansas City. Tom knew it and I knew it. He had $6,000, and I let him have the $10,000 to make the deal with. His brother Ed took 'em on to market three weeks ago. He ought to be back 'most any day now with the money. When he comes Tom'll pay that note.'

The bank examiner was shocked. It was, perhaps, his duty to step out to the telegraph office and wire the situation to the Comptroller. But he did not. He talked pointedly and effectively to Longley for three minutes. He succeeded in making the banker understand that he stood upon the border of a catastrophe. And then he offered a tiny loophole of escape.

'I am going to Hilldale's to-night,' he told Longley, 'to examine a bank there. I will pass through Chaparosa on my way back. At twelve tomorrow I shall call at this bank. If this loan has been cleared out of the way by that time it will not be mentioned in my report. If not – I will have to do my duty.'

With that the examiner bowed and departed.

The President of the First National lounged in his chair half an hour longer, and then he lit a mild cigar, and went over to Tom Merwin's house. Merwin, a ranchman in brown duck, with a contemplative eye, sat with his feet upon a table, plaiting a rawhide quirt.

'Tom,' said Longley, leaning against the table, 'you heard anything from Ed yet?'

'Not yet,' said Merwin, continuing his plaiting. 'I guess Ed'll be along back now in a few days.'

'There was a bank examiner,' said Longley, 'nosing around our place to-day, and he bucked a sight about that note of yours. You know I know it's all right, but the thing *is* against the banking laws. I was pretty sure you'd have paid it off before the bank was examined again, but the son-of-a-gun slipped in on us, Tom. Now, I'm short of cash myself just now, or I'd let you have the money to take it up with. I've got till twelve o'clock to-morrow, and then I've got to show the cash in place of that note or—'

'Or what, Bill?' asked Merwin, as Longley hesitated.

'Well, I suppose it means be jumped on with both of Uncle Sam's feet.'

'I'll try to raise the money for you on time,' said Merwin, interested in his plaiting.

'All right, Tom,' concluded Longley, as he turned toward the door; 'I knew you would if you could.'

Merwin threw down his whip and went to the only other bank in town, a private one, run by Cooper & Craig.

'Cooper,' he said, to the partner by that name, 'I've got to have $10,000 to-day or to-morrow. I've got a house and lot here that's worth about $6,000 and that's all the actual collateral. But I've got a cattle deal on that's sure to bring me in more than that much profit within a few days.'

Cooper began to cough.

'Now, for God's sake don't say no.' said Merwin. 'I owe that much money on a call loan. It's been called, and the man that called it is a man I've laid on the same blanket with in cow-camps and ranger-camps for ten years. He can call anything I've got. He can call the blood out of my veins and it'll come. He's got to have the money. He's in a devil of a— Well, he needs the money, and I've got to get it for him. You know my word's good, Cooper.'

'No doubt of it,' assented Cooper, urbanely, 'but I've a partner, you know. I'm not free in making loans. And even if you had the best security in your hands, Merwin, we couldn't accommodate you in less than a week. We're just making a shipment of $15,000 to Myer Brothers in Rockdell, to buy cotton with. It goes down on the narrow gauge to-night. That leaves our cash quite short at present. Sorry we can't arrange it for you.'

Merwin went back to his little bar office and plaited at his quirt again.

About four o'clock in the afternoon he went to the First National and leaned over the railing of Longley's desk.

'I'll try to get that money for you to-night – I mean to-morrow, Bill.'

'All right, Tom,' said Longley, quietly.

At nine o'clock that night Tom Merwin stepped cautiously out of the small frame house in which he lived. It was near the edge of the little town, and few citizens were in the neighborhood at that hour. Merwin wore two six-shooters in a belt and a slouch hat. He moved swiftly down a lonely street, and then followed the sandy road that ran parallel to the narrow-gauge track until he reached the water-tank, two miles below the town. There Tom Merwin stopped, tied a black silk handkerchief about the lower part of his face, and pulled his hat down low.

In ten minutes the night train for Rockdell pulled up at the tank, having come from Chaparosa.

With a gun in each hand Merwin raised himself from behind a clump of chaparral and started for the engine. But before he had taken three steps, two long, strong arms clasped him from behind, and he was lifted from his feet and thrown, face downward, upon the grass. There was a heavy knee pressing against his back, and an iron hand grasping each of his wrists. He was held thus, like a child, until the engine had taken water, and until the train had moved, with accelerating speed, out of sight. Then he was released, and rose to his feet to face Bill Longley.

'The case never needed to be fixed up this way, Tom,' said Longley. 'I saw Cooper this evening, and he told me what you and him talked about. Then I went down to your house to-night and saw you come out with your guns on, and I followed you. Let's go back, Tom.'

They walked away together, side by side.

' 'Twas the only chance I saw,' said Merwin, presently. 'You called your loan, and I tried to answer you. Now, what'll you do, Bill, if they sock it to you?'

'What would you have done if they'd socked it to you?' was the answer Longley made.

'I never thought I'd lay in a bush to stick up a train,' remarked Merwin; 'but a call loan's different. A call's a call with me. We've got twelve hours yet, Bill, before his spy jumps onto you. We've got to raise them spondulicks somehow. Maybe we can – Great Sam Houston! do you hear that?'

Merwin broke into a run, and Longley kept with him, hearing only a rather pleasing whistle somewhere in the night rendering the lugubrious air of 'The Cowboy's Lament.'

'It's the only tune he knows,' shouted Merwin, as he ran. 'I'll bet –'

They were at the door of Merwin's house. He kicked it open and fell over an old valise lying in the middle of the floor. A sunburned, firmjawed youth, stained by travel, lay upon the bed puffing at a brown cigarette.

'What's the word, Ed?' gasped Merwin.

'So, so,' drawled that capable youngster. 'Just got in on the 9:30. Sold the bunch for fifteen, straight. Now, buddy, you want to quit kickin' a valise around that's got $29,000 in greenbacks in its in'ards.'

THE PRINCESS AND THE PUMA

THERE HAD TO BE A KING AND QUEEN, of course. The king was a terrible old man who wore six-shooters and spurs, and shouted in such a tremendous voice that the rattlers on the prairie would run into their holes under the prickly pear. Before there was a royal family they called the man 'Whispering Ben.' When he came to own 50,000 acres of land and more cattle than he could count, they called him O'Donnell 'the Cattle King.'

The queen had been a Mexican girl from Laredo. She made a good, mild, Coloradoclaro wife, and even succeeded in teaching Ben to modify his voice sufficiently while in the house to keep the dishes from being broken. When Ben got to be king she would sit on the gallery of Espinosa Ranch and weave rush mats. When wealth became so irresistible and oppressive that uphol-stered chairs and a centre table were brought down from San Antone in the wagons, she bowed her smooth, dark head, and shared the fate of the Danaë.

To avoid *lèse-majesté* you have been presented first to the king and queen. They do not enter the story, which might be called 'The Chronicle of the Princess, the Happy Thought, and Lion that Bungled his Job.'

Josefa O'Donnell was the surviving daughter, the princess. From her mother she inherited warmth of nature and a dusky, semi-tropic beauty. From Ben O'Donnell the royal she acquired a store in intrepidity, common sense, and the faculty of ruling. The combination was worth going miles to see. Josefa while riding her pony at a gallop could put five out of six bullets through a tomato-can swinging at the end of a string. She could play for hours with a white kitten she owned, dressing it in all manner of absurd clothes. Scorning a pencil, she could tell you out of her head what 1545 two-year-olds would bring on the hoof, at $8.50 per head. Roughly speaking, the Espinosa Ranch is forty miles long and thirty broad – but mostly leased land. Josefa, on her pony, had prospected over every mile of it. Every cow-puncher on the range knew her by sight and was a loyal vassal. Ripley Givens, foreman of one of the Espinosa outfits, saw her one day, and made up his mind to form a royal matrimonial alliance. Presumptuous? No. In those days in the Nueces country a man was a man. And, after all, the title of cattle king does not presuppose blood royal. Often it only signifies that its owner wears the crown in token of his magnificent qualities in the art of cattle stealing.

One day Ripley Givens rode over to the Double Elm Ranch to inquire about a bunch of strayed yearlings. He was late in setting out on his return trip, and it was sundown when he struck the White Horse Crossing of the Nueces. From there to his own camp it was sixteen miles. To the Espinosa ranch-house it was twelve. Givens was tired. He decided to pass the night at the Crossing.

There was a fine water hole in the river-bed. The banks were thickly covered with great trees, undergrown with brush. Back from the water hole fifty yards was a stretch of curly mesquite grass – supper for his horse and bed for himself. Givens staked his horse, and spread out his saddle blankets to dry. He sat down with his back against a tree and rolled a cigarette. From somewhere in the dense timber along the river came a sudden, rageful, shivering wail. The pony danced at the end of his rope and blew a whistling snort of comprehending fear. Givens puffed at his cigarette, but he reached leisurely for his pistol-belt, which lay on the grass, and twirled the cylinder of his weapon tentatively. A great gar plunged with a loud splash into the water hole. A little brown rabbit skipped around a bunch of catclaw and sat twitching his whiskers and looking humorously at Givens. The pony went on eating grass.

It is well to be reasonably watchful when a Mexican lion sings soprano along the arroyos at sundown. The burden of his song may be that young calves and fat lambs are scarce, and that he has a carnivorous desire for your acquaintance.

In the grass lay an empty fruit can, cast there by some former sojourner. Givens caught sight of it with a grunt of satisfaction. In his coat pocket tied behind his saddle was a handful or two of ground coffee. Black coffee and cigarettes! What ranchero could desire more?

In two minutes he had a little fire going clearly. He started, with his can, for the water hole. When within fifteen yards of its edge he saw, between the bushes, a side-saddled pony with down-dropped reins cropping grass a little distance to his left. Just rising from her hands and knees on the brink of the water hole was Josefa O'Donnell. She had been drinking water, and she brushed the sand from the palms of her hands. Ten yards away, to her right, half concealed by a clump of sacuista, Givens saw the crouching form of the Mexican lion. His amber eyelids glared hungrily; six feet from them was the tip of the tail stretched straight, like a pointer's. His hind-quarters rocked with the motion of the cat tribe preliminary to leaping.

Givens did what he could. His six-shooter was thirty-five yards away lying on the grass. He gave a loud yell, and dashed between the lion and the princess.

The 'rucus,' as Givens called it afterward, was brief and somewhat confused. When he arrived on the line of attack he saw a dim streak in the air, and heard a couple of faint cracks. Then a hundred pounds of Mexican lion plumped down upon his head and flattened him, with a heavy jar, to the ground. He remembered calling out: 'Let up, now – no fair gouging!' and then he crawled from under the lion like a worm, with his mouth full of grass and dirt, and a big lump on the back of his head where it had struck the root of a water-elm. The lion lay motionless. Givens, feeling aggrieved, and suspicious of fouls, shook his fist at the lion, and shouted: 'I'll rastle you again for twenty —' and then he got back to himself.

Josefa was standing in her tracks, quietly reloading her silver-mounted .38. It had not been a difficult shot. The lion's head made an easier mark than a tomato-can swinging at the end of a string. There was a provoking, teasing, maddening smile upon her mouth and in her dark eyes. The would-be-rescuing knight felt the fire of his fiasco burn down to his soul. Here had been his chance, the chance that he had dreamed of; and Momus, and not Cupid, had presided over it. The satyrs in the wood were, no doubt, holding their sides in hilarious, silent laughter. There had been something like vaudeville – say Signor Givens and his funny knockabout act with the stuffed lion.

'Is that you, Mr. Givens?' said Josefa, in her deliberate saccharine contralto. 'You nearly spoiled my shot when you yelled. Did you hurt your head when you fell?'

'Oh, no,' said Givens, quietly; 'that didn't hurt.' He stooped ignominiously and dragged his best Stetson hat from under the beast. It was crushed and wrinkled to a fine comedy effect. Then he knelt down and softly stroked the fierce, open-jawed head of the dead lion.

'Poor old Bill?' he exclaimed, mournfully.

'What's that?' asked Josefa, sharply.

'Of course you didn't know, Miss Josefa,' said Givens, with an air of one allowing magnanimity to triumph over grief. 'Nobody can blame you. I tried to save him, but I couldn't let you know in time.'

'Save who?'

'Why, Bill. I've been looking for him all day. You see, he's been our camp pet for two years. Poor old fellow, he wouldn't have hurt a cotton-tail rabbit. It'll break the boys all up when they hear about it. But you couldn't tell of course, that Bill was just trying to play with you.'

Josefa's black eyes burned steadily upon him. Ripley Givens met the test successfully. He stood rumpling the yellow-brown curls on his head pensively. In his eyes was regret, not unmingled with a gentle reproach. His smooth features were set to a pattern of indisputable sorrow. Josefa wavered.

'What was your pet doing here?' she asked, making a last stand. 'There's no camp near the White Horse Crossing.'

'The old rascal ran away from camp yesterday,' answered Givens, readily. 'It's a wonder the coyotes didn't scare him to death. You see, Jim Webster, our horse wrangler, brought a little terrier pup into camp last week. The pup made life miserable for Bill – he used to chase him around and chew his hind legs for hours at a time. Every night when bedtime came Bill would sneak under one of the boys' blankets and sleep to keep the pup from finding him. I reckon he must have been worried pretty desperate or he wouldn't have run away. He was always afraid to get out of sight of camp.'

Josefa looked at the body of the fierce animal. Givens gently patted one of the formidable paws that could have killed a yearling calf with one blow. Slowly a red flush widened upon the dark olive face of the girl. Was it the signal of shame of the true sportsman who has brought down ignoble quarry? Her eyes grew softer, and the lowered lids drove away all their bright mockery.

'I'm very sorry,' she said, humbly; 'but he looked so big, and jumped so high that—'

'Poor old Bill was hungry,' interrupted Givens, in quick defence of the deceased. 'We always made him jump for his supper in camp. He would lie down and roll over for a piece of meat. When he saw you he thought he was going to get something to eat from you.'

Suddenly Josefa's eyes opened wide.

'I might have shot you!' she exclaimed. 'You ran right in between. You risked your life to save your pet! That was fine, Mr. Givens. I like a man who is kind to animals.'

Yes; there was even admiration in her gaze now. After all, there was a hero rising out of the ruins of the anti-climax. The look on Givens's face would have secured him a high position in the S.P.C.A.

'I always loved 'em,' said he; 'horses, dogs, Mexican lions, cows, alligators—'

'I hate alligators,' instantly demurred Josefa; 'crawly, muddy things!'

'Did I say alligators?' said Givens. 'I meant antelopes, of course.'

Josefa's conscience drove her to make further amends. She held out her hand penitently. There was a bright, unshed drop in each of her eyes.

'Please forgive me. Mr. Givens, won't you? I'm only a girl, you know, and I was frightened at first. I'm very, very sorry I shot Bill. You don't know how ashamed I feel. I wouldn't have done it for anything.'

Givens took the proffered hand. He held it for a time while he allowed the generosity of his nature to overcome his grief at the loss of Bill. At last it was clear that he had forgiven her.

'Please don't speak of it any more, Miss Josefa. 'Twas enough to frighten any young lady the way Bill looked. I'll explain it all right to the boys.'

'Are you really sure you don't hate me?' Josefa came closer to him impulsively. Her eyes were sweet – oh, sweet and pleading with gracious penitence. 'I would hate any one who would kill my kitten. And how daring and kind of you to risk being shot when you tried to save him! How very few men would have done that!' Victory wrested from defeat! Vaudeville turned into drama! Bravo, Ripley Givens!

It was now twilight. Of course Miss Josefa could not be allowed to ride on to the ranch-house alone. Givens resaddled his pony in spite of that animal's reproachful glances, and rode with her. Side by side they galloped across the smooth grass, the princess and the man who was kind to animals. The prairie odors of fruitful earth and delicate bloom were thick and sweet around them. Coyotes yelping over there on the hill! No fear. And yet—

Josefa rode closer. A little hand seemed to grope. Givens found it with his own. The ponies kept an even gait. The hands lingered together, and the owner of one explained.

'I never was frightened before, but just think! How terrible it would be to meet a really wild lion! Poor Bill! I'm so glad you came with me!'

O'Donnell was sitting on the ranch gallery.

'Hello, Rip!' he shouted— 'that you?'

'He rode in with me,' said Josefa. 'I lost my way and was late.'

'Much obliged,' called the cattle king. 'Stop over, Rip, and ride to camp in the morning.'

But Givens would not. He would push on to camp. There was a bunch of steers to start off on the trail at daybreak. He said good-night, and trotted away.

An hour later, when thelights were out, Josefa, in her night-robe, came to her door and called to the king in his own room across the brick-paved hallway:

'Say, Pop, you know that old Mexican lion they call the "Gotch-eared Devil" – the one that killed Gonzales, Mr. Martin's sheep herder, and about fifty calves on the Salada range? Well, I settled his hash this afternoon over at the White Horse Crossing. Put two balls in his head with my .38 while he was on the jump. I knew him by the slice gone from his left ear that old Gonzales cut off with his machete. You couldn't have made a better shot yourself, Daddy.'

'Bully for you!' thundered Whispering Ben from the darkness of the royal chamber.

THE INDIAN SUMMER OF DRY VALLEY JOHNSON

DRY VALLEY JOHNSON SHOOK THE BOTTLE. You have to shake the bottle before using; for sulphur will not dissolve. Then Dry Valley saturated a small sponge with the liquid and rubbed it carefully into the roots of his hair. Besides sulphur there was sugar of lead in it and tincture of nux vomica and bay rum. Dry Valley found the recipe in a Sunday newspaper. You must next be told why a strong man came to fall victim to a Beauty Hint.

Dry Valley had been a sheepman. His real name was Hector, but he had been rechristened after his range to distinguish him from 'Elm Creek' Johnson, who ran sheep further down the Frio.

Many years of living face to face with sheep on their own terms wearied Dry Valley Johnson. So, he sold his ranch for eighteen thousand dollars and moved to Santa Rosa to live a life of gentlemanly ease. Being a silent and melancholy person of thirty-five – or perhaps thirty-eight – he soon became that cursed and earthcumbering thing – an elderlyish bachelor with a hobby. Some one gave him his first strawberry to eat, and he was done for.

Dry Valley bought a four-room cottage in the village, and a library on strawberry culture. Behind the cottage was a garden of which he made a strawberry patch. In his old gray woolen shirt, his brown duck trousers and high-heeled boots he sprawled all day on a canvas cot under a live-oak tree at his back door studying the history of the seductive scarlet berry.

The school teacher, Miss De Witt, spoke of him as 'a fine, presentable man, for all his middle age.' But the focus of Dry Valley's eyes embraced no women. They were merely beings who flew skirts as a signal for him to lift awkwardly his heavy, round-crowned, broad-brimmed felt Stetson whenever he met them, and then hurry past to get back to his beloved berries.

And all this recitative by the chorus is only to bring us to the point where you may be told why Dry Valley shook up the insoluble sulphur in the bottle. So long-drawn and inconsequential a thing is history – the anamorphous shadow of a milestone reaching down the road between us and the setting sun.

When his strawberries were beginning to ripen Dry Valley bought the heaviest buggy whip in the Santa Rosa store. He sat for many hours under the live-oak tree plaiting and weaving in an extension to its lash. When it was done he could snip a leaf from a bush twenty feet away with the cracker. For the bright, predatory eyes of Santa Rosa youth were watching the ripening berries, and Dry Valley was arming himself against their expected raids. No greater care had he taken of his tender lambs during his ranching days than he did of his cherished fruit, warding it from the hungry wolves that whistled and howled and shot their marbles and peered through the fence that surrounded his property.

In the house next to Dry Valley's lived a widow with a pack of children that gave the husbandman frequent anxious misgivings. In the woman there was a strain of the Spanish. She had wedded one of the name of O'Brien. Dry Valley was a connoisseur in cross strains; and he foresaw trouble in the offspring of this union.

Between the two homesteads ran a crazy picket fence overgrown with morning glory and wild gourd vines. Often he could see little heads with mops of black hair and flashing dark eyes dodging in and out between the pickets, keeping tabs on the reddening berries.

Late one afternoon Dry Valley went to the post office. When he came back, like Mother Hubbard he found the deuce to pay. The descendants of Iberian bandits and Hibernian cattle raiders had swooped down upon his strawberry patch. To the outraged vision of Dry Valley there seemed to be a sheep corral full of them; perhaps they numbered five or six. Between the rows of green plants they were stooped, hopping about like toads, gobbling silently and voraciously his finest fruit.

Dry Valley slipped into the house, got his whip, and charged the marauders. The lash curled about the legs of the nearest – a greedy ten-year-old – before they knew they were discovered. His screech gave warning; and the flock scampered for the fence like a drove of *javelis* flushed in the chaparral. Dry Valley's whip drew a toll of two more elfin shrieks before they dived through the vine-clad fence and disappeared.

Dry Valley, less fleet, followed them nearly to the pickets. Checking his useless pursuit, he rounded a bush, dropped his whip and stood, voiceless, motionless, the capacity of his powers consumed by the act of breathing and preserving the perpendicular.

Behind the bush stood Panchita O'Brien, scorning to fly. She was nineteen, the oldest of the raiders. Her night-black hair was gathered back in a wild mass and tied with a scarlet ribbon. She stood, with reluctant feet, yet nearer the brook than to the river; for childhood had environed and detained her.

She looked at Dry Valley Johnson for a moment with magnificent insolence, and before his eyes slowly crunched a luscious berry between her white teeth. Then she turned and walked slowly to the fence with a swaying, conscious motion, such as a duchess might make use of in leading a promenade. There she turned again and grilled Dry Valley Johnson once more in the dark flame of her audacious eyes, laughed a trifle school-girlishly, and twisted herself with pantherish quickness between the pickets to the O'Brien side of the wild gourd vine.

Dry Valley picked up his whip and went into the house. He stumbled as he went up the two wooden steps. The old Mexican woman who cooked his meals and swept his house called him to supper as he went through the rooms. Dry Valley went on, stumbled down the front steps, out the gate and down the road into a mesquite thicket at the edge of town. He sat down in the grass and laboriously plucked the spines from a prickly pear, one by one. This was his attitude of thought, acquired in the days when his problems were only those of wind and wool and water.

A thing had happened to the man – a thing that, if you are eligible, you must pray may pass you by. He had become enveloped in the Indian Summer of the Soul.

Dry Valley had had no youth. Even his childhood had been one of dignity and seriousness. At six he had viewed the frivolous gambols of the lambs on his father's ranch with disapproval. His life as a young man had been wasted. The divine fires and impulses, the glorious exaltations and despairs, the glow and enchantment of youth had passed above his head. Never a thrill of Romeo had he known; he was but a melancholy Jaques of the forest with a rudder philosophy lacking the bitter-sweet flavor of experience that tempered the veteran years of the rugged ranger of Arden. And now in his sere and yellow leaf one scornful look from the eyes of Panchita O'Brien had flooded the autumnal landscape with a tardy and delusive summer heat.

But a sheepman is a hardy animal. Dry Valley Johnson had weathered too many northers to turn his back on a later summer, spiritual or real. Old? He would show them.

By the next mail went an order to San Antonio for an outfit of the latest clothes, colors and styles and prices no object. The next day went the recipe for the hair restorer clipped from a newspaper; for Dry Valley's sunburned auburn hair was beginning to turn silvery above his ears.

Dry Valley kept indoors closely for a week except for frequent sallies after youthful strawberry snatchers. Then, a few days later, he suddenly emerged brilliantly radiant in the hectic glow of his belated midsummer madness.

A jay-bird-blue tennis suit covered him outwardly, almost as far as his wrists and ankles. His shirt was ox-blood; his collar winged and tall; his necktie a floating oriflamme; his shoes a venomous bright tan, pointed and shaped on penitential lasts. A little flat straw hat with a striped band desecrated his weather-beaten head. Lemon-colored kid gloves protected his rough hands from the benignant May sunshine. This sad and optic-smiting creature teetered out of its den, smiling foolishly and smoothing its gloves for men and angels to see. To such a pass had Dry Valley Johnson been brought by Cupid, who always shoots game that is out of season with an arrow from the quiver of Momus. Reconstructing mythology, he had risen, a prismatic macaw, from the ashes of the gray-brown phoenix that had folded its tired wings to roost under the tree of Santa Rosa.

Dry Valley paused in the street to allow Santa Rosans within sight of him to be stunned; and then deliberately and slowly, as his shoes required, entered Mrs. O'Brien's gate.

Not until the eleven months' drought did Santa Rosa cease talking about Dry Valley Johnson's courtship of Panchita O'Brien. It was an unclassifiable procedure; something like a combination of cake-walking, deaf-and-dumb oratory, postage stamp flirtation, and parlor charades. It lasted two weeks and then came to a sudden end.

Of course Mrs. O'Brien favored the match as soon as Dry Valley's intentions were disclosed. Being the mother of a woman child, and therefore a charter member of the Ancient Order of the Rat-trap, she joyfully decked out Panchita for the sacrifice. The girl was temporarily dazzled by having her dresses lengthened and her hair piled up on her head, and came near forgetting that she was only a slice of cheese. It was nice, too, to have as good a match as Mr. Johnson paying you attentions and to see the other girls fluttering the curtains at their windows to see you go by with him.

Dry Valley bought a buggy with yellow wheels and a fine trotter in San Antonio. Every day he drove out with Panchita. He was never seen to speak to her when they were walking or driving. The consciousness of his clothes kept his mind busy; the knowledge that he could say nothing of interest kept him dumb; the feeling that Panchita was there kept him happy.

He took her to parties and dances, and to church. He tried – oh, no man ever tried so hard, to be young as Dry Valley did. He could not dance; but he invented a smile which he wore on these joyous occasions, a smile that, in him, was as great a concession to mirth and gaiety as turning hand-springs would be in another. He began to seek the company of the young men in the town – even of the boys. They accepted him as a decided damper, for his attempts at sportiveness were so forced that they might as well have essayed their games in a cathedral. Neither he nor any other could estimate what progress he had made with Panchita.

The end came suddenly in one day, as often disappears the false afterglow before a November sky and wind.

Dry Valley was to call for the girl one afternoon at six for a walk. An afternoon walk in Santa Rose was a feature of social life that called for the pink of one's wardrobe. So Dry Valley began gorgeously to array himself; and so early that he finished early, and went over to the O'Brien cottage. As he neared the porch on the crooked walk from the gate he heard sounds of revelry within. He stopped and looked through the honeysuckle vines in the open door.

Panchita was amusing her younger brothers and sisters. She wore a man's clothes – no doubt those of the late Mr. O'Brien. On her head was the smallest brother's straw hat decorated with an ink-striped paper band. On her hands were flapping yellow cloth gloves, roughly cut out and sewn for the masquerade. The same material covered her shoes, giving them the semblance of tan leather. High collar and flowing necktie were not omitted.

Panchita was an actress. Dry Valley saw his affectedly youthful gait, his limp where the right shoe hurt him, his forced smile, his awkward simulation of a gallant air, all reproduced with startling fidelity. For the first time a mirror had been held up to him. The corroboration of one of the youngsters calling, 'Mamma, come and see Pancha do like Mr. Johnson,' was not needed.

As softly as the caricatured tans would permit, Dry Valley tiptoed back to the gate and home again.

Twenty minutes after the time appointed for the walk Panchita tripped demurely out her gate in a thin, trim white lawn and sailor hat. She strolled up the sidewalk and slowed her steps at Dry Valley's gate, her manner expressing wonder at his unusual delinquency.

Then out of his door and down the walk strode – not the polychromatic victim of a lost summer time, but the sheepman, rehabilitated. He wore his old gray woolen shirt, open at the throat, his brown duck trousers stuffed into his run-over boots, and his white felt sombrero on the back of his head. Twenty years or fifty he might look; Dry Valley cared not. His light blue eyes met Panchita's dark ones with a cold flash in them. He came as far as the gate. He pointed with his long arm to her house.

'Go home,' said Dry Valley. 'Go home to your mother. I wonder lightnin' don't strike a fool like me. Go home and play in the sand. What business have you got cavortin' around with grown men? I reckon I was locoed to be makin' a he poll-parrot out of myself for a kid like you. Go home and don't let me see you no more. Why I done it, will somebody tell me? Go home, and let me try and forget it.'

Panchita obeyed and walked slowly towards her home, saying nothing. For some distance she kept her head turned and her large eyes fixed intrepidly upon Dry Valley's. At her gate she stood for a moment looking back at him, then ran suddenly and swiftly into the house.

Old Antonia was building a fire in the kitchen stove. Dry Valley stopped at the door and laughed harshly.

'I'm a pretty looking old rhinoceros to be gettin' stuck on a kid ain't I, 'Tonia?' said he.

'Not verree good thing,' agreed Antonia, sagely, 'for too much old man to likee *muchacha*.'

'You bet it ain't,' said Dry Valley, grimly. 'It's dum foolishness; and, besides, it hurts.'

He brought at one armful the regalia of his aberration – the blue tennis suit, shoes, hat, gloves, and all, and threw them in a pile at Antonia's feet.

'Give them to your old man,' said he, 'to hunt antelope in.'

Just as the first star presided palely over the twilight Dry Valley got his biggest strawberry book and sat on the back steps to catch the last of the reading light. He thought he saw the figure of someone in his strawberry patch. He laid aside the book, got his whip, and hurried forth to see.

It was Panchita. She had slipped through the picket fence and was halfway across the patch. She stopped when she saw him and looked at him without wavering.

A sudden rage – a humiliating flush of unreasoning wrath – came over Dry Valley. For this child he had made himself a motley to the view. He had tried to bribe Time to turn backward for himself; he had – been made a fool of. At last he had seen his folly. There was a gulf between him and youth over which he could not build a bridge even with yellow gloves to protect his hands. And the sight of his torment coming to pester him with her elfin pranks – coming to plunder his strawberry vines like a mischievous school-boy – roused all his anger.

'I told you to keep away from here,' said Dry Valley. 'Go back to your home.'

Panchita moved slowly toward him.

Dry Valley cracked his whip.

'Go back home,' said Dry Valley, savagely, 'and play theatricals some more. You'd make a fine man. You've made a fine one of me.'

She came a step nearer, silent, and with that strange, defiant, steady shine in her eye that had always puzzled him. Now it stirred his wrath.

His whiplash whistled through the air. He saw a red streak suddenly come through her white dress above her knee where it had struck.

Without flinching and with the same unchanging dark glow in her eyes, Panchita came steadily toward him through the strawberry vines. Dry Valley's trembling hand released his whip handle. When within a yard of him Panchita stretched out her arms.

'God kid!' stammered Dry Valley, 'do you mean—?'

But the seasons are versatile; and it may have been Springtime after all, instead of Indian Summer, that struck Dry Valley Johnson.

CHRISTMAS BY INJUNCTION

CHEROKEE WAS THE CIVIC FATHER of Yellowhammer. Yellowhammer was a new mining town constructed mainly of canvas and undressed pine. Cherokee was a prospector. One day while his burro was eating quartz and pine burrs Cherokee turned up with his pick a nugget weighing thirty ounces. He staked his claim and then, being a man of breadth and hospitality, sent out invitations to his friends in three states to drop in and share his luck.

Not one of the invited guests sent regrets. They rolled in from the Gila country, from Salt River, from the Pecos, from Albuquerque and Phoenix and Santa Fé, and from the camps intervening.

When a thousand citizens had arrived and taken up claims they named the town Yellowhammer, appointed a vigilance committee, and presented Cherokee with a watch-chain made of nuggets.

Three hours after the presentation ceremonies Cherokee's claim played out. He had located a pocket instead of a vein. He abandoned it and staked others one by one. Luck had kissed her hand to him. Never afterwards did he turn up enough dust in Yellowhammer to pay his bar bill. But his thousand invited guests were mostly prospering, and Cherokee smiled and congratulated them.

Yellowhammer was made up of men who took off their hats to a smiling loser; so they invited Cherokee to say what he wanted.

'Me?' said Cherokee, 'oh, grubstakes will be about the thing. I reckon I'll prospect along up in the Mariposas. If I strike it up there I will most certainly let you all know about the facts. I never was any hand to hold out cards on my friends.'

In May Cherokee packed his burro and turned its thoughtful, mouse-colored forehead to the north. Many citizens escorted him to the undefined limits of Yellowhammer and bestowed upon him shouts of commendation and farewells. Five pocket flasks without an air bubble between contents and cork were forced upon him; and he was bidden to consider Yellowhammer in perpetual commission for his bed, bacon and eggs, and hot water for shaving in the event that luck did not see fit to warm her hands by his campfire of the Mariposas.

The name of the father of Yellowhammer was given him by the gold hunters in accordance with their popular system of nomenclature. It was not necessary for a citizen to exhibit his baptismal certificate in order to acquire a cognomen. A man's name was his personal property. For convenience in calling him up to the bar and in designating him among other blue-shirted bipeds, a temporary appellation, title or epithet was conferred upon him by the public. Personal peculiarities formed the source of the majority of such informal baptisms. Many were easily dubbed geographically from the regions from which they confessed to have hailed. Some announced themselves to be 'Thompsons,' and 'Adamses,' and the like, with a brazenness and loudness that cast a cloud upon their titles. A few vaingloriously and shamelessly uncovered their proper and indisputable names. This was held to be unduly arrogant, and did not win popularity. One man who said he was Chesterton L. C. Belmont, and proved it by letters, was given till sundown to leave the town. Such names as 'Shorty,' 'Bow-legs,' 'Texas,' 'Lazy Bill,' 'Thirsty Rogers,' 'Limping Riley,' 'The Judge,' and 'California Ed' were in favor. Cherokee derived his title from the fact that he claimed to have lived for a time with that tribe in the Indian Nation.

On the twentieth day of December Baldy, the mail rider, brought Yellow-hammer a piece of news.

'What do I see in Albuquerque,' said Baldy, to the patrons of the bar, 'but Cherokee all embellished and festooned up like the Czar of Turkey, and lavishin' money in bulk. Him and me seen the elephant and the owl, and we had specimens of this seidlitz powder wine; and Cherokee he audits all the bills, C.O.D. His pockets looked like a pool table's after a fifteen-ball run.'

'Cherokee must have struck pay ore,' remarked California Ed. 'Well, he's white. I'm much obliged to him for his success.'

'Seems like Cherokee would ramble down to Yellowhammer and see his friends,' said another, slightly aggrieved. 'But that's the way. Prosperity is the finest cure there is for lost forgetfulness.'

'You wait,' said Baldy; 'I'm comin' to that. Cherokee strikes a three-foot vein up in the Mariposas that assays a trip to Europe to the ton, and he closes it out to a syndicate outfit for a hundred thousand hasty dollars in cash. Then he buys himself a baby sealskin overcoat and a red sleigh, and what do you think he takes it in his head to do next?'

'Chuck-a-luck,' said Texas, whose ideas of recreation were the gamester's.

'Come and Kiss Me, Ma Honey,' sang Shorty, who carried tintypes in his pocket and wore a red necktie while working on his claim.

'Bought a saloon?' suggested Thirsty Rogers.

'Cherokee took me to a room,' continued Baldy, 'and showed me. He's got that room full of drums and dolls and skates and bags of candy and jumping-jacks and toy lambs and whistles and such infantile truck. And what do you think he's goin' to do with them inefficacious knick-knacks? Don't surmise none – Cherokee told me. He's goin' to load 'em up in his red sleigh and – wait a minute, don't order no drinks yet – he's goin' to drive down here to Yellowhammer and give the kids – the kids of this here town – the biggest Christmas tree and the biggest cryin' doll and Little Giant Boys' Tool Chest blowout that ever seen west of Cape Hatteras.'

Two minutes of absolute silence ticked away in the wake of Baldy's words. It was broken by the House, who, happily conceiving the moment to be ripe for extending hospitality, sent a dozen whisky glasses spinning down the bar, with the slower traveling bottle bringing up the rear.

'Didn't you tell him?' asked the miner called Trinidad.

'Well, no,' answered Baldy, pensively; 'I never exactly seen my way to.

'You see, Cherokee had this Christmas mess already bought and paid for; and he was all flattered up with self-esteem over his idea; and we had in a way flew the flume with that fizzy wine I speak of; so I never let on.'

'I cannot refrain from a certain amount of surprise,' said the Judge, as he hung his ivory-handled cane on the bar, 'that our friend Cherokee should possess such an erroneous conception of – ah – his, as it were, own town.'

'Oh, it ain't the eighth wonder of the terrestrial world,' said Baldy. 'Cherokee's been gone from Yellowhammer over seven months. Lots of things could happen in that time. How's he to know there there ain't a single kid in this town, and so far as emigration is concerned, none expected?'

'Come to think of it,' remarked California Ed, 'it's funny some ain't drifted in. Town ain't settled enough yet for to bring in the rubber-ring brigade, I reckon.'

'To top off this Christmas-tree splurge of Cherokee's,' went on Baldy, 'he's goin' to give an imitation of Santa Claus. He's got a white wig and whiskers that disfigure him up exactly like the pictures of this William Cullen Longfellow in the books, and a red suit of fur-trimmed outside underwear, and eight-ounces gloves, and a stand-up, lay-down croshayed red cap. Ain't it a shame that a outfit like that can't get a chance to connect with a Annie and Willie's prayer layout?'

'When does Cherokee allow to come over with his truck?' inquired Trinidad.

'Mornin' before Christmas,' said Baldy. 'And he wants you folks to have a room fixed up and a tree hauled and ready. And such ladies to assist as can stop breathin' long enough to let it be a surprise for the kids.'

The unblessed condition of Yellowhammer had been truly described. The voice of childhood had never gladdened its flimsy structures; the patter of restless little feet had never consecrated the one rugged highway between the two rows of tents and rough buildings. Later they would come. But now Yellowhammer was but a mountain camp, and nowhere in it were the roguish, expectant eyes, opening wide at dawn of the enchanting day; the eager, small hands to reach for Santa's bewildering hoard; the elated, childish voicings of the season's joy, such as the coming good things of the warm-hearted Cherokee deserved.

Of women there were five in Yellowhammer. The assayer's wife, the proprietress of the Lucky Strike Hotel, and a laundress whose washtub panned out an ounce of dust a day. These were the permanent feminines; the remaining two were the Spangler Sisters, Misses Fanchon and Erma, of the Transcontinental Comedy Company, then playing in the repertoire at the (improvised) Empire Theatre. But of children there were none. Sometimes Miss Fanchon enacted with spirit and address the part of robustious childhood; but between her delineation and the visions of adolescence that the fancy offered as eligible recipients of Cherokee's holiday stores there seemed to be fixed a gulf.

Christmas would come on Thursday. On Tuesday morning Trinidad, instead of going to work, sought the Judge at the Lucky Strike Hotel.

'It'll be a disgrace to Yellowhammer,' said Trinidad, 'if it throws Cherokee down on his Christmas-tree blowout. You might say that that man made this town. For one, I'm goin' to see what can be done to give Santa Claus a square deal.'

'My coöperation,' said the Judge, 'would be gladly forthcoming. I am indebted to Cherokee for past favors. But, I do not see – I have heretofore regarded the absence of children rather as a luxury – but in this instance – still, I do not see—'

'Look at me,' said Trinidad, 'and you'll see old Ways and Means with the fur on. I'm goin' to hitch up a team and rustle a load of kids for Cherokee's Santa Claus act, if I have to rob an orphan asylum.'

'Eureka!' cried the Judge, enthusiastically.

'No, you didn't,' said Trinidad, decidedly. 'I found it myself. I learned about that Latin word at school.'

'I will accompany you,' declared the Judge, waving his cane. 'Perhaps such eloquence and gift of language as I may possess will be of benefit in persuading our young friends to lend themselves to our project.'

Within an hour Yellowhammer was acquainted with the theme of Trinidad and the Judge, and approved it. Citizens who knew of families with offspring within a forty-mile radius of Yellowhammer came forward and contributed their information. Trinidad made careful notes of all such and then hastened to secure a vehicle and team.

The first stop scheduled was at a double loghouse fifteen miles out from Yellowhammer. A man opened the door at Trinidad's hail, and then came down and leaned upon the rickety gate. The doorway was filled with a close mass of youngsters, some ragged, all full of curiosity and health.

'It's this way,' explained Trinidad. 'We're from Yellowhammer, and we

come kidnappin' in a gentle kind of a way. One of our leading citizens is
stung with the Santa Claus affliction, and he's due in town to-morrow with
half the folderols that's painted red and made in Germany. The youngest kid
we got in Yellowhammer packs a forty-five and a safety razor. Consequently
we're mighty shy on anybody to say 'Oh' and 'Ah' when we light the candles
on the Christmas tree. Now, partner, if you'll loan us a few kids we guarantee
to return 'em safe and sound on Christmas Day. And they'll come back
loaded down with a good time and Swiss Family Robinsons and cornucopias
and red drums and similar testimonials. What do you say?'

'In other words,' said the Judge, 'we have discovered for the first time in
our embryonic but progressive little city the inconveniences of the absence
of adolescence. The season of the year having approximately arrived during
which it is a custom to bestow frivolous but often appreciated gifts upon the
young and tender —'

'I understand,' said the parent, packing his pipe with a forefinger. 'I guess
I needn't detain you gentlemen. Me and the old woman have got seven kids,
so to speak; and runnin' my mind over the bunch, I don't appear to hit upon
none that we could spare for you to take over to your doin's. The old woman
has got some popcorn candy and ragdolls hid in the clothes chest, and we
allow to give Christmas a little whirl of our own in a insignificant sort of
style. No, I couldn't, with any degree of avidity, seem to fall in with the idea
of lettin' none of 'em go. Thank you kindly, gentlemen.'

Down the slope they drove and up another foothill to the ranchhouse of
Wiley Wilson. Trinidad recited his appeal and the Judge boomed out his
ponderous antiphony. Mrs. Wiley gathered her two rosy-cheeked youngster
close to her skirts and did not smile until she had seen Wiley laugh and
shake his head. Again a refusal.

Trinidad and the Judge vainly exhausted more than half their list before
twilight set in among the hills. They spent the night at a stage road hostelry,
and set out again early the next morning. The wagon had not acquired a
single passenger.

'It's creepin' upon my faculties,' remarked Trinidad, 'that borrowin' kids
at Christmas is somethin' like tryin' to steal butter from a man that's got hot
pancakes a-comin'.'

'It is undoubtedly an indisputable fact,' said the Judge, 'that the – ah –
family ties seem to be more coherent and assertive at that period of the year.'

On the day before Christmas they drove thirty miles, making four fruitless
halts and appeals. Everywhere they found 'kids' at a premium.

The sun was low when the wife of a section boss on a lonely railroad
huddled her unavailable progeny behind her and said:

'There's a woman that's just took charge of the railroad eatin' house down
at Granite Junction. I hear she's got a little boy. Maybe she might let him
go.'

Trinidad pulled up his mules at Granite Junction at five o'clock in the
afternoon. The train had just departed with its load of fed and appeased
passengers.

On the steps of the eating house they found a thin and glowering boy of
ten smoking a cigarette. The dining-room had been left in chaos by the
peripatetic appetites. A youngish woman reclined, exhausted, in a chair. Her
face wore sharp lines of worry. She had once possessed a certain style of

beauty that would never wholly leave her and would never wholly return. Trinidad set forth his mission.

'I'd count it a mercy if you'd take Bobby for a while,' she said, wearily. 'I'm on the go from morning till night, and I don't have time to 'tend to him. He's learning bad habits from the men. It'll be the only chance he'll have to get any Christmas.'

The men went outside and conferred with Bobby. Trinidad pictured the glories of the Christmas tree and presents in lively colors.

'And, moreover, my young friend,' added the Judge, 'Santa Claus himself will personally distribute the offerings that will typify the gifts conveyed by the shepherds of Bethlehem to—'

'Aw, come off,' said the boy, squinting his small eyes. 'I ain't no kid. There ain't any Santa Claus. It's your folks that buys toys and sneaks 'em in when you're asleep. And they make marks in the soot in the chimney with the tongs to look like Santa's sleigh tracks.'

'That might be so,' argued Trinidad, 'but Christmas trees ain't no fairy tale. This one's goin' to look like the ten-cent store in Albuquerque, all strung up in redwood. There's tops and drums and Noah's arks and—'

'Oh, rats!' said Bobby, wearily. 'I cut them out long ago. I'd like to have a rifle – not a target one – a real one, to shoot wildcats with; but I guess you won't have any of them on your old tree.'

'Well, I can't say for sure,' said Trinidad, diplomatically; 'it might be. You go along with us and see.'

The hope thus held out, though faint, won the boy's hesitating consent to go. With this solitary beneficiary for Cherokee's holiday bounty, the canvassers spun along the homeward road.

In Yellowhammer the empty storeroom had been transformed into what might have passed as the bower of an Arizona fairy. The ladies had done their work well. A tall Christmas tree, covered to the topmost branch with candle, spangles, and toys sufficient for more than a score of children, stood in the centre of the floor. Near sunset anxious eyes had begun to scan the street for the returning team of child-providers. At noon that day Cherokee had dashed into town with his new sleigh piled high with bundles and boxes and bales of all sizes and shapes. So intent was he upon the arrangements for his altruistic plans that the dearth of childhood did not receive his notice. No one gave away the humiliating state of Yellowhammer, for the efforts of Trinidad and the Judge were expected to supply the deficiency.

When the sun went down Cherokee, with many winks and arch grins on his seasoned face, went into retirement with the bundle containing the Santa Claus raiment and a package containing special and undisclosed gifts.

'When the kids are rounded up,' he instructed the volunteer arrangement committee, 'light up the candles on the tree and set 'em to playin' "Pussy Wants a Corner" and "King William." When they get good and at it, why – old Santa'll slide in the door. I reckon there'll be plenty of gifts to go 'round.'

The ladies were flitting about the tree, giving it final touches that were never final. The Spangler Sisters were there in costume as Lady Violet de Vere and Marie, the maid, in their new drama, 'The Miner's Bride.' The theatre did not open until nine, and they were welcome assistants of the Christmas-tree committee. Every minute heads would pop out the door to look and listen for the approach of Trinidad's team. And now this became an anxious function, for night had fallen and it would soon be necessary to light the candles on the tree, and Cherokee was apt to make an irruption at any time in his Kriss Kringle garb.

At length the wagon of the child 'rustlers' rattled down the street to the door. The ladies, with little screams of excitement, flew to the lighting of the candles. The men of Yellowhammer passed in and out restlessly or stood about the room in embarrassed groups.

Trinidad and the Judge, bearing the marks of protracted travel, entered, conducting between them a single impish boy, who stared with sullen, pessimistic eyes at the gaudy tree.

'Where are the other children?' asked the assayer's wife, the acknowledged leader of all social functions.

'Ma'am,' said Trinidad with a sigh, 'prospectin' for kids at Christmas time is like huntin' in limestone for silver. This parental business is one that I haven't no chance to comprehend. It seems that fathers and mothers are willin' for their offsprings to be drownded, stole, fed on poison oak, and et by catamounts 364 days in the year; but on Christmas Day they insists on enjoyin' the exclusive mortification of their company. This here young biped, ma'am, is all that washed out of our two days' manoeuvres.'

'Oh, the sweet little boy!' cooed Miss Erma, trailing her De Vere robes to centre of stage.

'Aw, shut up,' said Bobby, with a scowl. 'Who's a kid? You ain't, you bet.'

'Fresh brat!' breathed Miss Erma, beneath her enamelled smile.

'We done the best we could,' said Trinidad. 'It's tough on Cherokee, but it can't be helped.'

Then the door opened and Cherokee entered in the conventional dress of Saint Nick. A white rippling beard and flowing hair covered his face almost to his dark and shining eyes. Over his shoulder he carried a pack.

No one stirred as he came in. Even the Spangler Sisters ceased their coquettish poses and stared curiously at the tall figure. Bobby stood with his hands in his pockets gazing gloomily at the effeminate and childish tree. Cherokee put down his pack and looked wonderingly about the room. Perhaps he fancied that a bevy of eager children were being herded somewhere, to be loosed upon his entrance. He went up to Bobby and extended his red-mittened hand.

'Merry Christmas, little boy,' said Cherokee. 'Anything on the tree you want they'll get it down for you. Won't you shake hands with Santa Claus?'

'There ain't any Santa Claus,' whined the boy. 'You've got old false billy goat's whiskers on your face. I ain't no kid. What do I want with dolls and tin horses? The driver said you'd have a rifle, and you haven't. I want to go home.'

Trinidad stepped into the breach. He shook Cherokee's hand in warm greeting.

'I'm sorry, Cherokee,' he explained. 'There never was a kid in Yellowhammer. We tried to rustle a bunch of 'em for your swaree, but this sardine was all we could catch. He's a atheist, and he don't believe in Santa Claus. It's a shame for you to be out all this truck. But me and the Judge was sure we could round up a wagonful of candidates for your gimcracks.'

'That's all right,' said Cherokee, gravely. 'The expense don't amount to nothin' worth mentionin'. We can dump the stuff down a shaft or throw it away. I don't know what I was thinkin' about; but it never occurred to my cogitations that there wasn't any kids in Yellowhammer.'

Meanwhile the company had relaxed into a hollow but praiseworthy imitation of a pleasure gathering.

Bobby had retreated to a distant chair, and was coldly regarding the scene with ennui plastered thick upon him. Cherokee, lingering with his original idea, went over and sat beside him.

'Where do you live, little boy?' he asked, respectfully.

'Granite Junction,' said Bobby without emphasis.

The room was warm. Cherokee took off his cap, and then removed his beard and wig.

'Say!' exclaimed Bobby, with a show of interest, 'I know your mug, all right.'

'Did you ever see me before?' asked Cherokee.

'I don't know; but I've seen your picture lots of times.'

'Where?'

The boy hesitated. 'On the bureau at home,' he answered.

'Let's have your name, if you please, buddy.'

'Robert Lumsden. The picture belongs to my mother. She puts it under her pillow of nights. And once I saw her kiss it. I wouldn't. But women are that way.'

Cherokee rose and beckoned to Trinidad.

'Keep this boy by you till I come back,' he said. 'I'm going to shed these Christmas duds, and hitch up my sleigh. I'm goin' to take this kid home.'

'Well, infidel,' said Trinidad, taking Cherokee's vacant chair, 'and so you are too superannuated and effete to yearn for such mockeries as candy and toys, it seems.'

'I don't like you,' said Bobby, with acrimony. 'You said there would be a rifle. A fellow can't even smoke. I wish I was at home.'

Cherokee drove his sleigh to the door, and they lifted Bobby in beside him. The team of fine horses sprange away prancingly over the hard snow, Cherokee had his $500 overcoat of baby sealskin. The laprobe that he drew about them was as warm as velvet.

Bobby slipped a cigarette from his pocket and was trying to snap a match.

'Throw that cigarette away,' said Cherokee, in a quiet but new voice.

Bobby hesitated, and then dropped the cylinder overboard.

'Throw the box, too,' commanded the new voice.

More reluctantly the boy obeyed.

'Say,' said Bobby, presently, 'I like you. I don't know why. Nobody never made me do anything I didn't want to do before.'

'Tell me, kid,' said Cherokee, not using his new voice, 'are you sure your mother kissed that picture that looks like me?'

'Dead sure. I seen her do it.'

'Didn't you remark somethin' a while ago about wanting a rifle?'

'You bet I did. Will you get me one?'

'To-morrow – silver-mounted.'

Cherokee took out his watch.

'Half-past nine. We'll hit the Junction plumb on time with Christmas Day. Are you cold? Sit closer, son.'

A CHAPARRAL PRINCE

NINE O'CLOCK AT LAST, and the drudging toil of the day was ended. Lena climbed to her room in the third half-story of the Quarrymen's Hotel. Since daylight she had slaved, doing the work of a full-grown woman, scrubbing the floors, washing the heavy ironstone plates and cups, making the beds, and supplying the insatiate demands for wood and water in that turbulent and depressing hostelry.

The din of the day's quarrying was over – the blasting and drilling, the creaking of the great cranes, the shouts of the foremen, the backing and shifting of the flat-cars hauling the heavy blocks of limestone. Down in the hotel office three or four of the laborers were growling and swearing over a belated game of checkers. Heavy odors of stewed meat, hot grease, and cheap coffee hung like a depressing fog about the house.

Lena lit the stump of a candle and sat limply upon her wooden chair. She was eleven years old, thin and ill-nourished. Her back and limbs were sore and aching. But the ache in her heart made the biggest trouble. The last straw had been added to the burden upon her small shoulders. They had taken away Grimm. Always at night, however tired she might be, she had turned to Grimm for comfort and hope. Each time had Grimm whispered to her that the prince or the fairy would come and deliver her out of the wicked enchantment. Every night she had taken fresh courage and strength from Grimm.

To whatever tale she read she found an analogy in her own condition. The woodcutter's lost child, the unhappy goose girl, the persecuted step-daughter, the little maiden imprisoned in the witch's hut – all these were but transparent disguises for Lena, the overworked kitchenmaid in the Quarrymen's Hotel. And always when the extremity was direst came the good fairy or the gallant prince to the rescue.

So, here in the ogre's castle, enslaved by a wicked spell, Lena had leaned upon Grimm and waited, longing for the powers of goodness to prevail. But on the day before Mrs. Maloney had found the book in her room and had carried it away, declaring sharply that it would not do for servants to read at night; they lost sleep and did not work briskly the next day. Can one only eleven years old, living away from one's mama, and never having any time to play, live entirely deprived of Grimm? Just try it once and you will see what a difficult thing it is.

Lena's home was in Texas, away up among the little mountains on the Pedernales River, in a little town called Fredericksburg. They are all German people who live in Fredericksburg. Of evenings they sit at little tables along the sidewalk and drink beer and play pinochle and scat. They are very thrifty people.

Thriftiest among them was Peter Hildesmuller, Lena's father. And that is why Lena was sent to work in the hotel at the quarries, thirty miles away. She earned three dollars every week there, and Peter added her wages to his well-guarded store. Peter had an ambition to become as rich as his neighbor, Hugo Heffelbauer, who smoked a meerschaum pipe three feet long and had wiener schnitzel and hassenpfeffer for dinner every day in the week. And now Lena was quite old enough to work and assist in the accumulation of riches. But conjecture, if you can, what it means to be sentenced at eleven years of age from a home in the pleasant little Rhine village to hard labor in the ogre's castle, where you must fly to serve the ogres, while they devour cattle and sheep, growling fiercely as they stamp white limestone dust from their great shoes for you to sweep and scour with your weak, aching fingers. And then – to have Grimm taken away from you!

Lena raised the lid of an old empty case that had once contained canned corn and got out a sheet of paper and a piece of pencil. She was going to write a letter to her mamma. Tommy Ryan was going to post it for her at Ballinger's. Tommy was seventeen, worked in the quarries, went home to Ballinger's every night, and was now waiting in the shadows under Lena's window for her to throw her letter out to him. That was the only way she could send a letter to Fredericksburg. Mrs. Maloney did not like for her to write letters.

The stump of candle was burning low, so Lena hastily bit the wood from around the lead of her pencil and began. This is the letter she wrote:

Dearest Mamma: I want so much to see you. And Gretel and Claus and Heinrich and little Adolf. I am so tired. I want to see you. To-day I was slapped by Mrs. Maloney and had no supper. I could not bring in enough wood, for my hand hurt. She took my book yesterday. I mean 'Grimms's Fairy Tales,' which Uncle Leo gave me. It did not hurt any one for me to read the book. I try to work as well as I can, but there is so much to do. I read only a little bit every night. Dear mamma, I shall tell you what I am going to do. Unless you send for me to-morrow to bring me home I shall go to a deep place I know in the river and drown. It is wicked to drown, I suppose, but I wanted to see you, and there is no one else. I am very tired, and Tommy is waiting for the letter. You will excuse me, mamma, if I do it.

Your respectful and loving daughter,
Lena

Tommy was still waiting faithfully when the letter was concluded, and when Lena dropped it out she saw him pick it up and start up the steep hillside. Without undressing she blew out the candle and curled herself upon the mattress on the floor.

At 10:30 o'clock old man Ballinger came out of the house in his stocking feet and leaned over the gate, smoking his pipe. He looked down the big road, white in the moonshine, and rubbed one ankle with the toe of his other foot. It was time for the Fredericksburg mail to come pattering up the road.

Old man Ballinger had waited only a few minutes when he heard the lively hoofbeats of Fritz's team of little black mules, and very soon afterward his covered spring wagon stood in front of the gate. Fritz's big spectacles flashed in the moonlight and his tremendous voice shouted a greeting to the postmaster of Ballinger's. The mail-carrier jumped out and took the bridles from the mules, for he always fed them oats at Ballinger's.

While the mules were eating from their feed bags old man Ballinger brought out the mail sack and threw it into the wagon.

Fritz Bergmann was a man of three sentiments – or to be more accurate – four, the pair of mules deserving to be reckoned individually. Those mules were the chief interest and joy of his existence. Next came the Emperor of Germany and Lena Hildesmuller.

'Tell me,' said Fritz, when he was ready to start, 'contains the sacks a letter to Frau Hildesmuller from the little Lena at the quarries? One came in the last mail to say that she is a little sick, already. Her mamma is very anxious to hear again.'

'Yes,' said old man Ballinger, 'that's a letter for Mrs. Helterskelter, or some sich name. Tommy Ryan brung it over when he come. Her little gal workin' over thar, you say?'

'In the hotel,' shouted Fritz, as he gathered up the lines; 'eleven years old and not bigger as a frankfurter. The close-fist of a Peter Hildesmuller! – some day shall I with a big club pound that man's dummkopf – all in and out the town. Perhaps in this letter Lena will say that she is yet feeling better. So, her mamma will be glad. *Auf wiedersehen*, Herr Ballinger – your feets will take cold out in the night air.'

'So long, Fritzy,' said old man Ballinger. 'You got a nice cool night for your drive.'

Up the road went the little black mules at their steady trot, while Fritz thundered at them occasional words of endearment and cheer.

These fancies occupied the mind of the mailcarrier until he reached the big post-oak forest, eight miles from Ballinger's. Here his ruminations were scattered by the sudden flash and report of pistols and a whooping as if from a whole tribe of Indians. A band of galloping centaurs closed in around the mail wagon. One of them leaned over the front wheel, covered the driver with his revolver, and ordered him to stop. Others caught at the bridles of Donder and Blitzen.

'Donnerwetter!' shouted Fritz, with all his tremendous voice – 'wass ist? Release your hands from dose mules. Ve vas der United States mail!'

'Hurry up, Dutch!' drawled a melancholy voice. 'Don't you know when you're in a stick-up? Reverse your mules and climb out of the cart.'

It is due to the breadth of Hondo Bill's demerit and the largeness of his achievements to state that the holding up of the Fredericksburg mail was not perpetuated by way of an exploit. As the lion while in the pursuit of prey commensurate to his prowess might set a frivolous foot upon a casual rabbit in his path, so Hondo Bill and his gang had swooped sportively upon the pacific transport of Meinherr Fritz.

The real work of their sinister night ride was over. Fritz and his mail bag and his mules came as a gentle relaxation, grateful after the arduous duties of their profession. Twenty miles to the southeast stood a train with a killed engine, hysterical passengers, and a looted express and mail car. That represented the serious occupation of Hondo Bill and his gang. With a fairly rich prize of currency and silver the robbers were making a wide detour to the west through the less populous country, intending to seek safety in Mexico by means of some fordable spot on the Rio Grande. The booty from the train had melted the desperate bushrangers to jovial and happy skylarkers.

Trembling with outraged dignity and no little personal apprehension, Fritz climbed out to the road after replacing his suddenly removed spectacles. The band had dismounted and were singing, capering, and whooping, thus expressing their satisfied delight in the life of a jolly outlaw. Rattlesnake Rogers, who stood at the heads of the mules, jerked a little too vigorously at the rein of the tender-mouthed Donder, who reared and emitted a loud, protesting snort of pain. Instantly Fritz, with a scream of anger, flew at the bulky Rogers and began assiduously to pommel that surprised free-booter with his fists.

'Villain!' shouted Fritz, 'dog, bigstiff! Dot mule he has a soreness by his mouth. I vill knock off your shoulders mit your head – robber-mans!'

'Yi-yi!' howled Rattlesnake, roaring with laughter and ducking his head, 'somebody git this here sourkrout off'n me!'

One of the band jerked Fritz back by the coat-tail, and the woods rang with Rattlesnake's vociferous comments.

'The dog-goned little wienerwurst,' he yelled, amiably. 'He's not so much of a skunk, for a Dutchman. Took up for his animile plum quick, didn't he? I like to see a man like his hoss, even if it is a mule. The dad-blamed little Limburger he went for me, didn't he! Whoa, now, muley – I ain't a-goin' to hurt your mouth agin any more.'

Perhaps the mail would not have been tampered with had not Ben Moody, the lieutenant, possessed certain wisdom that seemed to promise more spoils.

'Say, Cap,' he said, addressing Hondo Bill, 'there's liable to be good pickings in these mail sacks. I've done some hoss tradin' with these Dutchmen around Fredericksburg, and I know the style of the varmints. There's big money goes through the mails to that town. Them Dutch risk a thousand dollars sent wrapped in a piece of paper before they'd pay the banks to handle the money.'

Hondo Bill, six feet two, gentle of voice and impulsive in action, was dragging the sacks from the rear of the wagon before Moody had finished his speech. A knife shone in his hand, and they heard the ripping sound as it bit through the tough canvas. The outlaws crowded around and began tearing open letters and packages, enlivening their labors by swearing affably at the writers, who seemed to have conspired to confute the prediction of Ben Moody. Not a dollar was found in the Fredericksburg mail.

'You ought to be ashamed of yourself,' said Hondo Bill to the mail-carrier in solemn tones, 'to be packing around such a lot of old, trashy paper as this. What d'you mean by it, anyhow? Where do you Dutchers keep your money at?'

The Ballinger mail sack opened like a cocoon under Hondo's knife. It contained but a handful of mail. Fritz had been fuming with terror and excitement until this sack was reached. He now remembered Lena's letter. He addressed the leader of the band, asking him that particular missive be spared.

'Much obliged, Dutch,' he said to the disturbed carrier. 'I guess that's the letter we want. Got spondulicks in it, ain't it? Here she is. Make a light, boys.'

Hondo found and tore open the letter to Mrs. Hildesmuller. The others stood about, lighting twisted-up letters one from another. Hondo gazed with mute disapproval at the single sheet of paper covered with the angular German script.

'Whatever is this you've humbugged us with, Dutchy? You call this here a valuable letter? That's a mighty low-down trick to play on your friends what come along to help you distribute your mail.'

'That's Chiny writin',' said Sandy Grundy, peering over Hondo's shoulder.

'You're off your kazip,' declared another of the gang, an effective youth, covered with silk handkerchiefs and nickel plating. 'That's shorthand. I seen 'em do it once in court.'

'Ach, no, no, no – dot is German,' said Fritz. 'It is no more as a little girl writing a letter to her mamma. One poor little girl, sick and vorking hard avay from home. Ach! it is a shame. Good Mr. Robber-man, you vill please let me have dot letter?'

'What the devil do you take us for, old Pretzels' said Hondo with sudden and surprising severity. 'You ain't presumin' to insinuate that we gents ain't possessed of sufficient politeness for to take an interest in the miss's health are you? Now, you go on, and you read that scratchin' out loud and in plain United States language to this here company of educated society.'

Hondo twirled his six-shooter by its trigger guard and stood towering above the little German, who at once began to read the letter, translating the simple words into English. The gang of rovers stood in absolute silence, listening intently.

'How old is that kid?' asked Hondo when the letter was done.

'Eleven,' said Fritz.

'And where is she at?'

'At dose rock quarries – working. Ach, mein Gott – little Lena, she speak of drowning. I do not know if she vill do it, but if she shall I schwear I vill dot Peter Hildesmuller shoot mit a gun.'

'You Dutchers,' said Hondo Bill, his voice swelling with fine contempt, 'make me plenty tired. Hirin' out your kids to work when they ought to be playin' dolls in the sand. You're a hell of a sect of people. I reckon we'll fix your clock for a while just to show what we think of your old cheesy nation. Here, boys!'

Hondo Bill parleyed aside briefly with his band, and then they seized Fritz and conveyed him off the road to one side. Here they bound him fast to a tree with a couple of lariats. His team they tied to another tree near by.

'We ain't going to hurt you bad,' said Hondo, reassuringly. '"Twon't hurt you to be tied up for a while. We will now pass you the time of day, as it is up to us to depart. Ausgespielt – nixcumrous, Dutchy. Don't get any more impatience.'

Fritz heard a great squeaking of saddles as the men mounted their horses. Then a loud yell and a great clatter of hoofs as they galloped pell-mell back along the Fredericksburg road.

For more than two hours Fritz sat against his tree, tightly but not painfully bound. Then from the reaction after his exciting adventure he sank into slumber. How long he slept he knew not, but he was at last awakened by a rough shake. Hands were untying his ropes. He was lifted to his feet, dazed, confused in mind, and weary of body. Rubbing his eyes, he looked and saw that he was again in the midst of the same band of terrible bandits. They shoved him up to the seat of his wagon and placed the lines in his hands.

'Hit it out for home, Dutch,' said Hondo Bill's voice, commandingly. 'You've given us lots of trouble and we're pleased to see the back of your neck. Spiel! Zwei bier! Vamoose!'

Hondo reached out and gave Blitzen a smart cut with his quirt.

The little mules sprang ahead, glad to be moving again. Fritz urged them along, himself dizzy and muddled over his fearful adventure.

According to schedule time, he should have reached Fredericksburg at daylight. As it was, he drove down the long street of the town at eleven o'clock a.m. He had to pass Peter Hildesmuller's house on his way to the post-office. He stopped his team at the gate and called. But Frau Hildesmuller was watching for him. Out rushed the whole family of Hildesmullers.

Frau Hildesmuller, fat and flushed, inquired if he had a letter from Lena, and then Fritz raised his voice and told the tale of his adventure. He told the contents of the letter that the robber had made him read, and then Frau Hildesmuller broke into wild weeping. Her little Lena drown herself! Why had they sent her from home? What could be done? Perhaps it would be too late by the time they could send for her now. Peter Hildesmuller dropped his meerschaum on the walk and it shivered into pieces.

'Woman!' he roared at his wife, 'why did you let that child go away? It is your fault if she comes home to us no more.'

Every one knew that it was Peter Hildesmuller's fault, so they paid no attention to his words.

A moment afterward a strange, faint voice was heard to call: 'Mamma!' Frau Hildesmuller at first thought it was Lena's spirit calling, and then she rushed to the rear of Fritz's covered wagon, and, with a loud shriek of joy, caught up Lena herself, covering her pale little face with kisses and smothering her with hugs. Lena's eyes were heavy with the deep slumber of exhaustion but she smiled and lay close to the one she had longed to see. There among the mail sacks, covered in a nest of strange blankets and comforters, she had lain asleep until wakened by the voices around her.

Fritz stared at her with eyes that bulged behind his spectacles.

'Gott in Himmel!' he shouted. 'How did you get in that wagon? Am I going crazy as well as to be murdered and hanged by robbers this day?'

'You brought her to us, Fritz,' cried Frau Hildesmuller. 'How can we ever thank you enough?'

'Tell mamma how you came in Fritz's wagon,' said Frau Hildesmuller.

'I don't know,' said Lena. 'But I know how I got away from the hotel. The Prince brought me.'

'By the Emperor's crown!' shouted Fritz, 'we are all going crazy.'

'I always knew he would come,' said Lena, sitting down on her bundle of bedclothes on the sidewalk. 'Last night he came with his armed knights and captured the ogre's castle. They broke the dishes and kicked down the doors. They pitched Mr. Maloney into a barrel of rain water and threw flour all over Mrs. Maloney. The workmen in the hotel jumped out of the windows and ran into the woods when the knights began firing their guns. They wakened me up and I peeped down the stair. And then the Prince came up and wrapped me in the bedclothes and carried me out. He was so tall and strong and fine. His face was as rough as a scrubbing brush, and he talked soft and kind and smelled of schnapps. He took me on his horse before him and we rode away among the knights. He held me close and I went to sleep that way, and didn't wake up till I got home.'

'Rubbish!' cried Fritz Bergmann. 'Fairy tales! How did you come from the quarries to my wagon?'

'The Prince brought me,' said Lena, confidently.

And to this day the good people of Fredericksburg haven't been able to make her give any other explanation.

THE REFORMATION OF CALLIOPE

CALLIOPE CATESBY WAS IN HIS HUMORS AGAIN. Ennui was upon him. This goodly promontory, the earth – particularly that portion of it known as Quicksand – was to him no more than a pestilent congregation of vapors. Overtaken by the megrims, the philosopher may seek relief in soliloquy; my lady find solace in tears; the flaccid Easterner scold at the millinery bills of his women folk. Such recourse was insufficient to the denizens of Quicksand. Calliope, especially, was wont to express his ennui according to his lights.

Over night Calliope had hung out signals of approaching low spirits. He had kicked his own dog on the porch of the Occidental Hotel, and refused to apologize. He had become capricious and fault-finding in conversation. While strolling about he reached often for twigs of mesquite and chewed the leaves fiercely. That was always an ominous act. Another symptom alarming to those who were familiar with the different stages of his doldrums was his increasing politeness and a tendency to use formal phrases. A husky softness succeeded the usual penetrating drawl in his tones. A dangerous courtesy marked his manners. Later, his smile became crooked, the left side of his mouth slanting upward, and Quicksand got ready to stand from under.

At this stage Calliope generally began to drink. Finally, about midnight, he was seen going homeward, saluting those whom he met with exaggerated but inoffensive courtesy. Not yet was Calliope's melancholy at the danger point. He would seat himself at the window of the room he occupied over Silvester's tonsorial parlors and there chant lugubrious and tuneless ballads until morning, accompanying the noises by appropriate maltreatment of a jingling guitar. More magnanimous than Nero, he would thus give musical warning of the forthcoming municipal upheaval that Quicksand was scheduled to endure.

A quiet, amiable man was Calliope Catesby at other times – quiet to indolence, and amiable to worthlessness. At best he was a loafer and a nuisance; at worst he was the Terror of Quicksand. His ostensible occupation was something subordinate in the real estate line; he drove the beguiled Easterner in buckboards out to look over lots and ranch property. Originally he came from one of the Gulf States, his lank six feet, slurring rhythm of speech, and sectional idioms giving evidence of his birthplace.

And yet, after taking on Western adjustments, this languid pine-box whittler, cracker barrel hugger, shady corner lounger of the cotton fields and sumac hills of the South became famed as a bad man among men who had made a life-long study of the art of truculence.

At nine the next morning Calliope was fit. Inspired by his own barbarous melodies and the contents of his jug, he was ready primed to gather fresh laurels from the diffident brow of Quicksand. Encircled and criss-crossed with cartridge belts, abundantly garnished with revolvers, and copiously drunk, he poured forth into Quicksand's main street. Too chivalrous to surprise and capture a town by silent sortie, he paused at the nearest corner and emitted his slogan – that fearful, brassy yell, so reminiscent of the steam piano, that has gained for him the classic appellation that had superseded his own baptismal name. Following close upon his vociferation came three shots from his forty-five by way of limbering up the guns and testing his aim. A yellow dog, the personal property of Colonel Swazey, the proprietor of the Occidental, fell feet upward in the dust with one farewell yelp. A Mexican who was crossing the street from the Blue Front grocery, carrying in his hand a bottle of kerosene, was stimulated to a sudden and admirable burst of speed, still grasping the neck of the shattered bottle. The new gilt weathercock on Judge Riley's lemon and ultra-marine two-story residence shivered, flapped, and hung by a splinter, the sport of the wanton breezes.

The artillery was in trim. Calliope's hand was steady. The high, calm ecstasy of habitual battle was upon him, though slightly embittered by the sadness of Alexander in that his conquests were limited to the small world of Quicksand.

Down the street went Calliope, shooting right and left. Glass fell like hail; dogs vamosed; chickens flew, squawking; feminine voices shrieked concernedly to youngsters at large. The din was perforated at intervals by the *staccato* of the Terror's guns, and was drowned periodically by the brazen screech that Quicksand knew so well. The occasion of Calliope's low spirits were legal holidays in Quicksand. All along the main street in advance of his coming clerks were putting up shutters and closing doors. Business would languish for a space. The right of way was Calliope's, and as he advanced, observing the dearth of opposition and the few opportunities for distraction, his ennui perceptibly increased.

But some four squares farther down lively preparations were being made to minister to Mr. Catesby's love for interchange of compliments and repartee. On the previous night numerous messengers had hastened to advise Buck Patterson, the city marshal, of Calliope's impending eruption. The patience of that official, often strained in extending leniency toward the disturber's misdeeds, had been overtaxed. In Quicksand some indulgence was accorded the natural ebullition of human nature. Providing that the lives of the more useful citizens were not recklessly squandered, or too much property needlessly laid waste, the community sentiment was against a too strict enforcement of the law. But Calliope had raised the limit. His outbursts had been too frequent and too violent to come within the classification of a normal and sanitary relaxation of spirit.

Buck Patterson had been expecting and awaiting in his little ten-by-twelve frame office that preliminary yell announcing that Calliope was feeling blue. When the signal came the City Marshal rose to his feet and buckled on his guns. Two deputy sheriffs and three citizens who had proven the edible qualities of fire also stood up, ready to bandy with Calliope's leaden jocularities.

'Gather that fellow in,' said Buck Patterson, setting for the lines of the campaign. 'Don't have no talk, but shoot as soon as you can get a show. Keep behind cover and bring him down. He's a nogood 'un. It's up to Calliope to turn up his toes this time, I reckon. Go to him all spraddled out, boys. And don't git too reckless, for what Calliope shoots at he hits.'

Buck Patterson, tall, muscular, and solemn-faced, with his bright 'City Marshal' badge shining on the breast of his blue flannel shirt, gave his posse directions for the onslaught upon Calliope. The plan was to accomplish the downfall of the Quicksand Terror without loss to the attaching party, if possible.

The splenetic Calliope, unconscious of retributive plots, was steaming

down the channel, cannonading on either side, when he suddenly became
aware of breakers ahead. The City Marshal and one of the deputies rose up
behind some dry-goods boxes half a square to the front and opened fire. At
the same time the rest of the posse, divided, shelled him from two side streets
up which they were cautiously manoeuvring from a well-executed detour.

The first volley broke the lock of one of Calliope's guns, cut a neat underbit
in his right ear, and exploded a cartridge in his crossbelt, scorching his ribs
as it bursts. Feeling braced up by this unexpected tonic to his spiritual
depression, Calliope executed a fortissimo note from his upper registers, and
returned the fire like an echo. The upholders of the law dodged at his flash,
but a trifle too late to save one of the deputies a bullet just above the elbow,
and the marshal a bleeding cheek from a splinter that a ball tore from a box
he had ducked behind.

And now Calliope met the enemy's tactics in kind. Choosing with a rapid
eye the street from which the weakest and least accurate fire had come, he
invaded it a double-quick, abandoning the unprotected middle of the street.
With rare cunning the opposing force in that direction – one of the deputies
and two of the valorous volunteers – waited, concealed by beer barrels, until
Calliope had passed their retreat, and then peppered him from the rear. In
another moment they were reinforced by the marshal and his other men,
and then Calliope felt that in order to successfully prolong the delights of
the controversy he must find some means of reducing the great odds against
him. His eye fell upon a structure that seemed to hold out this promise,
providing he could reach it.

Not far away was the little railroad station, its building a strong box house,
ten by twenty feet, resting upon a platform four feet above ground. Windows
were in each of its walls. Something like a fort it might become to a man
thus sorely pressed by superior numbers.

Calliope made a bolt and rapid spurt for it, the marshal's crowd 'smoking'
him as he ran. He reached the haven in safety, the station agent leaving the
building by a window, like a flying squirrel, as the garrison entered the door.

Patterson and his supporters halted under protection of a pile of lumber
and held consultations. In the station was an unterrified desperado who was
an excellent shot and carried an abundance of ammunition. For thirty yards
on each side of the besieged was a stretch of bare, open ground. It was a sure
thing that the man who attempted to enter that unprotected area would be
stopped by one of Calliope's bullets.

The City Marshal was resolved. He had decided that Calliope Catesby
should no more wake the echoes of Quicksand with his strident whoop. He
had so announced. Officially and personally he felt imperatively bound to
put the soft pedal on that instrument of discord. It played bad tunes.

Standing near was a hand truck used in the manipulation of small freight.
It stood by a shed full of sacked wool, a consignment from one of the sheep
ranches. On this truck the marshal and his men piled three heavy sacks of
wool. Stooping low, Buck Patterson started for Calliope's fort, slowly pushing
this loaded truck before him for protection. The posse, scattering broadly,
stood ready to nip the besieged in case he should show himself in an effort
to repel the juggernaut of justice that was creeping upon him. Only once did
Calliope make demonstration. He fired from a window and soft tufts of wool
spurted from the marshal's trustworthy bulwark. The return shots from the

posse pattered against the window frame of the fort. No loss resulted on either side.

The marshal was too deeply engrossed in steering his protected battleship to be aware of the approach of the morning train until he was within a few feet of the platform. The train was coming up on the other side of it. It stopped only one minute at Quicksand. What an opportunity it would offer to Calliope! He had only to step out the other door, mount the train, and away.

Abandoning his breastworks, Buck, with his gun ready, dashed up the steps and into the room, driving open the closed door with one heave of his weighty shoulder. The members of the posse heard one shot fired inside, and then there was silence.

At length the wounded man opened his eyes. After a blank space he again could see and hear and feel and think. Turning his eyes about, he found himself lying on a wooden bench. A tall man with a perplexed countenance, wearing a big badge with 'City Marshal' engraved upon it, stood over him. A little old woman in black, with a wrinkled face and sparkling black eyes was holding a wet handkerchief against one of his temples. He was trying to get these facts fixed in his mind and connected with past events, when the old woman began to talk.

'There now, great, big, strong man! That bullet never tetched ye! Jest skeeted along the side of your head and sort of paralyzed ye for a spell. I've heerd of sech things afor! con-cussion is what they names it. Abel Wadkins used to kill squirrels that way – barkin' em, Abe called it. You jest been barked, sir, and you'll be all right in a little bit. Feel lots better already, don't ye! You just lay still a while longer and let me bathe your head. You don't know me, I reckon, and 'tain't surprisin' that you shouldn't. I come in on that train from Alabama to see my son. Big son, ain't he? Lands! you wouldn't hardly think he'd ever been a baby, would ye? This is my son, sir.'

Half turning, the old woman looked up at the standing man, her worn face lighting with a proud and wonderful smile. She reached out one veined and calloused hand and took one of her son's. Then smiling cheerily down at the prostrate man, she continued to dip the handkerchief in the waiting-room tin washbasin and gently apply it to his temple. She had the benevolent garrulity of old age.

'I ain't seen my son before,' she continued, 'in eight years. One of my nephews, Elkanah Price, he's a conductor on one of them railroads, and he got me a pass to come out here. I can stay a whole week on it, and then it'll take me back again. Jest think, now, that little boy of mine has got to be a officer – a city marshal of a whole town! That's something like a constable, ain't it? I never knowed he was a officer; he didn't say nothin' about it in his letters. I reckon he thought his old mother'd be skeered about the danger he was in. But, laws! I never was much of a hand to git skeered. 'Tain't no use. I heard them guns a-shootin' while I was gittin' off them cars, and I see smoke a-comin' out of the depot, but I jest walked right along. Then I see son's face lookin' out through the window. I knowed him at oncet. He met me at the door, and squeezed me 'most to death. And there you was, sir, a-lyin' there jest like you was dead, and I 'lowed we'd see what might be done to help sot you up.'

'I think I'll sit up now,' said the concussion patient. 'I'm feeling pretty fair by this time.'

He sat, somewhat weakly yet, leaning against the wall. He was a rugged man, big-boned and straight. His eyes, steady and keen, seemed to linger upon the face of the man standing so still above him. His look wandered often from the face he studied to the marshal's badge upon the other's breast.

'Yes, yes, you'll be all right,' said the old woman, patting his arm, 'if you don't get to cuttin' up agin, and havin' folks shootin' at you. Son told me about you, sir, while you was layin' senseless on the floor. Don't you take it as meddlesome fer an old woman with a son as big as you to talk about it. And you mustn't hold no grudge ag'in my son for havin' to shoot at ye. A officer has got to take up for the law – it's his duty – and them that acts bad and lives wrong has to suffer. Don't blame my son any, sir – 'tain't his fault. He's always been a good boy – good when he was growin' up, and kind and 'bedient and well-behaved. Won't you let me advise you, sir, not to do so no more? Be a good man, and leave liquor alone and live peaceably and godly. Keep away from bad company and work honest and sleep sweet.'

The black-mittened hand of the old pleader gently touched the breast of the man she addressed. Very earnest and candid her old, worn face looked. In her rusty black dress and antique bonnet she sat, near the close of a long life, and epitomized the experience of the world. Still the man to whom she spoke gazed above her head, contemplating the silent son of the old mother.

'What does the marshal say?' he asked. 'Does he believe the advice is good? Suppose the marshal speaks up and says if the talk's right?'

The tall man moved uneasily. He fingered the badge on his breast for a moment, and then he put an arm around the old woman and drew her close to him. She smiled the unchanging mother smile of three-score years, and patted his big brown hand with her crooked, mittened fingers while her son spake.

'I say this,' he said, looking squarely into the eyes of the other man, 'that if I was in your place I'd follow it. If I was a drunken, desp'rate character, without shame or hope, I'd follow it. If I was in your place and you was in mine I'd say: "Marshal, I'm willin' to swear if you'll give me the chance I'll quit the racket. I'll drop the tanglefoot and the gun play, and won't play hoss no more. I'll be a good citizen and go to work and quit my foolishness. So help me God!" That's what I'd say to you if you was marshal and I was in your place.'

'Hear my son talkin',' said the old woman softly. 'Hear him, sir. You promise to be good and he won't do you no harm. Forty-one year ago his heart first beat ag'in mine, and it's beat true ever since.'

The other man rose to his feet, trying his limbs and stretching his muscles.

'Then,' said he, 'if you was in my place and said that, and I was marshal, I'd say: "Go free, and do your best to keep your promise." '

'Lawsy!' exclaimed the old woman, in a sudden flutter, 'ef I didn't clear forget that trunk of mine! I see a man settin' it on the platform jest as I seen son's face in the window, and it went plum out of my head. There's eight jars of home-made quince jam in that trunk that I made myself. I wouldn't have nothin' happen to them jars for a red apple.'

Away to the door she trotted, spry and anxious, and then Calliope Catesby spoke out to Buck Patterson:

'I just couldn't help it, Buck. I seen her through the window a-comin' in.

She had never heard a word 'bout my tough ways. I didn't have the nerve to let her know I was a worthless cuss bein' hunted down by the community. There you was lyin' where my shot laid you, like you was dead. The idea struck me sudden, and I just took your badge off and fastened it onto myself, and I fastened my reputation onto you. I told her I was the marshal and you was a holy terror. You can take your badge back now, Buck.'

With shaking fingers Calliope began to unfasten the disc of metal from his shirt.

'Easy there!' said Buck Patterson. 'You keep that badge right where it is, Calliope Catesby. Don't you dare to take it off till the day your mother leaves this town. You'll be city marshal of Quicksand as long as she's here to know it. After I stir around town a bit and put 'em on I'll guarantee that nobody won't give the thing away to her. And say, you leather-headed, rip-roarin', low-down son of a locoed cyclone, you follow that advice she gave me! I'm goin' to take some of it myself, too.'

'Buck,' said Calliope, feelingly, 'ef I don't I hope I may —'

'Shut up,' said Buck. 'She's a-comin' back.'

THE FOUR MILLION

TOBIN'S PALM

TOBIN AND ME, THE TWO OF US, went down to Coney one day, for there was four dollars between us, and Tobin had need of distractions. For there was Katie Mahorner, his sweetheart, of County Sligo, lost since she started for America three months before with two hundred dollars, her own savings, and one hundred dollars from the sale of Tobin's inherited estate, a fine cottage and pig on the Bog Shannaugh. And since the letter that Tobin got saying that she had started to come to him not a bit of news had he heard or seen of Katie Mahorner. Tobin advertised in the papers, but nothing could be found of the colleen.

So, to Coney me and Tobin went, thinking that a turn at the chutes and the smell of the popcorn might raise the heart in his bosom. But Tobin was a hard-headed man, and the sadness stuck in his skin. He ground his teeth at the crying balloons; he cursed the moving pictures; and, though he would drink whenever asked, he scorned Punch and Judy, and was for licking the tintype men as they came.

So I gets him down a side way on a board walk where the attractions were some less violent. At a little six by eight stall Tobin halts, with a more human look in his eye.

' 'Tis here,' says he, 'I will be diverted. I'll have the palm of me hand investigated by the wonderful palmist of the Nile, and see if what is to be will be.'

Tobin was a believer in signs and the unnatural in nature. He possessed illegal convictions in his mind along the subjects of black cats, lucky numbers and the weather predictions in the papers.

We went into the enchanted chicken coop, which was fixed, mysterious with red cloth and pictures of hands with lines crossing 'em like a railroad centre. The sign over the door says it is Madame Zozo the Egyptian Palmist. There was a fat woman inside in a red jumper with pothooks and beasties embroidered upon it. Tobin gives her ten cents and extends one of his hands. She lifts Tobin's hand, which is own brother to the hoof of a drayhorse, and examines it to see whether 'tis a stone in the frog or a cast shoe he has come for.

'Man,' says this Madame Zozo, 'the line of your fate shows—'

' 'Tis not me foot at all,' says Tobin, interrupting. 'Sure, 'tis no beauty but ye hold the palm of me hand.'

'The line shows,' says the Madame, 'that ye've not arrived at your time of life without bad luck. And there's more to come. The mount of Venus – or is that a stone bruise? – shows that ye've been in love. There's been trouble in your life on account of your sweetheart.'

' 'Tis Katie Mahorner she has references with,' whispers Tobin to me in a loud voice to one side.

'I see,' says the palmist, 'a great deal of sorrow and tribulation with one whom ye cannot forget. I see the lines of designation point to the letter K and the letter M in her name.'

'Whist!' says Tobin to me; 'do ye hear that?'

'Look out,' goes on the palmist, 'for a dark man and a light woman; for they'll both bring ye trouble. Ye'll make a voyage upon the water very soon, and have a financial loss. I see one line that brings good luck. There's a man coming into your life who will fetch ye good fortune. Ye'll know him when ye see him by his crooked nose.'

'Is his name set down?' asks Tobin. ' 'Twill be convenient in the way of greeting when he backs up to dump off the good luck.'

'His name,' says the palmist, thoughtful looking, 'is not spelled out by the lines, but they indicate 'tis a long one, and the letter "o" should be in it. There's no more to tell. Good-evening. Don't block up the door.'

' 'Tis wonderful how she knows,' says Tobin as we walk to the pier.

As we squeezed through the gates a nigger man sticks his lighted segar against Tobin's ear, and there is trouble. Tobin hammers his neck, and the women squeal, and by presence of mind I drag the little man out of the way before the police comes. Tobin is always in an ugly mood when enjoying himself.

On the boat going back, when the man calls 'Who wants the good-looking waiter?' Tobin tried to plead guilty, feeling the desire to blow the foam off a crock of suds, but when he felt in his pocket he found himself discharged for lack of evidence. Somebody had disturbed his change during the commotion. So we sat, dry, upon the stools, listening to the Dagoes fiddling on deck. If anything, Tobin was lower in spirits and less congenial with his misfortunes than when we started.

On a seat against the railing was a young woman dressed suitable for red automobiles, with hair the color of an unsmoked meerschaum. In passing by Tobin kicks her foot without intentions, and, being polite to ladies when in drink, he tries to give his hat a twist while apologizing. But he knocks it off, and the wind carries it overboard.

Tobin came back and sat down, and I began to look out for him, for the man's adversities were becoming frequent. He was apt, when pushed so close by hard luck, to kick the best dressed man he could see, and try to take command of the boat.

Presently Tobin grabs my arm and says, excited: 'Jawn,' says he, 'do ye know what we're doing? We're taking a voyage upon the water.'

'There now,' says I; 'subdue yeself. The boat'll land in ten minutes more.'

'Look,' says he, 'at the light lady upon the bench. And have ye forgotten the nigger man that burned me ear? And isn't the money I had gone – a dollar sixty-five it was?'

I thought he was no more than summing up his catastrophes so as to get violent with good excuse, as men will do, and I tried to make him understand such things was trifles.

'Listen,' says Tobin. 'Ye've no ear for the gift of prophecy or the miracles of the inspired. What did the palmist lady tell ye out of me hand? 'Tis coming true before your eyes. "Look out," says she, "for a dark man and a light woman; they'll bring ye trouble." Have ye forgot the nigger man, though he got some of it back from me fist? Can ye show me a lighter woman than the blonde lady that was the cause of me hat falling in the water? And where's the dollar sixty-five I had in me vest when we left the shooting gallery?'

The way Tobin put it, it did seem to corroborate the art of prediction, though it looked to me that these accidents could happen to any one at Coney without the implication of palmistry.

Tobin got up and walked around on deck, looking close at the passengers out of his little red eyes. I asked him the interpretation of his movements. Ye never know what Tobin has in his mind until he begins to carry it out.

'Ye should know,' says he, 'I'm working out the salvation promised by the lines in me palm. I'm looking for the crooked-nosed man that's to bring the good luck. 'Tis all that will save us. Jawn, did ye ever see a straighter-nosed gang of hellions in the days of your life?'

'Twas the nine-thirty boat, and we landed and walked up-town through Twenty-second Street, Tobin being without his hat.

On a street corner, standing under a gas-light and looking over the elevated road at the moon, was a man. A long man he was, dressed decent, with a segar between his teeth, and I saw that his nose made two twists from bridge to end, like the wriggle of a snake. Tobin saw it at the same time, and I heard him breathe hard like a horse when you take the saddle off. He went straight up to the man, and I went with him.

'Good-night to ye,' Tobin says to the man. The man takes out a segar and passes the compliments, sociable.

'Would ye hand us your name,' asks Tobin, 'and let us look at the size of it? It may be our duty to become acquainted with ye.'

'My name,' says the man, polite, 'is Friedenhausman – Maximus G. Friedenhausman.'

' 'Tis the right length,' says Tobin. 'Do you spell it with an "o" anywhere down the stretch of it?'

'I do not,' says the man.

'*Can* ye spell it with an "o"?' inquires Tobin, turning anxious.

'If your conscience,' says the man with the nose, 'is indisposed toward foreign idioms ye might, to please yourself, smuggle the letter into the penultimate syllable.'

' 'Tis well,' says Tobin. 'Ye're in the presence of Jawn Malone and Daniel Tobin.'

' 'Tis highly appreciated,' says the man, with a bow. 'And now since I cannot conceive that ye would hold a spelling bee upon the street corner, will ye name some reasonable excuse for being at large?'

'By the two signs,' answers Tobin, trying to explain, 'which ye display according to the reading of the Egyptian palmist from the sole of me hand, ye've been nominated to offset with good luck the lines of trouble leading to the nigger man and the blonde lady with her feet crossed in the boat, besides the financial loss of a dollar sixty-five, all so far fulfilled according to Hoyle.'

The man stopped smoking and looked at me.

'Have ye any amendments,' he asks, 'to offer to that statement, or are ye one too? I thought by the looks of ye ye might have him in charge.'

'None,' says I to him, 'except that as one horseshoe resembles another so are ye the picture of good luck as predicted by the hand of me friend. If not, then the lines of Danny's hand may have been crossed, I don't know.'

'There's two of ye,' says the man with the nose, looking up and down for the sight of a policeman. 'I've enjoyed your company immense. Goodnight.'

With that he shoves his segar in his mouth and moves across the street, stepping fast. But Tobin sticks close to one side of him and me at the other.

'What!' says he, stopping on the opposite sidewalk and pushing back his hat; 'do ye follow me? I tell ye,' he says, very loud, 'I'm proud to have met ye. But it is my desire to be rid of ye. I am off to me home.'

'Do,' says Tobin, leaning against his sleeve. 'Do be off to your home. And I will sit at the door of it till ye come out in the morning. For the dependence is upon ye to obviate the curse of the nigger man and the blonde lady and the financial loss of the one-sixty-five.'

' 'Tis a strange hallucination,' says the man, turning to me as a more reasonable lunatic. 'Hadn't ye better get him home?'

'Listen, man,' says I to him. 'Daniel Tobin is as sensible as he ever was. Maybe he is a bit deranged on account of having drink enough to disturb but not enough to settle his wits, but he is no more than following out the legitimate path of his superstitions and predicaments, which I will explain to you.' With that I relates the facts about the palmist lady and how the finger of suspicion points to him as an instrument of good fortune. 'Now, understand,' I concludes, 'my position in this riot. I am the friend of me friend Tobin, according to me interpretations. 'Tis easy to be a friend to the prosperous, for it pays; 'tis not hard to be friend to the poor, for ye get puffed up by gratitude and have your picture printed standing in front of a tenement with a scuttle of coal and an orphan in each hand. But it strains the art of friendship to be true friend to a born fool. And that's what I'm doing,' says I, 'for, in my opinion, there's no fortune to be read from the palm of me hand that wasn't printed there with the handle of a pick. And, though ye've got the crookedest nose in New York City, I misdoubt that all the fortune-tellers doing business could milk good luck from ye. But the lines of Danny's hand pointed to ye fair, and I'll assist him to experiment with ye until he's convinced ye're dry.'

After that the man turns, sudden, to laughing. He leans against a corner and laughs considerable. Then he claps me and Tobin on the backs of us and takes us by an arm apiece.

' 'Tis my mistake,' says he. 'How could I be expecting anything so fine and wonderful to be turning the corner upon me? I came near being found unworthy. Hard by,' says he, 'is a café, snug and suitable for the entertainment of idiosyncrasies. Let us go there and have a drink while we discuss the unavailability of the categorical.'

So saying, he marched me and Tobin to the back room of a saloon, and ordered the drinks, and laid the money on the table. He looks at me and Tobin like brothers of his, and we have the segars.

'Ye must know,' says the man of destiny, 'that me walk in life is one that is called the literary. I wander abroad be night seeking idiosyncrasies in the masses and truth in the heavens above. When ye came upon me I was in contemplation of the elevated road in conjunction with the chief luminary of night. The rapid transit is poetry and art: the moon but a tedious, dry body, moving by rote. But these are private opinions, for, in the business of literature, the conditions are reversed. 'Tis me hope to be writing a book to explain the strange things I have discovered in life.'

'Ye will put me in a book,' says Tobin, disgusted; 'will ye put me in a book?'

'I will not,' says the man, 'for the covers will not hold ye. Not yet. The best I can do is to enjoy ye meself, for the time is not ripe for destroying the limitations of print. Ye would look fantastic in type. All alone by meself must I drink this cup of joy. But, I thank ye, boys; I am truly grateful.'

'The talk of ye,' says Tobin, blowing through his moustache and pounding the table with his fist, 'is an eyesore to me patience. There was good luck promised out of the crook of your nose, but ye bear fruit like the bag of a drum. Ye resemble, with your noise of books, the wind blowing through a crack. Sure, now, I would be thinking the palm of me hand lied but for the coming true of the nigger man and the blonde lady and—'

'Whist!' says the long man; 'would ye be led astray by physiognomy? Me nose will do what it can within bounds. Let us have these glasses filled again, for 'tis good to keep idiosyncrasies well moistened, they being subject to deterioration in a dry moral atmosphere.'

So, the man of literature makes good, to my notion, for he pays, cheerful, for everything, the capital of me and Tobin being exhausted by prediction. But Tobin is sore, and drinks quiet, with the red showing in his eye.

By and by we moved out, for 'twas eleven o'clock, and stands a bit upon the sidewalk. And then the man says he must be going home, and invites me and Tobin to walk that way. We arrives on a side street two blocks away where there is a stretch of brick houses with high stoops and iron fences. The man stops at one of them and looks up at the top windows which he finds dark.

' 'Tis me humble dwelling,' says he, 'and I begin to perceive by the signs that me wife has retired to slumber. Therefore I will venture a bit in the way of hospitality. 'Tis me wish that ye enter the basement room, where we dine, and partake of a reasonable refreshment. There will be some fine cold fowl and cheese and a bottle or two of ale. Ye will be welcome to enter and eat, for I am indebted to ye for diversions.'

The appetite and conscience of me and Tobin was congenial to the proposition, though 'twas sticking hard in Danny's superstitions to think that a few drinks and a cold lunch should represent the good fortune promised by the palm of his hand.

'Step down the steps,' says the man with the crooked nose, 'and I will enter by the door above and let ye in. I will ask the new girl we have in the kitchen,' says he, 'to make ye a pot of coffee to drink before ye go. 'Tis fine coffee Katie Mahorner makes for a green girl just landed three months. Step in,' says the man, 'and I'll send her down to ye.'

THE GIFT OF THE MAGI

ONE DOLLAR AND EIGHTY-SEVEN CENTS. That was all. And sixty cents of it was in pennies. Pennies saved one and two at a time by bulldozing the grocer and the vegetable man and the butcher until one's cheeks burned with the silent imputation of parsimony that such close dealing implied. Three times Della counted it. One dollar and eighty-seven cents. And the next day would be Christmas.

There was clearly nothing to do but flop down on the shabby little couch and howl. So Della did it. Which instigates the moral reflection that life is made up of sobs, sniffles, and smiles, with sniffles predominating.

While the mistress of the home is gradually subsiding from the first stage to the second, take a look at the home. A furnished flat at $8 per week. It did not exactly beggar description, but it certainly had that word on the lookout for the mendicancy squad.

In the vestibule below was a letter-box into which no letter would go, and

an electric button from which no mortal finger could coax a ring. Also
appertaining thereunto was a card bearing the name 'Mr. James Dillingham
Young.'

The 'Dillingham' had been flung to the breeze during a former period of
prosperity when its possessor was being paid $30 per week. Now, when the
income was shrunk to $20, the letters of 'Dillingham' looked blurred, as
though they were thinking seriously of contracting to a modest and unas-
suming D. But whenever Mr. James Dillingham Young came home and
reached his flat above he was called 'Jim' and greatly hugged by Mrs. James
Dillingham Young, already introduced to you as Della. Which is all very
good.

Della finished her cry and attended to her cheeks with the powder rag.
She stood by the window and looked out dully at a gray cat walking a gray
fence in a gray backyard. Tomorrow would be Christmas Day, and she had
only $1.87 with which to buy Jim a present. She had been saving every
penny she could for months, with this result. Twenty dollars a week doesn't
go far. Expenses had been greater than she had calculated. They always are.
Only $1.87 to buy a present for Jim. Her Jim. Many a happy hour she had
spent planning for something nice for him. Something fine and rare and
sterling – something just a little bit near to being worthy of the honor of
being owned by Jim.

There was a pier-glass between the windows of the room. Perhaps you
have seen a pier-glass in an $8 flat. A very thin and very agile person may,
by observing his reflection in a rapid sequence of longitudinal strips, obtain
a fairly accurate conception of his looks. Della, being slender, had mastered
the art.

Suddenly she whirled from the window and stood before the glass. Her
eyes were shining brilliantly, but her face had lost its color within twenty
seconds. Rapidly she pulled down her hair and let it fall to its full length.

Now, there were two possessions of the James Dillingham Youngs in
which they both took a mighty pride. One was Jim's gold watch that had
been his father's and his grandfather's. The other was Della's hair. Had the
Queen of Sheba lived in the flat across the airshaft, Della would have let her
hair hang out the window some day to dry just to depreciate Her Majesty's
jewels and gifts. Had King Solomon been the janitor, with all his treasures
piled up in the basement, Jim would have pulled out his watch every time
he passed, just to see him pluck at his beard from envy.

So now Della's beautiful hair fell about her rippling and shining like a
cascade of brown waters. It reached below her knee and made itself almost
a garment for her. And then she did it up again nervously and quickly. Once
she faltered for a minute and stood still while a tear or two splashed on the
worn red carpet.

On went her old brown jacket; on went her old brown hat. With a whirl
of skirts and with the brilliant sparkle still in her eyes, she fluttered out the
door and down the stairs to the street.

Where she stopped the sign read: 'Mme. Sofronie. Hair Goods of All Kinds.'
One flight up Della ran, and collected herself, panting. Madame, large, too
white, chilly, hardly looked the 'Sofronie.'

'Will you buy my hair?' asked Della.

'I buy hair,' said Madame. 'Take yer hat off and let's have a sight at the
looks of it.'

Down rippled the brown cascade.

'Twenty dollars,' said Madame, lifting the mass with a practised hand.

'Give it to me quick,' said Della.

Oh, and the next two hours tripped by on rosy wings. Forget the hashed metaphor. She was ransacking the stores for Jim's present.

She found it at last. It surely had been made for Jim and no one else. There was no other like it in any of the stores, and she had turned all of them inside out. It was a platinum fob chain simple and chaste in design, properly proclaiming its value by substance alone and not by meretricious ornamentation – as all good things should do. It was even worthy of The Watch. As soon as she saw it she knew that it must be Jim's. It was like him. Quietness and value – the description applied to both. Twenty-one dollars they took from her for it, and she hurried home with the 87 cents. With that chain on his watch Jim might be properly anxious about the time in any company. Grand as the watch was, he sometimes looked at it on the sly on account of the old leather strap that he used in place of a chain.

When Della reached home her intoxication gave way a little to prudence and reason. She got out her curling irons and lighted the gas and went to work repairing the ravages made by generosity added to love. Which is always a tremendous task, dear friends – a mammoth task.

Within forty minutes her head was covered with tiny, close-lying curls that made her look wonderfully like a truant schoolboy. She looked at her reflection in the mirror long, carefully, and critically.

'If Jim doesn't kill me,' she said to herself, 'before he takes a second look at me, he'll say I look like a Coney Island chorus girl. But what could I do – oh! what could I do with a dollar and eighty-seven cents?'

At 7 o'clock the coffee was made and the frying-pan was on the back of the stove hot and ready to cook the chops.

Jim was never late. Della doubled the fob chain in her hand and sat on the corner of the table near the door that he always entered. Then she heard his step on the stair away down on the first flight, and she turned white for just a moment. She had a habit of saying little silent prayers about the simplest everyday things, and now she whispered: 'Please God, make him think I am still pretty.'

The door opened and Jim stepped in and closed it. He looked thin and very serious. Poor fellow, he was only twenty-two – and to be burdened with a family! He needed a new overcoat and he was without gloves.

Jim stopped inside the door, as immovable as a setter at the scent of quail. His eyes were fixed upon Della, and there was an expression in them that she could not read, and it terrified her. It was not anger, nor surprise, nor disapproval, nor horror, nor any of the sentiments that she had been prepared for. He simply stared at her fixedly with that peculiar expression on his face.

Della wriggled off the table and went for him.

'Jim, darling,' she cried, 'don't look at me that way. I had my hair cut off and sold it because I couldn't have lived through Christmas without giving you a present. It'll grow out again – you won't mind, will you? I just had to do it. My hair grows awfully fast. "Merry Christmas!" Jim, and let's be happy. You don't know what a nice – what a beautiful, nice gift I've got for you.'

'You've cut off your hair?' asked Jim, laboriously, as if he had not arrived at that patent fact yet even after the hardest mental labor.

'Cut it off and sold it,' said Della. 'Don't you like me just as well, anyhow? I'm me without my hair, ain't I?'

Jim looked about the room curiously.

'You say your hair is gone?' he said, with an air almost of idiocy.

'You needn't look for it,' said Della. 'It's sold, I tell you – sold and gone, too. It's Christmas Eve, boy. Be good to me, for it went for you. Maybe the hairs on my head were numbered,' she went on with a sudden serious sweetness, 'but nobody could ever count my love for you. Shall I put the chops on, Jim?'

Out of his trance Jim seemed quickly to wake. He enfolded his Della. For ten seconds let us regard with discreet scrutiny some inconsequential object in the other direction. Eight dollars a week or a million a year – what is the difference? A mathematician or a wit would give you the wrong answer. The magi brought valuable gifts, but that was not among them. This dark assertion will be illuminated later on.

Jim drew a package from his overcoat pocket and threw it upon the table.

'Don't make any mistake, Dell,' he said, 'about me. I don't think there's anything in the way of a haircut or a shave or a shampoo that could make me like my girl any less. But if you'll unwrap that package you may see why you had me going a while at first.'

White fingers and nimble tore at the string and paper. And then an ecstatic scream of joy; and then, alas! a quick feminine charge to hysterical tears and wails, necessitating the immediate employment of all the comforting powers of the lord of the flat.

For there lay The Combs – the set of combs, side and back, that Della had worshipped for long in a Broadway window. Beautiful combs, pure tortoise shell, with jewelled rims – just the shade to wear in the beautiful vanished hair. They were expensive combs, she knew, and her heart had simply craved and yearned over them without the least hope of possession. And now, they were hers, but the tresses that should have adorned the coveted adornments were gone.

But she hugged them to her bosom, and at length she was able to look up with dim eyes and a smile and say: 'My hair grows so fast, Jim!'

And then Della leaped up like a little singed cat and cried, 'Oh, oh!'

Jim had not yet seen his beautiful present. She held it out to him eagerly upon her open palm. The dull precious metal seemed to flash with a reflection of her bright and ardent spirit.

'Isn't it a dandy, Jim? I hunted all over town to find it. You'll have to look at the time a hundred times a day now. Give me your watch. I want to see how it looks on it.'

Instead of obeying, Jim tumbled down on the couch and put his hands under the back of his head and smiled.

'Dell,' said he, 'let's put our Christmas presents away and keep 'em a while. They're too nice to use just at present. I sold the watch to get the money to buy your combs. And now suppose you put the chops on.'

The magi, as you know, were wise men – wonderfully wise men – who brought gifts to the Babe in the manger. They invented the art of giving Christmas presents. Being wise, their gifts were no doubt wise ones, possibly bearing the privilege of exchange in case of duplication. And here I have lamely related to you the uneventful chronicle of two foolish children in a flat who most unwisely sacrificed for each other the greatest treasures of their house. But in a last word to the wise of these days let it be said that of all who give gifts these two were the wisest. Of all who give and receive gifts, such as they are wisest. Everywhere they are wisest. They are the magi.

A COSMOPOLITE IN A CAFÉ

AT MIDNIGHT THE CAFÉ was crowded. By some chance the little table at which I sat had escaped the eye of incomers, and two vacant chairs at it extended their arms with venal hospitality to the influx of patrons.

And then a cosmopolite sat in one of them, and I was glad, for I held a theory that since Adam no true citizen of the world has existed. We hear of them, and we see foreign labels on much luggage, but we find travellers instead of cosmopolites.

I invoke your consideration of the scene – the marble-topped tables, the range of leather-upholstered wall seats, the gay company, the ladies dressed in demi-state toilets, speaking in an exquisite visible chorus of taste, economy, opulence or art; the sedulous and largess-loving *garçons*, the music wisely catering to all with its raids upon the composers; the *mélange* of talk and laughter – and, if you will, the Würzburger in the tall glass cones that bend to your lips as a ripe cherry sways on its branch to the beak of a robber jay. I was told by a sculptor from Mauch Chunk that the scene was truly Parisian.

My cosmopolite was named E. Rushmore Coglan, and he will be heard from next summer at Coney Island. He is to establish a new 'attraction' there, he informed me, offering kingly diversion. And then his conversation rang along parallels of latitude and longitude. He took the great, round world in his hand, so to speak, familiarly, contemptuously, and it seemed no larger than the seed of a Maraschìno cherry in a *table d'hôte* grape fruit. He spoke disrespectfully of the equator, he skipped from continent to continent, he derided the zones, he mopped up the high seas with his napkin. With a wave of his hand he would speak of a certain bazaar in Hyderabad. Whiff! He would have you on skis in Lapland. Zip! Now you rode the breakers with the Kanakas at Kealaikahiki. Presto! He dragged you through an Arkansas post-oak swamp, let you dry for a moment on the alkali plains of his Idaho ranch, then whirled you into the society of Viennese archdukes. Anon he would be telling you of a cold he acquired in a Chicago lake breeze and how old Escamila cured it in Buenos Ayres with a hot infusion of the *chuchula* weed. You would have addressed a letter to "E. Rushmore Coglan, Esq., the Earth, Solar System, the Universe,' and mailed it, feeling confident that it would be delivered to him.

I was sure that I had found at least one true cosmopolite since Adam, and I listened to his world-wide discourse fearful lest I should discover in it the local note of the mere globe-trotter. But his opinion never fluttered or drooped; he was as impartial to cities, countries, and continents as the winds or gravitation.

And as E. Rushmore Coglan prattled of this little planet I thought with glee of a great almost-cosmopolite who wrote for the whole world and dedicated himself to Bombay. In a poem he has to say that there is pride and rivalry between the cities of the earth, and that 'the men that breed from them, they traffic up and down, but cling to their cities' hem as a child to the mother's gown.' And whenever they walk 'by roaring streets unknown' they remember their native city 'most faithful, foolish, fond: making her mere-breathed name their bond upon their bond.' And my glee was roused because I had caught Mr. Kipling napping. Here I had found a man not made from dust; one who had no narrow boasts of birthplace or country, one who, if he bragged at all, would brag of his whole round globe against the Martians and the inhabitants of the Moon.

Expression on these subjects was precipitated from E. Rushmore Coglan by the third corner to our table. While Coglan was describing to me the topography along the Siberian Railway the orchestra glided into a medley. The concluding air was 'Dixie,' and as the exhilarating notes tumbled forth they were almost overpowered by a great clapping of hands from almost every table.

It is worth a paragraph to say that this remarkable scene can be witnessed every evening in numerous cafés in the City of New York. Tons of brew have been consumed over theories to account for it. Some have conjectured hastily that all Southerners in town hie themselves to cafés at nightfall. This applause of the 'rebel' air in a Northern city does puzzle a little; but it is not insolvable. The war with Spain, many years' generous mint and watermelon crops, a few long-shot winners at the New Orleans race track, and the brilliant banquets given by the Indiana and Kansas citizens who compose the Night Carolina Society have made the South rather a 'fad' in Manhattan. Your manicure will lisp softly that your left forefinger reminds her so much of a gentleman's in Richmond, Va. Oh, certainly; but many a lady has to work now – the war, you know.

When 'Dixie' was being played a dark-haired young man sprang up from somewhere with a Mosby guerrilla yell and waved frantically his soft-brimmed hat. Then he strayed through the smoke, dropped into the vacant chair at our table and pulled out cigarettes.

The evening was at the period when reserve is thawed. One of us mentioned three Würzburgers to the waiter; the dark-haired young man acknowledged his inclusion in the order by a smile and a nod. I hastened to ask him a question because I wanted to try out a theory I had.

'Would you mind telling me,' I began, 'whether you are from—'

The fist of E. Rushmore Coglan banged the table and I was jarred into silence.

'Excuse me,' said he, 'but that's a question I never like to hear asked. What does it matter where a man is from? Is it fair to judge a man by his post-office address? Why, I've seen Kentuckians who hated whiskey, Virginians who weren't descended from Pocohontas, Indianians who hadn't written a novel, Mexicans who didn't wear velvet trousers with silver dollars sewed along the seams, funny Englishmen, spendthrift Yankees, cold-blooded Southerners, narrow-minded Westerners, and New Yorkers who were too busy to stop for an hour on the street to watch a one-armed grocer's clerk do up cranberries in paper bags. Let a man be a man and don't handicap him with the label of any section.'

'Pardon me,' I said, 'but my curiosity was not altogether an idle one. I know the South, and when the band plays "Dixie" I like to observe. I have formed the belief that the man who applauds that air with special violence and ostensible sectional loyalty is invariably a native of either Secaucus, N. J., or the district between Murray Hill Lyceum and the Harlem River, this city.

I was about to put my opinion to the test by inquiring of this gentleman when you interrupted with your own – larger theory, I must confess.'

And now the dark-haired young man spoke to me, and it became evident that his mind also moved along its own set of grooves.

'I should like to be a periwinkle,' said he, mysteriously, 'on the top of a valley, and sing too-ralloo-ralloo.'

This was clearly too obscure, so I turned again to Coglan.

'I've been around the world twelve times,' said he. 'I know an Esquimau in Upernavik who sends to Cincinnati for his neckties, and I saw a goat-herder in Uruguay who won a prize in a Battle Creek breakfast food puzzle competition. I pay rent on a room in Cairo, Egypt, and another in Yokahama all the year around. I've got slippers waiting for me in a tea-house in Shanghai, and I don't have to tell 'em how to cook my eggs in Rio Janeiro or Seattle. It's a mighty little old world. What's the use of bragging about being from the North, or the South, or the old manor house in the dale, or Euclid Avenue, Cleveland, or Pike's Peak, or Fairfax County, Va., or Hooligan's Flats or any place? It'll be a better world when we quit being fools about some mildewed town or ten acres of swampland just because we happened to be born there.'

'You seem to be a genuine cosmopolite,' I said, admiringly. 'But it also seems that you would decry patriotism.'

'A relic of the stone age,' declared Cogland, warmly. 'We are all brothers – Chinamen, Englishmen, Zulus, Patagonians and the people in the bend of the Kaw River. Some day all this pretty pride in one's city or state or section or country will be wiped out, and we'll all be citizens of the world, as we ought to be.'

'But while you are wandering in foreign lands,' I persisted, 'do not your thoughts revert to some spot – some dear and —'

'Nary a spot,' interrupted E. R. Coglan, flippantly. 'The terrestrial, globular, planetary hunk of matter, slightly flattened at the poles, and known as the Earth, is my abode. I've met a good many object-bound citizens of this country abroad. I've seen men from Chicago sit in a gondola in Venice on a moonlight night and brag about their drainage canal. I've seen a Southerner on being introduced to the King of England hand that monarch, without batting his eyes, the information that his grand-aunt on his mother's side was related by marriage to the Perkinses, of Charleston. I knew a New Yorker who was kidnapped for ransom by some Afghanistan bandits. His people sent over the money and he came back to Kabul with the agent. "Afghanistan?" the natives said to him through an interpreter. "Well, not so slow, do you think?" "Oh, I don't know,' says he, and he begins to tell them about a cab driver at Sixth Avenue and Broadway. Those ideas don't suit me. I'm not tied down to anything that isn't 8,000 miles in diameter. Just put me down as E. Rushmore Coglan, citizen of the terrestrial sphere.'

My cosmopolite made a large adieu and left me, for he thought he saw some one through the chatter and smoke whom he knew. So I was left with the would-be periwinkle, who was reduced to Würzburger without further ability to voice his aspirations to perch, melodious, upon the summit of a valley.

I sat reflecting upon my evident cosmopolite and wondering how the poet had managed to miss him. He was my discovery and I believed in him. How was it? 'The men that breed from them they traffic up and down, but cling to their cities' hem as a child to the mother's gown.'

Not so E. Rushmore Coglan. With the whole world for his—

My meditations were interrupted by a tremendous noise and conflict in another part of the café. I saw above the heads of the seated patrons E. Rushmore Coglan and a stranger to me engaged in terrific battle. They fought between the tables like Titans, and glasses crashed, and men caught their hats up and were knocked down, and a brunette screamed, and a blonde began to sing 'Teasing.'

My cosmopolite was sustaining the pride and reputation of the Earth when the waiters closed in on both combatants with their famous flying wedge formation and bore them outside, still resisting.

I called McCarthy, one of the French *garçons*, and asked him the cause of the conflict.

'The man with the red tie' (that was my cosmopolite), said he, 'got hot on account of things said about the bum sidewalks and water supply of the place he come from by the other guy.'

'Why,' said I, bewildered, 'that man is a citizen of the world – a cosmopolite. He—'

'Originally from Mattawamkeag, Maine, he said,' continued McCarthy, 'and he wouldn't stand for no knockin' the place.'

BETWEEN ROUNDS

THE MAY MOON SHONE BRIGHT upon the private boarding-house of Mrs. Murphy. By reference to the almanac a large amount of territory will be discovered upon which its rays also fell. Spring was in its heyday, with hay fever soon to follow. The parks were green with new leaves and buyers for the Western and Southern trade. Flowers and summer-resort agents were blowing; the air and answers to Lawson were growing milder; hand-organs, fountains and pinochle were playing everywhere.

The windows of Mrs. Murphy's boarding-house were open. A group of boarders were seated on the high stoop upon round, flat mats like German pancakes.

In one of the second-floor front windows Mrs. McCaskey awaited her husband. Supper was cooling on the table. Its heat went into Mrs. McCaskey.

At nine McCaskey came. He carried his coat on his arm and his pipe in his teeth; and he apologized for disturbing the boarders on the steps as he selected spots of stone between them on which to set his size 9, width Ds.

As he opened the door of his room he received a surprise. Instead of the usual stove-lid or potato-masher for him to dodge, came only words.

Mr. McCaskey reckoned that the benign May moon had softened the breast of his spouse.

'I heard ye,' came the oral substitutes for kitchenware. 'Ye can apollygize to riff-raff of the streets for settin' yer unhandy feet on the tails of their frocks, but ye'd walk on the neck of yer wife the length of a clothesline without so much as a "Kiss me fut," and I'm sure it's that long from rubberin' out the windy for ye and the victuals cold such as there's money to buy after drinkin' up yer wages at Gallegher's every Saturday evenin', and the gas man here twice to-day for his.'

'Woman,' said Mr. McCaskey, dashing his coat and hat upon a chair, 'the noise of ye is an insult to me appetite. When ye run down politeness ye take the mortar from between the bricks of the foundations of society. 'Tis no more than exercisin' the acrimony of a gentleman when we ask the dissent of ladies blockin' the way for steppin' between them. Will ye bring the pig's face of ye out of the windy and see to the food?'

Mrs. McCaskey arose heavily and went to the stove. There was something in her manner that warned Mr. McCaskey. When the corners of her mouth went down suddenly like a barometer it usually foretold a fall of crockery and tinware.

'Pig's face, is it?' said Mrs. McCaskey, and hurled a stewpan full of bacon and turnips at her lord.

Mr. McCaskey was no novice at repartee. He knew what should follow the entrée. On the table was a roast sirloin of pork, garnished with shamrocks. He retorted with this, and drew the appropriate return of a bread pudding in an earthen dish. A hunk of Swiss cheese accurately thrown by her husband struck Mrs. McCaskey below one eye. When she replied with a well-aimed coffee-pot full of a hot, black, semi-fragrant liquid the battle, according to courses, should have ended.

But Mr. McCaskey was no 50-cent *table d'hôter*. Let cheap Bohemians consider coffee the end, if they would. Let them make that *faux pas*. He was foxier still. Finger-bowls were not beyond the compass of his experience. They were not to be had in the Pension Murphy; but their equivalent was at hand. Triumphantly he sent the granite-ware wash-basin at the head of his matrimonial adversary. Mrs. McCaskey dodged in time. She reached for a flatiron, with which, as a sort of cordial, she hoped to bring the gastronomical duel to a close. But a loud, wailing scream downstairs caused both her and Mr. McCaskey to pause in a sort of involuntary armistice.

On the sidewalk at the corner of the house Policeman Cleary was standing with one ear upturned, listening to the crash of household utensils.

' 'Tis Jawn McCaskey and his missis at it again,' meditated the policeman. 'I wonder shall I go up and stop the row. I will not. Married folks they are; and few pleasures they have. 'Twill not last long. Sure, they'll have to borrow more dishes to keep it up with.'

And just then came the loud scream below stairs, betokening fear or dire extremity. ' 'Tis probably the cat,' said Policeman Cleary, and walked hastily in the other direction.

The boarders on the steps were fluttered. Mr. Toomey, an insurance solicitor by birth and an investigator by profession, went inside to analyze the scream. He returned with the news that Mrs. Murphy's little boy, Mike, was lost. Following the messenger, out bounced Mrs. Murphy – two hundred pounds in tears and hysterics, clutching the air and howling to the sky for the loss of thirty pounds of freckles and mischief. Bathos, truly; but Mr. Toomey sat down at the side of Miss Purdy, millinery, and their hands came together in sympathy. The two old maids, Misses Walsh, who complained every day about the noise in the halls, inquired immediately if anybody had looked behind the clock.

Major Griggs, who sat by his fat wife on the top step, arose and buttoned his coat. 'The little one lost?' he exclaimed. 'I will scour the city.' His wife never allowed him out after dark. But now she said: 'Go, Ludovic!' in a baritone voice. 'Whoever can look upon that mother's grief without springing to her relief has a heart of stone.' 'Give me some thirty or – sixty cents, my love,' said the Major. 'Lost children sometimes stray far. I may need car-fares.'

Old man Denny, hall room, fourth floor back, who sat on the lowest step, trying to read a paper by the street lamp, turned over a page to follow up the article about the carpenter's strike. Mrs. Murphy shrieked to the moon: 'Oh, ar-r-Mike, f'r Gawd's sake, where is me little bit av a boy?'

'When'd ye see him last?' asked old man Denny, with one eye on the report of the Building Trades League.

'Oh,' wailed Mrs. Murphy, ' 'twas yesterday, or maybe four hours ago! I dunno. But it's lost he is, me little boy Mike. He was playin' on the sidewalk only this mornin' – or was it Wednesday? I'm that busy with work, 'tis hard to keep up with dates. But I've looked the house over from top to cellar, and it's gone he is. Oh, for the love av Hiven—'

Silent, grim, colossal, the big city has ever stood against its revilers. They call it hard as iron; they say that no pulse of pity beats in its bosom; they compare its streets with lonely forests and deserts of lava. But beneath the hard crust of the lobster is found a delectable and luscious food. Perhaps a different simile would have been wiser. Still, nobody should take offence. We would call no one a lobster without good and sufficient claws.

No calamity so touches the common heart of humanity as does the straying of a little child. Their feet are so uncertain and feeble; the ways are so steep and strange.

Major Griggs hurried down to the corner, and up the avenue into Billy's place. 'Gimme a rye-high,' he said to the servitor. 'Haven't seen a bow-legged, dirty-faced little devil of a six-year-old lost kid around here anywhere, have you?'

Mr. Toomey retained Miss Purdy's hand on the steps. 'Think of that dear dear little babe,' said Miss Purdy, 'lost from his mother's side – perhaps already fallen beneath the iron hoofs of galloping steeds – oh, isn't it dreadful?'

'Ain't that right?' agreed Mr. Toomey, squeezing her hand. 'Say I start out and help look for um!'

'Perhaps,' said Miss Purdy, 'you should. But, oh, Mr. Toomey, you are so dashing – so reckless – suppose in your enthusiasm some accident should befall you, then what—'

Old man Denny read on about the arbitration agreement, with one finger on the lines.

In the second floor front Mr. and Mrs. McCaskey came to the window to recover their second wind. Mr. McCaskey was scooping turnips out of his vest with a crooked forefinger, and his lady was wiping an eye that the salt of the roast pork had not benefited. They heard the outcry below, and thrust their heads out of the window.

' 'Tis little Mike is lost,' said Mrs. McCaskey, in a hushed voice, 'the beautiful, little, trouble-making angel of a gossoon!'

'The bit of a boy mislaid?' said Mr. McCaskey, leaning out of the window. 'Why, now, that's bad enough, entirely. The childer, they be different. If 'twas a woman I'd be willin', for they leave peace behind 'em when they go.'

Disregarding the thrust, Mrs. McCaskey caught her husband's arm.

'Jawn,' she said, sentimentally, 'Missis Murphy's little bye is lost. 'Tis a great city for losing little boys. Six years old he was. Jawn, 'tis the same age our little bye would have been if we had had one six years ago.'

'We never did,' said Mr. McCaskey, lingering with the fact.

'But if we had, Jawn, think what sorrow would be in our hearts this night, with out little Phelan run away and stolen in the city nowheres at all.'

'Ye talk foolishness,' said Mr. McCaskey. ' 'Tis Pat he would be named, after me old father in Cantrim.'

'Ye lie!' said Mrs. McCaskey, without anger. 'Me brother was worth tin dozen bog-trotting McCaskeys. After him would the bye be named.' She leaned over the window-sill and looked down at the hurrying and bustle below.

'Jawn,' said Mrs. McCaskey, softly, 'I'm sorry I was hasty wid ye.'

' 'Twas hasty puddin', as ye say,' said her husband, 'and hurry-up turnips and get-a-move-on-ye coffee. 'Twas what ye could call a quick lunch, all right, and tell no lie.'

Mrs. McCaskey slipped her arm inside her husband's and took his rough hand in hers.

'Listen at the cryin' of poor Mrs. Murphy,' she said. ' 'Tis an awful thing for a bit of a bye to be lost in this great big city. If 'twas our little Phelan, Jawn, I'd be breakin' me heart.'

Awkwardly Mr. McCaskey withdrew his hand. But he laid it around the nearing shoulder of his wife.

' 'Tis foolishness, of course,' said he, roughly, 'but I'd be cut up some meself if our little – Pat was kidnapped or anything. But there never was any children for us. Sometimes I've been ugly and hard with ye, Judy. Forget it.'

They leaned together, and looked down at the heart-drama being acted below.

Long they sat thus. People surged along the sidewalk, crowding, questioning, filling the air with rumors, and inconsequent surmises. Mrs. Murphy plowed back and forth in their midst, like a soft mountain down which plunged an audible cataract of tears. Couriers came and went.

Loud voices and a renewed uproar were raised in front of the boarding-house.

'What's up now, Judy?' asked Mr. McCaskey.

' 'Tis Missis Murphy's voice,' said Mrs. McCaskey, harking. 'She says she's after finding little Mike asleep behind the roll of linoleum under the bed in her room.'

Mr. McCaskey laughed loudly.

'That's yer Phelan,' he shouted, sardonically. 'Divil a bit would a Pat have done that trick. If the bye we never had is strayed and stole, by the powers, call him Phelan, and see him hide out under the bed like a mangy pup.'

Mrs. McCaskey arose heavily, and went toward the dish closet, with the corners of her mouth drawn down.

Policeman Cleary came back around the corner as the crowd dispersed. Surprised, he upturned an ear toward the McCaskey apartment, where the crash of irons and chinaware and the ring of hurled kitchen utensils seemed as loud as before. Policeman Cleary took out his timepiece.

'By the deported snakes!' he exclaimed. 'Jawn McCaskey and his lady have been fightin' for an hour and a quarter by the watch. The missis could give him forty pounds weight. Strength to his arm.'

Policeman Cleary strolled back around the corner.

Old man Denny folded his paper and hurried up the steps just as Mrs.
Murphy was about to lock the door for the night.

THE SKYLIGHT ROOM

FIRST MRS. PARKER WOULD SHOW you the double parlors. You would not dare to
interrupt her description of their advantages and of the merits of the
gentleman who had occupied them for eight years. Then you would manage
to stammer forth the confession that you were neither a doctor nor a dentist.
Mrs. Parker's manner of receiving the admission was such that you could
never afterward entertain the same feeling toward your parents, who had
neglected to train you up in one of the professions that fitted Mrs. Parker's
parlors.

Next you ascended one flight of stairs and looked at the second-floor-back
at $8. Convinced by her second-floor manner that it was worth the $12 that
Mr. Toosenberry always paid for it until he left to take charge of his brother's
orange plantation in Florida near Palm Beach, where Mrs. McIntyre always
spent the winters that had the double front room with private bath, you
managed to babble that you wanted something still cheaper.

If you survived Mrs. Parker's scorn, you were taken to look at Mr. Skidder's
large hall room on the third floor. Mr. Skidder's room was not vacant. He
wrote plays and smoked cigarettes in it all day long. But every room-hunter
was made to visit his room to admire the lambrequins. After each visit, Mr.
Skidder, from the fright caused by possible eviction, would pay something
on his rent.

Then – oh, then – if you still stood on one foot, with your hot hand
clutching the three moist dollars in your pocket, and hoarsely proclaimed
your hideous and culpable poverty, nevermore would Mrs. Parker be cicerone
of yours. She would honk loudly the word 'Clara,' she would show you her
back, and march downstairs. Then Clara, the colored maid, would escort you
up to the carpeted ladder that served for the fourth flight, and show you the
Skylight Room. It occupied 7 × 8 feet of floor space in the middle of the hall.
On each side of it was a dark lumber closet or storeroom.

In it was an iron cot, a washstand and a chair. A shelf was the dresser. Its
four bare walls seemed to close in upon you like the sides of a coffin. Your
hand crept to your throat, you gasped, you looked up as from a well – and
breathed once more. Through the glass of the little skylight you saw a square
of blue infinity.

'Two dollars, suh,' Clara would say in her half-contemptuous, half-
Tuskegeenial tones.

One day Miss Leeson came hunting for a room. She carried a typewriter
made to be lugged around by a much larger lady. She was a very little girl,
with eyes and hair that had kept on growing after she had stopped and that
always looked as if they were saying: 'Goodness me! Why didn't you keep
up with us?'

Mrs. Parker showed her the double parlors. 'In this closet,' she said, 'one
could keep a skeleton or anaesthetic or coal —'

'But I am neither a doctor nor a dentist,' said Miss Leeson, with a shiver.

Mrs. Parker gave her the incredulous, pitying, sneering, icy stare that she kept for those who failed to qualify as doctors or dentists, and led the way to the second-floor-back.

'Eight dollars?' said Miss Leeson. 'Dear me! I'm not Hetty if I do look green. I'm just a poor little working girl. Show me something higher and lower.'

Mr. Skidder jumped and strewed the floor with cigarette stubs at the rap on his door.

'Excuse me, Mr. Skidder,' said Mrs. Parker, with her demon's smile at his pale looks. 'I didn't know you were in. I asked the lady to have a look at your lambrequins.'

'They're too lovely for anything,' said Miss Leeson, smiling in exactly the way the angels do.

After they had gone Mr. Skidder got very busy erasing the tall, black-haired heroine from his latest (unproduced) play and inserted a small, roguish one with heavy, bright hair and vivacious features.

'Anna Held'll jump at it,' said Mr. Skidder to himself, putting his feet up against the lambrequins and disappearing in a cloud of smoke like an aërial cuttlefish.

Presently the tocsin call of 'Clara!' sounded to the world the state of Miss Leeson's purse. A dark goblin seized her, mounted a Stygian stairway, thrust her into a vault with a glimmer of light in its top and muttered the menacing and cabalistic words 'Two dollars!'

'I'll take it!' sighed Miss Leeson, sinking down upon the squeaky iron bed.

Every day Miss Leeson went out to work. At night she brought home papers with handwriting on them and made copies with her typewriter. Sometimes she had no work at night, and then she would sit on the steps of the high stoop with the other roomers. Miss Leeson was not intended for a skylight room when the plans were drawn for her creation. She was gay-hearted and full of tender, whimsical fancies. Once she let Mr. Skidder read to her three acts of his great (unpublished) comedy, 'It's No Kid; or, The Heir of the Subway.'

There was rejoicing among the gentlemen roomers whenever Miss Leeson had time to sit on the steps for an hour or two. But Miss Longnecker, the tall blonde who taught in a public school and said, 'Well, really!' to everything you said, sat on the top step and sniffed. And Miss Dorn, who shot at the moving ducks at Coney every Sunday and worked in a department store, sat on the bottom step and sniffed. Miss Leeson sat on the middle step and the men would quickly group around her.

Especially Mr. Skidder, who had cast her in his mind for the star part in a private, romantic (unspoken) drama in real life. And especially Mr. Hoover, who was forty-five, fat, flush and foolish. And especially very young Mr. Evans, who set up a hollow cough to induce her to ask him to leave off cigarettes. The men voted her 'the funniest and jolliest ever,' but the sniffs on the top step and the lower step were implacable.

I pray you to let the drama halt while Chorus stalks to the footlights and drops an epicedian tear upon the fatness of Mr. Hoover. Tune the pipes to the tragedy of tallow, the bane of bulk, the calamity of corpulence. Tried out, Falstaff might have rendered more romance to the ton than would have Romeo's rickety ribs to the ounce. A lover may sigh, but he must not puff. To the train of Momus are the fat men remanded. In vain beats the faithfullest heart above a 52-inch belt. Avaunt, Hoover! Hoover, forty-five, flush and foolish, might carry off Helen herself; Hoover, forty-five, flush, foolish and fat is meat for perdition. There was never a chance for you, Hoover.

As Mrs. Parker's roomers sat thus one summer's evening, Miss Leeson looked up into the firmament and cried with her little gay laugh:

'Why, there's Billy Jackson! I can see him from down here, too.'

All looked up – some at the windows of skyscrapers, some casting about for an airship, Jackson-guided.

'It's that star,' explained Miss Leeson, pointing with a tiny finger. 'Not the big one that twinkes – the steady blue one near it. I can see it every night through my skylight. I named it Billy Jackson.'

'Well, really!' said Miss Longnecker. 'I didn't know you were an astronomer, Miss Leeson.'

'Oh, yes,' said the small star gazer, 'I know as much as any of them about the style of sleeves they're going to wear next fall in Mars.'

'Well, really!' said Miss Longnecker. 'The star you refer to is Gamma, of the constellation Cassiopeia. It is nearly of the second magnitude, and its meridian passage is—'

'Oh,' said the very young Mr. Evans, 'I think Billy Jackson is a much better name for it.'

'Same here,' said Mr. Hoover, loudly breathing defiance to Miss Longnecker. 'I think Miss Leeson has just as much right to name stars as any of those old astrologers had.'

'Well, really!' said Miss Longnecker.

'I wonder whether it's a shooting star,' remarked Miss Dorn. 'I hit nine ducks and a rabbit out of ten in the gallery at Coney Sunday.'

'He doesn't show up very well from down here,' said Miss Leeson. 'You ought to see him from my room. You know you can see stars even in the daytime from the bottom of a well. At night my room is like the shaft of a coal mine, and it makes Billy Jackson look like the big diamond pin that Night fastens her kimono with.'

There came a time after that when Miss Leeson brought no formidable papers home to copy. And when she went out in the morning, instead of working, she went from office to office and let her heart melt away in the drip of cold refusals transmitted through insolent office boys. This went on.

There came an evening when she wearily climbed Mrs. Parker's stoop at the hour when she always returned from her dinner at the restaurant. But she had had no dinner.

As she stepped into the hall Mr. Hoover met her and seized his chance. He asked her to marry him, and his fatness hovered above her like an avalanche. She dodged, and caught the balustrade. He tried for her hand, and she raised it and smote him weakly in the face. Step by step she went up, dragging herself by the railing. She passed Mr. Skidder's door as he was red-inking a stage direction for Myrtle Delorme (Miss Leeson) in his (unaccepted) comedy, to 'pirouette across the stage from L to the side of the Count.' Up the carpeted ladder she crawled at last and opened the door of the skylight room.

She was too weak to light the lamp or to undress. She fell upon the iron cot, her fragile body scarcely hollowing the worn springs. And in that Erebus of a room she slowly raised her heavy eyelids, and smiled.

For Billy Jackson was shining down on her, calm and bright and constant through the skylight. There was no world about her. She was sunk in a pit of blackness, with but that small square of pallid light framing the star that she had so whimsically and oh, so ineffectually, named. Miss Longnecker must be right: it was Gamma, of the constellation Cassiopeia, and not Billy Jackson. And yet she could not let it be Gamma.

As she lay on her back, she tried twice to raise her arm. The third time she got two thin fingers to her lips and blew a kiss out of the black pit to Billy Jackson. Her arm fell back limply.

'Good-bye, Billy,' she murmured, faintly. 'You're millions of miles away and you won't even twinkle once. But you kept where I could see you most of the time up there when there wasn't anything else but darkness to look at, didn't you? . . . Millions of miles. . . . Good-bye, Billy Jackson.'

Clara, the colored maid, found the door locked at 10 the next day, and they forced it open. Vinegar, and the slapping of wrists and burnt feathers proving of no avail, some one ran to 'phone for an ambulance.

In due time it backed up to the door with much gong-clanging, and the capable young medico, in his white linen coat, ready, active, confident, with his smooth face half debonair, half grim, danced up the steps.

'Ambulance call to 49,' he said, briefly. 'What's the trouble?'

'Oh, yes, doctor,' sniffed Mrs. Parker, as though her trouble that there should be trouble in the house was the greater. 'I can't think what can be the matter with her. Nothing we could do would bring her to. It's a young woman, a Miss Elsie – yes, a Miss Elsie Leeson. Never before in my house —'

'What room?' cried the doctor in a terrible voice, to which Mrs. Parker was a stranger.

'The skylight room. It—'

Evidently the ambulance doctor was familiar with the location of skylight rooms. He was gone up the stairs, four at a time. Mrs. Parker followed slowly, as her dignity demanded.

On the first landing she met him coming back bearing the astronomer in his arms. He stopped and let loose the practised scalpel of his tongue, not loudly. Gradually Mrs. Parker crumpled as a stiff garment that slips down from a nail. Ever afterwards there remained crumples in her mind and body. Sometimes her curious roomers would ask her what the doctor said to her.

'Let that be,' she would answer. 'If I can get forgiveness for having heard it I will be satisfied.'

The ambulance physician strode with his burden through the pack of hounds that follow the curiosity chase, and even they fell back along the sidewalk abashed, for his face was that of one who bears his own dead.

They noticed that he did not lay down upon the bed prepared for it in the ambulance the form that he carried, and all that he said was: 'Drive like h—l, Wilson,' to the driver.

That is all. Is it a story? In the next morning's paper I saw a little news item, and the last sentence of it may help you (as it helped me) to weld the incidents together.

It recounted the reception into Bellevue Hospital of a young woman who had been removed from No. 49 East — Street, suffering from debility induced by starvation. It concluded with these words:

'Dr. William Jackson, the ambulance physician who attended the case, says the patient will recover.'

A SERVICE OF LOVE

WHEN ONE LOVES ONE'S ART no service seems too hard.

That is our premise. This story shall draw a conclusion from it, and show at the same time that the premise is incorrect. That will be a new thing in logic, and a feat in story-telling somewhat older than the great wall of China.

Joe Larrabee came out of the post-oak flats of the Middle West pulsing with a genius for pictorial art. At six he drew a picture of the town pump with a prominent citizen passing it hastily. This effort was framed and hung in the drug-store window by the side of the ear of corn with an uneven number of rows. At twenty he left for New York with a flowing necktie and a capital tied up somewhat closer.

Delia Caruthers did things in six octaves so promisingly in a pine-tree village in the South that her relatives chipped in enough in her chip hat for her to go 'North' and 'finish.' They could not see her f—, but that is our story.

Joe and Delia met in an atelier where a number of art and music students had gathered to discuss chiaroscuro, Wagner, music, Rembrandt's works, pictures, Waldteufel, wall paper, Chopin and Oolong.

Joe and Delia became enamored one of the other, or each of the other, as you please, and in a short time were married – for (see above), when one loves one's Art no service seems too hard.

Mr. and Mrs. Larrabee began housekeeping in a flat. It was a lonesome flat – something like the A sharp way down at the left-hand end of the keyboard. And they were happy; for they had their Art, and they had each other. And my advice to the rich young man would be – sell all thou hast, and give it to the poor – janitor for the privilege of living in a flat with your Art and your Delia.

Flat-dwellers shall indorse my dictum that theirs is the only true happiness. If a home is happy it cannot fit too close – let the dresser collapse and become a billiard table; let the mantel turn to a rowing machine, the escritoire to a spare bedchamber, the washstand to an upright piano; let the four walls come together, if they will, so you and your Delia are between. But if home be the other kind, let it be wide and long – enter you at the Golden Gate, hang your hat on Hatteras, your cape on Cape Horn and go out by the Labrador.

Joe was painting in the class of the great Magister – you know his fame. His fees are high; his lessons are light – his high-lights have brought him renown. Delia was studying under Rosenstock – you know his repute as a disturber of the piano keys.

They were mighty happy as long as their money lasted. So is every – but I will not be cynical. Their aims were very clear and defined. Joe was to become capable very soon of turning out pictures that old gentlemen with thin side-whiskers and thick pocketbooks would sandbag one another in his studio for the privilege of buying. Delia was to become familiar and then contemptuous with Music, so that when she saw the orchestra seats and boxes unsold she could have sore throat and lobster in a private dining-room and refuse to go on the stage.

But the best, in my opinion, was the home life in the little flat – the ardent, voluble chats after the day's study; the cozy dinners and fresh, light breakfasts; the interchange of ambitions – ambitions interwoven each with the other's or else inconsiderable – the mutual help and inspiration; and – overlook my artlessness – stuffed olives and cheese sandwiches at 11 p.m.

But after a while Art flagged. It sometimes does, even if some switchman doesn't flag it. Everything going out and nothing coming in, as the vulgarians say. Money was lacking to pay Mr. Magister and Herr Rosenstock their prices. When one loves one's Art no service seems too hard. So, Delia said she must give music lessons to keep the chafing dish bubbling.

For two or three days she went out canvassing for pupils. One evening she came home elated.

'Joe, dear,' she said, gleefully, 'I've a pupil. And, oh, the loveliest people. General – General A. B. Pinkney's daughter – on Seventy-first Street. Such a splendid house, Joe – you ought to see the front door! Byzantine I think you would call it. And inside! Oh, Joe, I never saw any thing like it before.

'My pupil is his daughter Clementina. I dearly love her already. She's a delicate thing – dresses always in white; and the sweetest, simplest manners! Only eighteen years old. I'm to give three lessons a week; and, just think, Joe! $5 a lesson. I don't mind it a bit; for when I get two or three more pupils I can resume my lessons with Herr Rosenstock. Now, smooth out that wrinkle between your brows, dear, and let's have a nice supper.'

'That's all right for you, Dele,' said Joe, attacking a can of peas with a carving knife and a hatchet, 'but how about me? Do you think I'm going to let you hustle for wages while I philander in the regions of high art? Not by the bones of Benvenuto Cellini! I guess I can sell papers or lay cobblestones, and bring in a dollar or two.'

Delia came and hung about his neck.

'Joe, dear, you are silly. You must keep on at your studies. It is not as if I had quit my music and gone to work at something else. While I teach I learn. I am always with my music. And we can live as happily as millionaires on $15 a week. You mustn't think of leaving Mr. Magister.'

'All right,' said Joe, reaching for the blue scalloped vegetable dish. 'But I hate for you to be giving lessons. It isn't Art. But you're a trump and a dear to do it.'

'When one loves one's Art no service seems too hard,' said Delia.

'Magister praised the sky in that sketch I made in the park,' said Joe. 'And Tinkle gave me permission to hang two of them in his window. I may sell one if the right kind of a moneyed idiot sees them.'

'I'm sure you will,' said Delia, sweetly. 'And now let's be thankful for Gen. Pinkney and this veal roast.'

During all of the next week the Larrabees had an early breakfast. Joe was enthusiastic about some morning-effect sketches he was doing in Central Park, and Delia packed him off breakfasted, coddled, praised and kissed at 7 o'clock. Art is an engaging mistress. It was most times 7 o'clock when he returned in the evening.

At the end of the week Delia, sweetly proud but languid, triumphantly tossed three five-dollar bills on the 8 × 10 (inches) centre table of the 8 × 10 (feet) flat parlor.

'Sometimes,' she said, a little wearily, 'Clementina tries me. I'm afraid she doesn't practise enough, and I have to tell her the same things so often. And then she always dresses entirely in white, and that does get monotonous. But

Gen. Pinkney is the dearest old man! I wish you could know him, Joe. He comes in sometimes when I am with Clementina at the piano – he is a widower, you know – and stands there pulling his white goatee. ''And how are the semiquavers and the demisemiquavers progressing?'' he always asks.

'I wish you could see the wainscoting in that drawing room, Joe! And those Astrakhan rug portières. And Clementina has such a funny little cough. I hope she is stronger than she looks. Oh, I really am getting attached to her, she is so gentle and high bred. Gen. Pinkney's brother was once Minister to Bolivia.'

And then Joe, with the air of Monte Cristo, drew forth a ten, a five, a two and a one – all legal tender notes – and laid them beside Delia's earnings.

'Sold that watercolor of the obelisk to a man from Peoria,' he announced, overwhelmingly.

'Don't joke with me,' said Delia – 'not from Peoria!'

'All the way. I wish you could see him, Dele. Fat man with a woolen muffler and a quill toothpick. He saw the sketch in Tinkle's window and thought it was a windmill at first. He was game, though, and bought it anyhow. He ordered another – an oil sketch of the Lackawanna freight depot – to take back with him. Music lessons! Oh, I guess Art is still in it.'

'I'm so glad you've kept on,' said Delia, heartily. 'You're bound to win, dear. Thirty-three dollars! We never had so much to spend before. We'll have oysters tonight.'

'And filet mignon with champignons,' said Joe. 'Where is the olive fork?'

On the next Saturday evening Joe reached home first. He spread his $18 on the parlor table and washed what seemed to be a great deal of dark paint from his hands.

Half an hour later Delia arrived, her right hand tied up in a shapeless bundle of wraps and bandages.

'How is this?' asked Joe after the usual greetings. Delia laughed, but not very joyously.

'Clementina,' she explained, 'insisted upon a Welsh rabbit after her lesson. She is such a queer girl. Welsh rabbits at 5 in the afternoon. The General was there. You should have seen him run for the chafing dish, Joe, just as if there wasn't a servant in the house. I know Clementina isn't in good health; she is so nervous. In serving the rabbit she spilled a great lot of it, boiling hot, over my hand and wrist. It hurt awfully, Joe. And the dear girl was so sorry! But Gen. Pinkney! – Joe, that old man nearly went distracted. He rushed downstairs and sent somebody – they said the furnace man or somebody in the basement – out to a drug store for some oil and things to bind it up with. It doesn't hurt so much now.'

'What's this?' asked Joe, taking the hand tenderly and pulling at some white strands beneath the bandages.

'It's something soft,' said Delia, 'that had oil on it. Oh, Joe, did you sell another sketch?' She had seen the money on the table.

'Did I?' said Joe; 'just ask the man from Peoria. He got his depot to-day, and he isn't sure but he thinks he wants another parkscape, and a view on the Hudson. What time this afternoon did you burn your hand, Dele?'

'Five o'clock, I think,' said Dele, plaintively. 'The iron – I mean the rabbit came off the fire about that time. You ought to have seen Gen. Pinkney, Joe, when —'

'Sit down here a moment, Dele,' said Joe. He drew her to the couch, sat beside her and put his arm across her shoulders.

'What have you been doing for the last two weeks, Dele?' he asked.

She braved it for a moment or two with an eye full of love and stubborness, and murmured a phrase or two vaguely of Gen. Pinkney; but at length down went her head and out came the truth and tears.

'I couldn't get any pupils,' she confessed. 'And I couldn't bear to have you give up your lessons; and I got a place ironing shirts in that big Twenty-fourth Street laundry. And I think I did very well to make up both General Pinkney and Clementina, don't you, Joe? And when a girl in the laundry set down a hot iron on my hand this afternoon I was all the way home making up that story about the Welsh rabbit. You're not angry, are you, Joe? And if I hadn't got the work you mightn't have sold your sketches to that man from Peoria.'

'He wasn't from Peoria,' said Joe, slowly.

'Well, it doesn't matter where he was from. How clever you are, Joe – and – kiss me, Joe – and what made you ever suspect that I wasn't giving music lessons to Clementina?'

'I didn't,' said Joe, 'until to-night. And I wouldn't have then, only I sent up this cotton waste and oil from the engine-room this afternoon for a girl upstairs who had her hand burned with a smoothing-iron. I've been firing the engine in that laundry for the last two weeks.'

'And then you didn't—'

'My purchaser from Peoria,' said Joe, 'and Gen. Pinkney are both creations of the same art – but you wouldn't call it either painting or music.'

And then they both laughed, and Joe began:

'When one loves one's Art no service seems—'

But Delia stopped him with her hand on his lips. 'No,' she said – 'just "When one loves." '

THE COMING-OUT OF MAGGIE

EVERY SATURDAY NIGHT the Clover Leaf Social Club gave a hop in the hall of the Give and Take Athletic Association on the East Side. In order to attend one of these dances you must be a member of the Give and Take – or, if you belong to the division that starts off with the right foot in waltzing, you must work in Rhinegold's paper-box factory. Still, any Clover Leaf was privileged to escort or be escorted by an outsider to a single dance. But mostly each Give and Take brought the paper-box girl that he affected; and few strangers could boast of having shaken a foot at the regular hops.

Maggie Toole, on account of her dull eyes, broad mouth and left-handed style of footwork in the two-step, went to the dances with Anna McCarty and her 'fellow.' Anna and Maggie worked side by side in the factory, and were the greatest chums ever. So Anna always made Jimmy Burns take her by Maggie's house every Saturday night so that her friend could go to the dance with them.

The Give and Take Athletic Association lived up to its name. The hall of the association in Orchard Street was fitted out with muscle-making inventions. With the fibres thus builded up the members were wont to engage the police and rival social athletic organizations in joyous combat. Between these more serious occupations the Saturday night hops with the paper-box factory girls came as a refining influence and as an efficient screen. For sometimes the tip went 'round, and if you were among the elect that tiptoed up the dark back stairway you might see as neat and satisfying a little welter-weight affair to a finish as ever happened inside the ropes.

On Saturdays Rhinegold's paper-box factory closed at 3 p.m. On one such afternoon Anna and Maggie walked homeward together. At Maggie's door Anna said, as usual: 'Be ready at seven sharp, Mag, and Jimmy and me'll come by for you.'

But what was this? Instead of the customary humble and grateful thanks from the non-escorted one there was to be perceived a high poised head, a prideful dimpling at the corners of a broad mouth, and almost a sparkle in a dull brown eye.

'Thanks, Anna,' said Maggie; 'but you and Jimmy needn't bother to-night. I've a gentleman friend that's coming round to escort me to the hop.'

The comely Anna pounced upon her friend, shook her, chided and beseeched her. Maggie Toole catch a fellow! Plain, dear, loyal, unattractive Maggie, so sweet as a chum so unsought for a two-step or a moonlit bench in the little park. How was it? When did it happen? Who was it?

'You'll see to-night,' said Maggie, flushed with the wine of the first grapes she had gathered in Cupid's vineyard. 'He's swell all right. He's two inches taller than Jimmy, and an up-to-date dresser. I'll introduce him, Anna, just as soon as we get to the hall.'

Anna and Jimmy were among the first Clover Leafs to arrive that evening. Anna's eyes were brightly fixed upon the door of the hall to catch the first glimpse of her friend's 'catch.'

At 8.30 Miss Toole swept into the hall with the escort. Quickly her triumphant eye discovered her chum under the wing of her faithful Jimmy.

'Oh, gee!' cried Anna, 'Mag ain't made a hit – oh, no! Swell fellow? well, I guess! Style? Look at 'um.'

'Go as far as you like,' said Jimmy, with sandpaper in his voice. 'Cop him out if you want him. These new guys always win out with the push. Don't mind me. He don't squeeze all the lines, I guess. Huh!'

'Shut up, Jimmy. You know what I mean. I'm glad for Mag. First fellow she ever had. Oh, here they come.'

Across the floor Maggie sailed like a coquettish yacht convoyed by a stately cruiser. And truly, her companion justified the encomiums of the faithful chum. He stood two inches taller than the average Give and Take athlete; his dark hair curled; his eyes and his teeth flashed whenever he bestowed his frequent smiles. The young men of the Clover Leaf Club pinned not their faith to the graces of person as much as they did to its prowess, its achievements in hand-to-hand conflicts, and its preservation from the legal duress that constantly menaced it. The member of the association who would bind a paper-box maiden to his conquering chariot scorned to employ Beau Brummell airs. They were not considered honorable methods of warfare. The swelling biceps, the coat straining at its buttons over the chest, the air of conscious conviction of the supereminence of the male in the cosmogony of creation, even a calm display of bow legs as subduing and enchanting agents in the gentle tourneys of Cupid – these were the approved arms and ammunition of the Clover Leaf gallants. They viewed, then, the genuflexions and alluring poses of this visitor with their chins at a new angle.

'A friend of mine, Mr. Terry O'Sullivan,' was Maggie's formula of introduction. She led him around the room, presenting him to each new-arriving Clover Leaf. Almost was she pretty now, with the unique luminosity in her eyes that comes to a girl with her first suitor and a kitten with its first mouse.

'Maggie Toole's got a fellow at last,' was the word that went round among the paper-box girls. 'Pipe Mag's floor-walker' – thus the Give and Takes expressed their indifferent contempt.

Usually at the weekly hops Maggie kept a spot on the wall warm with her back. She felt and showed so much gratitude whenever a self-sacrificing partner invited her to dance that his pleasure was cheapened and diminished. She had even grown used to noticing Anna joggle the reluctant Jimmy with her elbow as a signal for him to invite her chum to walk over his feet through a two-step.

But to-night the pumpkin had turned to a coach and six. Terry O'Sullivan was a victorious Prince Charming, and Maggie Toole winged her first butterfly flight. And though our tropes of fairyland be mixed with those of entomology they shall not spill one drop of ambrosia from the rose-crowned melody of Maggie's one perfect night.

The girls besieged her for introduction to her 'fellow.' The Clover Leaf young men, after two years of blindness, suddenly perceived charms in Miss Toole. They flexed their compelling muscles before her and bespoke her for the dance.

Thus she scored; but to Terry O'Sullivan the honors of the evening fell thick and fast. He shook his curls; he smiled and went easily through the seven motions for acquiring grace in your own room before an open window ten minutes each day. He danced like a faun; he introduced manner and style and atmosphere; his words came trippingly upon his tongue, and – he waltzed twice in succession with the paper-box girl that Dempsey Donovan brought.

Dempsey was the leader of the association. He wore a dress suit, and could chin the bar twice with one hand. He was one of 'Big Mike' O'Sullivan's lieutenants, and was never troubled by trouble. No cop dared to arrest him. Whenever he broke a pushcart man's head or shot a member of the Heinrick B. Sweeney Outing and Literary Association in the kneecap, an officer would drop around and say:

'The Cap'n'd like to see ye a few minutes round to the office whin ye have time, Dempsey, me boy.'

But there would be sundry gentlemen there with large gold fob chains and black cigars; and somebody would tell a funny story, and then Dempsey would go back and work half an hour with the six-pound dumbbells. So, doing a tight-rope act on a wire stretched across Niagara was a safe terpsichorean performance compared with waltzing twice with Dempsey Donovan's paper-box girl. At 10 o'clock the jolly round face of 'Big Mike' O'Sullivan shone at the door for five minutes upon the scene. He always looked in for five minutes, smiled at the girls and handed out real perfectos to the delighted boys.

Dempsey Donovan was at his elbow instantly, talking rapidly. 'Big Mike' looked carefully at the dancers, smiled, shook his head and departed.

The music stopped. The dancers scattered to the chairs along the walls.

Terry O'Sullivan, with his entrancing bow, relinquished a pretty girl in blue to her partner and started back to find Maggie. Dempsey intercepted him in the middle of the floor.

Some fine instinct that Rome must have bequeathed to us caused nearly every one to turn and look at them – there was a subtle feeling that two gladiators had met in the arena. Two or three Give and Takes with tight coat sleeves drew nearer.

'One moment, Mr. O'Sullivan,' said Dempsey. 'I hope you're enjoying yourself. Where did you say you lived?'

The two gladiators were well matched. Dempsey had, perhaps, ten pounds of weight to give away. The O'Sullivan had breadth and quickness. Dempsey had a glacial eye, a dominating slit of mouth, an indestructible jaw, a complexion like a belle's and the coolness of a champion. The visitor showed more fire in his contempt and less control over his conspicuous sneer. They were enemies by the law written when the rocks were molten. They were each too splendid, too mighty, too incomparable to divide pre-eminence. One only must survive.

'I live on Grand,' said O'Sullivan, insolently; 'and no trouble to find me at home. Where do you live?'

Dempsey ignored the question.

'You say your name's O'Sullivan,' he went on. 'Well, "Big Mike" says he never saw you before.'

'Lots of things he never saw,' said the favorite of the hop.

'As a rule,' went on Dempsey, huskily sweet, 'O'Sullivans in this district know one another. You escorted one of our lady members here, and we want a chance to make good. If you've got a family tree let's see a few historical O'Sullivan buds come out on it. Or do you want us to dig it out of you by the roots?'

'Suppose you mind your own business,' suggested O'Sullivan, blandly.

Dempsey's eye brightened. He held up an inspired forefinger as though a brilliant idea had struck him.

'I've got it now,' he said, cordially. 'It was just a little mistake. You ain't no O'Sullivan. You are a ring-tailed monkey. Excuse us for not recognizing you at first.'

O'Sullivan's eye flashed. He made a quick movement, but Andy Geoghan was ready and caught his arm.

Dempsey nodded at Andy and William McMahan, the secretary of the club, and walked rapidly toward a door at the rear of the hall. Two other members of the Give and Take Association swiftly joined the little group. Terry O'Sullivan was now in the hands of the Board of Rules and Social Referees. They spoke to him briefly and softly, and conducted him out through the same door at the rear.

This movement on the part of the Clover Leaf members requires a word of elucidation. Back of the association hall was a small room rented by the club. In this room personal difficulties that arose on the ballroom floor were settled, man to man, with the weapons of nature, under the supervision of the Board. No lady could say that she had witnessed a fight at a Clover Leaf hop in several years. Its gentlemen members guaranteed that.

So easily and smoothly had Dempsey and the Board done their preliminary work that many in the hall had not noticed the checking of the fascinating

O'Sullivan's social triumph. Among these was Maggie. She looked about for her escort.

'Smoke up!' said Rose Cassidy. 'Wasn't you on? Demps Donovan picked a scrap with your Lizzie-boy, and they're waltzed out to the slaughter room with him. How's my hair look done up this way, Mag?'

Maggie laid a hand on the bosom of her cheese-cloth waist.

'Gone to fight with Dempsey!' she said, breathlessly. 'They've got to be stopped. Dempsey Donovan can't fight him. Why, he'll – he'll kill him!'

'Ah, what do you care?' said Rose. 'Don't some of 'em fight every hop?'

But Maggie was off, darting her zig-zag way through the maze of dancers. She burst through the rear door into the dark hall and then threw her solid shoulder against the door of the room of single combat. It gave way, and in the instant that she entered her eye caught the scene – the Board standing about with open watches; Dempsey Donovan in his shirt sleeves dancing light-footed, with the wary grace of the modern pugilist, within easy reach of his adversary; Terry O'Sullivan standing with arms folded and a murderous look in his dark eyes. And without slacking the speed of her entrance she leaped forward with a scream – leaped in time to catch and hang upon the arm of O'Sullivan that was suddenly uplifted, and to whisk from it the long, bright stiletto that he had drawn from his bosom.

The knife fell and rang upon the floor. Cold steel drawn in the rooms of the Give and Take Association! Such a thing had never happened before. Every one stood motionless for a minute. Andy Geoghan kicked the stiletto with the toe of his shoe curiously, like an antiquarian who has come upon some ancient weapon unknown to his learning.

And then O'Sullivan hissed something unintelligible between his teeth. Dempsey and the Board exchanged looks. And then Dempsey looked at O'Sullivan without anger, as one looks at a stray dog, and nodded his head in the direction of the door. 'The back stairs, Giuseppi,' he said, briefly. 'Somebody'll pitch your hat down after you.'

Maggie walked up to Dempsey Donovan. There was a brilliant spot of red in her cheeks, down which slow tears were running. But she looked him bravely in the eye.

'I knew it, Dempsey,' she said, as her eyes grew dull even in their tears. 'I knew he was a Guinea. His name's Tony Spinelli. I hurried in when they told me you and him was scrappin'. Them Guineas always carries knives. But you don't understand, Dempsey. I never had a fellow in my life. I got tired of comin' with Anna and Jimmy every night, so I fixed it with him to call himself O'Sullivan, and brought him along. I knew there'd be nothin' doin' for him if he came as a Dago. I guess I'll resign from the club now.'

Dempsey turned to Andy Geoghan.

'Chuck that cheese slicer out of the window,' he said, 'and tell 'em inside that Mr. O'Sullivan has had a telephone message to go down to Tammany Hall.'

And then he turned back to Maggie.

'Say, Mag,' he said, 'I'll see you home. And how about next Saturday night? Will you come to the hop with me if I call around for you?'

It was remarkable how quickly Maggie's eyes could change from dull to a shining brown.

'With you, Dempsey?' she stammered. 'Say – will a duck swim?'

MAN ABOUT TOWN

THERE ARE TWO OR THREE THINGS that I wanted to know. I do not care about a mystery. So I began to inquire.

It took me two weeks to find out what women carry in dress suit cases. And then I began to ask why a mattress is made in two pieces. This serious query was at first received with suspicion because it sounded like a conundrum. I was at last assured that its double form of construction was designed to make lighter the burden of woman, who make up beds. I was so foolish as to persist, begging to know why, then, they were not made in two equal pieces; whereupon I was shunned.

The third draught that I craved from the fount of knowledge was enlightenment concerning the character known as A Man About Town. He was more vague in my mind than a type should be. We must have a concrete idea of anything, even if it be an imaginary idea, before we can comprehend it. Now, I have a mental picture of John Doe that is as clear as a steel engraving. His eyes are weak blue; he wears a brown vest and a shiny black serge coat. He stands always in the sunshine chewing something; and he keeps half-shutting his pocket knife and opening it again with his thumb. And, if the Man Higher Up is ever found, take my assurance for it, he will be a large, pale man with blue wristlets showing under his cuffs, and he will be sitting to have his shoes polished within sound of a bowling alley, and there will be somewhere about him turquoises.

But the canvas of my imagination, when it came to limning the Man About Town, was blank. I fancied that he had a detachable sneer (like the smile of the Cheshire cat) and attached cuffs; and that was all. Whereupon I asked a newspaper reporter about him.

'Why,' said he, 'a "Man About Town" is something between a "rounder" and a "clubman." He isn't exactly – well, he fits in between Mrs. Fish's receptions and private boxing bouts. He doesn't – well, he doesn't belong either to the Lotos Club or to the Jerry McGeoghegan Galvanized Iron Workers' Apprentices' Left Hook Chowder Association. I don't exactly know how to describe him to you. You'll see him everywhere there's anything doing. Yes, I suppose he's a type. Dress clothes every evening; knows the ropes; calls every policeman and waiter in town by their first names. No; he never travels with the hydrogen derivatives. You generally see him alone or with another man.'

My friend the reporter left me, and I wandered further afield. By this time the 3126 electric lights on the Rialto were alight. People passed, but they held me not. Paphian eyes rayed upon me, and left me unscathed. Diner, heimgangers, shop-girls, confidence men, panhandlers, actors, highwaymen, millionaires, and outlanders hurried, skipped, strolled, sneaked, swaggered, and scurried by me; but I took no note of them. I knew them all; I had read their hearts; they had served. I wanted my Man About Town. He was a type, and to drop him would be an error – a typograph – but no! let us continue.

Let us continue with a moral digression. To see a family reading the Sunday paper gratifies. The sections have been separated. Papa is earnestly scanning the page that pictures the young lady exercising before an open window, and bending – but there, there! Mamma is interested in trying to guess the missing letters in the word N–w Yo–k. The oldest girls are eagerly perusing the financial reports, for a certain young man remarked last Sunday night that he had taken a flyer in Q., X. & Z. Willie, the eighteen-year-old son, who attends the New York public school, is absorbed in the weekly article describing how to make over an old shirt, for he hopes to take a prize in sewing on graduation day.

Grandma is holding to the cosmic supplement with a two-hours', grip; and little Tottie, the baby, is rocking along the best she can with the real estate transfers. This view is intended to be reassuring, for it is desirable that a few lines of this story be skipped. For it introduces strong drink.

I went into a café to – and while it was being mixed I asked the man who grabs up your hot Scotch spoon as soon as you lay it down what he understood by the term, epithet, description, designation, characterization or appellation, viz.: a 'Man about Town.'

'Why,' said he, carefully, 'it means a fly guy that's wise to the all-night push – see? It's a hot sport that you can't bump to the rail anywhere between the Flatirons – see? I guess that's about what it means.'

I thanked him and departed.

On the sidewalk a Salvation lassie shook her contribution receptacle gently against my waistcoat pocket.

'Would you mind telling me,' I asked her, 'if you ever meet with the character commonly denominated as "A Man About Town" during your daily wanderings?'

'I think I know whom you mean,' she answered, with a gentle smile. 'We see them in the same places night after night. They are the devil's body guard, and if the soldiers of any army are as faithful as they are, their commanders are well served. We go among them, diverting a few pennies from their wickedness to the Lord's service.'

She shook the box again and I dropped a dime into it.

In front of a glittering hotel a friend of mine, a critic, was climbing from a cab. He seemed at leisure; and I put my question to him. He answered me conscientiously, as I was sure he would.

'There is a type of "Man About Town" in New York,' he answered. 'The term is quite familiar to me, but I don't think I was ever called upon to define the character before. It would be difficult to point you out an exact specimen. I would say, offhand, that it is a man who had a hopeless case of the peculiar New York disease of wanting to see and know. At 6 o'clock each day life begins with him. He follows rigidly the conventions of dress and manners; but in the business of poking his nose into places where he does not belong he could give pointers to a civet cat or a jackdaw. He is the man who has chased Bohemia about the town from rathskeller to roof garden and from Hester Street to Harlem until you can't find a place in the city where they don't cut their spaghetti with a knife. Your "Man About Town" has done that. He is always on the scent of something new. He is curiosity, impudence, and omnipresence. Hansoms were made for him, and gold-banded cigars; and the curse of music at dinner. There are not so many of him; but his minority report is adopted everywhere.

'I'm glad you brought up the subject; I've felt the influence of this nocturnal blight upon our city, but I never thought to analyze it before. I can see now that your "Man About Town" should have been classified long ago. In his wake spring up wine agents and cloak models; and the orchestra plays "Let's All Go Up to Maud's" for him, by request, instead of Händel. He makes his rounds every evening; while you and I see the elephant once a week. When the cigar store is raided, he winks at the officer, familiar with his ground, and walks away immune, while you and I search among the Presidents for names, and among the stars for addresses to give the desk sergeant.'

My friend, the critic, paused to acquire breath for fresh eloquence. I seized my advantage.

'You have classified him,' I cried with joy. 'You have painted his portrait in the gallery of city types. But I must meet one face to face. I must study the Man About Town at first hand. Where shall I find him? How shall I know him?'

Without seeming to hear me, the critic went on. And his cab-driver was waiting for his fare, too.

'He is the sublimated essence of Butt-in; the refined, intrinsic extract of Rubber; the concentrated, purified, irrefutable, unavoidable spirit of Curiosity and Inquisitiveness. A new sensation is the breath in his nostrils when his experience is exhausted he explores new fields with the indefatigability of a—'

'Excuse me,' I interrupted, 'but can you produce one of this type? It is a new thing to me. I must study it. I will search the town over until I find one. Its habitat must be here on Broadway.'

'I am about to dine here,' said my friend. 'Come inside, and if there is a Man About Town present I will point him out to you. I know most of the regular patrons here.'

'I am not dining yet,' I said to him. 'You will excuse me. I am going to find my Man About Town this night if I have to rake New York from the Battery to Little Coney Island.'

I left the hotel and walked down Broadway. The pursuit of my type gave a pleasant savor of life and interest to the air I breathed. I was glad to be in a city so great, so complex and diversified. Leisurely and with something of an air I strolled along with my heart expanding at the thought that I was a citizen of great Gotham, a sharer in its magnificence and pleasures, a partaker in its glory and prestige.

I turned to cross the street. I heard something buzz like a bee, and then I took a long, pleasant ride with Santos-Dumont.

When I opened my eyes I remembered a smell of gasoline, and I said aloud: 'Hasn't it passed yet?'

A hospital nurse laid a hand that was not particularly soft upon my brow that was not at all fevered. A young doctor came along, grinned, and handed me a morning newspaper.

'Want to see how it happened?' he asked, cheerily. I read the article. Its headlines began where I heard the buzzing leave off the night before. It closed with these lines:

'—Bellevue Hospital, where it was said that his injuries were not serious. He appeared to be a typical Man About Town.'

THE COP AND THE ANTHEM

ON HIS BENCH IN MADISON SQUARE Soapy moved uneasily. When wild geese honk high of nights, and when women without sealskin coats grow kind to their husbands, and when Soapy moves uneasily on his bench in the park, you may know that winter is near at hand.

A dead leaf fell in Soapy's lap. That was Jack Frost's card. Jack is kind to the regular denizens of Madison Square, and gives fair warning of his annual call. At the corners of four streets he hands his pasteboard to the North Wind, footman of the mansion of All Outdoors, so that the inhabitants thereof may make ready.

Soapy's mind became cognizant of the fact that the time had come for him to resolve himself into a singular Committee of Ways and Means to provide against the coming rigor. And therefore he moved uneasily on his bench.

The hibernatorial ambitions of Soapy were not of the highest. In them were no considerations of Mediterranean cruises, of soporific Southern skies or drifting in the Vesuvian Bay. Three months on the Island was what his soul craved. Three months of assured board and bed and congenial company, safe from Boreas and bluecoats, seemed to Soapy the essence of things desirable.

For years the hospitable Blackwell's had been his winter quarters. Just as his more fortunate fellow New Yorkers had bought their tickets to Palm Beach and the Riviera each winter, so Soapy had made his humble arrangements for his annual hegira to the Island. And now the time was come. On the previous night three Sabbath newspapers, distributed beneath his coat, about his ankles and over his lap, had failed to repulse the cold as he slept on his bench near the spurting fountain in the ancient square. So the Island loomed big and timely in Soapy's mind. He scorned the provisions made in the name of charity for the city's dependents. In Soapy's opinion the Law was more benign than Philanthropy. There was an endless round of institutions, municipal and eleemosynary, on which he might set out and receive lodging and food accordant with the simple life. But to one of Soapy's proud spirit the gifts of charity are encumbered. If not in coin you must pay in humiliation of spirit for every benefit received at the hands of philanthropy. As Caesar had his Brutus, every bed of charity must have its toll of a bath, every loaf of bread its compensation of a private and personal inquisition. Wherefore it is better to be a guest of the law, which, though conducted by rules, does not meddle unduly with a gentleman's private affairs.

Soapy, having decided to go to the Island, at once set about accomplishing his desire. There were many easy ways of doing this. The pleasantest was to dine luxuriously at some expensive restaurant; and then, after declaring insolvency, be handed over quietly and without uproar to a policeman. An accommodating magistrate would do the rest.

Soapy left his bench and strolled out of the square and across the level sea of asphalt, where Broadway and Fifth Avenue flow together. Up Broadway he turned, and halted at a glittering café, where are gathered together nightly the choicest products of the grape, the silkworm, and the protoplasm.

Soapy had confidence in himself from the lowest button of his vest upward.

He was shaven, and his coat was decent and his neat black, ready-tied four-in-hand had been presented to him by a lady missionary on Thanksgiving Day. If he could reach a table in the restaurant unsuspected, success would be his. The portion of him that would show above the table would raise no doubt in the waiter's mind. A roasted mallard duck, thought Soapy, would be about the thing – with a bottle of Chablis, and then Camembert, a demi-tasse and a cigar. One dollar for the cigar would be enough. The total would not be so high as to call forth any supreme manifestation of revenge from the café management; and yet the meat would leave him filled and happy for the journey to his winter refuge.

But as Soapy set foot inside the restaurant door the head waiter's eye fell upon his frayed trousers and decadent shoes. Strong and ready hands turned him about and conveyed him in silence and haste to the sidewalk and averted the ignoble fate of the menaced mallard.

Soapy turned off Broadway. It seemed that his route to the coveted Island was not to be an epicurean one. Some other way of entering limbo must be thought of.

At a corner of Sixth Avenue electric lights and cunningly displayed wares behind plate-glass made a shop window conspicuous. Soapy took a cobblestone and dashed it through the glass. People came running around the corner, a policeman in the lead. Soapy stood still, with his hands in his pockets, and smiled at the sight of brass buttons.

'Where's the man that done that?' inquired the officer, excitedly.

'Don't you figure out that I might have had something to do with it?' said Soapy, not without sarcasm, but friendly, as one greets good fortune.

The policeman's mind refused to accept Soapy even as a clue. Men who smash windows do not remain to parley with the law's minions. They take to their heels. The policeman saw a man halfway down the block running to catch a car. With drawn club he joined in the pursuit. Soapy, with disgust in his heart, loafed along, twice unsuccessful.

On the opposite side of the street was a restaurant of no great pretensions. It catered to large appetites and modest purses. Its crockery and atmosphere were thick; its soup and napery thin. Into this place Soapy took his accusive shoes and telltale trousers without challenge. At a table he sat and consumed beefsteak, flapjacks, doughnuts and pie. And then to the waiter he betrayed the fact that the minutest coin and himself were strangers.

'Now, get busy and call a cop,' said Soapy. 'And don't keep a gentleman waiting.'

'No cop for youse,' said the waiter, with a voice like butter cakes and an eye like the cherry in a Manhattan cocktail. 'Hey, Con!'

Neatly upon his left ear on the callous pavement two waiters pitched Soapy. He arose joint by joint, as a carpenter's rule opens, and beat the dust from his clothes. Arrest seemed but a rosy dream. The Island seemed very far away. A policeman who stood before a drug store two doors away laughed and walked down the street.

Five blocks Soapy travelled before his courage permitted him to woo capture again. This time the opportunity presented what he fatuously termed to himself a 'cinch.' A young woman of a modest and pleasing guise was standing before a show window gazing with sprightly interest at its display of shaving mugs and inkstands, and two yards from the window a large policeman of severe demeanor leaned against a water plug.

It was Soapy's design to assume the rôle of the despicable and execrated 'masher.' The refined and elegant appearance of his victim and the contiguity of the conscientious cop encouraged him to believe that he would soon feel the pleasant official clutch upon his arm that would insure his winter quarters on the right little, tight little isle.

Soapy straightened the lady missionary's ready-made tie, dragged his shrinking cuffs into the open, set his hat at a killing cant and sidled toward the young woman. He made eyes at her, was taken with sudden coughs and 'hems,' smiled, smirked and went brazenly through the impudent and contemptible litany of the 'masher.' With half an eye Soapy saw that the policeman was watching him fixedly. The young woman moved away a few steps, and again bestowed her absorbed attention upon the shaving mugs. Soapy followed, boldly stepping to her side, raised his hat and said:

'Ah there, Bedelia! Don't you want to come and play in my yard?'

The policeman was still looking. The persecuted young woman had but to beckon a finger and Soapy would be practically en route for his insular haven. Already he imagined he could feel the cozy warmth of the station-house. The young woman faced him and, stretching out a hand, caught Soapy's coat sleeve.

'Sure, Mike,' she said, joyfully, 'if you'll blow me to a pail of suds. I'd have spoke to you sooner, but the cop was watching.'

With the young woman playing the clinging ivy to his oak Soapy walked past the policeman overcome with gloom. He seemed doomed to liberty.

At the next corner he shook off his companion and ran. He halted in the district where by night are found the lightest streets, hearts, vows and librettos. Women in furs and men in greatcoats moved gaily in the wintry air. A sudden fear seized Soapy that some dreadful enchantment had rendered him immune to arrest. The thought brought a little of panic upon it, and when he came upon another policeman lounging grandly in front of a transplendent theatre he caught at the immediate straw of 'disorderly conduct.'

On the sidewalk Soapy began to yell drunken gibberish at the top of his harsh voice. He danced, howled, raved, and otherwise disturbed the welkin.

The policeman twirled his club, turned his back to Soapy and remarked to a citizen.

' 'Tis one of them Yale lads celebratin' the goose egg they give to the Hartford College. Noisy; but no harm. We've instructions to lave them be.'

Disconsolate, Soapy ceased his unavailing racket. Would never a policeman lay hands on him? In his fancy the Island seemed an unattainable Arcadia. He buttoned his thin coat against the chilling wind.

In a cigar store he saw a well-dressed man lighting a cigar at a swinging light. His silk umbrella he had set by the door on entering. Soapy stepped inside, secured the umbrella and sauntered off with it slowly. The man at the cigar light followed hastily.

'My umbrella,' he said, sternly.

'Oh, is it?' sneered Soapy, adding insult to petit larceny. 'Well, why don't you call a policeman? I took it. Your umbrella! Why don't you call a cop? There stands one on the corner.'

The umbrella owner slowed his steps. Soapy did likewise, with a presentiment that luck would again run against him. The policeman looked at the two curiously.

'Of course,' said the umbrella man – 'that is – well, you know how these mistakes occur – I – if it's your umbrella I hope you'll excuse me – I picked it up this morning in a restaurant – If you recognize it as yours, why – I hope you'll—'

'Of course it's mine,' said Soapy, viciously.

The ex-umbrella man retreated. The policeman hurried to assist a tall blonde in an opera cloak across the street in front of a street car that was approaching two blocks away.

Soapy walked eastward through a street damaged by improvements. He hurled the umbrella wrathfully into an excavation. He muttered against the men who wear helmets and carry clubs. Because he wanted to fall into their clutches, they seemed to regard him as a king who could do no wrong.

At length Soapy reached one of the avenues to the east where the glitter and turmoil was but faint. He set his face down this toward Madison Square, for the homing instinct survives even when the home is a park bench.

But on an unusually quiet corner Soapy came to a standstill. Here was an old church, quaint and rambling and gabled. Through one violet-stained window a soft light glowed, where, no doubt, the organist loitered over the keys, making sure of his mastery of the coming Sabbath anthem. For there drifted out to Soapy's ears sweet music that caught and held him transfixed against the convolutions of the iron fence.

The moon was above, lustrous and serene; vehicles and pedestrians were few; sparrows twittered sleepily in the eaves – for a little while the scene might have been a country churchyard. And the anthem that the organist played cemented Soapy to the iron fence, for he had known it well in the days when his life contained such things as mothers and roses and ambitions and friends and immaculate thoughts and collars.

The conjunction of Soapy's receptive state of mind and the influences about the old church wrought a sudden and wonderful change in his soul. He viewed with swift horror the pit into which he had tumbled, the degraded days, unworthy desires, dead hopes, wrecked faculties and base motives that made up his existence.

And also in a moment his heart responded thrillingly to this novel mood. An instantaneous and strong impulse moved him to battle with his desperate fate. He would pull himself out of the mire; he would make a man of himself again; he would conquer the evil that had taken possession of him. There was time; he was comparatively young yet: he would resurrect his old eager ambitions and pursue them without faltering. Those solemn but sweet organ notes had set up a revolution in him. Tomorrow he would go into the roaring downtown district and find work. A fur importer had once offered him a place as driver. He would find him to-morrow and ask for the position. He would be somebody in the world. He would—

Soapy felt a hand laid on his arm. He looked quickly around into the broad face of a policeman.

'What are you doin' here?' asked the officer.

'Nothin',' said Soapy.

'Then come along,' said the policeman.

'Three months on the Island,' said the Magistrate in the Police Court the next morning.

AN ADJUSTMENT OF NATURE

IN AN ART EXHIBITION the other day I saw a painting that had been sold for $5,000. The painter was a young scrub out of the West named Kraft, who had a favorite food and a pet theory. His pabulum was an unquenchable belief in the Unerring Artistic Adjustment of Nature. His theory was fixed around corned-beef hash with poached egg. There was a story behind the picture, so I went home and let it drip out of a fountain-pen. The idea of Kraft – but that is not the beginning of the story.

Three years ago Kraft, Bill Judkins (a poet), and I took our meals at Cypher's on Eighth Avenue. I say 'took.' When we had money, Cypher got it 'off of' us, as he expressed it. We had no credit; we went in, called for food and ate it. We paid or we did not pay. We had confidence in Cypher's sullenness and smouldering ferocity. Deep down in his sunless soul he was either a prince, a fool, or an artist. He sat at a worm-eaten desk, covered with files of waiter's checks so old that I was sure the bottomest was one for clams that Henry Hudson had eaten and paid for. Cypher had the power, in common with Napoleon III and the goggle-eyed perch, of throwing a film over his eyes, rendering opaque the windows of his soul. Once when we left him unpaid, with egregious excuses, I looked back and saw him shaking with inaudible laughter behind his film. Now and then we paid up back scores.

But the chief thing at Cypher's was Milly. Milly was a waitress. She was a grand example of Kraft's theory of the artistic adjustment of nature. She belonged, largely, to waiting, as Minerva did to the art of scrapping, or Venus to the science of serious flirtation. Pedestalled and in bronze she might have stood with the noblest of her heroic sisters as 'Liver-and-Bacon Enlivening the World.' She belonged to Cypher's. You expected to see her colossal figure loom through that reeking blue cloud of smoke from frying fat just as you expect the Palisades to appear through a drifting Hudson River fog. There amid the steam of vegetables and the vapors of acres of 'ham and,' the crash of crockery, the clatter of steel, the screaming of 'short orders,' the cries of the hungering and all the horrid tumult of feeding man, surrounded by swarms of the buzzing winged beasts bequeathed us by Pharaoh, Milly steered her magnificent way like some great liner cleaving among the canoes of howling savages.

Our Goddess of Grub was built on lines so majestic that they could be followed only with awe. Her sleeves were always rolled above her elbows. She could have taken us three musketeers in her two hands and dropped us out of the window. She had seen fewer years than any of us, but she was of such superb Evehood and simplicity that she mothered us from the beginning. Cypher's store of eatables she poured out upon us with royal indifference to price and quantity, as from a cornucopia that knew no exhaustion. Her voice rang like a great silver bell; her smile was many-toothed and frequent; she seemed like a yellow sunrise on mountain tops. I never saw her but I thought of the Yosemite. And yet, somehow, I could never think of her as existing outside of Cypher's. There nature had placed her and she had taken root and grown mightily. She seemed happy, and took her few poor dollars on Saturday nights with the flushed pleasure of a child that receives an unexpected donation.

It was Kraft who first voiced the fear that each of us must have held latently. It came up apropos, of course, of certain questions of art at which we were hammering. One of us compared the harmony existing between a Haydn symphony and pistache ice cream to the exquisite congruity between Milly and Cypher's.

'There is a certain fate hanging over Milly,' said Kraft, 'and if it overtakes her she is lost to Cypher's and to us.'

'She will grow fat?' asked Judkins, fearsomely.

'She will go to night school and become refined?' I ventured, anxiously.

'It is this,' said Kraft, punctuating in a puddle of spilled coffee with a stiff forefinger. 'Caesar had his Brutus – the cotton has its bollworm, the chorus girl has her Pittsburger, the summer boarder has his poison ivy, the hero has his Carnegie medal, art has its Morgan, the rose has its—'

'Speak,' I interrupted, much perturbed. 'You do not think that Milly will begin to lace?'

'One day,' concluded Kraft, solemnly, 'there will come to Cypher's for a plate of beans a millionaire lumberman from Wisconsin, and he will marry Milly.'

'Never!' exclaimed Judkins and I, in horror.

'A lumberman,' repeated Kraft, hoarsely.

'And a millionaire lumberman!' I sighed, despairingly.

'From Wisconsin!' groaned Judkins.

We agreed that the awful fate seemed to menace her. Few things were less improbable. Milly, like some vast virgin stretch of pine woods, was made to catch the lumberman's eye. And well we knew the habits of the Badgers, once fortune smiled upon them. Straight to New York they hie, and lay their goods at the feet of the girl who serves them beans in a beanery. Why, the alphabet itself connives. The Sunday Newspaper's headliner's work is cut for him.

'Winsome Waitress Wins Wealthy Wisconsin Woodsman.'

For a while we felt that Milly was on the verge of being lost to us.

It was our love of the Unerring Artistic Adjustment of Nature that inspired us. We could not give her over to a lumberman, doubly accursed by wealth and provincialism. We shuddered to think of Milly, with her voice modulated and her elbows covered, pouring tea in the marble teepee of a tree murderer. No! In Cypher's she belonged – in the bacon smoke, the cabbage perfume, the grand, Wagnerian chorus of hurled ironstone china and rattling casters.

Our fears must have been prophetic, for on that same evening the wildwood discharged upon us Milly's preordained confiscator – our fee to adjustment and order. But Alaska and not Wisconsin bore the burden of the visitation.

We were at our supper of beef stew and dried apples when he trotted in as if on the heels of a dog team, and made one of the mess at our table. With the freedom of the camps he assaulted our ears and claimed the fellowship of men lost in the wilds of a hash house. We embraced him as a specimen, and in three minutes we had all but died for one another as friends.

He was rugged and bearded and wind-dried. He had just come off the 'trail,' he said, at one of the North River ferries. I fancied I could see the snow dust of Chilcoot yet powdering his shoulders. And then he strewed the table with the nuggets, stuffed ptarmigans, bead work and seal pelts of the returned Klondiker, and began to prate to us of his millions.

'Bank drafts for two millions,' was his summing up, 'and a thousand a day piling up from my claims. And now I want some beef stew and canned peaches. I never got off the train since I mushed out of Seattle, and I'm hungry. The stuff the niggers feed you on pullmans don't count. You gentlemen order what you want.'

And then Milly loomed up with a thousand dishes on her bare arm – loomed up big and white and pink and awful as Mount Saint Elias – with a smile like day breaking in a gulch. And the Klondiker threw down his pelts and nuggets as dross, and let his jaw fall halfway, and stared at her. You could almost see the diamond tiaras on Milly's brow and the hand-embroidered silk Paris gowns that he meant to buy for her.

At last the bollworm had attacked the cotton – the poison ivy was reaching out its tendrils to entwine the summer boarder – the millionaire lumberman, thinly disguised as the Alaskan miner, was about to engulf our Milly and upset Nature's adjustment.

Kraft was the first to act. He leaped up and pounded the Klondiker's back. 'Come out and drink,' he shouted. 'Drink first and eat afterward.' Judkins seized one arm and I the other. Gaily, roaringly, irresistibly, in jolly-good-fellow style, we dragged him from the restaurant to a café, stuffing his pockets with his embalmed birds and indigestible nuggets.

There he rumbled a roughly good-humored protest. 'That's the girl for my money,' he declared. 'She can eat out of my skillet the rest of her life. Why, I never see such a fine girl. I'm going back there and ask her to marry me. I guess she won't want to sling hash any more when she sees the pile of dust I've got.'

'You'll take another whiskey and milk now,' Kraft persuaded, with Satan's smile. 'I thought you up-country fellows were better sports.'

Kraft spent his puny store of coin at the bar and then gave Judkins and me such an appealing look that we went down to the last dime we had in toasting our guest.

Then, when our ammunition was gone and the Klondiker, still somewhat sober, began to babble again of Milly, Kraft whispered into his ear such a polite, barked insult relating to people who were miserly with their funds, that the miner crashed down handful after handful of silver and notes, calling for all the fluids in the world to drown the imputation.

Thus the work was accomplished. With his own guns we drove him from the field. And then we had him carted to a distant small hotel and put to bed with his nuggets and baby seal-skins stuffed around him.

'He will never find Cypher's again,' said Kraft. 'He will propose to the first white apron he sees in a dairy restaurant to-morrow. And Milly – I mean the Natural Adjustment – is saved!'

And back to Cypher's went we three, and finding customers scarce, we joined hands and did an Indian dance with Milly in the centre.

This, I say, happened three years ago. And about that time a little luck descended upon us three, and we were enabled to buy costlier and less wholesome food than Cypher's. Our paths separated, and I saw Kraft no more and Judkins seldom.

But, as I said, I saw a painting the other day that was sold for $5,000. The title was 'Boadicea,' and the figures seemed to fill all out-of-doors. But of all the picture's admirers who stood before it, I believe I was the only one who longed for Boadicea to stalk from her frame bringing me corned-beef hash with poached egg.

I hurried away to see Kraft. His satanic eyes were the same, his hair was worse tangled, but his clothes had been made by a tailor.

'I didn't know,' I said to him.

'We've bought a cottage in the Bronx with the money,' said he. 'Any evening at 7.'

'Then,' said I, 'when you led us against the lumberman – the – Klondiker – it wasn't altogether on account of the Unerring Artistic Adjustment of Nature?'

'Well, not altogether,' said Kraft, with a grin.

MEMOIRS OF A YELLOW DOG

I DON'T SUPPOSE IT WILL KNOCK any of you people off your perch to read a contribution from an animal. Mr. Kipling and a good many others have demonstrated the fact that animals can express themselves in remunerative English, and no magazine goes to press nowadays without an animal story in it, except the old-style monthlies that are still running pictures of Bryan and the Mont Pelée horror.

But you needn't look for any stuck-up literature in my piece, such as Bearoo, the bear, and Snakoo, the snake, and Tammanoo, the tiger, talk in the jungle books. A yellow dog that's spent most of his life in a cheap New York flat, sleeping in a corner on an old sateen underskirt (the one she spilled port wine on at the Lady Longshoremen's banquet), mustn't be expected to perform any tricks with the art of speech.

I was born a yellow pup; date, locality, pedigree and weight unknown. The first thing I can recollect, an old woman had me in a basket at Broadway and Twenty-third trying to sell me to a fat lady. Old Mother Hubbard was boosting me to beat the band as a genuine Pomeranian-Hambletonian-Red-Irish-Cochin-China-Stoke-Pogis fox terrier. The fat lady chased a V around among the samples of gros grain flannelette in her shopping bag till she cornered it, and gave up. From that moment I was a pet – a mamma's own wootsey quidlums. Say, gentle reader, did you ever have a 200-pound woman breathing a flavor of Camembert cheese and Peau d'Espagne pick you up and wallop her nose all over you, remarking all the time in an Emma Eames tone of voice: 'Oh, oo's um oodlum; doodlum, woodlum, toodlum, bitsy-witsy skoodlums?'

From pedigreed yellow pup I grew up to be an anonymous yellow cur looking like a cross between an Angora cat and a box of lemons. But my mistress never tumbled. She thought that the two primeval pups that Noah chased into the ark were but a collateral branch of my ancestors. It took two policemen to keep her from entering me at the Madison Square Garden for the Siberian bloodhound prize.

I'll tell you about that flat. The house was the ordinary thing in New York, paved with Parian marble in the entrance hall and cobblestones above the first floor. Our flat was three – well, not flights – climbs up. My mistress rented it unfurnished, and put in the regular things – 1903 antique upholstered parlor set, oil chromo of geishas in a Harlem tea house, rubber plant and husband.

By Sirius! there was a biped I felt sorry for. He was a little man with sandy hair and whiskers a good deal like mine. Henpecked? – well, toucans and flamingoes and pelicans all had their bills in him. He wiped the dishes and listened to my mistress tell about the cheap, ragged things the lady with the squirrel-skin coat on the second floor hung out on her line to dry. And every evening while she was getting supper she made him take me out on the end of a string for a walk.

If men knew how women pass the time when they are alone they'd never marry. Laura Lean Jibbey, peanut brittle, a little almond cream on the neck muscles, dishes unwashed, half an hour's talk with the iceman, reading a package of old letters, a couple of pickles and two bottles of malt extract, one hour peeking through a hole in the window shade into the flat across the air-shaft – that's about all there is to it. Twenty minutes before time for him to come home from work she straightens up the house, fixes her rat so it won't show, and gets out a lot of sewing for a ten-minute bluff.

I led a dog's life in that flat. 'Most all day I lay there in my corner watching that fat woman kill time. I slept sometimes and had pipe dreams about being out chasing cats into basements and growling at old ladies with black mittens, as a dog was intended to do. Then she would pounce upon me with a lot of that drivelling poodle palaver and kiss me on the nose – but what could I do? A dog can't chew cloves.

I began to feel sorry for Hubby, dog my cats if I didn't. We looked so much alike that people noticed it when we went out; so we shook the streets that Morgan's cab drives down, and took to climbing the piles of last December's snow on the streets where cheap people live.

One evening when we were thus promenading, and I was trying to look like a prize St. Bernard, and the old man was trying to look like he wouldn't have murdered the first organ-grinder he heard play Mendelssohn's wedding-march, I looked up at him and said, in my way:

'What are you looking so sour about, you oakum trimmed lobster? She don't kiss you. You don't have to sit on her lap and listen to talk that would make the book of a musical comedy sound like the maxims of Epictetus. You ought to be thankful you're not a dog. Brace up, Benedick, and bid the blues begone.'

The matrimonial mishap looked down at me with almost canine intelligence in his face.

'Why, doggie,' says he, 'good doggie. You almost look like you could speak. What is it, doggie – cats.'

Cats! Could speak!

But, of course, he couldn't understand. Humans were denied the speech of animals. The only common ground of communication upon which dogs and men can get together is in fiction.

In the flat across the hall from us lived a lady with a black-and-tan terrier. Her husband strung it and took it out every evening, but he always came home cheerful and whistling. One day I touched noses with the black-and-tan in the hall, and I struck him for an elucidation.

'See here, Wiggle-and-Skip,' I says, 'you know that it ain't the nature of a real man to play dry nurse to a dog in public. I never saw one leashed to a bow-wow yet that didn't look like he'd like to lick every other man that looked at him. But your boss comes in every day as perky and set up as an amateur prestidigitator doing the egg trick. How does he do it? Don't tell me he likes it.'

'Him?' says the black-and-tan. 'Why, he uses Nature's Own Remedy. He gets spifflicated. At first when we go out he's as shy as the man on the steamer who would rather play pedro when they make 'em all jackpots. By the time we've been in eight saloons he don't care whether the thing on the end of his line is a dog or a catfish. I've lost two inches of my tail trying to sidestep those swinging doors.'

The pointer I got from that terrier – Vaudeville please copy – set me to thinking.

One evening about 6 o'clock my mistress ordered him to get busy and do the ozone act for Lovey. I have concealed it until now, but that is what she called me. The black-and-tan was called 'Tweetness.' I consider that I have the bulge on him as far as you could chase a rabbit. Still 'Lovey' is something of a nomenclatural tin can on the tail of one's self-respect.

At a quiet place on a safe street I tightened the line of my custodian in front of an attractive, refined saloon. I made a dead-ahead scramble for the doors, whining like a dog in the press despatches that lets the family know that little Alice is bogged while gathering lilies in the brook.

'Why, darn my eyes,' says the old man, with a grin; 'darn my eyes if the saffron-colored son of a seltzer lemonade ain't asking me in to take a drink. Lemme see – how long's it been since I saved shoe leather by keeping one foot on the foot-rest? I believe I'll —'

I knew I had him. Hot Scotches he took, sitting at a table. For an hour he kept the Campbells coming. I sat by his side rapping for the waiter with my tail, and eating free lunch such as mamma in her flat never equalled with her homemade truck bought at a delicatessen store eight minutes before papa comes home.

When the products of Scotland were all exhausted except the rye bread the old man unwound me from the table leg and played me outside like a fisherman plays a salmon. Out there he took off my collar and threw it into the street.

'Poor doggie,' says he; 'good doggie. She shan't kiss you any more. 'S a darned shame. Good doggie, go away and get run over by a street car and be happy.'

I refused to leave. I leaped and frisked around the old man's legs happy as a pug on a rug.

'You old flea-headed woodchuck-chaser,' I said to him – 'you moon-baying, rabbit-pointing, egg-stealing old beagle, can't you see that I don't want to leave you? Can't you see that we're both Pups in the Wood and the missis is the cruel uncle after you with the dish towel and me with the flea liniment and a pink bow to tie on my tail. Why not cut that all out and be pards forever more?'

Maybe you'll say he didn't understand – maybe he didn't. But he kind of got a grip on the Hot Scotches, and stood still for a minute, thinking.

'Doggie,' says he, finally, 'we don't live more than a dozen lives on this earth, and very few of us live to be more than 300. If I ever see that flat any more I'm a flat, and if you do you're flatter; and that's no flattery. I'm offering 60 to 1 that Westward Ho wins out by the length of a dachshund.'

There was no string, but I frolicked along with my master to the

Twenty-third Street ferry. And the cats on the route saw reason to give thanks that prehensile claws had been given to them.

On the Jersey side my master said to a stranger who stood eating a currant bun:

'Me and my doggie, we are bound for the Rocky Mountains.'

But what pleased me most was when my old man pulled both of my ears until I howled, and said:

'You common, monkey-headed, rat-tailed, sulphur-colored son of a door mat, do you know what I'm going to call you?'

I thought of 'Lovey,' and I whined dolefully.

'I'm going to call you "Pete," ' says my master; and if I'd had five tails I couldn't have done enough wagging to do justice to the occasion.

THE LOVE-PHILTRE OF IKEY SCHOENSTEIN

THE BLUE LIGHT DRUG STORE is downtown, between the Bowery and First Avenue, where the distance between the two streets is the shortest. The Blue Light does not consider that pharmacy is a thing of bric-à-brac, scent and ice-cream soda. If you ask it for pain-killer it will not give you a bonbon.

The Blue Light scorns the labor-saving arts of modern pharmacy. It macerates its opium and percolates its own laudanum and paregoric. To this day pills are made behind its tall prescription desk – pills rolled out on its own pill-tile, divided with a spatula, rolled with the finger and thumb, dusted with calcined magnesia and delivered in little round pasteboard pill-boxes. The store is on a corner about which coveys of ragged-plumed, hilarious children play and become candidates for the cough drops and soothing syrups that wait for them inside.

Ikey Schoenstein was the night clerk of the Blue Light and the friend of his customers. Thus it is on the East Side, where the heart of pharmacy is not glacé. There, as it should be, the druggist is a counsellor, a confessor, an adviser, an able and willing missionary and mentor whose learning is respected, whose occult wisdom is venerated and whose medicine is often poured, untasted, into the gutter. Therefore Ikey's corniform, bespectacled nose and narrow, knowledge-bowed figure was well known in the vicinity of the Blue Light, and his advice and notice were much desired.

Ikey roomed and breakfasted at Mrs. Riddle's two squares away. Mrs. Riddle had a daughter named Rosy. The circumlocution has been in vain – you must have guessed it – Ikey adored Rosy. She tinctured all his thoughts; she was the compound extract of all that was chemically pure and officinal – the dispensatory contained nothing equal to her. But Ikey was timid, and his hopes remained insoluble in the menstruum of his backwardness and fears. Behind his counter he was a superior being, calmly conscious of special knowledge and worth; outside he was a weak-kneed, purblind, motorman-cursed rambler, with ill-fitting clothes stained with chemicals and smelling of socotrine aloes and valerianate of ammonia.

The fly in Ikey's ointment (thrice welcome, pat trope!) was Chunk McGowan.

Mr. McGowan was also striving to catch the bright smiles tossed about by Rosy. But he was no out-fielder as Ikey was; he picked them off the bat. At

the same time he was Ikey's friend and customer, and often dropped in at
the Blue Light Drug Store to have a bruise painted with iodine or get a cut
rubber-plastered after a pleasant evening spent along the bowery.

One afternoon McGowan drifted in in his silent, easy way, and sat, comely,
smooth-faced, hard, indomitable, good-natured, upon a stool.

'Ikey,' said he, when his friend had fetched his mortar and sat opposite,
grinding gum benzoin to a powder, 'get busy with your ear. It's drugs for me
if you've got the line I need.'

Ikey scanned the countenance of Mr. McGowan for the usual evidence of
conflict, but found none.

'Take your coat off,' he ordered. 'I guess already that you have been stuck
in the ribs with a knife. I have many times told you those Dagoes would do
you up.'

Mr. McGowan smiled. 'Not them,' he said. 'Not any Dagoes. But you've
located the diagnosis all right enough – it's under my coat, near the ribs. Say!
Ikey – Rosy and me are goin' to run away and get married tonight.'

Ikey's left forefinger was doubled over the edge of the mortar, holding it
steady. He gave it a wild rap with the pestle, but felt it not. Meanwhile Mr.
McGowan's smile faded to a look of perplexed gloom.

'That is,' he continued, 'if she keeps in the notion until the time comes.
We've been layin' pipes for the getaway for two weeks. One day she says she
will; the same evenin' she says nixy. We've agreed on to-night, and Rosy's
stuck to the affirmative this time for two whole days. But it's five hours yet
till the time, and I'm afraid she'll stand me up when it comes to the scratch.'

'You said you wanted drugs,' remarked Ikey.

Mr. McGowan looked ill at ease and harassed – a condition opposed to his
usual line of demeanor. He made a patent-medicine almanac into a roll and
fitted it with unprofitable carefulness about his finger.

'I wouldn't have this double handicap make a false start to-night for a
million,' he said. 'I've got a little flat up in Harlem all ready, with chrysan-
themums on the table and a kettle ready to boil. And I've engaged a pulpit
pounder to be ready at his house for us at 9.30. It's got to come off. And if
Rosy don't change her mind again!' – Mr. McGowan ceased, a prey to his
doubts.

'I don't see then yet,' said Ikey, shortly, 'what makes it that you talk of
drugs, or what I can be doing about it.'

'Old man Riddle don't like me a little bit,' went on the uneasy suitor, bent
upon marshalling his arguments. 'For a week he hasn't let Rosy step outside
the door with me. If it wasn't for losin' a boarder they'd have bounced me
long ago. I'm makin' $20 a week and she'll never regret flyin' the coop with
Chunk McGowan.'

'You will excuse me, Chunk,' said Ikey. 'I must make a prescription that
is to be called for soon.'

'Say,' said McGowan, looking up suddenly, 'say, Ikey, ain't there a drug
of some kind – some kind of powders that'll make a girl like you better if
you give 'em to her?'

Ikey's lip beneath his nose curled with the scorn of superior enlightenment;
but before he could answer, McGowan continued:

'Tim Lacy told me he got some once from a croaker uptown and fed 'em
to his girl in soda water. From the very first dose he was ace-high and

everybody else looked like thirty cents to her. They was married in less than two weeks.'

Strong and simple was Chunk McGowan. A better reader of men than Ikey was could have seen that his tough frame was strung upon fine wires. Like a good general who was about to invade the enemy's territory he was seeking to guard every point against possible failure.

'I thought,' went on Chunk, hopefully, 'that if I had one of them powders to give Rosy when I see her at supper to-night it might brace her up and keep her from reneging on the proposition to skip. I guess she don't need a mule team to drag her away, but women are better at coaching than they are at running bases. If the stuff'll work just for a couple of hours it'll do the trick.'

'When is this foolishness of running away to be happening?' asked Ikey.

'Nine o'clock,' said Mr. McGowan. 'Supper's at seven. At eight Rosy goes to bed with a headache, at nine old Parvenzano lets me through to his backyard, where there's a board off Riddle's fence, next door. I go under her window and help her down the fire-escape. We've got to make it early on the preacher's account. It's all dead easy if Rosy don't balk when the flag drops. Can you fix me one of them powders, Ikey?'

Ikey Schoenstein rubbed his nose slowly.

'Chunk,' said he, 'it is of drugs of that nature that pharmaceutists must have much carefulness. To you alone of my acquaintance would I intrust a powder like that. But for you I shall make it, and you shall see how it makes Rosy to think of you.'

Ikey went behind the prescription desk. There he crushed to a powder two soluble tablets, each containing a quarter of a grain of morphia. To them he added a little sugar of milk to increase the bulk, and folded the mixture neatly in a white paper. Taken by an adult this powder would insure several hours of heavy slumber without danger to the sleeper. This he handed to Chunk McGowan, telling him to administer it in a liquid if possible, and received the hearty thanks of the backyard Lochinvar.

The subtlety of Ikey's action becomes apparent upon recital of his subsequent move. He sent a messenger for Mr. Riddle and disclosed the plans of Mr. McGowan for eloping with Rosy. Mr. Riddle was a stout man, brick-dusty of complexion and sudden in action.

'Much obliged,' he said, briefly, to Ikey. 'The lazy Irish loafer! My own room's just above Rosy's. I'll just go up there myself after supper and load the shot-gun and wait. If he comes in my backyard he'll go away in an ambulance instead of a bridal chaise.'

With Rosy held in the clutches of Morpheus for a many-hours deep slumber, and the blood-thirsty parent waiting, armed and forewarned, Ikey felt that his rival was close, indeed, upon discomfiture.

All night in the Blue Light Drug Store he waited at his duties for chance news of the tragedy, but none came.

At eight o'clock in the morning the day clerk arrived and Ikey started hurriedly for Mrs. Riddle's to learn the outcome. And, lo! as he stepped out of the store who but Chunk McGowan sprang from a passing street car and grasped his hand – Chunk McGowan with a victor's smile and flushed with joy.

'Pulled it off,' said Chunk with Elysium in his grin. 'Rosy hit the fire-escape on time to a second, and we was under the wire at the Reverend's at

9.30¼. She's up at the flat – she cooked eggs this mornin' in a blue kimono – Lord! how lucky I am! You must pace up some day, Ikey, and feed with us. I've got a job down near the bridge, and that's where I'm heading for now.'

'The – the – powder?' stammered Ikey.

'Oh, that stuff you gave me!' said Chunk, broadening his grin; 'well, it was this way. I sat down at the supper table last night at Riddle's, and I looked at Rosy, and I says to myself, "Chunk, if you get the girl get her on the square – don't try any hocus-pocus with a thoroughbred like her." And I keeps the paper you give me in my pocket. And then my lamps fall on another party present, who, I says to myself, is failin' in a proper affection toward his comin' son-in-law, so I watches my chance and dumps that powder in old man Riddle's coffee – see?'

MAMMON AND THE ARCHER

OLD ANTHONY ROCKWALL, retired manufacturer and proprietor of Rockwall's Eureka Soap, looked out the library window of his Fifth Avenue mansion and grinned. His neighbor to the right – the aristocratic clubman, G. Van Schuylight Suffolk-Jones – came out to his waiting motor-car, wrinkling a contumelious nostril, as usual, at the Italian renaissance sculpture of the soap palace's front elevation.

'Stuck-up old statuette of nothing doing!' commented the ex-Soap King. 'The Eden Musée'll get that old frozen Nesselrode yet if he don't watch out. I'll have this house painted red, white, and blue next summer and see if that'll make his Dutch nose turn up any higher.'

And then Anthony Rockwall, who never cared for bells, went to the door of his library and shouted 'Mike!' in the same voice that had once chipped off pieces of the welkin on the Kansas prairies.

'Tell my son,' said Anthony to the answering menial, 'to come in here before he leaves the house.'

When young Rockwall entered the library the old man laid aside his newspaper, looked at him with a kindly grimness on his big, smooth, ruddy countenance, rumpled his mop of white hair with one hand and rattled the keys in his pocket with the other.

'Richard,' said Anthony Rockwall, 'what do you pay for the soap that you use?'

Richard, only six months home from college, was startled a little. He had not yet taken the measure of this sire of his, who was as full of unexpectedness as a girl at her first party.

'Six dollars a dozen, I think, dad.'

'And your clothes?'

'I suppose about sixty dollars, as a rule.'

'You're a gentleman,' said Anthony, decidedly. 'I've heard of these young bloods spending $24 a dozen for soap, and going over the hundred mark for clothes. You've got as much money to waste as any of 'em, and yet you stick to what's decent and moderate. Now I use the old Eureka – not only for sentiment, but it's the purest soap made. Whenever you pay more than 10 cents a cake for soap you buy bad perfumes and labels. But 50 cents is doing very well for a young man in your generation, position and condition. As I said, you're a gentleman. They say it takes three generations to make one. They're off. Money'll do it as slick as soap grease. It's made you one. By hokey! it's almost made one of me. I'm nearly as impolite and disagreeable and ill-mannered as these two old knickerbocker gents on each side of me that can't sleep of nights because I bought in between 'em.'

'There are some things that money can't accomplish,' remarked young Rockwall, rather gloomily.

'Now, don't say that,' said old Anthony, shocked. 'I bet my money on money every time. I've been through the encyclopaedia down to Y looking for something you can't buy with it; and I expect to have to take up the appendix next week. I'm for money against the field. Tell me something money won't buy.'

'For one thing,' answered Richard, rankling a little, 'it won't buy one into the exclusive circles of society.'

'Oho! won't it?' thundered the champion of the root of evil. 'You tell me where your exclusive circles would be if the first Astor hadn't had the money to pay for his steerage passage over?'

Richard sighed.

'And that's what I was coming to,' said the old man, less boisterously. 'That's why I asked you to come in. There's something going wrong with you, boy. I've been noticing it for two weeks. Out with it. I guess I could lay my hands on eleven millions within twenty-four hours, besides the real estate. If it's your liver, there's the *Rambler* down in the bay, coaled, and ready to steam down to the Bahamas in two days.'

'Not a bad guess, dad; you haven't missed it far.'

'Ah,' said Anthony, keenly; 'what's her name?'

Richard began to walk up and down the library floor. There was enough comradeship and sympathy in this crude old father of his to draw his confidence.

'Why don't you ask her?' demanded old Anthony. 'She'll jump at you. You've got the money and the looks, and you're a decent boy. Your hands are clean. You've got no Eureka soap on 'em. You've been to college, but she'll overlook that.'

'I haven't had a chance,' said Richard.

'Make one,' said Anthony. 'Take her for a walk in the park, or a straw ride, or walk home with her from church. Chance! Pshaw!'

'You don't know the social mill, dad. She's part of the stream that turns it. Every hour and minute of her time is arranged for days in advance. I must have that girl, dad, or this town is a blackjack swamp forevermore. And I can't write it – I can't do that.'

'Tut!' said the old man. 'Do you mean to tell me that with all the money I've got you can't get an hour or two of a girl's time for yourself?'

'I've put it off too late. She's going to sail for Europe at noon day after to-morrow for a two years' stay. I'm to see her alone to-morrow evening for a few minutes. She's at Larchmont now at her aunt's. I can't go there. But I'm allowed to meet her with a cab at the Grand Central Station to-morrow evening at the 8.30 train. We drive down Broadway to Wallack's at a gallop, where her mother and a box party will be waiting for us in the lobby. Do you think she would listen to a declaration from me during that six or eight minutes under those circumstances. No. And what chance would I have in the theatre or afterward? None. No, dad, this is one tangle that your money can't unravel. We can't buy one minute of time with cash; if we could, rich people would live longer. There's no hope of getting a talk with Miss Lantry before she sails.'

'All right, Richard, my boy,' said old Anthony, cheerfully. 'You may run along down to your club now. I'm glad it ain't your liver. But don't forget to burn a few punk sticks in the joss house to the great god Mazuma from time to time. You say money won't buy time? Well, of course, you can't order eternity wrapped up and delivered at your residence for a price, but I've seen Father Time get pretty bad stone bruises on his heels when he walked through the gold diggings.'

That night came Aunt Ellen, gentle, sentimental, wrinkled, sighing, oppressed by wealth, in to Brother Anthony at his evening paper, and began discourse on the subject of lovers' woes.

'He told me all about it,' said Brother Anthony, yawning. 'I told him my bank account was at his service. And then he began to knock money. Said money couldn't help. Said the rules of society couldn't be bucked for a yard by a team of ten-millionaires.'

'Oh, Anthony,' sighed Aunt Ellen, 'I wish you would not think so much of money. Wealth is nothing where a true affection is concerned. Love is all-powerful. If he only had spoken earlier! She could not have refused our Richard. But now I fear it is too late. He will have no opportunity to address her. All your gold cannot bring happiness to your son.'

At eight o'clock the next evening Aunt Ellen took a quaint old gold ring from a moth-eaten case and gave it to Richard.

'Wear it to-night, nephew,' she begged. 'Your mother gave it to me. Good luck in love she said it brought. She asked me to give it to you when you had found the one you loved.'

Young Rockwall took the ring reverently and tried it on his smallest finger. It slipped as far as the second joint and stopped. He took it off and stuffed it into his vest pocket, after the manner of man. And then he 'phoned for his cab.

At the station he captured Miss Lantry out of the gabbing mob at eight thirty-two.

'We mustn't keep mamma and the others waiting,' said she.

'To Wallack's Theatre as fast as you can drive!' said Richard, loyally.

They whirled up Forty-second to Broadway, and then down the white-starred lane that leads from the soft meadows of sunset to the rocky hills of morning.

At Thirty-fourth Street young Richard quickly thrust up the trap and ordered the cabman to stop.

'I've dropped a ring,' he apologized, as he climbed out. 'It was my mother's, and I'd hate to lose it. I won't detain you a minute – I saw where it fell.'

In less than a minute he was back in the cab with the ring.

But within that minute a crosstown car had stopped directly in front of the cab. The cab-man tried to pass to the left, but a heavy express wagon cut him off. He tried the right and had to back away from a furniture van that had no business to be there. He tried to back out, but dropped his reins and swore dutifully. He was blockaded in a tangled mess of vehicles and horses.

One of those street blockades had occurred that sometimes tie up commerce and movement quite suddenly in the big city.

'Why don't you drive on?' said Miss Lantry impatiently. 'We'll be late.'

Richard stood up in the cab and looked around. He saw a congested flood of wagons, trucks, cabs, vans and street cars filling the vast space where Broadway, Sixth Avenue, and Thirty-fourth Street cross one another as a twenty-six inch maiden fills her twenty-two inch girdle. And still from all the cross streets they were hurrying and rattling toward the converging point at full speed, and hurling themselves into the straggling mass, locking wheels and adding their drivers' imprecations to the clamor. The entire traffic of Manhattan seemed to have jammed itself around them. The oldest New Yorker among the thousands of spectators that lined the sidewalks had not witnessed a street blockade of the proportions of this one.

'I'm very sorry,' said Richard, as he resumed his seat, 'but it looks as if we are stuck. They won't get this jumble loosened up in an hour. It was my fault. If I hadn't dropped the ring we—'

'Let me see the ring,' said Miss Lantry. 'Now that it can't be helped, I don't care. I think theatres are stupid, anyway.'

At 11 o'clock that night somebody tapped lightly on Anthony Rockwall's door.

'Come in,' shouted Anthony, who was in a red dressing-gown, reading a book of piratical adventures.

Somebody was Aunt Ellen, looking like a gray-haired angel that had been left on earth by mistake.

'They're engaged, Anthony,' she said, softly. 'She has promised to marry our Richard. On their way to the theatre there was a street blockade, and it was two hours before their cab could get out of it.

'And oh, Brother Anthony, don't ever boast of the power of money again. A little emblem of true love – a little ring that symbolized unending and unmercenary affection – was the cause of our Richard finding his happiness. He dropped it in the street, and got out to recover it. And before they could continue the blockade occurred. He spoke to his love and won her there while the cab was hemmed in. Money is dross compared with true love, Anthony.'

'All right,' said old Anthony. 'I'm glad the boy has got what he wanted. I told him I wouldn't spare any expense in the matter if—'

'But, Brother Anthony, what good could your money have done?'

'Sister,' said Anthony Rockwall. 'I've got my pirate in a devil of a scrape. His ship has just been scuttled, and he's too good a judge of the value of money to let drown. I wish you would let me go on with this chapter.'

The story should end here. I wish it would as heartily as you who read it wish it did. But we must go to the bottom of the well for truth.

The next day a person with red hands and a blue polka-dot necktie, who called himself Kelly, called at Anthony Rockwall's house, and was at once received in the library.

'Well,' said Anthony, reaching for his check-book, 'it was a good bilin' of soap. Let's see – you had $5,000 in cash.'

'I paid out $300 more of my own,' said Kelly. 'I had to go a little above the estimate. I got the express wagons and cabs mostly for $5; but the trucks and two-horse teams mostly raised me to $10. The motormen wanted $10, and some of the loaded teams $20. The cops struck me hardest – $50 I paid two, and the rest $20 and $25. But didn't it work beautiful, Mr. Rockwall? I'm glad William A. Brady wasn't onto that little outdoor vehicle mob scene. I

wouldn't want William to break his heart with jealousy. And never a
rehearsal, either! The boys was on time to the fraction of a second. It was
two hours before a snake could get below Greeley's statue.'

'Thirteen hundred – there you are, Kelly,' said Anthony, tearing off a
check. 'Your thousand, and the $300 you were out. You don't despise money,
do you, Kelly?'

'Me?' said Kelly. 'I can lick the man that invented poverty.'

Anthony called Kelly when he was at the door.

'You didn't notice,' said he, 'anywhere in the tie-up, a kind of a fat boy
without any clothes on shooting arrows around with a bow, did you?'

'Why, no,' said Kelly, mystified. 'I didn't. If he was like you say, maybe
the cops pinched him before I got there.'

'I thought the little rascal wouldn't be on hand,' chuckled Anthony.
'Good-by, Kelly.'

SPRINGTIME À LA CARTE

IT WAS A DAY IN MARCH.

Never, never begin a story this way when you write one. No opening
could possibly be worse. It is unimaginative, flat dry, and likely to consist of
mere wind. But in this instance it is allowable. For the following paragraph,
which should have inaugurated the narrative, is too wildly extravagant and
preposterous to be flaunted in the face of the reader without preparation.

Sarah was crying over her bill of fare.

Think of a New York girl shedding tears on the menu card!

To account for this you will be allowed to guess that the lobsters were all
out, or that she had sworn ice-cream off during Lent, or that she had ordered
onions, or that she had just come from a Hackett matinée. And then, all
these theories being wrong, you will please let the story proceed.

The gentleman who announced that the world was an oyster which he
with his sword would open made a larger hit than he deserved. It is not
difficult to open an oyster with a sword. But did you ever notice any one try
to open the terrestrial bivalve with a typewriter? Like to wait for a dozen raw
opened that way?

Sarah had managed to pry apart the shells with her unhandy weapon far
enough to nibble a wee bit at the cold and clammy world within. She knew
no more shorthand than if she had been a graduate in stenography just let
slip upon the world by a business college. So, not being able to stenog, she
could not enter that bright galaxy of office talent. She was a free-lance
typewriter and canvassed for odd jobs of copying.

The most brilliant and crowning feat of Sarah's battle with the world was
the deal she made with Schulenberg's Home Restaurant. The restaurant was
next door to the old red brick in which she hall-roomed. One evening after
dining at Schulenberg's 40-cent, five-course *table d'hôte* (served as fast as you
throw the five baseballs at the colored gentleman's head) Sarah took away
with her the bill of fare. It was written in an almost unreadable script neither
English nor German, and so arranged that if you were not careful you began
with a toothpick and rice pudding and ended with soup and the day of the
week.

The next day Sarah showed Schulenberg a neat card on which the menu was beautifully typewritten with the viands temptingly marshalled under their right and proper heads from 'hors d'oeuvre' to 'not responsible for over-coats and umbrellas.'

Schulenberg became a naturalized citizen on the spot. Before Sarah left him she had him willingly committed to an agreement. She was to furnish typewritten bills of fare for the twenty-one tables in the restaurant – a new bill for each day's dinner, and new ones for breakfast and lunch as often as changes occurred in the food or as neatness required.

In return for this Schulenberg was to send three meals per diem to Sarah's hall room by a waiter – an obsequious one if possible – and furnish her each afternoon with a pencil draft of what Fate had in store for Schulenberg's customers on the morrow.

Mutual satisfaction resulted from the agreement. Schulenberg's patrons now knew what the food they ate was called even if its nature sometimes puzzled them. And Sarah had food during a cold, dull winter, which was the main thing with her.

And then the almanac lied, and said that spring had come. Spring comes when it comes. The frozen snows of January still lay like adamant in the cross-town streets. The hand-organs still played 'In the Good Old Summertime,' with their December vivacity and expression. Men began to make thirty-day notes to buy Easter dresses. Janitors shut off steam. And when these things happen one may know that the city is still in the clutches of winter.

One afternoon Sarah shivered in her elegant hall bedroom; 'house heated; scrupulously clean; conveniences; seen to be appreciated.' She had no work to do except Schulenberg's menu cards. Sarah sat in her squeaky willow rocker, and looked out the window. The calendar on the wall kept crying to her: 'Springtime is here, Sarah – springtime is here, I tell you. Look at me, Sarah, my figures show it. You've got a neat figure yourself, Sarah – a – nice springtime figure – why do you look out the window so sadly?'

Sarah's room was at the back of the house. Looking out the window she could see the windowless rear brick wall of the box factory on the next street. But the wall was clearest crystal; and Sarah was looking down a grassy lane shaded with cherry trees and elms and bordered with raspberry bushes and Cherokee roses.

Spring's real harbingers are too subtle for the eye and ear. Some must have the flowering crocus, the wood-starring dogwood, the voice of bluebird – even so gross a reminder as the farewell handshake of the retiring buckwheat and oyster before they can welcome the Lady in Green to their dull bosoms. But to old earth's choicest kind there come straight, sweet messages from his newest bride, telling them they shall be no stepchildren unless they choose to be.

On the previous summer Sarah had gone into the country and loved a farmer.

(In writing your story never hark back thus. It is bad art, and cripples interest. Let it march, march.)

Sarah stayed two weeks at Sunnybrook Farm. There she learned to love old Farmer Franklin's son Walter. Farmers have been loved and wedded and turned out to grass in less time. But young Walter Franklin was a modern agriculturist. He had a telephone in his cow house, and he could figure up exactly what effect next year's Canada wheat crop would have on potatoes planted in the dark of the moon.

It was in this shaded and raspberried lane that Walter had wooed and won her. And together they had sat and woven a crown of dandelions for her hair. He had immoderately praised the effect of the yellow blossoms against her brown tresses; and she had left the chaplet there, and walked back to the house swinging her straw sailor in her hands.

They were to marry in the spring – at the very first signs of spring, Walter said. And Sarah came back to the city to pound her typewriter.

A knock at the door dispelled Sarah's visions of that happy day. A waiter had brought the rough pencil draft of the Home Restaurant's next day fare in old Schulenberg's angular hand.

Sarah sat down to her typewriter and slipped a card between the rollers. She was a nimble worker. Generally in an hour and a half the twenty-one menu cards were written and ready.

To-day there were more changes on the bill of fare than usual. The soups were lighter; pork was eliminated from the entrées, figuring only with Russian turnips among the roasts. The gracious spirit of spring pervaded the entire menu. Lamb, that lately capered on the greening hillsides, was becoming exploited with the sauce that commemorated its gambols. The song of the oyster, though not silenced, was *dimuendo con amore*. The frying-pan seemed to be held, inactive, behind the beneficent bars of the broiler. The pie list swelled; the richer puddings had vanished; the sausage, with his drapery wrapped about him, barely lingered in a pleasant thanatopsis with the buckwheats and the sweet but doomed maple.

Sarah's fingers danced like midgets above a summer stream. Down through the courses she worked, giving each item its position according to its length with an accurate eye.

Just above the desserts came the list of vegetables. Carrots and peas, asparagus on toast, the perennial tomatoes and corn and succotash, lima beans, cabbage – and then—

Sarah was crying over her bill of fare. Tears from the depths of some divine despair rose in her heart and gathered to her eyes. Down went her head on the little typewriter stand; and the keyboard rattled a dry accompaniment to her moist sobs.

For she had received no letter from Walter in two weeks, and the next item on the bill of fare was dandelions – dandelions with some kind of egg – but bother the egg! – dandelions, with whose golden blooms Walter had crowned her his queen of love and future bride – dandelions, the harbingers of spring, her sorrow's crown of sorrow – reminder of her happiest days.

Madam, I dare you to smile until you suffer this test: Let the Marechal Niel roses that Percy brought you on the night you gave him your heart be served as a salad with French dressing before your eyes at a Schulenberg *table d'hôte*. Had Juliet so seen her love tokens dishonored the sooner would she have sought the lethean herbs of the good apothecary.

But what witch is Spring! Into the great cold city of stone and iron a message had to be sent. There was none to convey it but the little hardy courier of the fields with his rough green coat and modest air. He is a true soldier of fortune, this *dent-de-lion* – this lion's tooth, as the French chefs call him. Flowered, he will assist at love-making, wreathed in my lady's

nut-brown hair; young and callow and unblossomed, he goes into the boiling
pot and delivers the word of his sovereign mistress.

By and by Sarah forced back her tears. The cards must be written. But,
still in a faint, golden glow from her dandelion dream, she fingered the
typewriter keys absently for a little while, with her mind and heart in the
meadow lane with her young farmer. But soon she came swiftly back to the
rock-bound lanes of Manhattan, and the typewriter began to rattle and jump
like a strike-breaker's motor car.

At 6 o'clock the waiter brought her dinner and carried away the typewritten
bill of fare. When Sarah ate she set aside, with a sigh, the dish of dandelions
with its crowning ovarious accompaniment. As this dark mass had been
transformed from a bright and love-indorsed flower to be an ignominious
vegetable, so had her summer hopes wilted and perished. Love may, as
Shakespeare said, feed on itself: but Sarah could not bring herself to eat the
dandelions that had graced, as ornaments, the first spiritual banquet of her
heart's true affection.

At 7.30 the couple in the next room began to quarrel: the man in the room
above sought for A on his flute; the gas went a little lower; three coal wagons
started to unload – the only sound of which the phonograph is jealous; cats
on the back fences slowly retreated toward Mukden. By these signs Sarah
knew that it was time for her to read. She got out 'The Cloister and the
Hearth,' the best non-selling book of the month, settled her feet on her
trunk, and began to wander with Gerard.

The front door bell rang. The landlady answered it. Sarah left Gerard and
Denys treed by a bear and listened. Oh, yes; you would, just as she did!

And then a strong voice was heard in the hall below, and Sarah jumped
for her door, leaving the book on the floor and the first round easily the
bear's.

You have guessed it. She reached the top of the stairs just as her farmer
came up, three at a jump, and reaped and garnered her, with nothing left for
the gleaners.

'Why haven't you written – oh, why?' cried Sarah.

'New York is a pretty large town,' said Walter Franklin. 'I came in a week
ago to your old address. I found that you went away on a Thursday. That
consoled some; it eliminated the possible Friday bad luck. But it didn't
prevent my hunting for you with police and otherwise ever since!'

'I wrote!' said Sarah, vehemently.

'Never got it!'

'Then how did you find me?'

The young farmer smiled a springtime smile.

'I dropped into that Home Restaurant next door this evening,' said he. 'I
don't care who knows it; I like a dish of some kind of green at this time of
the year. I ran my eye down that nice typewritten bill of fare looking for
something in that line. When I got below cabbage I turned my chair over
and hollered for the proprietor. He told me where you lived.'

'I remember,' sighed Sarah, happily. 'That was dandelions below cabbage.'

'I'd know that cranky capital W 'way above the line that your typewriter
makes anywhere in the world,' said Franklin.

'Why, there's no W in dandelions,' said Sarah in surprise.

The young man drew the bill of fare from his pocket and pointed to a line.

Sarah recognised the first card she had typewritten that afternoon. There

was still the rayed splotch in the upper right-hand corner where a tear had
fallen. But over the spot where one should have read the name of the meadow
plant, the clinging memory of their golden blossoms had allowed her fingers
to strike strange keys.

Between the red cabbage and the stuffed green peppers was the item:
'DEAREST WALTER, WITH HARD-BOILED EGG.'

THE GREEN DOOR

SUPPOSE YOU SHOULD BE WALKING down Broadway after dinner, with ten minutes
allotted to the consummation of your cigar while you are choosing between
a diverting tragedy and something serious in the way of vaudeville. Suddenly
a hand is laid upon your arm. You turn to look into the thrilling eyes of a
beautiful woman, wonderful in diamonds and Russian sables. She thrusts
hurriedly into your hand an extremely hot buttered roll, flashes out a tiny
pair of scissors, snips off the second button of your overcoat, meaningly
ejaculates the one word, 'parallelogram!' and swiftly flies down a cross street,
looking back fearfully over her shoulder.

That would be pure adventure. Would you accept it? Not you. You would
flush with embarrassment; you would sheepishly drop the roll and continue
down Broadway, fumbling feebly for the missing button. This you would do
unless you are one of the blessed few in whom the pure spirit of adventure
is not dead.

True adventurers have never been plentiful. They who are set down in
print as such have been mostly business men with newly invented methods.
They have been out after the things they wanted – golden fleeces, holy grails,
lady loves, treasure, crowns and fame. The true adventurer goes forth aimless
and uncalculating to meet and greet unknown fate. A fine example was the
Prodigal Son – when he started back home.

Half-adventurers – brave and splendid figures – have been numerous. From
the Crusades to the Palisades they have enriched the arts of history and
fiction and the trade of historical fiction. But each of them had a prize to
win, a goal to kick, an axe to grind, a race to run, a new thrust in tierce to
deliver, a name to carve, a crow to pick – so they were not followers of true
adventure.

In the big city the twin spirits Romance and Adventure are always abroad
seeking worthy wooers. As we roam the streets they slyly peep at us and
challenge us in twenty different guises. Without knowing why, we look up
suddenly to see in a window a face that seems to belong to our gallery of
intimate portraits; in a sleeping thoroughfare we hear a cry of agony and fear
coming from an empty and shuttered house; instead of at our familiar curb
a cab-driver deposits us before a strange door, which one, with a smile, opens
for us and bids us enter; a slip of paper, written upon, flutters down to our
feet from the high lattices of Chance; we exchange glances of instantaneous
hate, affection, and fear with hurrying strangers in the passing crowds; a
sudden souse of rain – and our umbrella may be sheltering the daughter of
the Full Moon and first cousin of the Sidereal System; at every corner
handkerchiefs drop, fingers beckon, eyes besiege, and the lost, the lonely,
the rapturous, the mysterious, the perilous changing clues of adventure are

slipped into our fingers. But few of us are willing to hold and follow them. We are grown stiff with the ramrod of convention down our backs. We pass on; and some day we come, at the end of a very dull life, to reflect that our romance has been a pallid thing of a marriage or two, a satin rosette kept in a safe-deposit drawer, and a lifelong feud with a steam radiator.

Rudolf Steiner was a true adventurer. Few were the evenings on which he did not go forth from his hall bedchamber in search of the unexpected and the egregious. The most interesting thing in life seemed to him to be what might lie just around the next corner. Sometimes his willingness to tempt fate led him into strange paths. Twice he had spent the night in a station-house; again and again he had found himself the dupe of ingenious and mercenary tricksters; his watch and money had been the price of one flattering allurement. But with undiminished ardor he picked up every glove cast before him into the merry lists of adventure.

One evening Rudolf was strolling along a cross-town street in the older central part of the city. Two streams of people filled the sidewalks – the home-hurrying, and that restless contingent that abandons home for the specious welcome of the thousand-candle-power *table d'hôte*.

The young adventurer was of pleasing presence, and moved serenely and watchfully. By daylight he was a salesman in a piano store. He wore his tie drawn through a topaz ring instead of fastened with a stick pin; and once he had written to the editor of a magazine that 'Junie's Love Test,' by Miss Libbey, had been the book that had most influenced his life.

During his walk a violent chattering of teeth in a glass case on the sidewalk seemed at first to draw his attention (with a qualm) to a restaurant before which it was set; but a second glance revealed the electric letters of a dentist's sign high above the next door. A giant negro, fantastically dressed in a red embroidered coat, yellow trousers and a military cap, discreetly distributed cards to those of the passing crowd who consented to take them.

This mode of dentistic advertising was a common sight to Rudolf. Usually he passed the dispenser of the dentist's cards without reducing his store; but to-night the African slipped one into his hand so deftly that he retained it there smiling a little at the successful feat.

When he had travelled a few yards further he glanced at the card indifferently. Surprised, he turned it over and looked again with interest. One side of the card was blank; on the other was written in ink three words, 'The Green Door.' And then Rudolf saw, three steps in front of him, a man throw down the card the negro had given him as he passed. Rudolf picked it up. It was printed with the dentist's name and address and the usual schedule of 'plate work' and 'bridge work' and 'crowns,' and specious promises of 'painless' operations.

The adventurous piano salesman halted at the corner and considered. Then he crossed the street, walked down a block, recrossed and joined the upward current of people again. Without seeming to notice the negro as he passed the second time, he carelessly took the card that was handed him. Ten steps away he inspected it. In the same handwriting that appeared on the first card 'The Green Door' was inscribed upon it. Three or four cards were tossed to the pavement by pedestrians both following and leading him. These fell blank side up. Rudolf turned them over. Every one bore the printed legend of the dental 'parlors.'

Rarely did the arch sprite Adventure need to beckon twice to Rudolf Steiner, his true follower. But twice it had been done, and the quest was on.

Rudolf walked slowly back to where the giant negro stood by the case of rattling teeth. This time as he passed he received no card. In spite of his gaudy and ridiculous garb, the Ethiopian displayed a natural barbaric dignity as he stood, offering the cards suavely to some, allowing others to pass unmolested. Every half minute he chanted a harsh, unintelligible phrase akin to the jabber of car conductors and grand opera. And not only did he withhold a card this time but it seemed to Rudolf that he received from the shining and massive black countenance a look of cold, almost contemptuous disdain.

The look stung the adventurer. He read in it a silent accusation that he had been found wanting. Whatever the mysterious written words on the cards might mean, the black had selected him twice from the throng for their recipient; and now seemed to have condemned him as deficient in the wit and spirit to engage the enigma.

Standing aside from the rush, the young man made a rapid estimate of the building in which he conceived that his adventure must lie. Five stories high it rose. A small restaurant occupied the basement.

The first floor, now closed, seemed to house millinery or furs. The second floor, by the winking electric letters, was the dentist's. Above this a polyglot babel of signs struggled to indicate the abodes of palmists, dressmakers, musicians, and doctors. Still higher up draped curtains and milk bottles white on the window sills proclaimed the regions of domesticity.

After concluding his survey Rudolf walked briskly up the high flight of stone steps into the house. Up two flights of the carpeted stairway he continued; and at its top paused. The hallway there was dimly lighted by two pale jets of gas – one far to his right, the other nearer, to his left. He looked toward the nearer light and saw, within its wan halo, a green door. For one moment he hesitated; then he seemed to see the contumelious sneer of the African juggler of cards; and then he walked straight to the green door and knocked against it.

Moments like those that passed before his knock was answered measure the quick breath of true adventure. What might not be behind those green panels! Gamesters at play; cunning rogues baiting their traps with subtle skill; beauty in love with courage, and thus planning to be sought by it; danger, death, love, disappointment, ridicule – any of these might respond to that temerarious rap.

A faint rustle was heard inside, and the door slowly opened. A girl not yet twenty stood there white-faced and tottering. She loosed the knob and swayed weakly, groping with one hand. Rudolf caught her and laid her on a faded couch that stood against the wall. He closed the door and took a swift glance around the room by the light of a flickering gas jet. Neat, but extreme poverty was the story that he read.

The girl lay still, as if in a faint. Rudolf looked around the room excitedly for a barrel. People must be rolled upon a barrel who – no, no; that was for drowned persons. He began to fan her with his hat. That was successful, for he struck her nose with the brim of his derby and she opened her eyes. And then the young man saw that hers, indeed, was the one missing face from his heart's gallery of intimate portraits. The frank, gray eyes, the little nose, turning pertly outward; the chestnut hair, curling like the tendrils of a pea vine, seemed the right end and reward of all his wonderful adventures. But the face was woefully thin and pale.

The girl looked at him calmly, and then smiled.

'Fainted, didn't I?' she asked, weakly. 'Well, who wouldn't? You try going without anything to eat for three days and see!'

'Himmel!' exclaimed Rudolf, jumping up. 'Wait till I come back.'

He dashed out the green door and down the stairs. In twenty minutes he was back again kicking at the door with his toe for her to open it. With both arms he hugged an array of wares from the grocery and the restaurant. On the table he laid them – bread and butter, cold meats, cakes, pies, pickles, oysters, a roasted chicken, a bottle of milk and one of red-hot tea.

'This is ridiculous,' said Rudolf, blusteringly, 'to go without eating. You must quit making election bets of this kind. Supper is ready.' He helped her to a chair at the table and asked: 'Is there a cup for the tea?' 'On the shelf by the window,' she answered. When he turned again with the cup he saw her, with eyes shining rapturously, beginning upon a huge dill pickle that she had rooted out from the paper bags with a woman's unerring instinct. He took it from her, laughingly, and poured the cup full of milk. 'Drink that first,' he ordered, 'and then you shall have some tea, and then a chicken wing. If you are very good you shall have a pickle to-morrow. And now, if you'll allow me to be your guest we'll have supper.'

He drew up the other chair. The tea brightened the girl's eyes and brought back some of her color. She began to eat with a sort of dainty ferocity like some starved wild animal. She seemed to regard the young man's presence and the aid he had rendered her as a natural thing – not as though she undervalued the conventions; but as one whose great stress gave her the right to put aside the artificial for the human. But gradually, with the return of strength and comfort, came also a sense of the little conventions that belong; and she began to tell him her little story. It was one of a thousand such as the city yawns at every day – the shop girl's story of insufficient wages, further reduced by 'fines' that go to swell the store's profits; of time lost through illness; and then of lost positions, lost hope, and – the knock of the adventurer upon the green door.

But to Rudolf the history sounded as big as the Iliad or the crisis in 'Junie's Love Test.'

'To think of you going through all that,' he exclaimed.

'It was something fierce,' said the girl, solemnly.

'And you have no relatives or friends in the city?'

'None whatever.'

'I am all alone in the world, too,' said Rudolf, after a pause.

'I am glad of that,' said the girl, promptly; and somehow it pleased the young man to hear that she approved of his bereft condition.

Very suddenly her eyelids dropped and she sighed deeply.

'I'm awfully sleepy,' she said, 'and I feel so good.'

Rudolf rose and took his hat.

'Then I'll say good-night. A long night's sleep will be fine for you.'

He held out his hand, and she took it and said 'good-night.' But her eyes asked a question so eloquently, so frankly and pathetically that he answered it with words.

'Oh, I'm coming back to-morrow to see how you are getting along. You can't get rid of me so easily.'

Then, at the door, as though the way of his coming had been so much less important than the fact that he had come, she asked: 'How did you come to knock at my door?'

He looked at her for a moment, remembering the cards, and felt a sudden jealous pain. What if they had fallen into other hands as adventurous as his? Quickly he decided that she must never know the truth. He would never let her know that he was aware of the strange expedient to which she had been driven by her great distress.

'One of our piano tuners lives in this house,' he said. 'I knocked at your door by mistake.'

The last thing he saw in the room before the green door closed was her smile.

At the head of the stairway he paused and looked curiously about him. And then he went along the hallway to its other end; and, coming back, ascended to the floor above and continued his puzzled explorations. Every door that he found in the house was painted green.

Wondering, he descended to the sidewalk. The fantastic African was still there. Rudolf confronted him with his two cards in his hand.

'Will you tell me why you gave me these cards and what they mean?' he asked.

In a broad, good-natured grin the negro exhibited a splendid advertisement of his master's profession.

'Dar it is, boss,' he said, pointing down the street. 'But I 'spect you is a little late for de fust act.'

Looking the way he pointed Rudolf saw above the entrance to a theatre the blazing electric sign of its new play, 'The Green Door.'

'I'm informed dat it's a fust-rate show, sah,' said the negro. 'De agent what represents it pussented me with a dollar, sah, to distribute a few of his cards along with de doctah's. May I offer you one of de doctah's cards, suh?'

At the corner of the block in which he lived Rudolf stopped for a glass of beer and a cigar. When he had come out with his lighted weed he buttoned his coat, pushed back his hat and said, stoutly, to the lamp post on the corner:

'All the same, I believe it was the hand of Fate that doped out the way for me to find her.'

Which conclusion, under the circumstances, certainly admits Rudolf Steiner to the ranks of the true followers of Romance and Adventure.

FROM THE CABBY'S SEAT

THE CABBY HAS HIS POINT OF VIEW. It is more single-minded, perhaps, than that of a follower of any other calling. From the high, swaying seat of his hansom he looks upon his fellow-men as nomadic particles, of no account except when possessed of migratory desires. He is Jehu, and you are goods in transit. Be you President or vagabond, to cabby you are only a Fare. He takes you up, cracks his whip, joggles your vertebrae and sets you down.

When time for payment arrives, if you exhibit a familiarity with legal rates you come to know what contempt is; if you find that you have left your pocketbook behind you are made to realize the mildness of Dante's imagination.

It is not an extravagant theory that the cabby's singleness of purpose and concentrated view of life are the results of the hansom's peculiar construction. The cock-of-the-roost sits aloft like Jupiter on an unsharable seat, holding your fate between two thongs of inconstant leather. Helpless, ridiculous, confined, bobbing like a toy mandarin, you sit like a rat in a trap – you, before whom butlers cringe on solid land – and must squeak upward through a slit in your peripatetic sarcophagus to make your feeble wishes known.

Then, in a cab, you are not even an occupant; you are contents. You are a cargo at sea, and the 'cherub that sits up aloft' has Davy Jones's street and number of heart.

One night there were sounds of revelry in the big brick tenement house next door but one to McGary's Family Café. The sounds seemed to emanate from the apartments of the Walsh family. The sidewalk was obstructed by an assortment of interested neighbors, who opened a lane from time to time for a hurrying messenger bearing from McGary's goods pertinent to festivity and diversion. The sidewalk contingent was engaged in comment and discussion from which it made no effort to eliminate the news that Norah Walsh was being married.

In the fulness of time there was an eruption of the merry-makers to the sidewalk. The uninvited guests enveloped and permeated them, and upon the night air rose joyous cries, congratulations, laughter, and unclassified noises born of McGary's oblations to the hymeneal scene.

Close to the curb stood Jerry O'Donovan's cab. Night-hawk was Jerry called; but no more lustrous or cleaner hansom than his ever closed its doors upon point lace and November violets. And Jerry's horse! I am within bounds when I tell you that he was stuffed with oats until one of those old ladies who leave their dishes unwashed at home and go about having expressmen arrested, would have smiled – yes, smiled – to have seen him.

Among the shifting, sonorous, pulsing crowd glimpses could be had of Jerry's high hat, battered by the winds and rains of many years; of his nose like a carrot, battered by the frolicsome, athletic progeny of millionaires and by contumacious fares; of his brass-buttoned green coat, admired in the vicinity of McGary's. It was plain that Jerry had usurped the functions of his cab, and was carrying a 'load.' Indeed, the figure may be extended and he be likened to a bread-wagon if we admit the testimony of a youthful spectator, who was heard to remark 'Jerry has got a bun.'

From somewhere among the throng in the street or else out of the thin stream of pedestrians a young woman tripped and stood by the cab. The professional hawk's eye of Jerry caught the movement. He made a lurch for the cab, overturning three or four onlookers and himself – no! he caught the cap of a water-plug and kept his feet. Like a sailor shinning up the ratlins during a squall Jerry mounted to his professional seat. Once he was there McGary's liquids were baffled. He seesawed on the mizzenmast of his craft as safe as a Steeple Jack rigged to the flagpole of a skyscraper.

'Step in, lady,' said Jerry, gathering his lines.

The young woman stepped into the cab; the doors shut with a bang; Jerry's whip cracked in the air; the crowd in the gutter scattered, and the fine hansom dashed away 'crosstown.

When the oat-spry horse had hedged a little his first spurt of speed Jerry broke the lid of his cab and called down through the aperture in the voice of a cracked megaphone, trying to please:

'Where, now, will ye be drivin' to?'

'Anywhere you please,' came up the answer, musical and contented.

' 'Tis drivin' for pleasure she is,' thought Jerry. And then he suggested as a matter of course:

'Take a thrip around in the park, lady. 'Twill be ilegant cool and fine.'

'Just as you like,' answered the fare, pleasantly.

The cab headed for Fifth Avenue and sped up that perfect street. Jerry bounced and swayed in his seat. The potent fluids of McGary were disquieted and they sent new fumes to his head. He sang an ancient song of Killisnook and brandished his whip like a baton.

Inside the cab the fare sat up straight on the cushions, looking to right and left at the lights and houses. Even in the shadowed hansom her eyes shone like stars at twilight.

When they reached Fifty-ninth Street Jerry's head was bobbing and his reins were slack. But his horse turned in through the park gate and began the old familiar nocturnal round. And then the fare leaned back, entranced, and breathed deep the clean, wholesome odors of grass and leaf and bloom. And the wise beast in the shafts, knowing his ground, struck into his by-the-hour gait and kept to the right of the road.

Habit also struggled successfully against Jerry's increasing torpor. He raised the hatch of his storm-tossed vessel and made the inquiry that cabbies do make in the park.

'Like shtop at the Cas-sino, lady? Gezzer r'freshm's, 'n lish'n the music. Ev'body shtops.'

'I think that would be nice,' said the fare.

They reined up with a plunge at the Casino entrance. The cab doors flew open. The fare stepped directly upon the floor. At once she was caught in a web of ravishing music and dazzled by a panorama of lights and colors. Some one slipped a little square card into her hand on which was printed a number – 34. She looked around and saw her cab twenty yards away already lining up in its place among the waiting mass of carriages, cabs, and motor cars. And then a man who seemed to be all shirtfront danced backward before her; and next she was seated at a little table by a railing over which climbed a jessamine vine.

There seemed to be a wordless invitation to purchase; she consulted a collection of small coins in a thin purse, and received from them license to order a glass of beer. There she sat, inhaling and absorbing it all – the new-colored, new-shaped life in a fairy palace in an enchanted wood.

At fifty tables sat princes and queens clad in all the silks and gems of the world. And now and then one of them would look curiously at Jerry's fare. They saw a plain figure dressed in a pink silk of the kind that is tempered by the word 'foulard,' and a plain face that wore a look of love of life that the queens envied.

Twice the long hands of the clocks went round. Royalties thinned from their *al fresco* thrones, and buzzed or clattered away in their vehicles of state. The music retired into cases of wood and bags of leather and baize. Waiters removed cloths pointedly near the plain figure sitting almost alone.

Jerry's fare rose, and held out her numbered card simply:

'Is there anything coming on the ticket?' she asked.

A waiter told her it was her cab check, and that she should give it to the man at the entrance. This man took it, and called the number. Only three hansoms stood in line. The driver of one of them went and routed out Jerry asleep in his cab. He swore deeply, climbed to the captain's bridge and steered his craft to the pier. His fare entered, and the cab whirled into the cool fastnesses of the park along the shortest homeward cuts.

At the gate a glimmer of reason in the form of sudden suspicion seized upon Jerry's beclouded mind. One or two things occurred to him. He stopped his horse, raised the trap and dropped his phonographic voice, like a lead plummet, through the aperture:

'I want to see four dollars before goin' any further on th' thrip. Have ye got th' dough?'

'Four dollars!' laughed the fare, softly, 'dear me, no. I've only got a few pennies and a dime or two.

Jerry shut down the trap and slashed his oat-fed horse. The clatter of hoofs strangled but could not drown the sound of his profanity. He shouted choking and gurgling curses at the starry heavens; he cut viciously with his whip at passing vehicles; he scattered fierce and everchanging oaths and imprecations along the streets, so that a late truck driver, crawling homeward, heard and was abashed. But he knew his recourse, and made for it at a gallop.

At the house with the green lights beside the steps he pulled up. He flung wide the cab doors and tumbled heavily to the ground.

'Come on, you,' he said, roughly.

His fare came forth with the Casino dreamy smile still on her plain face. Jerry took her by the arm and led her into the police station. A gray-moustached sergeant looked keenly across the desk. He and the cabby were no strangers.

'Sargeant,' began Jerry in his old raucous, martyred, thunderous tones of complaint. 'I've got a fare here that—'

Jerry paused. He drew a knotted, red hand across his brow. The fog set up by McGary was beginning to clear away.

'A fare, sargeant,' he continued, with a grin, 'that I want to introduce to ye. It's me wife that I married at ould man Walsh's this evening. And a devil of a time we had, 'tis thrue. Shake hands wit th' sargeant, Norah, and we'll be off to home.'

Before stepping into the cab Norah sighed profoundly.

'I've had such a nice time, Jerry,' said she.

AN UNFINISHED STORY

WE NO LONGER GROAN AND HEAP ASHES upon our heads when the flames of Tophet are mentioned. For, even the preachers have begun to tell us that God is radium, or ether or some scientific compound, and that the worst we wicked ones may expect is a chemical reaction. This is a pleasing hypothesis; but there lingers yet some of the old, goodly terror of orthodoxy.

There are but two subjects upon which one may discourse with a free imagination, and without the possibility of being controverted. You may talk of your dreams; and you may tell what you heard a parrot say. Both Morpheus and the bird are incompetent witnesses; and your listener dare not attack your recital. The baseless fabric of a vision, then, shall furnish my theme

– chosen with apologies and regrets instead of the more limited field of pretty Polly's small talk.

I had a dream that was so far removed from the higher criticism that it had to do with the ancient, respectable, and lamented bar-of-judgment theory.

Gabriel had played his trump; and those of us who could not follow suit were arraigned for examination. I noticed at one side a gathering of professional bondsmen in solemn black and collars that buttoned behind; but it seemed there was some trouble about their real estate titles; and they did not appear to be getting any of us out.

A fly cop – an angel policeman – flew over to me and took me by the left wing. Near at hand was a group of very prosperous-looking spirits arraigned for judgment.

'Do you belong with that bunch?' the policeman asked.

'Who are they?' was my answer.

'Why,' said he, 'they are —'

But this irrelevant stuff is taking up space that the story should occupy.

Dulcie worked in a department store. She sold Hamburg edging, or stuffed peppers, or automobiles, or other little trinkets such as they keep in department stores. Of what she earned, Dulcie received six dollars per week. The remainder was credited to her and debited to somebody else's account in the ledger kept by G— Oh, primal energy, you say, Reverend Doctor— Well, then, in the Ledger of Primal Energy.

During her first year in the store, Dulcie was paid five dollars per week. It would be instructive to know how she lived on that amount. Don't care? Very well; probably you are interested in larger amounts. Six dollars is a larger amount. I will tell you how she lived on six dollars per week.

One afternoon at six, when Dulcie was sticking her hat pin within an eighth of an inch of her *medulla oblongata*, she said to her chum, Sadie – the girl that waits on you with her left side:

'Say, Sade, I made a date for dinner this evening with Piggy.'

'You never did!' exclaimed Sadie, admiringly. 'Well, ain't you the lucky one? Piggy's an awful swell; and he always takes a girl to swell places. He took Blanche up to the Hoffman House one evening, where they have swell music, and you see a lot of swells. You'll have a swell time, Dulce.'

Dulcie hurried homeward. Her eyes were shining, and her cheeks showed the delicate pink of life's – real life's – approaching dawn. It was Friday; and she had fifty cents left of her week's wages.

The streets were filled with the rush-hour floods of people. The electric lights of Broadway were glowing – calling moths from miles, from leagues, from hundreds of leagues out of darkness around to come in and attend the singeing school. Men in accurate clothes, with faces like those carved on cherry stones by the old salts in sailors' homes, turned and stared at Dulcie as she sped, unheeding, past them. Manhattan, the night-blooming cereus, was beginning to unfold its dead-white, heavy-odored petals.

Dulcie stopped in a store where goods were cheap and bought an imitation lace collar with her fifty cents. That money was to have been spent otherwise – fifteen cents for supper, ten cents for breakfast, ten cents for lunch. Another dime was to be added to her small store of savings; and five cents was to be squandered for licorice drops – the kind that made your cheek look like the toothache, and last as long. The licorice was an extravagance – almost a carouse – but what is life without pleasures?

Dulcie lived in a furnished room. There is this difference between a furnished room and a boarding-house. In a furnished room, other people do not know it when you go hungry.

Dulcie went up to her room – the third-floor-back in a West Side brownstone-front. She lit the gas. Scientists tell us that the diamond is the hardest substance known. Their mistake. Landladies know of a compound beside which the diamond is as putty. They pack it in the tips of gas-burners; and one may stand on a chair and dig at it in vain until one's fingers are pink and bruised. A hairpin will not remove it; therefore let us call it immovable.

So Dulcie lit the gas. In its one-fourth-candle-power glow we will observe the room.

Couch-bed, dresser, table, washstand, chair – of this much the landlady was guilty. The rest was Dulcie's. On the dresser were her treasures – a gilt china vase presented to her by Sadie, a calendar issued by a pickle works, a book on the divination of dreams, some rice powder in a glass dish, and a cluster of artificial cherries tied with a pink ribbon.

Against the wrinkly mirror stood pictures of General Kitchener, William Muldoon, the Duchess of Marlborough, and Benvenuto Cellini. Against one wall was a plaster of Paris plaque of an O'Callahan in a Roman helmet. Near it was a violent oleograph of a lemon-colored child assaulting an inflammatory butterfly. This was Dulcie's final judgment in art; but it had never been upset. Her rest had never been disturbed by whispers of stolen copes; no critic had elevated his eyebrows at her infantile entomologist.

Piggy was to call for her at seven. While she swiftly makes ready, let us discreetly face the other way and gossip.

For the room, Dulcie paid two dollars per week. On week-days her breakfast cost ten cents; she made coffee and cooked an egg over the gaslight while she was dressing. On Sunday mornings she feasted royally on veal chops and pineapple fritters at 'Billy's' restaurant, at a cost of twenty-five cents – and tipped the waitress ten cents. New York presents so many temptations for one to run into extravagance. She had her lunches in the department-store restaurant at a cost of sixty cents for the week; dinners were $1.05. The evening papers – show me a New Yorker going without his daily paper! – came to six cents; and two Sunday papers – one for the personal column and the other to read – were ten cents. The total amounts to $4.76. Now, one has to buy clothes, and—

I give it up. I hear of wonderful bargains in fabrics, and of miracles performed with needle and thread; but I am in doubt. I hold my pen poised in vain when I would add to Dulcie's life some of those joys that belong to woman by virtue of all the unwritten, sacred, natural, inactive ordinances of the equity of heaven. Twice she had been to Coney Island and had ridden the hobby-horses. 'Tis a weary thing to count your pleasures by summers instead of by hours.

Piggy needs but a word. When the girls named him, an undeserving stigma was cast upon the noble family of swine. The words-of-three-letters lesson in the old blue spelling book begins with Piggy's biography. He was fat; he had the soul of a rat, the habits of a bat, and the magnanimity of a cat. . . . He wore expensive clothes; and was a connoisseur in starvation. He could look at a shop-girl and tell you to an hour how long it had been since she had eaten anything more nourishing than marshmallows and tea. He hung about the shopping districts, and prowled around in department stores with his

invitations to dinner. Men who escort dogs upon the streets at the end of a
string look down upon him. He is a type; I can dwell upon him no longer;
my pen is not the kind intended for him; I am no carpenter.

At ten minutes to seven Dulcie was ready. She looked at herself in the
wrinkly mirror. The reflection was satisfactory. The dark blue dress, fitting
without a wrinkle, the hat with its jaunty black feather, the but-slightly-
soiled gloves – all representing self-denial, even of food itself – were vastly
becoming.

Dulcie forgot everything else for a moment except that she was beautiful,
and that life was about to lift a corner of its mysterious veil for her to observe
its wonders. No gentleman had ever asked her out before. Now she was
going for a brief moment into the glitter and exalted show.

The girls said that Piggy was a 'spender.' There would be a grand dinner,
and music, and splendidly dressed ladies to look at and things to eat that
strangely twisted the girls' jaws when they tried to tell about them. No doubt
she would be asked out again.

There was a blue pongee suit in a window that she knew – by saving
twenty cents a week instead of ten in – let's see— Oh, it would run into
years! But there was a second-hand store in Seventh Avenue where—

Somebody knocked at the door. Dulcie opened it. The landlady stood there
with a spurious smile, sniffing for cooking by stolen gas.

'A gentleman's downstairs to see you,' she said. 'Name is Mr. Wiggins.'

By such epithet was Piggy known to unfortunate ones who had to take
him seriously.

Dulcie turned to the dresser to get her handkerchief; and then she stopped
still, and bit her underlip hard. While looking in her mirror she had seen
fairyland and herself, a princess, just awakening from a long slumber. She
had forgotten one that was watching her with sad, beautiful, stern eyes – the
only one there was to approve or condemn what she did. Straight and slender
and tall, with a look of sorrowful reproach on his handsome, melancholy
face, General Kitchener fixed his wonderful eyes on her out of his gilt
photograph frame on the dresser.

Dulcie turned like an automatic doll to the landlady.

'Tell him I can't go,' she said, dully. 'Tell him I'm sick, or something. Tell
him I'm not going out.'

After the door was closed and locked, Dulcie fell upon her bed, crushing
her black tip, and cried for ten minutes. General Kitchener was her only
friend. He was Dulcie's ideal of a gallant knight. He looked as if he might
have a secret sorrow, and his wonderful moustache was a dream, and she was
a little afraid of that stern yet tender look in his eyes. She used to have little
fancies that he would call at the house sometime, and ask for her, with his
sword clanking against his high boots. Once, when a boy was rattling a piece
of chain against a lamp post she had opened the window and looked out. But
there was no use. She knew that General Kitchener was away over in Japan,
leading his army against the savage Turks; and he would never step out of
his gilt frame for her. Yet one look from him had vanquished Piggy that
night. Yes, for that night.

When her cry was over Dulcie got up and took off her best dress, and put
on her old blue kimono. She wanted no dinner. She sang two verses of
'Sammy.' Then she became intensely interested in a little red speck on the

side of her nose. And after that was attended to, she drew up a chair to the rickety table, and told her fortune with an old deck of cards.

'The horrid, impudent thing!' she said aloud. 'And I never gave him a word or a look to make him think it!'

At nine o'clock Dulcie took a tin box of crackers and a little pot of raspberry jam out of her trunk and had a feast. She offered General Kitchener some jam on a cracker; but he only looked at her as the sphinx would have looked at a butterfly – if there are butterflies in the desert.

'Don't eat if you don't want to,' said Dulcie. 'And don't put on so many airs and scold so with your eyes. I wonder if you'd be so superior and snippy if you had to live on six dollars a week.'

It was not a good sign for Dulcie to be rude to General Kitchener. And then she turned Benvenuto Cellini face downward with a severe gesture. But that was not inexcusable; for she had always thought he was Henry VIII, and she did not approve of him.

At half-past nine Dulcie took a last look at the pictures on the dresser, turned out the light and skipped into bed. It's an awful thing to go to bed with a good-night look at General Kitchener, William Muldoon, the Duchess of Marlborough, and Benvenuto Cellini.

This story doesn't really get anywhere at all. The rest of it comes later – sometime when Piggy asks Dulcie again to dine with him, and she is feeling lonelier than usual, and General Kitchener happens to be looking the other way; and then—

As I said before, I dreamed that I was standing near a crowd of prosperous-looking angels, and a policeman took me by the wing and asked if I belonged with them.

'Who are they?' I asked.

'Why,' said he, 'they are the men who hired working-girls, and paid 'em five or six dollars a week to live on. Are you one of the bunch?'

'Not on your immortality,' said I. 'I'm only a fellow that set fire to an orphan asylum, and murdered a blind man for his pennies.'

THE CALIPH, CUPID AND THE CLOCK

PRINCE MICHAEL, OF THE ELECTORATE VALLELUNA, sat on his favorite bench in the park. The coolness of the September night quickened the life in him like a rare, tonic wine. The benches were not filled; for park loungers, with their stagnant blood, are prompt to detect and fly home from the crispness of early autumn. The moon was just clearing the roofs of the range of dwellings that bounded the quadrangle on the east. Children laughed and played about the fine-sprayed fountain. In the shadowed spots fauns and hamadryads wooed, unconscious of the gaze of mortal eyes. A hand-organ – Philomel by the grace of our stage carpenter, Fancy – fluted and droned in a side street. Around the enchanted boundaries of the little park street cars spat and mewed and the stilted trains roared like tigers and lions prowling for a place to enter. And above the trees shone the great, round, shining face of an illuminated clock in the tower of an antique public building.

Prince Michael's shoes were wrecked far beyond the skill of the carefullest cobbler. The ragman would have declined any negotiations concerning his clothes. The two weeks' stubble on his face was gray and brown and red and greenish yellow – as if it had been made up from individual contributions from the chorus of a musical comedy. No man existed who had money enough to wear so bad a hat as his.

Prince Michael sat on his favorite bench and smiled. It was a diverting thought to him that he was wealthy enough to buy every one of those closed-ranged, bulky, window-lit mansions that faced him, if he chose. He could have matched gold, equipages, jewels, art treasures, estates and acres with any Croesus in this proud city of Manhattan, and scarcely have entered upon the bulk of his holdings. He could have sat at table with reigning sovereigns. The social world, the world of art, the fellowship of the elect, adulation, imitation, the homage of the fairest, honors from the highest, praise from the wisest, flattery, esteem, credit, pleasure, fame – all the honey of life was waiting in the comb in the hive of the world for Prince Michael, of the Electorate of Valleluna, whenever he might choose to take it. But his choice was to sit in rags and dinginess on a bench in a park. For he had tasted of the fruit of the tree of life, and, finding it bitter in his mouth had stepped out of Eden for a time to seek distraction close to the unarmored, beating heart of the world.

These thoughts strayed dreamily through the mind of Prince Michael, as he smiled under the stubble of his polychromatic beard. Lounging thus, clad as the poorest of mendicants in the parks, he loved to study humanity. He found in altruism more pleasure than his riches, his station and all the grosser sweets of life had given him. It was his chief solace and satisfaction to alleviate individual distress, to confer favors upon worthy ones who had need of succor, to dazzle unfortunates by unexpected and bewildering gifts of truly royal magnificence, bestowed, however, with wisdon and judiciousness.

And as Prince Michael's eye rested upon the glowing face of the great clock in the tower, his smile, altruistic as it was, became slightly tinged with contempt. Big thoughts were the Prince's; and it was always with a shake of his head that he considered the subjugation of the world to the arbitrary measures of Time. The comings and goings of people in hurry and dread, controlled by the little metal moving hands of a clock, always made him sad.

By and. by came a young man in evening clothes and sat upon the third bench from the Prince. For half an hour he smoked cigars with nervous haste, and then he fell to watching the face of the illuminated clock above the trees. His perturbation was evident, and the Prince noted, in sorrow, that its cause was connected, in some manner, with the slowly moving hands of the timepiece.

His Highness arose and went to the young man's bench.

'I beg your pardon for addressing you,' he said, 'but I perceive that you are disturbed in mind. If it may serve to mitigate the liberty I have taken I will add that I am Prince Michael, heir to the throne of the Electorate of Valleluna. I appear incognito, of course, as you may gather from my appearance. It is a fancy of mine to render aid to others whom I think worthy of it. Perhaps the matter that seems to distress you is one that would more readily yield to our mutual efforts.'

The young man looked up brightly at the Prince. Brightly, but the perpendicular line of perplexity between his brows was not smoothed away.

He laughed, and even then it did not. But he accepted the momentary diversion.

'Glad to meet you, Prince,' he said, good humoredly. 'Yes, I'd say you were incog. all right. Thanks for your offer of assistance – but I don't see where your butting-in would help things any. It's a kind of private affair, you know – but thanks all the same.'

Prince Michael sat at the young man's side. He was often rebuffed but never offensively. His courteous manner and words forbade that.

'Clocks,' said the Prince, 'are shackles on the feet of mankind. I have observed you looking persistently at that clock. Its face is that of a tyrant, its numbers are false as those on a lottery ticket; its hands are those of a bunco steerer, who makes an appointment with you to your ruin. Let me entreat you to throw off its humiliating bonds and cease to order your affairs by that insensate monitor of brass and steel.'

'I don't usually,' said the young man. 'I carry a watch except when I've got my radiant rags on.'

'I know human nature as I do the trees and grass,' said the Prince, with earnest dignity. 'I am a master of philosophy, a graduate in art, and I hold the purse of a Fortunatus. There are few mortal misfortunes that I cannot alleviate or overcome. I have read your countenance, and found in it honesty and nobility as well as distress. I beg of you to accept my advice or aid. Do not belie the intelligence I see in your face by judging from my appearance of my ability to defeat your troubles.'

The young man glanced at the clock again and frowned darkly. When his gaze strayed from the glowing horologue of time it rested intently upon a four-story red brick house in the row of dwellings opposite to where he sat. The shades were drawn, and the lights in many rooms shone dimly through them.

'Ten minutes to nine!' exclaimed the young man, with an impatient gesture of despair. He turned his back upon the house and took a rapid step or two in a contrary direction.

'Remain!' commanded Prince Michael, in so potent a voice that the disturbed one wheeled around with a somewhat chagrined laugh.

'I'll give her the ten minutes and then I'm off,' he muttered, and then aloud to the Prince: 'I'll join you in confounding all clocks, my friend, and throw in women, too.'

'Sit down,' said the Prince, calmly. 'I do not accept your addition. Women are the natural enemies of clocks, and, therefore, the allies of those who would seek liberation from these monsters that measure our follies and limit our pleasures. If you will so far confide in me I would ask you to relate to me your story.'

The young man threw himself upon the bench with a reckless laugh.

'Your Royal Highness, I will,' he said, in tones of mock deference. 'Do you see yonder house – the one with the three upper windows lighted? Well, at 6 o'clock I stood in that house with the young lady I am – that is, I was – engaged to. I had been doing wrong, my dear Prince – I had been a naughty boy, and she had heard of it. I wanted to be forgiven of course – we are always wanting women to forgive us, aren't we, Prince?

' "I want time to think it over," said she. "There is one thing certain; I will either fully forgive you, or I will never see your face again. There will be no half-way business. At half-past eight," she said, "at exactly half-past eight you may be watching the middle upper window of the top floor. If I decide to forgive I will hang out of that window a white silk scarf. You will know by that that all is as was before, and you may come to me. If you see no scarf you may consider that everything between us is ended forever." That,' concluded the young man, bitterly, 'is why I have been watching that clock. The time for the signal to appear has passed twenty-three minutes ago. Do you wonder that I am a little disturbed, my Prince of Rags and Whiskers?'

'Let me repeat to you,' said Prince Michael, in his even, well-modulated tones, 'that women are the natural enemies of clocks. Clocks are an evil, women a blessing. The signal may yet appear.'

'Never, on your principality!' exclaimed the young man, hopelessly. 'You don't know Marian – of course. She's always on time, to the minute. That was the first thing about her that attracted me. I've got the mitten instead of the scarf. I ought to have known at 8.31 that my goose was cooked. I'll go West on the 11.45 to-night with Jack Milburn. The jig's up. I'll try Jack's ranch awhile and top off with the Klondike and whiskey. Good-night – er – er – Prince.'

Prince Michael smiled his enigmatic, gentle, comprehending smile and caught the coat sleeve of the other. The brilliant light in the Prince's eyes was softening to a dreamier, cloudy translucence.

'Wait,' he said solemnly, 'till the clock strikes. I have wealth and power and knowledge above most men, but when the clock strikes I am afraid. Stay by me until then. This woman shall be yours. You have the word of the hereditary Prince of Valleluna. On the day of your marriage I will give you $100,000 and a palace on the Hudson. But there must be no clocks in that palace – they measure our follies and limit our pleasures. Do you agree to that?'

'Of course,' said the young man, cheerfully, 'they're a nuisance, anyway – always ticking and striking and getting you late for dinner.'

He glanced again at the clock in the tower. The hands stood at three minutes to nine.

'I think,' said Prince Michael, that I will sleep a little. The day has been fatiguing.'

He stretched himself upon a bench with the manner of one who had slept thus before.

'You will find me in this park on any evening when the weather is suitable,' said the Prince, sleepily. 'Come to me when your marriage day is set and I will give you a check for the money.'

'Thanks, Your Highness,' said the young man, seriously. 'It doesn't look as if I would need that palace on the Hudson, but I appreciate your offer, just the same.'

Prince Michael sank into deep slumber. His battered hat rolled from the bench to the ground. The young man lifted it, placed it over the frowsy face and moved one of the grotesquely relaxed limbs into a more comfortable position. 'Poor devil!' he said, as he drew the tattered clothes closer about the Prince's breast.

Sonorous and startling came the stroke of 9 from the clock tower. The young man sighed again, turned his face for one last look at the house of his relinquished hopes – and cried aloud profane words of holy rapture.

From the middle upper window blossomed in the dusk a waving, snowy, fluttering, wonderful, divine emblem of forgiveness and promised joy.

By came a citizen, rotund, comfortable, home-hurrying, unknowing of the delights of waving silken scarfs on the borders of dimly-lit parks.

'Will you oblige me with the time, sir?' asked the young man; and the citizen, shrewdly conjecturing his watch to be safe, dragged it out and announced:

'Twenty-nine and a half minutes past eight, sir.'

And then, from habit, he glanced at the clock in the tower, and made further oration.

'By George! that clock's half an hour fast! First time in ten years I've known it to be off. This watch of mine never varies a—'

But the citizen was talking to vacancy. He turned and saw his hearer a fast receding black shadow flying in the direction of a house with three lighted upper windows.

And in the morning came along two policemen on their way to the beats they owned. The park was deserted save for one dilapidated figure that sprawled, asleep, on a bench. They stopped and gazed upon it.

'It's Dopy Mike,' said one. 'He hits the pipe every night. Park bum for twenty years. On his last legs, I guess.'

The other policeman stooped and looked at something crumpled and crisp in the hand of the sleeper.

'Gee!' he remarked. 'He's doped out a fifty-dollar bill, anyway. Wish I knew the brand of hop that he smokes.'

And then 'Rap, rap, rap!' went the club of realism against the shoe soles of Prince Michael, of the Electorate of Valleluna.

SISTERS OF THE GOLDEN CIRCLE

THE RUBBERNECK AUTO was about ready to start. The merry top-riders had been assigned to their seats by the gentlemanly conductor. The sidewalk was blockaded with sightseers who had gathered to stare at sightseers, justifying the natural law that every creature on earth is preyed upon by some other creature.

The megaphone man raised his instrument of torture; the inside of the great automobile began to thump and throb like the heart of a coffee drinker. The top-riders nervously clung to the seats; the old lady from Valparaiso, Indiana, shrieked to be put ashore. But, before a wheel turns, listen to a brief preamble through the cardiaphone, which shall point out to you an object of interest on life's sightseeing tour.

Swift and comprehensive is the recognition of the white man for white man in African wilds; instant and sure is the spiritual greeting between mother and babe; unhesitatingly do master and dog commune across the slight gulf between animal and man; immeasurably quick and sapient are the brief messages between one and one's beloved. But all these instances set forth only slow and groping interchange of sympathy and thought beside one other instance which the Rubberneck coach shall disclose. You shall learn (if you have not learned already) what two beings of all earth's living inhabitants most quickly look into each other's hearts and souls when they meet face to face.

The gong whirred, and the Glaring-at-Gotham car.moved majestically upon its instructive tour.

On the highest, rear seat was James Williams, of Cloverdale, Missouri, and his Bride.

Capitalize it, friend typo – that last word – word of words in the epiphany of life and love. The scent of the flowers, the booty of the bee, the primal drip of spring waters, the overture of the lark, the twist of lemon peel on the cocktail of creation – such is the bride. Holy is the wife; revered the mother; galliptious is the summer girl – but the bride is the certified check among the wedding presents that the gods send in when man is married to mortality.

The car glided up the Golden Way. On the bridge of the great cruiser the captain stood, trumpeting the sights of the big city to his passengers. Wide-mouthed and open-eared they heard the sights of the metropolis thundered forth to their eyes. Confused, delirious with excitement and provincial longings, they tried to make ocular responses to the megaphonic ritual. In the solemn spires of spreading cathedrals they saw the home of the Vander-bilts; in the busy bulk of the Grand Central depot they viewed, wonderingly, the frugal cot of Russell Sage. Bidden to observe the highlands of the Hudson, they gaped, unsuspecting at the upturned mountains of a new-laid sewer.

To many the elevated railroad was the Rialto, on the stations of which uniformed men sat and made chop suey of your tickets. And to this day in the outlying districts many have it that Chuck Connors, with his hand on his heart, leads reform; and that but for the noble municipal efforts of one Parkhurst, a district attorney, the notorious 'Bishop' Potter gang would have destroyed law and order from the Bowery to the Harlem River.

But I beg you to observe Mrs. James Williams – Hattie Chalmers that was – once the belle of Cloverdale. Pale-blue is the bride's, if she will; and this color she had honored. Willingly had the moss rosebud loaned to her cheeks of its pink – and as for the violet! – her eyes wiĦ do very well as they are, thank you. A useless strip of white chaf – oh, no, he was guiding the auto car – of white chiffon – or perhaps it was grenadine or tulle – was tied beneath her chin, pretending to hold her bonnet in place. But you know as well as I do that the hat pins did the work.

And on Mrs. James Williams's face was recorded a little library of the world's best thoughts in three volumes. Volume No. 1 contained the belief that James Williams was about the right sort of thing. Volume No. 2 was an essay on the world, declaring it to be a very excellent place. Volume No. 3 disclosed the belief that in occupying the highest seat in a Rubberneck auto they were travelling the pace that passes all understanding.

James Williams, you would have guessed, was about twenty-four. It will gratify you to know that your estimate was so accurate. He was exactly twenty-three years, eleven months and twenty-nine days old. He was well built, active, strong-jawed, good-natured, and rising. He was on his wedding trip.

Dear kind fairy, please cut out those orders for money and 40 H. P. touring cars and fame and a new growth of hair and the presidency of the boat club. Instead of any of them turn backward – oh, turn backward and give us just a teeny-weeny bit of our wedding trip over again. Just an hour, dear fairy, so we can remember how the grass and poplar trees looked and the bow of those bonnet strings tied beneath her chin – even if it was the hat pins that did the work. Can't do it? Very well; hurry up with that touring car and the oil stock, then.

Just in front of Mrs. James Williams sat a girl in a loose tan jacket and a straw hat adorned with grapes and roses. Only in dream and milliners' shops do we, alas! gather grapes and roses at one swipe. This girl gazed with large blue eyes, credulous, when the megaphone man roared his doctrine that millionaires were things about which we should be concerned. Between blasts she resorted to Epictetian philosophy in the form of pepsin chewing gum.

At this girl's right hand sat a young man about twenty-four. He was well built, active, strong-jawed, and good-natured. But if his description seems to follow that of James Williams, divest it of anything Cloverdalian. This man belonged to hard streets and sharp corners. He looked keenly about him, seeming to begrudge the asphalt under the feet of those upon whom he looked down from his perch.

While the megaphone barks at a famous hostelry, let me whisper you through the low-tuned cardiaphone to sit tight; for now things are about to happen, and the great city will close over them again as over a scrap of ticker tape floating down from the den of a Broad Street bear.

The girl in the tan jacket twisted around to view the pilgrims on the last seat. The other passengers she had absorbed; the seat behind her was her Bluebeard's chamber.

Her eyes met those of Mrs. James Williams. Between two ticks of a watch they exchanged their life's experiences, histories, hopes and fancies. And all, mind you, with the eye, before two men could have decided whether to draw steel or borrow a match.

The bride leaned forward low. She and the girl spoke rapidly together, their tongues moving quickly like those of two serpents – a comparison that is not meant to go further. Two smiles and a dozen nods closed the conference.

And now in the broad, quiet avenue in front of the Rubberneck car a man in dark clothes stood with uplifted hand. From the sidewalk another hurried to join him.

The girl in the fruitful hat quickly seized her companion by the arm and whispered in his ear. That young man exhibited proof of ability to act promptly. Crouching low, he slid over the edge of the car, hung lightly for an instant, and then disappeared. Half a dozen of the top-riders observed his feat wonderingly, but made no comment, deeming it prudent not to express surprise at what might be the conventional manner of alighting in this bewildering city. The truant passenger dodged a hansom and then floated past, like a leaf on a stream between a furniture van and a florist's delivery wagon.

The girl in the tan jacket turned again, and looked into the eyes of Mrs. James Williams. Then she faced about and sat still while the Rubberneck auto stopped at the flash of the badge under the coat of the plainclothes man.

'What's eating you?' demanded the megaphonist, abandoning his professional discourse for pure English.

'Keep her at anchor for a minute,' ordered the officer. 'There's a man on board we want – a Philadelphia burglar called "Pinky" McGuire. There he is on the back seat. Look out for the side, Donovan.'

Donovan went to the hind wheel and looked up at James Williams.

'Come down, old sport,' he said pleasantly. 'We've got you. Back to

Sleepytown for yours. It ain't a bad idea, hidin' on a Rubberneck, though. I'll remember that.'

Softly through the megaphone came the advice of the conductor:

'Better step off, sir, and explain. The car must proceed on its tour.'

James Williams belonged among the level heads. With necessary slowness he picked his way through the passengers down to the steps at the front of the car. His wife followed, but she first turned her eyes and saw the escaped tourist glide from behind the furniture van and slip behind a tree on the edge of the little park, not fifty feet away.

Descended to the ground, James Williams faced his captors with a smile. He was thinking what a good story he would have to tell in Cloverdale about having been mistaken for a burglar. The Rubberneck coach lingered, out of respect for its patrons. What could be a more interesting sight than this?

'My name is James Williams, of Cloverdale, Missouri,' he said, kindly, so that they would not be too greatly mortified. 'I have letters here that will show —'

'You'll come with us, please,' announced the plainclothes man. ' "Pinky" McGuire's descriptions fits you like flannel washed in hot suds. A detective saw you on the Rubberneck up at Central Park and 'phoned down to take you in. Do your explaining at the station-house.'

James Williams's wife — his bride of two weeks — looked him in the face with a strange, soft radiance in her eyes and a flush on her cheeks, looked him in the face and said:

'Go with 'em quietly, "Pinky," and maybe it'll be in your favor.'

And then as the Glaring-at-Gotham car rolled away she turned and threw a kiss — his wife threw a kiss — at some one high up on the seats of the Rubberneck.

'Your girl gives you good advice, McGuire,' said Donovan. 'Come on now.'

And then madness descended upon and occupied James Williams. He pushed his hat far upon the back of his head.

'My wife seems to think I am a burglar,' he said, recklessly. 'I never heard of her being crazy; therefore I must be. And if I'm crazy, they can't do anything to me for killing you two fools in my madness.'

Whereupon he resisted so cheerfully and industriously that cops had to be whistled for, and afterwards the reserves, to disperse a few thousand delighted spectators.

At the station-house the desk sergeant asked for his name.

'McDoodle, the Pink, or Pinky the Brute, I forget which,' was James Williams's answer. 'But you can bet I'm a burglar; don't leave that out. And you might add that it took five of 'em to pluck the Pink. I'd especially like to have that in the records.'

In an hour came Mrs. James Williams, with Uncle Thomas, of Madison Avenue, in a respect-compelling motor car and proofs of the hero's innocence — for all the world like the third act of a drama backed by an automobile mfg. co.

After the police had sternly reprimanded James Williams for imitating a copyrighted burglar and given him as honorable a discharge as the department was capable of, Mrs. Williams rearrested him and swept him into an angle of the station-house. James Williams regarded her with one eye. He always said that Donovan closed the other while somebody was holding his good right hand. Never before had he given her a word of reproach or of reproof.

'If you can explain,' he began rather stiffly, 'why you—'

'Dear,' she interrupted, 'listen. It was an hour's pain and trial for you. I did it for her – I mean the girl who spoke to me on the coach. I was so happy, Jim – so happy with you that I didn't dare refuse that happiness to another. Jim, they were married only this morning – those two; and I wanted him to get away. While they were struggling with you I saw him slip from behind his tree and hurry across the park. That's all of it, dear – I had to do it.'

Thus does one sister of the plain gold band know another who stands in the enchanted light that shines but once and briefly for each one. By rice and satin bows does mere man become aware of weddings. But bride knoweth bride at the glance of an eye. And between them swiftly passes comfort and meaning in a language that man and widows wot not of.

THE ROMANCE OF A BUSY BROKER

PITCHER, CONFIDENTIAL CLERK in the office of Harvey Maxwell, broker, allowed a look of mild interest and surprise to visit his usually expressionless countenance when his employer briskly entered at half-past nine in company with his young lady stenographer. With a snappy 'Good-morning, Pitcher,' Maxwell dashed at his desk as though he were intending to leap over it, and then plunged into the great heap of letters and telegrams waiting there for him.

The young lady had been Maxwell's stenographer for a year. She was beautiful in a way that was decidedly unstenographic. She forewent the pomp of the alluring pompadour. She wore no chains, bracelets, or lockets. She had not the air of being about to accept an invitation to luncheon. Her dress was gray and plain, but it fitted her figure with fidelity and discretion. In her neat black turban hat was the gold-green wing of a macaw. On this morning she was softly and shyly radiant. Her eyes were dreamily bright, her cheeks genuine peach-blow, her expression a happy one, tinged with reminiscence.

Pitcher, still mildly curious, noticed a difference in her ways this morning. Instead of going straight into the adjoining room, where her desk was, she lingered, slightly irresolute, in the outer office. Once she moved over by Maxwell's desk, near enough for him to be aware of her presence.

The machine sitting at that desk was no longer a man; it was a busy New York broker, moved by buzzing wheels and uncoiling springs.

'Well – what is it? Anything?' asked Maxwell, sharply. His opened mail lay like a bank of stage snow on his crowded desk. His keen gray eye, impersonal and brusque, flashed upon her half impatiently.

'Nothing,' answered the stenographer, moving away with a little smile.

'Mr. Pitcher,' she said to the confidential clerk, 'did Mr. Maxwell say anything yesterday about engaging another stenographer?'

'He did,' answered Pitcher. 'He told me to get another one. I notified the agency yesterday afternoon to send over a few samples this morning. It's 9.45 o'clock, and not a single picture hat or piece of pineapple chewing gum has showed up yet.'

'I will do the work as usual, then,' said the young lady, 'until some one comes to fill the place.' And she went to her desk at once and hung the black turban hat with the gold-green macaw wing in its accustomed place.

He who has been denied the spectacle of a busy Manhattan broker during a rush of business is handicapped for the profession of anthropology. The poet sings of the 'crowded hour of glorious life.' The broker's hour is not only crowded, but minutes and seconds are hanging to all the straps and packing both front and rear platforms.

And this day was Harvey Maxwell's busy day. The ticker began to reel out jerkily its fitful coils of tape, the desk telephone had a chronic attack of buzzing. Men began to throng into the office and call at him over the railing, jovially, sharply, viciously, excitedly. Messenger boys ran in and out with messages and telegrams. The clerks in the office jumped about like sailors during a storm. Even Pitcher's face relaxed into something resembling animation.

On the Exchange there were hurricanes and landslides and snowstorms and glaciers and volcanoes, and those elemental disturbances were reproduced in miniature in the broker's offices. Maxwell shoved his chair against the wall and transacted business after the manner of a toe dancer. He jumped from ticker to 'phone, from desk to door with the trained agility of a harlequin.

In the midst of this growing and important stress the broker became suddenly aware of a high-rolled fringe of golden hair under a nodding canopy of velvet and ostrich tips, an imitation sealskin sacque and a string of beads as large as hickory nuts, ending near the floor with a silver heart. There was a self-possessed young lady connected with these accessories; and Pitcher was there to construe her.

'Lady from the Stenographer's Agency to see about the position,' said Pitcher.

Maxwell turned half around, with his hands full of papers and ticker tape. 'What position?' he asked, with a frown.

'Position of stenographer,' said Pitcher. 'You told me yesterday to call them up and have one sent over this morning.'

'You are losing your mind, Pitcher,' said Maxwell. 'Why should I have given you any such instructions? Miss Leslie has given perfect satisfaction during the year she has been here. The place is hers as long as she chooses to retain it. There's no place open here, madam. Countermand that order with the agency, Pitcher, and don't bring any more of 'em here.'

The silver heart left the office, swinging and banging itself independently against the office furniture as it indignantly departed. Pitcher seized a moment to remark to the bookkeeper that the 'old man' seemed to get more absent-minded and forgetful every day of the world.

The rush and pace of business grew fiercer and faster. On the floor they were pounding half a dozen stocks in which Maxwell's customers were heavy investors. Orders to buy and sell were coming and going as swift as the flight of swallows. Some of his own holdings were imperilled, and the man was working like some high-geared, delicate, strong machine – strung to full tension, going at full speed, accurate, and never hesitating, with the proper word and decision and act ready and prompt as clockwork. Stocks and bonds, loans and mortgages, margins and securities – here was a world of finance, and there was no room in it for the human world or the world of nature.

When the luncheon hour drew near there came a slight lull in the uproar.

Maxwell stood by his desk with his hands full of telegrams and memoranda, with a fountain pen over his right ear and his hair hanging in disorderly strings over his forehead. His window was open, for the beloved janitress, Spring had turned on a little warmth through the waking registers of the earth.

And through the window came a wandering – perhaps a lost – odor – a delicate, sweet odor of lilac that fixed the broker for a moment immovable. For this odor belonged to Miss Leslie; it was her own, and hers only.

The odor brought her vividly, almost tangibly before him. The world of finance dwindled suddenly to a speck. And she was in the next room – twenty steps away.

'By George, I'll do it now,' said Maxwell, half aloud. 'I'll ask her now. I wonder I didn't do it long ago.'

He dashed into the inner office with the haste of a short trying to cover. He charged upon the desk of the stenographer.

She looked up at him with a smile. A soft pink crept over her cheek, and her eyes were kind and frank. Maxwell leaned one elbow on her desk. He still clutched fluttering papers with both hands and the pen was above his ear.

'Miss Leslie,' he began, hurriedly, 'I have but a moment to spare. I want to say something in that moment. Will you be my wife? I haven't had time to make love to you in the ordinary way, but I really do love you. Talk quick, please – those fellows are clubbing the stuffing out of Union Pacific.'

'Oh, what are you talking about?' exclaimed the young lady. She rose to her feet and gazed upon him, round-eyed.

'Don't you understand?' said Maxwell, restively. 'I want you to marry me. I love you, Miss Leslie. I wanted to tell you, and I snatched a minute when things had slackened up a bit. They're calling me for the 'phone now. Tell 'em to wait a minute, Pitcher. Won't you, Miss Leslie?'

The stenographer acted very queerly. At first she seemed overcome with amazement; then tears flowed from her wondering eyes; and then she smiled sunnily through them, and one of her arms slid tenderly about the broker's neck.

'I know now,' she said, softly. 'It's this old business that has driven everything else out of your head for the time. I was frightened at first. Don't you remember, Harvey? We were married last evening at 8 o'clock in the Little Church around the Corner.'

AFTER TWENTY YEARS

THE POLICEMAN ON THE BEAT moved up the avenue impressively. The impressiveness was habitual and not for show, for spectators were few. The time was barely 10 o'clock at night, but chilly gusts of wind with a taste of rain in them had well nigh depeopled the streets.

Trying doors as he went, twirling his club with many intricate and artful movements, turning now and then to cast his watchful eye adown the pacific thoroughfare, the officer, with his stalwart form and slight swagger, made a fine picture of a guardian of the peace. The vicinity was one that kept early hours. Now and then you might see the lights of a cigar store or of an all-night lunch counter; but the majority of the doors belonged to business places that had long since been closed.

When about midway of a certain block the policeman suddenly slowed his walk. In the doorway of a darkened hardware store a man leaned, with an unlighted cigar in his mouth. As the policeman walked up to him the man spoke up quickly.

'It's all right, officer,' he said, reassuringly. 'I'm just waiting for a friend. It's an appointment made twenty years ago. Sounds a little funny to you, doesn't it? Well, I'll explain if you'd like to make certain it's all straight. About that long ago there used to be a restaurant where this store stands – "Big Joe" Brady's restaurant.'

'Until five years ago,' said the policeman. 'It was torn down then.'

The man in the doorway struck a match and lit his cigar. The light showed a pale, square-jawed face with keen eyes, and a little white scar near his right eyebrow. His scarfpin was a large diamond, oddly set.

'Twenty years ago to-night,' said the man, 'I dined here at "Big Joe" Brady's with Jimmy Wells, my best chum, and the finest chap in the world. He and I were raised here in New York, just like two brothers, together. I was eighteen and Jimmy was twenty. The next morning I was to start for the West to make my fortune. You couldn't have dragged Jimmy out of New York; he thought it was the only place on earth. Well, we agreed that night that we would meet here again exactly twenty years from that date and time, no matter what our conditions might be or from what distance we might have to come. We figured that in twenty years each of us ought to have our destiny worked out and our fortunes made, whatever they were going to be.'

'It sounds pretty interesting,' said the policeman. 'Rather a long time between meets, though, it seems to me. Haven't you heard from your friend since you left?'

'Well, yes, for a time we corresponded,' said the other. 'But after a year or two we lost track of each other. You see, the West is a pretty big proposition, and I kept hustling around over it pretty lively. But I know Jimmy will meet me here if he's alive, for he always was the truest, staunchest old chap in the world. He'll never forget. I came a thousand miles to stand in this door to-night, and it's worth it if my old partner turns up.'

The waiting man pulled out a handsome watch, the lids of it set with small diamonds.

'Three minutes to ten,' he announced. 'It was exactly ten o'clock when we parted here at the restaurant door.'

'Did pretty well out West, didn't you?' asked the policeman.

'You bet! I hope Jimmy has done half as well. He was a kind of plodder, though, good fellow as he was. I've had to compete with some of the sharpest wits going to get my pile. A man gets in a groove in New York. It takes the West to put a razor-edge on him.'

The policeman twirled his club and took a step or two.

'I'll be on my way. Hope your friend comes around all right. Going to call time on him sharp?'

'I should say not!' said the other. 'I'll give him half an hour at least. If Jimmy is alive on earth he'll be here by that time. So long, officer.'

'Good-night, sir,' said the policeman, passing on along his beat, trying doors as he went.

There was now a fine, cold drizzle falling, and the wind had risen from its uncertain puffs into a steady blow. The few foot passengers astir in that quarter hurried dismally and silently along with coat collars turned high and pocketed hands. And in the door of the hardware store the man who had come a thousand miles to fill an appointment, uncertain almost to absurdity, with the friend of his youth, smoked his cigar and waited.

About twenty minutes he waited, and then a tall man in a long overcoat, with collar turned up to his ears, hurried across from the opposite side of the street. He went directly to the waiting man.

'Is that you, Bob?' he asked, doubtfully.

'Is that you, Jimmy Wells?' cried the man in the door.

'Bless my heart!' exclaimed the new arrival, grasping both the other's hands with his own. 'It's Bob, sure as fate. I was certain I'd find you here if you were still in existence. Well, well, well! – twenty years is a long time. The old restaurant's gone, Bob; I wish it had lasted, so we could have had another dinner there. How has the West treated you, old man?'

'Bully; it has given me everything I asked it for. You've changed lots, Jimmy. I never thought you were so tall by two or three inches.'

'Oh, I grew a bit after I was twenty.'

'Doing well in New York, Jimmy?'

'Moderately. I have a position in one of the city departments. Come on, Bob; we'll go around to a place I know of, and have a good long talk about old times.'

The two men started up the street, arm in arm. The man from the West, his egotism enlarged by success, was beginning to outline the history of his career. The other, submerged in his overcoat, listened with interest.

At the corner stood a drug store, brilliant with electric lights. When they came into this glare each of them turned simultaneously to gaze upon the other's face.

The man from the West stopped suddenly and released his arm.

'You're not Jimmy Wells,' he snapped. 'Twenty years is a long time, but not long enough to change a man's nose from a Roman to a pug.'

'It sometimes changes a good man into a bad one,' said the tall man. 'You've been under arrest for ten minutes, 'Silky' Bob. Chicago thinks you may have dropped over our way and wires us she wants to have a chat with you. Going quietly, are you? That's sensible. Now, before we go to the station here's a note I was to hand to you. You may read it here at the window. It's from Patrolman Wells.'

The man from the West unfolded the little piece of paper handed him. His hand was steady when he began to read, but it trembled a little by the time he had finished. The note was rather short.

Bob: I was at the appointed place on time. When you struck the match to light your cigar I saw it was the face of the man wanted in Chicago. Somehow I couldn't do it myself, so I went around and got a plain clothes man to do the job.

                                                                    Jimmy

LOST ON DRESS PARADE

MR. TOWERS CHANDLER WAS PRESSING his evening suit in his hall bedroom. One iron was heating on a small gas stove; the other was being pushed vigorously back and forth to make the desirable crease that would be seen later on extending in straight lines from Mr. Chandler's patent leather shoes to the edge of his low-cut vest. So much of the hero's toilet may be intrusted to our confidence. The remainder may be guessed by those whom genteel poverty has driven to ignoble expedient. Our next view of him shall be as he descends the steps of his lodging-house immaculately and correctly clothed; calm, assured, handsome – in appearance the typical New York young clubman setting out, slightly bored, to inaugurate the pleasures of the evening.

Chandler's honorarium was $18 per week. He was employed in the office of an architect. He was twenty-two years old; he considered architecture to be truly an art; and he honestly believed – though he would not have dared to admit it in New York – that the Faltiron Building was inferior in design to the great cathedral in Milan.

Out of each week's earnings Chandler set aside $1. At the end of each ten weeks with the extra capital thus accumulated, he purchased one gentleman's evening from the bargain counter of stingy old Father Time. He arrayed himself in the regalia of millionaires and presidents; he took himself to the quarter where life is brightest and showiest, and there dined with taste and luxury. With ten dollars a man may, for a few hours, play the wealthy idler to perfection. The sum is ample for a well-considered meal, a bottle bearing a respectable label, commensurate tips, a smoke, cab fare, and the ordinary etceteras.

This one delectable evening culled from each dull seventy was to Chandler a source of renascent bliss. To the society bud comes but one début; it stands alone sweet in her memory when her hair has whitened; but to Chandler each ten weeks brought a joy as keen, as thrilling, as new, as the first had been. To sit among *bon vivants* under palms in the swirl of concealed music, to look upon the *habitués* of such a paradise and to be looked upon by them – what is a girl's first dance and short-sleeved tulle compared with this?

Up Broadway Chandler moved with the vespertine dress parade. For this evening he was an exhibit as well as a gazer. For the next sixty-nine evenings he would be dining in cheviot and worsted at dubious *table d'hôtes*, at whirlwind lunch counters, on sandwiches and beer in his hall bedroom. He was willing to do that, for he was a true son of the great city of razzle-dazzle, and to him one evening in the limelight made up for many dark ones.

Chandler protracted his walk until the forties began to intersect the great and glittering primrose way, for the evening was yet young, and when one is of the *beau monde* only one day in seventy, one loves to protract the pleasure. Eyes bright, sinister, curious, admiring, provocative, alluring were bent upon him, for his garb and air proclaimed him a devotee to the hour of solace and pleasure.

At a certain corner he came to a standstill, proposing to himself the question of turning back toward the showy and fashionable restaurant in which he usually dined on the evenings of his especial luxury. Just then a girl scuddled lightly around the corner, slipped on a patch of icy snow and fell plump upon the sidewalk.

Chandler assisted her to her feet with instant and solicitous courtesy. The girl hobbled to the wall of the building, leaned against it, and thanked him demurely.

'I think my ankle is strained,' she said. 'It twisted when I fell.'

'Does it pain you much?' inquired Chandler.

'Only when I rest my weight upon it. I think I will be able to walk in a minute or two.'

'If I can be of any further service,' suggested the young man, 'I will call a cab, or—'

'Thank you,' said the girl, softly but heartily. 'I am sure you need not trouble yourself any further. It was so awkward of me. And my shoe heels are horridly commonsense; I can't blame them at all.'

Chandler looked at the girl and found her swiftly drawing his interest. She was pretty in a refined way; and her eye was both merry and kind. She was inexpensively clothed in a plain black dress that suggested a sort of uniform such as shop-girls wear. Her glossy dark-brown hair showed its coils beneath a cheap hat of black straw whose only ornament was a velvet ribbon and bow. She could have posed as a model for the self-respecting working girl of the best type.

A sudden idea came into the head of the young architect. He would ask this girl to dine with him. Here was the element that his splendid but solitary periodic feats had lacked. His brief season of elegant luxury would be doubly enjoyable if he could add to it a lady's society. This girl was a lady, he was sure – her manner and speech settled that. And in spite of her extremely plain attire he felt that he would be pleased to sit at table with her.

These thoughts passed swiftly through his mind, and he decided to ask her. It was a breach of etiquette, of course, but oftentimes wage-earning girls waived formalities in matters of this kind. They were generally shrewd judges of men; and thought better of their own judgment than they did of useless conventions. His ten dollars, discreetly expended, would enable the two to dine very well indeed. The dinner would no doubt be a wonderful experience thrown into the dull routine of the girl's life; and her lively appreciation of it would add to his own triumph and pleasure.

'I think,' he said to her, with frank gravity, 'that your foot needs a longer rest than you suppose. Now, I am going to suggest a way in which you can give it that and at the same time do me a favor. I was on my way to dine all by my lonely self when you came tumbling around the corner. You come with me and we'll have a cozy dinner and a pleasant talk together, and by that time your game ankle will carry you home very nicely, I am sure.'

The girl looked quickly up into Chandler's clear, pleasant countenance. Her eyes twinkled once very brightly, and then she smiled ingenuously.

'But we don't know each other – it wouldn't be right, would it?' she said, doubtfully.

'There is nothing wrong about it,' said the young man, candidly. 'I'll introduce myself – permit me – Mr. Towers Chandler. After our dinner, which I will try to make as pleasant as possible, I will bid you good-evening, or attend you safely to your door, whichever you prefer.'

'But, dear me!' said the girl, with a glance at Chandler's faultless attire. 'In this old dress and hat!'

'Never mind that,' said Chandler, cheerfully. 'I'm sure you look more charming in them than any one we shall see in the most elaborate dinner toilette.'

'My ankle does hurt yet,' admitted the girl, attempting a limping step. 'I think I will accept your invitation, Mr. Chandler. You may call me – Miss Marian.'

'Come then, Miss Marian,' said the young architect, gaily, but with perfect courtesy; 'you will not have far to walk. There is a very respectable and good restaurant in the next block. You will have to lean on my arm – so – and walk slowly. It is lonely dining all by one's self. I'm just a little bit glad that you slipped on the ice.'

When the two were established at a well-appointed table, with a promising waiter hovering in attendance, Chandler began to experience the real joy that his regular outing always brought to him.

The restaurant was not so showy or pretentious as the one further down Broadway, which he always preferred, but it was nearly so. The tables were well filled with prosperous-looking diners, there was a good orchestra, playing softly enough to make conversation a possible pleasure, and the cuisine and service were beyond criticism. His companion, even in her cheap hat and dress, held herself with an air that added distinction to the natural beauty of her face and figure. And it is certain that she looked at Chandler, with his animated but self-possessed manner and his kindling and frank blue eyes, with something not far from admiration in her own charming face.

Then it was that the Madness of Manhattan, the Frenzy of Fuss and Feathers, the Bacillus of Brag, the Provincial Plague of Pose seized upon Towers Chandler. He was on Broadway, surrounded by pomp and style, and there were eyes to look at him. On the stage of that comedy he had assumed to play the one-night part of a butterfly of fashion and an idler of means and taste. He was dressed for the part, and all his good angels had not the power to prevent him from acting it.

So he began to prate to Miss Marian of clubs, of teas, of golf and riding and kennels and cotillions and tours abroad and threw out hints of a yacht lying at Larchmont. He could see that she was vastly impressed by this vague talk, so he endorsed his pose by random insinuations concerning great wealth, and mentioned familiarly a few names that are handled reverently by the proletariat. It was Chandler's short little day, and he was wringing from it the best that could be had, as he saw it. And yet once or twice he saw the pure gold of this girl shine through the mist that his egotism had raised between him and all objects.

'This way of living that you speak of,' she said, 'sounds so futile and purposeless. Haven't you any work to do in the world that might interest you more?'

'My dear Miss Marian,' he exclaimed – 'work! Think of dressing every day for dinner, of making half a dozen calls in an afternoon – with a policeman at every corner ready to jump into your auto and take you to the station, if you get up any greater speed than a donkey cart's gait. We do-nothings are the hardest workers in the land.'

The dinner was concluded, the waiter generously feed, and the two walked out to the corner where they had met. Miss Marian walked very well now; her limp was scarcely noticeable.

'Thank you for a nice time,' she said, frankly. 'I must run home now. I liked the dinner very much, Mr. Chandler.'

He shook hands with her, smiling cordially, and said something about a game of bridge at his club. He watched her for a moment, walking rather rapidly eastward, and then he found a cab to drive him slowly homeward.

In his chilly bedroom Chandler laid away his evening clothes for a sixty-nine days' rest. He went about it thoughtfully.

'That was a stunning girl,' he said to himself. 'She's all right, too, I'd be sworn, even if she does have to work. Perhaps if I'd told her the truth instead of all that razzle-dazzle we might – but, confound it! I had to play up to my clothes.'

Thus spoke the brave who was born and reared in the wigwams of the tribe of the Manhattans.

The girl, after leaving her entertainer, sped swiftly cross-town until she arrived at a handsome and sedate mansion two squares to the east, facing on that avenue which is the highway of Mammon and the auxiliary gods. Here she entered hurriedly and ascended to a room where a handsome young lady in an elaborate house dress was looking anxiously out the window.

'Oh, you madcap!' exclaimed the elder girl, when the other entered. 'When will you quit frightening us this way? It's two hours since you ran out in that rag of an old dress and Marie's hat. Mamma has been so alarmed. She sent Louis in the auto to try to find you. You are a bad, thoughtless Puss.'

The elder girl touched a button, and a maid came in a moment.

'Marie, tell mamma that Miss Marian has returned.'

'Don't scold, Sister. I only ran down to Mme. Theo's to tell her to use mauve insertion instead of pink. My costume and Marie's hat were just what I needed. Every one thought I was a shop-girl, I am sure.'

'Dinner is over, dear; you stayed so late.'

'I know. I slipped on the sidewalk and turned my ankle. I could not walk, so I hobbled into a restaurant and sat there until I was better. That is why I was so long.'

The two girls sat in the window seat, looking out at the lights and the stream of hurrying vehicles in the avenue. The younger one cuddled down with her head in her sister's lap.

'We will have to marry some day,' she said, dreamily – 'both of us. We have so much money that we will not be allowed to disappoint the public. Do you want me to tell you the kind of a man I could love, Sis?'

'Go on, you scatterbrain,' smiled the other.

'I could love a man with dark and kind blue eyes, who is gentle and respectful to poor girls, who is handsome and good and does not try to flirt. But I could love him only if he had an ambition, an object, some work to do in the world. I would not care how poor he was if I could help him build his way up. But, Sister dear, the kind of man we always meet – the man who lives an idle life between society and his clubs – I could not love a man like that, even if his eyes were blue and he were so kind to poor girls whom he met in the street.'

BY COURIER

IT WAS NEITHER THE SEASON nor the hour when the Park had frequenters; and it is likely that the young lady, who was seated on one of the benches at the side of the walk, had merely obeyed a sudden impulse to sit for a while and enjoy a foretaste of coming Spring.

She rested there, pensive and still. A certain melancholy that touched her countenance must have been of recent birth, for it had not yet altered the fine and youthful contours of her cheek, nor subdued the arch though resolute curve of her lips.

A tall young man came striding through the park along the path near which she sat. Behind him tagged a boy carrying a suit-case. At sight of the young lady, the man's face changed to red and back to pale again. He watched her countenance as he drew nearer, with hope and anxiety mingled on his own. He passed within a few yards of her, but he saw no evidence that she was aware of his presence or existence.

Some fifty yards further on he suddenly stopped and sat on a bench at one side. The boy dropped the suit-case and stared at him with wondering, shrewd eyes. The young man took out his handkerchief and wiped his brow. It was a good handkerchief, a good brow, and the young man was good to look at. He said to the boy:

'I want you to take a message to that young lady on that bench. Tell her I am on my way to the station, to leave for San Francisco, where I shall join that Alaska moose-hunting expedition. Tell her that, since she has commanded me neither to speak nor to write to her, I take this means of making one last appeal to her sense of justice, for the sake of what has been. Tell her that to condemn and discard one who has not deserved such treatment, without giving him her reasons or a chance to explain is contrary to her nature as I believe it to be. Tell her that I have thus, to a certain degree, disobeyed her injunctions, in the hope that she may yet be inclined to see justice done. Go, and tell her that.'

The young man dropped a half-dollar into the boy's hand. The boy looked at him for a moment with bright, canny eyes out of a dirty, intelligent face and then set off at a run. He approached the lady on the bench a little doubtfully, but unembarrassed. He touched the brim of an old plaid bicycle cap perched on the back of his head. The lady looked at him coolly, without prejudice or favor.

'Lady,' he said, 'dat gent on de oder bench sent yer a song and dance by me. If yer don't know de guy, and he's tryin' to do de Johnny act, say de word, and I'll call a cop in t'ree minutes. If yer does know him, and he's on de square, w'y I'll spiel yer de bunch of hot air he sent yer.'

The young lady betrayed a faint interest.

'A song and dance!' she said, in a deliberate, sweet voice that seemed to clothe her words in a diaphanous garment of impalpable irony. 'A new idea – in the troubadour line, I suppose. I – used to know the gentleman who sent you so I think it will hardly be necessary to call the police. You may execute your song and dance, but do not sing too loudly. It is a little early yet for open-air vaudeville, and we might attract attention.'

'Awe,' said the boy, with a shrug down the length of him, 'yer know what I mean, lady. 'Tain't a turn, it's wind. He told me to tell yer he's got his collars and cuffs in dat grip for a scoot clean out to 'Frisco. Den he's goin' to shoot snow-birds in de Klondike. He says you told him not to send 'round no more pink notes nor come hangin' over de garden gate, and he takes dis means of puttin' yer wise. He says yer refereed him out like a has-been, and never give him no chance to kick at de decision. He says yer swiped him, and never said why.'

The slightly awakened interest in the young lady's eyes did not abate. Perhaps it was caused by either the originality or the audacity of the snow-bird hunter, in thus circumventing her express commands against the ordinary modes of communication. She fixed her eye on a statue standing disconsolate in the dishevelled park, and spoke into the transmitter:

'Tell the gentleman that I need not repeat to him a description of my ideals. He knows what they have been and what they still are. So far as they touch on this case, absolute loyalty and truth are the ones paramount. Tell him that I have studied my own heart as well as one can, and I know its weakness as well as I do its needs. That is why I decline to hear his pleas, whatever they may be. I did not condemn him through hearsay or doubtful evidence, and that is why I made no charge. But, since he persists in hearing what he already well knows, you may convey the matter.

'Tell him that I entered the conservatory that evening from the rear, to cut a rose for my mother. Tell him I saw him and Miss Ashburton beneath the pink oleander. The tableau was pretty, but the pose and juxtaposition were too eloquent and evident to require explanation. I left the conservatory, and, at the same time, the rose and my ideal. You may carry that song and dance to your impressario.'

'I'm shy on one word, lady. Jux – jux – put me wise on that, will yer?'

'Juxtaposition – or you may call it propinquity – or, if you like, being rather too near for one maintaining the position of an ideal.'

The gravel spun from beneath the boy's feet. He stood by the other bench. The man's eyes interrogated him, hungrily. The boy's were shining with the impersonal zeal of the translater.

'De lady says dat she's on to de fact dat gals is dead easy when a feller come spielin' ghost stories and tryin' to make up, and dat's why she won't listen to no soft-soap. She says she caught yer dead to rights, huggin' a bunch o' calico in de hot-house. She side-stepped in to pull some posies and yer was squeezin' der oder gal to beat de band. She says it looked cute, all right all right, but it made her sick. She says yer better git busy, and make a sneak for de train.'

The young man gave a low whistle and his eyes flashed with a sudden thought. His hand flew to the inside pocket of his coat, and drew out a handful of letters. Selecting one, he handed it to the boy, following it with a silver dollar from his vest-pocket.

'Give that letter to the lady,' he said, 'and ask her to read it. Tell her that it should explain the situation. Tell her that, if she had mingled a little trust with her conception of the ideal, much heartache might have been avoided. Tell her that loyalty she prizes so much has never wavered. Tell her I am waiting for an answer.'

The messenger stood before the lady.

'De gent says he's had de ski-bunk put on him widout no cause. He says

he's no bum guy; and, lady, yer read dat letter, and I'll bet yer he's a white
sport, all right.'

The young lady unfolded the letter, somewhat doubtfully, and read it.

Dear Dr. Arnold: I want to thank you for your most kind and opportune
aid to my daughter last Friday evening, when she was overcome by an
attack of her old heart-trouble in the conservatory at Mrs. Waldron's
reception. Had you not been near to catch her as she fell and to render
proper attention, we might have lost her. I would be glad if you would
call and undertake the treatment of her case.

Gratefully yours,
Robert Ashburton

The young lady refolded the letter, and handed it to the boy.

'De gent wants an answer,' said the messenger. 'What's de word?'

The lady's eyes suddenly flashed on him, bright, smiling and wet.

'Tell that guy on the other bench,' she said, with a happy, tremulous
laugh, 'that his girl wants him.'

THE FURNISHED ROOM

RESTLESS, SHIFTING, FUGACIOUS as time itself is a certain vast bulk of the population
of the red brick district of the lower West Side. Homeless they have a
hundred homes. They flit from furnished room to furnished room, transients
forever – transients in abode, transients in heart and mind. They sing 'Home,
Sweet Home' in ragtime; they carry their *lares et penates* in a bandbox; their
vine is entwined about a picture hat; a rubber plant is their fig tree.

Hence the houses of this district, having had a thousand dwellers, should
have a thousand tales to tell, mostly dull ones, no doubt; but it would be
strange if there could not be found a ghost or two in the wake of all these
vagrant guests.

One evening after dark a young man prowled among these crumbling red
mansions, ringing their bells. At the twelfth he rested his lean hand-baggage
upon the step and wiped the dust from his hatband and forehead. The bell
sounded faint and far away in some remote, hollow depths.

To the door of this, the twelfth house whose bell he had rung, came a
housekeeper who made him think of an unwholesome, surfeited worm that
had eaten its nut to a hollow shell and now sought to fill the vacancy with
edible lodgers.

He asked if there was a room to let.

'Come in,' said the housekeeper. Her voice came from her throat; her
throat seemed lined with fur. 'I have the third-floor back, vacant since a
week back. Should you wish to look at it?'

The young man followed her up the stairs. A faint light from no particular
source mitigated the shadows of the halls. They trod noiselessly upon a stair
carpet that its own loom would have foresworn. It seemed to have become
vegetable; to have degenerated in that rank, sunless air to lush lichen or
spreading moss that grew in patches to the stair-case and was viscid under

the foot like organic matter. At each turn of the stairs were vacant niches in
the wall. Perhaps plants had once been set within them. If so they had died
in that foul and tainted air. It may be that statues of the saints had stood
there, but it was not difficult to conceive that imps and devils had dragged
them forth in the darkness and down to the unholy depths of some furnished
pit below.

'This is the room,' said the housekpeeper, from her furry throat. 'It's a
nice room. It ain't often vacant. I had some most elegant people in it last
summer – no trouble at all, and paid in advance to the minute. The water's
at the end of the hall. Sprowls and Mooney kept it three months. They done
a vaudeville sketch. Miss B'retta Sprowls – you may have heard of her – Oh,
that was just the stage names – right there over the dresser is where the
marriage certificate hung, framed. The gas is here, and you see there is plenty
of closet room. It's a room everybody likes. It never stays idle long.'

'Do you have many theatrical people rooming here?' asked the young man.

'They comes and goes. A good proportion of my lodgers is connected with
the theatres. Yes, sir, this is the theatrical district. Actor people never stays
long anywhere. I get my share. Yes, they comes and they goes.'

He engaged the room, paying for a week in advance. He was tired, he said,
and would take possession at once. He counted out the money. The room
had been made ready, she said, even to towels and water. As the housekeeper
moved away he put, for the thousandth time, the question that he carried
at the end of his tongue.

'A young girl – Miss Vashner – Miss Eloise Vashner – do you remember
such a one among your lodgers? She would be singing on the stage, most
likely. A fair girl, of medium height and slender, with reddish, gold hair and
dark mole near her left eyebrow.'

'No, I don't remember the name. Them stage people has names they
change as often as their rooms. They comes and they goes. No, I don't call
that one to mind.'

No. Always no. Five months of ceaseless interrogation and the inevitable
negative. So much time spent by day in questioning managers, agents, schools
and choruses; by night among the audiences of theatres from all-star casts
down to music halls so low that he dreaded to find what he most hoped for.
He who had loved her best had tried to find her. He was sure that since her
disappearance from home this great, water-girt city held her somewhere, but
it was like a monstrous quicksand, shifting its particles constantly, with no
foundation, its upper granules of to-day buried to-morrow in ooze and slime.

The furnished room received its latest guest with a first glow of pseudo-
hospitality, a hectic, haggard, perfunctory welcome like the specious smile
of a demirep. The sophistical comfort came in reflected gleams from the
decayed furniture, the ragged brocade upholstery of a couch and two chairs,
a foot-wide cheap pier glass between the two windows, from one or two gilt
picture frames and a brass bedstead in a corner.

The guest reclined, inert, upon a chair, while the room, confused in speech
as though it were an apartment in Babel, tried to discourse to him of its
divers tenantry.

A polychromatic rug like some brilliant-flowered, rectangular, tropical
islet lay surrounded by a billowy sea of soiled matting. Upon the gay.papered
wall were those pictures that pursue the homeless one from house to house
– The Huguenot Lovers, The First Quarrel, The Wedding Breakfast, Psyche

at the Fountain. The mantel's chastely severe outline was ingloriously veiled behind some pert drapery drawn rakishly askew like the sashes of the Amazonian ballet. Upon it was some desolate flotsam cast aside by the room's marooned when a lucky sail had borne them to a fresh port – a trifling vase or two, pictures of actresses, a medicine bottle, some stray cards out of a deck.

One by one, as the characters of a cryptograph became explicit, the little signs left by the furnished rooms' procession of guests developed a significance. The threadbare space in the rug in front of the dresser told that lovely women had marched in the throng. The tiny fingerprints on the wall spoke of little prisoners trying to feel their way to sun and air. A splattered stain, raying like the shadow of a bursting bomb, witnessed where a hurled glass or bottle had splintered with its contents against the wall. Across the pier glass had been scrawled with a diamond in staggering letters the name 'Marie.' It seemed that the succession of dwellers in the furnished room had turned in fury – perhaps tempted beyond forebearance by its garish coldness – and wreaked upon it their passions. The furniture was chipped and bruised; the couch, distorted by bursting springs, seemed a horrible monster that had been slain during the stress of some grotesque convulsion. Some more potent unheaval had cloven a great slice from the marble mantel. Each plank in the floor owned its particular cant and shriek as from a separate and individual agony. It seemed incredible that all this malice and injury had been wrought upon the room by those who had called it for a time their home; and yet it may have been the cheated home instinct surviving blindly, the resentful rage at false household gods that had kindled their wrath. A hut that is our own we can sweep and adorn and cherish.

The young tenant in the chair allowed these thoughts to file, soft-shod, through his mind, while there drifted into the room furnished sounds and furnished scents. He heard in one room a tittering and incontinent, slack laughter; in others the monologue of a scold, the rattling of dice, a lullaby, and one crying dully; above him a banjo tinkled with spirit. Doors banged somewhere; the elevated trains roared intermittently; a cat yowled miserably upon a back fence. And he breathed the breath of the house – a dank savor rather than a smell – a cold, musty effuvium as from underground vaults mingled with the reeking exhalations of linoleum and mildewed and rotten woodwork.

Then suddenly, as he rested there, the room was filled with the strong, sweet odor of mignonette. It came as upon a single buffet of wind with such sureness and fragrance and emphasis that it almost seemed a living visitant. And the man cried aloud: 'What, dear?' as if he had been called, and sprang up and faced about. The rich odor clung to him and wrapped him around. He reached out his arms for it, all his senses for the time confused and commingled. How could one be peremptorily called by an odor? Surely it must have been a sound. But, was it not the sound that had touched, that had caressed him?

'She has been in this room,' he cried, and he sprang to wrest from it a token, for he knew he would recognize the smallest thing that had belonged to her or that she had touched. This enveloping scent of mignonette, the odor that she had loved and made her own – whence came it?

The room had been but carelessly set in order. Scattered upon the flimsy dresser scarf were half a dozen hairpins – those discreet, indistinguishable friends of womankind, feminine of gender, infinite mood and uncommunicative of tense. These he ignored, conscious of their triumphant lack of identity. Ransacking the drawers of the dresser he came upon a discarded, tiny, ragged handkerchief. He pressed it to his face. It was racy and insolent with heliotrope; he hurled it to the floor. In another drawer he found odd buttons, a theatre programme, a pawnbroker's card, two lost marshmallows, a book on the divination of dreams. In the last was a woman's black satin hair bow, which halted him, poised between ice and fire. But the black satin hair bow also is femininity's demure, impersonal common ornament and tells no tales.

And then he traversed the room like a hound on the scent, skimming the walls, considering the corners of the bulging matting on his hands and knees, rummaging mantel and tables, the curtains and hangings, the drunken cabinet in the corner, for a visible sign, unable to perceive that she was there beside, around, against, within, above him, clinging to him, wooing him, calling him so poignantly through the finer senses that even his grosser ones became cognizant of the call. Once again he answered loudly: 'Yes, dear!' and turned, wild-eyed, to gaze on vacancy, for he could not yet discern form and color and love and outstretched arms in the odor of mignonette. Oh, God! whence that odor, and since when have odors had a voice to call? Thus he groped.

He burrowed in crevices and corners, and found corks and cigarettes. These he passed in passive contempt. But once he found in a fold of the matting a half-smoked cigar, and this he ground beneath his heel with a green and trenchant oath. He sifted the room from end to end. He found dreary and ignoble small records of many a peripatetic tenant; but of her whom he sought, and who may have lodged there, and whose spirit seemed to hover there, he found no trace.

And then he thought of the housekeeper.

He ran from the haunted room downstairs and to a door that showed a crack of light. She came out to his knock. He smothered his excitement as best he could.

'Will you tell me, madam,' he besought her, 'who occupied the room I have before I came?'

'Yes, sir. I can tell you again. 'Twas Sprowls and Mooney, as I said. Miss B'retta Sprowls it was in the theatres, but Missis Mooney she was. My house is well known for respectability. The marriage certificate hung, framed, on a nail over—'

'What kind of a lady was Miss Sprowls – in looks, I mean?'

'Why, black-haired, sir, short, and stout, with a comical face. They left a week ago Tuesday.'

'And before they occupied it?'

'Why, there was a single gentleman connected with the draying business. He left owing me a week. Before him was Missis Crowder and her two children, that stayed four months; and back of them was old Mr. Doyle, whose sons paid for him. He kept the room six months. That goes back a year, sir, and further I do not remember.'

He thanked her and crept back to his room. The room was dead. The essence that had vivified it was gone. The perfume of mignonette had departed. In its place was the old, stale odor of mouldy house furniture, of atmosphere in storage.

The ebbing of his hope drained his faith. He sat staring at the yellow, singing gaslight. Soon he walked to the bed and began to tear the sheets into strips. With the blade of his knife he drove them tightly into every crevice around windows and door. When all was snug and taut he turned out the light, turned the gas full on again and laid himself gratefully upon the bed.

It was Mrs. McCool's night to go with the can for beer. So she fetched it and sat with Mrs. Purdy in one of those subterranean retreats where housekeepers foregather and the worm dieth seldom.

'I rented out my third-floor this evening,' said Mrs. Purdy, across a fine circle of foam. 'A young man took it. He went up to bed two hours ago.'

'Now, did ye, Mrs. Purdy, ma'am?' said Mrs. McCool, with intense admiration. 'You do be a wonder for rentin' rooms of that kind. And did ye tell him, then?' she concluded in a husky whisper laden with mystery.

'Rooms,' said Mrs. Purdy, in her furriest tones, 'are furnished for to rent. I did not tell him, Mrs. McCool.'

' 'Tis right ye are, ma'am; 'tis by renting rooms we kape alive. Ye have the rale sense for business, ma'am. There be many people will rayjict the rentin' of a room if they be tould a suicide has been after dyin' in the bed of it.'

'As you say, we has our living to be making,' remarked Mrs. Purdy.

'Yis, ma'am; 'tis true. 'Tis just one wake ago this day I helped ye lay out the third-floor-back. A pretty slip of a colleen she was to be killin' herself wid the gas – a swate little face she had, Mrs. Purdy, ma'am.'

'She'd a-been called handsome, as you say,' said Mrs. Purdy, assenting but critical, 'but for that mole she had a-growin' by her left eyebrow. Do fill up your glass again, Mrs. McCool.'

THE BRIEF DÉBUT OF TILDY

IF YOU DO NOT KNOW BOGLE'S CHOP HOUSE and Family Restaurant it is your loss. For if you are one of the fortunate ones who dine expensively you should be interested to know how the other half consumes provisions. And if you belong to the half to whom waiters' checks are things of moment, you should know Bogle's, for there you get your money's worth – in quantity, at least.

Bogle's is situated in that highway of *bourgeoisie*, that boulevard of Brown-Jones-and-Robinson, Eighth Avenue. There are two rows of tables in the room, six in each row. On each table is a caster-stand, containing cruets of condiments and seasons. From the pepper cruet you may shake a cloud of something tasteless and melancholy, like volcanic dust. From the salt cruet you may expect nothing. Though a man should extract a sanguinary stream from the pallid turnip, yet will his prowess be balked when he comes to wrest salt from Bogle's cruets. Also upon each table stands the counterfeit of that benign sauce made 'from the recipe of a nobleman in India.'

At the cashier's desk sits Bogle, cold, sordid, slow, smouldering, and takes your money. Behind a mountain of toothpicks he makes your change, files your check, and ejects at you, like a toad, a word about the weather. Beyond a corroboration of his meteorological statement you would better not venture. You are not Bogle's friend; you are a fed, transient customer, and you and he may not meet again until the blowing of Gabriel's dinner horn. So take your change and go – to the devil if you like. There you have Bogle's sentiments.

The needs of Bogle's customers were supplied by two waitresses and a Voice. One of the waitresses was named Aileen. She was tall, beautiful, lively, gracious and learned in persiflage. Her other name? There was no more necessity for another name at Bogle's than there was for finger-bowls.

The name of the other waitress was Tildy. Why do you suggest Matilda? Please listen this time – Tildy – Tildy. Tildy was dumpy, plain-faced, and too anxious to please to please. Repeat the last clause to yourself once or twice, and make the acquaintance of the duplicate infinite.

The Voice at Bogle's was invisible. It came from the kitchen, and did not shine in the way of originality. It was a heathen Voice, and contented itself with vain repetitions of exclamations emitted by the waitresses concerning food.

Will it tire you to be told again that Aileen was beautiful? Had she donned a few hundred dollars' worth of clothes and joined the Easter parade, and had you seen her, you would have hastened to say so yourself.

The customers at Bogle's were her slaves. Six tables full she could wait upon at once. They who were in a hurry restrained their impatience for the joy of merely gazing upon her swiftly moving, graceful figure. They who had finished eating ate more that they might continue in the light of her smiles. Every man there – and they were mostly men – tried to make his impression upon her.

Aileen could successfully exchange repartee against a dozen at once. And every smile that she sent forth lodged, like pellets from a scatter-gun, in as many hearts. And all this while she would be performing astounding feats with orders of pork and beans, pot roasts, ham-and, sausage-and-the-wheats, and any quantity of things on the iron and in the pan and straight up and on the side. With all this feasting and flirting and merry exchange of wit Bogle's came mighty near being a salon, with Aileen for its Madame Recamier.

If the transients were entranced by the fascinating Aileen, the regulars were her adorers. There was much rivalry among many of the steady customers. Aileen could have had an engagement every evening. At least twice a week some one took her to a theatre or to a dance. One stout gentleman whom she and Tildy had privately christened 'The Hog' presented her with a turquoise ring. Another one known as 'Freshy,' who rode on the Traction Company's repair wagon, was going to give her a poodle as soon as his brother got the hauling contract in the Ninth. And the man who always ate spareribs and spinach and said he was a stock broker asked her to go to 'Parsifal' with him.

'I don't know where this place is,' said Aileen while talking it over with Tildy, 'but the wedding-ring's got to be on before I put a stitch into a travelling dress – ain't that right? Well, I guess!'

But, Tildy!

In steaming, chattering, cabbage-scented Bogle's there was almost a heart tragedy. Tildy with the blunt nose, the hay-colored hair, the freckled skin, the bag-o'-meal figure, had never had an admirer. Not a man followed her with his eyes when she went to and fro in the restaurant save now and then when they glared with the beast-hunger for food. None of them bantered her gaily to coquettish interchanges of wit. None of them loudly 'jollied' her of mornings as they did Aileen, accusing her, when the eggs were slow in coming, of late hours in the company of envied swains. No one had ever given her a turquoise ring or invited her upon a voyage to mysterious, distant 'Parsifal.'

Tildy was a good waitress, and the men tolerated her. They who sat at her tables spoke to her briefly with quotations from the bill of fare; and then raised their voices in honeyed and otherwise-flavored accents, eloquently addressed to the fair Aileen. They writhed in their chairs to gaze around and over the impending form of Tildy, that Aileen's pulchritude might season and make ambrosia of their bacon and eggs.

And Tildy was content to be the unwooed drudge if Aileen could receive the flattery and the homage. The blunt nose was loyal to the short Grecian. She was Aileen's friend; and she was glad to see her rule hearts and wean the attention of men from smoking pot-pie and lemon meringue. But deep below our freckles and hay-colored hair the unhandsomest of us dream of a prince or a princess, not vicarious, but coming to us alone.

There was a morning when Aileen tripped in to work with a slightly bruised eye; and Tildy's solicitude was almost enough to heal any optic.

'Fresh guy,' explained Aileen, 'last night as I was going home at Twenty-third and Sixth. Sashayed up, so he did, and made a break. I turned him down, cold, and he made a sneak; but followed me down to Eighteenth, and tried his hot air again. Gee! but I slapped him a good one side of the face. Then he give me that eye. Does it look real awful, Til! I should hate that Mr. Nicholson should see it when he comes in for his tea and toast at ten.'

Tildy listened to the adventure with breathless admiration. No man had ever tried to follow her. She was safe abroad at any hour of the twenty-four. What bliss it must have been to have had a man follow one and black one's eye for love!

Among the customers at Bogle's was a young man named Seeders, who worked in a laundry office. Mr. Seeders was thin and had light hair, and appeared to have been recently rough-dried and starched. He was too diffident to aspire to Aileen's notice; so he usually sat at one of Tildy's tables, where he devoted himself to silence and boiled weakfish.

One day when Mr. Seeders came in to dinner he had been drinking beer. There were only two or three customers in the restaurant. When Mr. Seeders had finished his weakfish he got up, put his arm around Tildy's waist, kissed her loudly and impudently, walked out upon the street, snapped his fingers in the direction of the laundry, and hied himself to play pennies in the slot machines at the Amusement Arcade.

For a few moments Tildy stood petrified. Then she was aware of Aileen shaking at her an arch forefinger, and saying:

'Why, Til, you naughty girl! Ain't you getting to be awful, Miss Slyboots. First thing I know you'll be stealing some of my fellows. I must keep an eye on you, my lady.'

Another thing dawned upon Tildy's recovering wits. In a moment she had advanced from a hopeless, lowly admirer to be an Eve-sister of the potent Aileen. She herself was now a man-charmer, a mark for Cupid, a Sabine who must be coy when the Romans were at their banquet boards. Man had found her waist achievable and her lips desirable. The sudden and amatory Seeders had, as it were, performed for her a miraculous piece of one-day laundry work. He had taken the sackcloth of her uncomeliness, had washed, dried, starched and ironed it, and returned it to her sheer embroidered lawn – the robe of Venus herself.

The freckles on Tildy's cheeks merged into a rosy flush. Now both Circe and Psyche peeped from her brightened eyes. Not even Aileen herself had been publicly embraced and kissed in the restaurant.

Tildy could not keep the delightful secret. When trade was slack she went and stood at Bogle's desk. Her eyes were shining; she tried not to let her words sound proud and boastful.

'A gentleman insulted me to-day,' she said. 'He hugged me around the waist and kissed me.'

'That so?' said Bogle, cracking open his business armor. 'After this week you get a dollar a week more.'

At the next regular meal when Tildy set food before customers with whom she had acquaintance she said to each of them modestly, as one whose merit needed no bolstering:

'A gentleman insulted me to-day in the restaurant. He put his arms around my waist and kissed me.'

The diners accepted the revelation in various ways – some incredulously, some with congratulations; others turned upon her the stream of badinage that had hitherto been directed at Aileen alone. And Tildy's heart swelled in her bosom, for she saw at last the towers of Romance rise above the horizon of the gray plain in which she had for so long travelled.

For two days Mr. Seeders came not again. During that time Tildy established herself firmly as a woman to be wooed. She bought ribbons, and arranged her hair like Aileen's and tightened her waist two inches. She had a thrilling but delightful fear that Mr. Seeders would rush in suddenly and shoot her with a pistol. He must have loved her desperately; and impulsive lovers are always blindly jealous.

Even Aileen had not been shot at with a pistol. And then Tildy rather hoped that he would not shoot at her, for she was always loyal to Aileen; and she did not want to over-shadow her friend.

At 4 o'clock on the afternoon of the third day Mr. Seeders came in. There were no customers at the tables. At the back end of the restaurant Tildy was refilling the mustard pots and Aileen was quartering pies. Mr. Seeders walked back to where they stood.

Tildy looked up and saw him, gasped, and pressed the mustard spoon against her heart. A red hair-bow was in her hair; she wore Venus's Eighth Avenue badge, the blue bead necklace with the swinging silver symbolic heart.

Mr. Seeders was flushed and embarrassed. He plunged one hand into his hip pocket and the other into a fresh pumpkin pie.

'Miss Tildy,' said he, 'I want to apologize for what I done the other evenin'. Tell you the truth, I was pretty well tanked up or I wouldn't of done it. I wouldn't do no lady that a-way when I was sober. So I hope, Miss Tildy, you'll accept my 'pology, and believe that I wouldn't of done it if I'd known what I was doin' and hadn't of been drunk.'

With this handsome plea Mr. Seeders backed away, and departed, feeling that reparation had been made.

But behind the convenient screen. Tildy had thrown herself flat upon a table among the butter chips and the coffee cups, and was sobbing her heart out – out and back again to the gray plain wherein travel they with blunt noses and hay-colored hair. From her knot she had torn the red hair-bow and cast it upon the floor. Seeders she despised utterly; she had but taken his kiss as that of a pioneer and prophetic prince who might have set the clocks going and the pages to running in fairyland. But the kiss had been maudlin and unmeant; the court had not stirred at the false alarm; she must forevermore remain the Sleeping Beauty.

Yet not all was lost. Aileen's arm was around her; and Tildy's red hand groped among the butter chips till it found the warm clasp of her friend's.

'Don't you fret, Til,' said Aileen, who did not understand entirely. 'That turnip-faced little clothespin of a Seeders ain't worth it. He ain't anything of a gentleman or he wouldn't ever of apologized.'